Fanny Blake was a publisher for many years, editing both fiction and non-fiction before becoming a freelance journalist and writer. She has written various non-fiction titles, acted as ghostwriter for a number of celebrities, and is a former books editor of *Woman & Home* magazine. She has been a judge of a number of literary prizes, including the Costa First Novel Award, the Desmond Elliott Award, the RNA Romantic Novel of the Year Award and the British Book Awards. She is also the commissioning editor for Quick Reads and a book reviewer. She has written eight previous novels, including *An Italian Summer* and *A Summer Reunion.*

Fanny Blake

The Long Way Home

**SIMON &
SCHUSTER**

London · New York · Sydney · Toronto · New Delhi

First published in Great Britain by Simon & Schuster UK Ltd, 2021

Copyright © Fanny Blake, 2021. All rights reserved

The right of Fanny Blake to be identified as author of
this work has been asserted in accordance with the
Copyright, Designs and Patents Act, 1988.

1 3 5 7 9 10 8 6 4 2

Simon & Schuster UK Ltd
1st Floor
222 Gray's Inn Road
London WC1X 8HB

Simon & Schuster Australia,Sydney
Simon & Schuster India,New Delhi

www.simonandschuster.co.uk
www.simonandschuster.com.au
www.simonandschuster.co.in

A CIP catalogue record for this book
is available from the British Library

Hardback ISBN: 978-1-4711-9359-0
eBook ISBN: 978-1-4711-9360-6
Audio ISBN: 978-1-3985-0406-6

Typeset in the UK by M Rules
Printed and bound in Great Britain by CPI Group (UK) Ltd, Croydon, CR0 4YY

For my family

1

Paris, 1954

A porter grabbed May's luggage and pushed ahead of her towards the taxi station. She followed, trying to keep close, fearful of losing him in this unfamiliar chaos. The Gare du Nord teemed with people and echoed with noise as they threaded through the crowd that surged around them. May felt disorientated by the Parisian spring light, slicing down from the high glass roof into the diffusion of steam, and by the hissing engines, whistles, shouts and incomprehensible tannoy announcements. Moments later she had tipped him (too much, probably, but she was too excited to care) and was handing the taxi driver a paper with Monsieur and Madame Dubois' address. He took the Gauloise from his mouth, said something she did not catch and they set off. Her heart was pounding.

The Paris streets were like nothing she had seen before. Bicycles and motor scooters wove between cars and vans, bells and horns blaring warnings while uniformed police-men with peaked pill-box hats stood in the centre of things, directing the traffic with batons. A green-and-white bus overtook them with the word DUBONNET running along the side of the roof. Green newspaper kiosks stood on street corners, bedecked with postcards and papers, and cafés were busy with tables set out on the pavements shaded by bright blue and green Pernod umbrellas. A green cross on the side of a building marked Pharmacie, striped awnings, unfamiliar words on buildings, in shop windows: a kaleidoscope of new impressions. Even the people looked different: women in elegant suits with nipped-in waists, hats at a jaunty angle; men in baggy dark suits or gaberdine macs. They passed monuments May had seen in pictures: the monumental Arc de Triomphe, the sycamore-lined Champs Elysées and the Louvre. They drove over a bridge that crossed the mighty Seine and passed the elaborate façade and towers of Notre Dame. This side of the river, the streets were narrower, darker, intriguing. May watched everything from the safety of the car, on the very edge of her seat.

Eventually they pulled up outside a once-elegant apartment building on the other side of the road from what looked like a huge park. The paintwork was peeling, the stonework grubby but it was beautiful. This was it. She had arrived. She stepped out of the cab and while the driver got her luggage, she counted out the right number of francs, not used to the unfamiliar coins. As he drove off, she pulled the bell by the heavy doors. What would her employers be like, she wondered with a sudden sense of misgiving.

More importantly what would their son, her charge, be like?

The door swung open to admit her to a courtyard. She stepped inside and waited, feeling very small as the apartment blocks reared up round her. A tabby cat, lying in a small patch of sunshine, stared at her and blinked. She could smell cooking and perhaps even – though she hoped not – drains. After what seemed an interminable wait, she heard footsteps on one of the interior stone stairways that led up into the building. A petite woman who looked like a ballet dancer stood in front of her, *soignée*, her dark hair scraped into a tight bun at the nape of her neck, her features aquiline but friendly. 'Miss May Campbell? I am Madame Dubois. Come wiz me,' she tried. 'My English is not so good.'

But May couldn't have cared less. After attending the lessons she was enrolled in, there wouldn't be any need for English between them. She was already entranced by the language and everything she had seen. Her adventure had begun.

2

Edinburgh, March 2019

As Isla opened the mirrored doors of the wardrobe, a faint drift of perfume brought her dead mother into the room. Memories rushed at her, prompted by the row of May's neatly hung clothes: her leaving all gussied-up for a night out with their father; a favourite coat pulled on against the Edinburgh weather; the dress she wore the previous Christmas; the old jacket she always put on for gardening. How much easier to shut the door on it all, to pretend nothing had changed. But everything had.

She glanced at the wall by the wardrobe and at the familiar pencil markings where May had once measured the heights of Isla and her two sisters as they grew up.

She, herself. Always the tallest. Her mother had disliked the fact that Isla had matched her in height by the age of fifteen. Her height had also set her apart from her sisters. And her red hair, like her father's. And her longing for independence.

Morag. Much shorter and wider, with dark hair and a fierce temper.

Lorna. As dark as Morag, but of slighter build. The baby of the family who worked out early on how to get her way.

Looking at those measurements made Isla catch her breath. All their childhood seemed encapsulated by them.

May's death had taken them all by surprise. A doughty Scottish woman who seemed as if she would go on forever had been struck down by a sudden fatal heart attack. Goodbyes were left unsaid, alongside a multitude of lingering regrets. Standing in her mother's bedroom that was so redolent of her, Isla longed for one last cup of tea and a final chance to unpick their differences. As it was, she would never know now why they had drifted apart over the years or be able to make up for it. The house felt diminished, but expectant too, as if their mother were about to walk through a door, be sitting in her favourite chair, or outside in the garden, swishing a stick at plants she didn't like.

The glowering sky made the room even more gloomy than Isla remembered. Faded photos of long-dead relatives and antique Scottish etchings collected by her father hung on the walls. The furniture was dark and heavy, the chintz curtains faded. She had never liked being in here, even when the sun shone. As a child, she would stand outside, hand poised to knock because she needed her mother, half-hoping not to be answered.

A branch scratched at the window, making her jump.

Dealing with their mother's affairs and organising the funeral was affecting all three sisters, tickling at the old tensions between them. So far emotions had been kept reined in, almost as if their mother was still with them, ready to correct anyone who stepped out of line. An unsentimental woman herself, she would not want them grieving her death. 'Part of life,' she'd say. 'And you must get on with yours.' The flowers; the hymns; the readings and speakers – all potential triggers for disagreement – had been strictly divided between them. No interference or comment allowed. In twenty-four hours, it would all be over. In the meantime, at Lorna's suggestion, they were looking for May's will.

Downstairs Isla could hear the sounds of Lorna going through the bureau in the sitting room while Morag searched their late father's study. May would have put a copy of her will somewhere safe. If they couldn't find it, Isla would call the solicitor in the morning. She sat on the edge of the bed, her mother's tweedy perfume rising from the pillow, the flowery edge of her brushed cotton nightdress peeking out from under it. She picked up the book on the bedside table, touched to think this history of Scottish gardens had been the last book her mother would have read. She flicked through the pages, removing the half-written letter that served as a bookmark. She immediately recognised her mother's scrawl. May would disapprove of her reading it but ... well, she wasn't here to stop her.

'*My dear girls* ...' she read. Isla stopped, surprised that it should be addressed to her and her sisters. What a strange coincidence. She took a breath and began to read on. '*Here's a list of everyone you might need to contact when I'm gone.*' She separated a second piece of paper from the first.

Their mother had always been a prodigious list maker: school uniform; holiday packing; the books she'd read; the things she needed to do; Christmas cards; party invitations. You name it. Life had been reduced to a series of tickings-off. This was just another: a list of everyone involved in her affairs from her accountant to the electricity company, from her solicitor to her bank details, almost as if she had a premonition of her impending death.

Isla returned to the letter. *'John Donaldson, the solicitor, has my will. There's a copy in your father's desk. Isla, dear, I'm leaving you the painting Daddy had in his study. It may not seem much, but one day you'll understand. After so long, I can't begin to tell—'*

That was it. Unfinished and unsigned. How extraordinary to find it at that moment, as if fate was putting it into her hands. Isla wondered what else her mother had been going to say. Had she had second thoughts about writing the letter at all? Or had she begun it the night before she died at the bridge table, never returning to finish it off. Leaving something so inconclusive was not in her mother's nature, but she had been taken without warning. Isla picked up the biro that lay by the bedside light and twirled it in her hand, thoughtful. May must have been the last person to touch it.

'Isla! Lorna!' Morag's voice carried up the stairs. 'I've found it.'

Isla shut the wardrobe doors and went downstairs, taking the letter with her, to find her sisters in the study. The leathery, smoky bookish smell was the same as ever. Shelves lined the walls, books piled higgledy-piggledy on them. A battered leather sofa and chair flanked the tiled fireplace. The old-fashioned lamps cast a flattering golden glow over everything. The last time Isla had seen her father he was sitting by this fire, reading, surrounded by a fug of sweet tobacco smoke from his pipe. Nothing much had changed. Even the tam o'shanter and blue-and-green tartan scarf still hung on the back of the door. Morag had opened the lid of his desk and scattered the contents of the cubby holes over it. She had the will in her hand.

'Let's have a look.' Before either of them could stop her, Lorna had snatched the envelope from her sister and was pulling out its contents. 'We might as well confirm what we already know. Her estate's divided between the three of us, and we'll be the executors.' She began to leaf through it with the focus of a bird of prey.

Her sisters couldn't have been more different, Isla thought, watching them. Morag's outdoors complexion was tanned and lined. She wore jeans and a fleece, indifferent to her appearance, unlike Lorna who was sleek and smart, not a hair out of place. Who knew how much she spent on looking her best?

'What? This can't be right.' Lorna's attention was on one particular page. She ran a perfectly manicured finger along one line then the next. 'But she can't do this to us.'

'What's happened?' Morag went to look over her shoulder.

'Look here.' Lorna pointed. 'There must be a mistake.'

'Let me see.' Morag took the will back and read it again. 'No! She can't do that to you, Isla.'

'What's happened?' Her sisters' shocked faces made her uneasy.

'You'd better read it for yourself.' Morag held the document out. 'But you won't like it.'

'I won't?' Isla took the will to the chair by the window, conscious the other two were quite still, watching her, waiting for a reaction. She had to read the relevant lines twice to make sure she had not made a mistake and, as she did so, a knot tightened in her stomach. 'I don't understand.' The hand holding the will dropped to her lap. Was that what her mother had been about to explain in the letter?

'You've been cut out.' Lorna's shock was tempered by a visible anger. 'Mum's left half her estate to Aunt Aggie and the other half to Morag and me. She's only left you that dreary picture that used to hang in here. What happened between you?'

Her sister's voice sounded far away as if the words were tumbling down a long tunnel towards her, losing their impact on arrival. Isla was only conscious of her disbelief, her hurt, the dawning realisation that her mother's dislike of her had not been imagined after all. All those years of treading on eggshells had obviously not been enough. But this! She blinked back tears. 'I need a few minutes.' She put the letter and the will on the desk and left the room, desperate to be on her own.

She ran up to her old childhood bedroom, now a pretty

but impersonal guest room. She lay on the bed, numbed, unable to process what had happened. She was hardly the first person to have a difficult relationship with their mother but this was far worse. This was a total rejection. But why?

There was a knock at the door before Morag put her head round it. 'Are you okay?'

Isla took a ragged breath and managed what felt like a feeble smile. 'Sort of. It was just the shock. I'm fine. Really.'

But she had never felt so far from fine.

3

Isla eventually went downstairs for a scratch supper of omelettes and salad that Morag and Lorna organised. They were joined by Aunt Aggie and Lorna's husband, Andrew, whom Lorna sniped at whenever she got the chance, making it quite clear she wished he had stayed at home. They all sat together in the dining room, picking at their food, each of them too preoccupied to eat.

As soon as she could, Aggie disappeared to the kitchen 'to clear up the debris'. Andrew took his chance and escaped to the living room a moment later with the second bottle of fine red wine he had brought with him and was now watching *Match of the Day* at full volume. Isla sometimes wondered how Lorna put up with him.

Lorna took a sip of her wine, brushed a crumb from her front. 'Of course we could always challenge the will, say Mum wasn't of sound mind.'

'But she *was*.' Morag poured herself another drink, clinking the bottle against the glass.

'We should sell Braemore.' Lorna ran her finger round the rim of her glass, as if she had been thinking whether or not to say so.

'But it's not ours to sell!' Morag looked shocked. 'What about Aunt Aggie?'

'There are some wonderful sheltered housing schemes,' said Lorna. 'And her share of Braemore would more than cover the cost of one of them.'

Money bought Lorna out of almost any tight corner, reflected Isla. 'You know she'd absolutely hate it. Besides, what's wrong with her going on living here?' She wanted to stand up for her aunt, who had reliably provided a port in a storm during Isla's rocky teenage years.

'Well, why don't you ask her?' suggested Morag. 'She's only in the kitchen.'

'Not yet.' Lorna's face was determined. 'We need to agree a way of persuading her first.'

Isla could imagine her chairing meetings of the local charities she was involved with. Terrifying.

'I don't understand why you want to get rid of the old place.'

Lorna shifted in her chair, her eyes defiant. 'Because it makes sense.'

They had grown up in Braemore, the house that had been in her father's family for generations. This was their family home. Isla knew every nook and cranny of the handsome Victorian farmhouse, from which boards on the upstairs landing creaked loudest to the hole behind one of the tiles in the sitting-room fireplace where she used to hide her pocket money. Most of the farmland had been sold off long ago, leaving the large grey stone building surrounded by an acre of private garden and several paddocks where Morag's pony had once grazed that were now rented to a neighbouring farmer. The house might be too big for Aggie alone, but it was home and full of memories and reminders of lives gone by. Despite everything, Isla wasn't ready to say goodbye to it either.

'No it doesn't. Isla?'

'I'm with Morag.' Though May had made sure it had nothing to do with her.

'Why do you both always make a point of disagreeing with me?' Lorna's hands were on her hips, like the recalcitrant schoolchild she once was.

'Only when you're in the wrong.' Morag looked at the posed family portrait on the heavy sideboard. They looked a perfect family – except Isla wasn't there. May had booked the photographer when she had been at a music exam. Isla had always suspected May had done it deliberately, although her mother had always denied it.

She couldn't wait for the evening to be over. If only May was here to answer her mounting questions. Instead she was with her sisters, their relationship twisting and turning back on itself like gnarled old tree roots. Isla had always yearned for that unquestioning familial affection, that undivided loyalty she had seen in other families. But long ago, she had recognised that was not them. She drummed her fingers on the table. 'I thought we were going to discuss things calmly and rationally.' Instead, she felt them heading towards the explosion they had been skirting round since they arrived.

'Don't be so saintly. Selling Braemore makes sense. We don't want it and it's far too big for Aggie.' The bit was between Lorna's neatly capped and whitened teeth.

'No! It's our family home.' Morag's voice was raised. 'I'm glad we'll be able to visit. I—'

'Everything all right, girls?' Andrew sauntered in, his rubicund face blurred with drink, an empty glass in hand. 'Not fighting already, are we?'

With the door open, they could hear the radio and the sounds of Aggie washing up coming from the kitchen.

'Go away, Andrew. This has nothing to do with you.' Lorna waved her hand dismissively. 'Why don't you help Aunt Aggie?'

His joviality disintegrated. 'I know when I'm not wanted.' He slammed the door as he left the room.

'That's the trouble. You don't.' Lorna muttered under her breath before turning to Morag. 'How often have you actually come here in the last five years?' She banged her palm on the table. 'Twice a year at most. I'm the only one who visits Mum and Aggie regularly. For my sins.'

'Only because you live a few miles away.' Morag zipped up her maroon fleece before wrapping her arms around herself.

'This is pointless,' said Isla, disliking how overtly hostile Lorna had been towards Andrew. 'Aggie owns half the house. You two own the rest. That's what Mum wanted.'

'People challenge wills all the time.'

'But we're not going to.' Morag was firm. 'Are we?' She turned to Isla for support.

'It's not up to me. But I don't think you can do that to Aggie, no.'

'Can't do what to me?' Aggie stood in the doorway, a spry woman of eighty-four, theatrical in a brilliant blue and pink kaftan, short grey hair gelled on end, inquisitive eyes, hand resting on a walking stick – another ancestral relic – with large rings on her fingers, a tea-towel over her shoulder. 'Thanks for the help, girls!'

'We were talking about the house,' said Lorna, suddenly sheepish.

'I'm so grateful,' said Aggie. 'I didn't expect May to leave it to me.'

'Well, technically speaking she's only left half of it to you.' Lorna didn't look at her sisters.

'She said she'd make sure I could stay here.' Aggie came to sit beside Isla, her hands on the table so the light bounced off her rings. 'It's going to be so different now.' Then she gave a mischievous smile. 'But at least I can start playing poker again. She banned me, you know? I might even ask a friend to live here with me.'

'Did she talk about why she wasn't leaving me anything?' Isla spoke quickly, aware Lorna was fuming beside her, but she had to know.

'Och, she'll have had her reasons, dear.' Uneasy, Aggie shifted in her chair and eyed the sideboard where a couple of bottles of whisky stood. 'I've just come in for a wee night cap.'

'But what were they?' Isla insisted, certain there was something Aggie wasn't saying.

Their aunt's eyes flicked nervously between them before she shook her head. 'You know what May was like. She kept herself to herself.'

'She only left me the picture that used to be in Dad's study. Why would she do that?' Isla heard her voice catch.

'It meant a lot to your father.' The shutters came down. 'Have I ever told you about the time—'

'Have you ever thought about moving somewhere smaller?' Lorna barged in with all the finesse of a charging bull.

'I'm not ready to move yet, dear.' Aggie crossed the room, took a glass from the corner cabinet and poured herself a generous slug of the malt. 'I'll see you in the morning.'

'Lorna, you shouldn't have.' Isla spoke as soon as the door closed behind her and before Lorna had time to push back.

'I had to. She was about to embark on one of her never-ending stories. And the whole thing's ridiculous. She'll be around for years and we'll never . . .' Lorna was red with fury now, her mouth a thin angry line. A pulse ticked by her right eye. 'You two have always sided against me. I've always been the baby to you.'

Isla could see the red mist descending on Morag. She closed her eyes, resigned to the inevitable.

'I don't think of you as the baby.' The words squeezed out of Morag. 'But your sense of entitlement is off the fucking scale. We're not going to a lawyer and we're not going to try to persuade Aggie to sell. We'll follow Mum's wishes to the letter. End of.' Morag helped her and Isla to another glass of wine, her hand shaking so she spilled some on the table.

All Isla wanted was to go home to Oxford and get on with her life.

'You're no better than me.' Lorna put down her glass. 'You and your middle-child complex. Nothing's ever fair, is it?'

'That's rich, coming from you.' Morag gave a superior smirk.

Lorna was on her feet and shoved her chair hard into the table.

'Will you two stop it. Please!' Isla shouted, snapping at last.

'Don't start trying to be peace-maker.' Morag turned on her suddenly.

Lorna was at the door. 'I'm leaving. You're pathetic. I just think it's sensible to sell, that's all. I'm not the one who turned this into something personal.'

'You never do take responsibility. Yes! Think about that for a second.' Morag paused to let her words sink in. 'Lucky you found a husband who can carry you. He's the one who's encouraged you to be so entitled. He should have put the brakes on years ago.'

The sisters stared at each other, appalled it had come to this.

'I'll leave you to deal with the probate then.' Lorna was icy. 'Everything can be done through the post or by email. I'll see you tomorrow at the funeral.' She opened the door. 'Andrew! It's time to go.'

Isla and Morag were left staring at each other. They

heard muttered words outside, the front door slamming, and a car start.

Morag spoke first. 'Perhaps I was a bit over the top, but honestly . . .'

'Yes, you were.'

'She pushed me too far. So – now we know her position. I'm not speaking to her about it again. It's too soon to sell. That's it.' She left the room and ran upstairs.

'Why didn't you just say *that*?' Isla shouted after her.

The bathroom door slammed shut.

Isla placed her hands on the mahogany table and stared at them, neat, long-fingered with even, unpolished nails. She waited until her heartbeat had slowed, unable to believe they had let the evening before their mother's funeral drift into this, the worst argument they'd had yet.

How would they ever come back from here?

4

London, June 2019

Three months after May's funeral, Isla was standing outside the Noel Coward theatre on St Martin's Lane, staring at her ex-husband's name. Ian Dansbridge. No matter how big or small it was on the poster, it was there. That was the main thing. Ian was still working (part-subsidised by his profitable sideline in antiques 'just in case'), still on the West End stage where he had always wanted to be. That of course had been at the heart of his leaving her. Even now, seeing his name there gave her the smallest frisson of ... what? Regret, resentment, but a real fondness too. Achieving his ambition of appearing in London's West End was no mean feat. Plenty of their contemporaries had dropped by the wayside long ago and found new avenues in life-coaching, alternative healing and one had even reinvented himself as an accountant.

'Come round after the show,' he'd said. 'We'll have dinner somewhere.'

The street was pulsing with people, umbrellas being

shaken and closed as their owners shuffled up the steps, past the bag check and into the theatre foyer. Isla joined them.

She had just got inside the doors when her phone rang. She looked at it, annoyed with herself for not turning it off sooner. Helen, their daughter.

Can't talk now She texted quickly. **Play starting. Will call after show**

The anticipatory buzz of the audience before curtain-up always excited her. Ian had got her a good seat in the centre of the stalls. She leafed through the programme, pausing only to study the pictures of the cast in rehearsal. In one, Ian looked focused, determined, and in another he was laughing. He had aged well. Good genes. He looked so like his father – tall, craggy and debonair. Isla and he had made a handsome couple. Something snagged inside her at the thought.

A series of trilling ringtones hushed the audience. The last of the phones blinked off as the theatre was plunged into darkness. When the lights went up, the actors were in place as if by magic and the play began.

Isla soon realised that this heavy-duty political drama was not for her. Ian's role as one of four politicians was small but crucial. She twisted her wrist stealthily until she could see the time. Only another two hours to go. She began to think what she would say to him when she went round after the show. 'Darling, you were wonderful.' What else? It wasn't that he wasn't wonderful, but he was nothing. This wasn't a role that demanded anything extraordinary from him. When they were married, he was ambitious, versatile. Now he was merely professional, dialling in the performance expected of him . . .

In the interval, a single glass of champagne stood in the bar with her name by it. A typical showy gesture of Ian's. She enjoyed the moment, taking in the atmosphere, listening to snippets of conversation, listening out for any praise for her ex.

The second half of the play picked up a bit but was still turgid, talky and old-fashioned. Watching him take the curtain call was a pleasure though. Ian eyed the house seats to check she was there. She raised her hands higher and clapped harder. How pleased he looked, confident the cast had done justice to the play. The rest of the audience applauded less enthusiastically.

Afterwards, she went outside and sheltered from the drizzle in a shop doorway while she returned Helen's call. Ian would be happy having a post-performance drink with his fellow cast-members until she turned up.

Helen picked up immediately. 'Mum! At last! I've got a bit of a problem.'

Isla knew what that meant. She waited to hear how she was going to be roped in to help.

'You know Mike's away on a shoot and I'm going to the States for a few days?'

A nasty sense of foreboding crept over Isla. 'Yes, I do. It's very exciting.' Helen's career as a scriptwriter was beginning to take off at last after years of working hard on countless TV soaps. That graft was about to pay dividends.

'Tilly's mum's phoned. She can't have Charlie to stay after all. I'll explain when I see you. So . . . can you possibly put off your trip to Edinburgh?'

'Can't we talk about this later?'

'Of course, but just say you will. Please.'

'I really don't think I can. Put off the trip, I mean.' She had carefully planned this journey to answer questions and mend fences. Instead of accepting May's ultimate rejection of her as she had hoped she'd be able to, as the months went past she had become increasingly obsessed with what lay behind it. Finding out might at least give her some sort of resolution or acceptance. They may not have been as close as some mothers and daughters, but nothing merited this slap in the face. Just as importantly, she wanted to be on speaking terms with both her sisters again, and them with each other. So she was going to stay with both of them in the hope she could bring that about. 'We'll talk later,' she said. 'Dad's expecting me. I've just seen him in the most terminally tedious play. He was great, of course.'

She added the last bit just for Helen.

There was a huddle of people at the stage door, hunched against the wet, waiting for the star of the show, an actor who had recently fronted a BBC spy drama that that had revived his flagging career. On her way up the white-washed stone staircase, she heard Ian's voice booming from a dressing room on the second floor. She opened the door to a long narrow nondescript room with lightbulb-framed mirrors, a dressing table down one side and rails of costumes at either end. Rain pattered onto a small window high in the wall.

'Darling, Isla,' he roared, still in costume. 'How wonderful to see you. It's been too long. Tom, have you met my first ex-wife?'

Tom, the actor they were all waiting for outside in the wet, was relaxing in a moth-eaten armchair. He looked over with a languid smile, the one that set the nation's hearts racing. 'I don't think so,' he said. 'Hello. Drink?' He passed Ian the bottle.

Isla's own heart fluttered faster for just a second, then she remembered who she was. A sixty-five-year-old ex-wife. *Get a grip!* She smiled. 'Thanks.'

She took the hard school chair Ian had pulled out from behind the costumes. They sat opposite each other in front of the mirror, the edges stuck about with good luck cards. There were a couple of dying bunches of flowers in brown water in vases, and a furry giraffe sat, legs splayed, among his make-up. She raised an eyebrow in its direction.

'Fan,' he said, shutting down that line of enquiry. 'So how did you enjoy the show?'

'Wonderful,' she said. 'So thought-provoking. And you were wonderful too.'

'Really?' He frowned. 'There was that bit in the second act. When I had to slip the papers to Tom. I'm not sure that works.'

'No, no. It did,' she said. 'It was terrific. Absolutely.' She had known him for long enough to know that agreeing with his doubts was the fastest route to an argument.

Twenty minutes later they were round the corner in Sheekeys where they were shown to a discreet table for two in a corner surrounded by black-and-white photographs of West End performers over the decades. Once they had ordered, they both relaxed.

'So,' he said. 'How are you? May's death must have hit hard, even though I know you weren't close.'

'Thank you for coming to the funeral.' To her horror, Isla felt tears welling. *Not here*, she told herself, biting the inside of her lip to stop them.

Since May's death, she had experienced similar over-whelming waves of emotion that crashed over her when least expected, making her feel utterly helpless. Thankfully, they retreated as swiftly as they came, but left her feeling like a limp rag. Once she had broken down in Sainsburys, unable to choose between two brands of frozen peas. Another time, she had been at work, talking to one of the Museum's trustees about funding when he suddenly asked, 'Would you like a Kleenex?' She had missed the crucial point of the conversation altogether and tears were rolling down her cheeks. Once or twice she had been overtaken by unprompted choking emotion when she was in the middle of a staff briefing or dealing with guests or suppliers. People were sympathetic, embarrassed, or just waited until she had regained control.

She had tried to see her relationship with her parents for what it was. The warmth and affection she held towards her father was in no doubt but it was hard to think about her mother. She knew so little about either of them but especially her. Bare facts yes, stuff about her life as Mrs Adair, housewife and mother to three daughters, but nothing about her feelings, her wants and desires – or why she batted those kind of questions away if they asked. Isla remembered her father shutting himself in his study for another evening and the accompanying click of their mother's bedroom door as she retired early for the night. Her bond with Aunt Aggie had been so much stronger.

Ian ignored her tears – if he noticed them at all.

'She was a funny old thing, your mum, but I was actually very fond of her. Could never quite make her out though.'

'She adored you.' She tried to steady her voice. All her family loved Ian, his behaviour towards her long ago written off as history. May especially had always encouraged him to keep in touch, inviting him to stay, as if his divorce had nothing to do with Isla. She didn't once stop to ask Isla what she felt about Ian's continued attachment to the family.

'Isla?' He wasn't good with emotion but he reached across the table and took her hand.

If she didn't change the subject she would break down and embarrass them both. 'Do you have to introduce me as your first ex-wife?' she said.

He looked taken aback, then smiled, withdrawing his hand. He understood. 'But you are. The first of three, and the only one who still talks to me.'

'Because I'm the only one who had your child.'

'Ah, sweet Helly.' He swilled the red wine round his glass and looked over the top of it at her. 'How is she? I spoke to her the other day but she's always so busy.'

'In a state about Charlie.'

'Ah, the school suspension.' He nodded, in the know. 'I don't remember Helly's old school being so bloody draconian.'

'Charlie's been suspended from school?' Warning lights started flashing in Isla's mind. 'Helen hasn't said anything to me.' She knew why not. Because Ian wouldn't make a fuss, whereas she wouldn't be able to help herself.

'Didn't she tell you?' He looked smug at having the inside info.

She didn't need to prompt him. He'd delight in being the one to tell her. She sipped her wine and waited.

'She's been suspended till the end of term because there were drugs found at some party she was at. The parents reported it to the school, who've come down on the girls like a ton of bricks.'

'What?!' Isla was shocked. 'Why would they do that? Couldn't they deal with it themselves? And anyway Charlie's not like that. Is she?' Stories of youngsters experimenting with drugs and with fatal results raced through her head.

'Bloody stupid, I agree. Getting caught I mean.' He sliced off the head of his plaice. 'It's all fine. Charlie had nothing to do with it – or so she says – but the school's drugs policy is fierce. Get caught in the vicinity of the stuff, and you're suspended. Supply it and you're expelled. Four of them apparently. Probably just for a spliff or two.' He shook his head. 'Remember when we—'

'—grew our own in the flat? Of course. How dumb were we, putting the pots in the kitchen window?' The police had spotted them from the street. No arrests. Just a warning and an order to throw them away.

They laughed. Isla relaxed.

No wonder Helen had been so on edge. Perhaps Isla should stay with Charlie after all. As she deliberated, Ian's attention was taken by an animated young woman in a red dress on the next table before he turned back. 'Don't make a fuss, will you? The poor child's had enough of that.'

She hated it when he advised her how to behave. 'Of course I'll talk to Helen when I see her tomorrow.'

'Just keep it low-key, that's all.' He lifted the skeleton from his fish, filleting it cleanly.

'I do know how to talk to her, Ian. I've had years of practice.'

'But sometimes you get it wrong.' He raised an eyebrow to elicit her agreement.

'Let's not talk about it now.' She would get the truth from Helen and make her decisions then.

'Fine. In fact, I do have other news.' He pulled a long face. 'Can I talk to you?'

'You know you can.' She readied herself for one of Ian's confessions that were always prefaced by those words. She had become his best listener and sometimes advisor over the years. She had never asked him to reciprocate, but she was happy for their confidences to remain a one-way street. She had her friend Mary to confide in when necessary.

He sighed. 'Fran's leaving me. Or to be more accurate, she's already left.'

Goodbye, wife number four.

'Oh, Ian. Not again.'

'I don't have much luck,' he said with a sidelong glance at the next table and the red dress.

She laughed. 'You have far too much and far more than you deserve.'

Did other ex-wives discuss what was once their greatest problem with the ex-husband who caused it? She had every sympathy with Fran. Ian had never been able to resist an attractive woman. Even at sixty-six, as they sat having dinner, his eye was wandering. He made a far better friend than a husband.

'I should have stayed with you. We'd make the perfect elderly couple.' His hand, flat on the table, was that of an old man. The realisation came with a shock to Isla. The years were catching up with both of them.

'I doubt that. Anyway I might be spoken for now.'

His face was a picture of astonishment vying with an unjustified possessiveness. 'Spoken for? By whom?'

'A lovely man I met. Tony. It's going well.' It felt odd telling Ian about another man, even though they split up long ago and there had been others since.

He sipped his wine for a little longer than necessary. 'Tony, eh? You never said.'

'You never asked.'

He smiled. 'I'm sorry but I'm pleased for you. Really.'

'We'll see. It's early days.' She wished she hadn't said anything. Then an idea struck her. 'I'm on my way to Scotland via the sisters, and he's coming up to meet me.' She ignored his wink. 'It's all fixed but Helen wants me to stay on longer to keep an eye on Charlie. I don't suppose *you*'d have her, would you?' That was the obvious solution. 'Just keep an eye on her for a few days.'

His eyebrows rose until they were briefly hidden by the still thick flop of hair. 'I don't think so! I've got another week of the run.'

Familial duties were not something he had ever taken too seriously. When it suited him, was the way he operated.

'But it would be such a help.' She never gave in to him that easily.

He turned down his lip. 'I really can't, darling. Don't you see? Have some of these fried courgettes.'

She saw exactly. The smooth running of his own life came before her or the journey that she had planned.

'I'm sure Helen and Charlie have friends who'll help out.' She spoke with a confidence she didn't feel.

'Why don't you take her with you?' He looked at her over the rim of his glass.

'To Scotland?!' That would make her trip very different to the one she had planned.

'Not necessarily. Couldn't you put her on a train home after a few days when Helly's back?'

Isla hesitated. How would she be able to focus on finding out more about May? What about the people she was staying with? Would they mind? But ... it was a solution. And whatever happened, Charlie would have to go home before Tony travelled up for their special weekend. The thought of their being together gave her a warm glow of anticipation. He may not have been in her life long but he had been stalwart and loving in his support, especially when May died. He had put up with her going on and on about her mother's bewildering lack of affection and how Isla blamed herself, the guilt she felt for never having addressed the issue and sorted it out. In return, she had been glad to be able to help him out financially while he got back on his feet. Not that he'd borrowed much and as soon as he found work, he'd pay her back. He'd made that part of the deal. However, the weekend in his choice of country hotel was a proper thank-you present for listening. Charlie absolutely couldn't be there for that.

'By the way, I thought I might go to Braemore myself for Aggie's birthday.' Having found the answer to Isla's dilemma, Ian had moved on already, and was watching to see what she felt about this latest idea. 'She asked me,' he added, on the defensive.

'Might you?'

'We-ell ...' His wavering hand showed his indecision. 'I've got an interview for a part.' He waited for the congratulation that didn't come. 'But I'd like to see the old bird again before she pops her clogs. You wouldn't mind if I go?'

'Since when have you taken any notice of what I mind?' She couldn't help smiling.

When they parted ways, they kissed before Ian dived into Leicester Square tube with a careless wave over his shoulder at her. Isla walked to her bus stop, her mind returning to Charlie. If Helen needed her help that badly, perhaps she really ought to overcome her misgivings and invite Charlie along with her.

Four or five days.

How bad could it be?

5

Helen ended her call and slammed the phone down on the kitchen counter. Isla could tell from her expression it was bad news. 'Keisha's mum was my last hope. Nobody'll have Charlie to stay – they're scared she'll be a bad influence – and our neighbour's going to be away so she can't keep an eye on her either. What the hell am I going to do? I worked so hard on the Netflix pilot, I can't not meet the producer and team behind the series. This could be a really big break for me. You know that, right?'

Isla looked around the living room. She'd taken the photo on the mantelpiece herself. It showed a happy family of three with Helen, hair blowing in the wind, looking up in adoration at Mike who was squinting into the sun, and ten-year-old Charlie smiling and happy on a sunny beach in Cornwall, her arms round a surfboard: a very different child from the surly creature who had surfaced at eleven thirty for breakfast that morning. That had been such a happy holiday of beaches, ice creams, fish and chips and laughter. All four of them together. What a difference a few years made.

'What shall I do now?' Helen was almost in tears.

From upstairs the pulsing bass beat of some unidentifiable music pounded through the floorboards to where Isla and Helen sat. Helen looked up and rolled her eyes but did nothing about it. Isla had made her confess that Ian had got the party episode spot on. All four girls thought to be smoking weed had indeed been suspended from school till the start of the new school year, including Charlie. 'I didn't tell you because I didn't want you to worry.' Helen gave her one of those commanding looks that said, *So don't start now.*

Isla stood up and stepped over Jock, her black Labrador and travelling companion, who opened an eye and thumped his tail on the floor. She looked out at the garden for a few minutes, bracing herself to speak.

'I could always take her with me.' There. She'd done it, her defences finally eroded by the thought of Charlie herself. They shouldn't be talking about her as if she was a parcel that needed to be stored somewhere for safekeeping. She was just a stroppy teenager but she was also Isla's only grandchild.

Helen's face lit up as she smiled with relief. 'Really? Would you?'

Isla knew immediately this was the right thing, whatever the consequences.

Helen jumped from her seat and hugged her mother hard. 'Thank you. I knew you'd come through.'

Of course she did.

'One condition.' Isla folded the newspaper and smoothed along the crease. 'We ask her first.'

'No need. I decide what's best for us.'

'If she's coming with me,' Isla insisted, 'it's only with her agreement. I'm not taking a reluctant passenger.' She fought the impulse to cave in under the force of her daughter's will.

But Helen's eyes were on the prize. 'Okay.' She went to the door and flung it open. 'Charlie! Turn the music down. We need you down here. Charlie!'

The music kept on thumping.

Isla looked down at her travelling companion. 'What do you think, Jock? Will this work?'

The old dog lifted his head at the mention of his own name then laid it down with a groan.

'That's not the answer I want, my friend.' She stroked the smooth velvet of his ear.

Helen was upstairs now. There was a sudden silence as the music was turned off. A shouted exchange and the slam of a door. Two pairs of footsteps on the stairs, one light and quick, the other stomping behind.

Charlie followed her mother into the room, which for the moment was obviously the last place on earth she wanted to be. The tension between mother and daughter was plain. Helen's face was tight, unsmiling. Charlie slouched, sullen in black leggings, a crop top and black Doc Martens that looked like space boots at the end of her skinny legs. Isla was surprised by the lip gloss and eye shadow that made her look older but no less vulnerable. Her mouth was wide with full bowed lips that turned up slightly at each corner. She had inherited Isla's pointy chin (once the bane of her life) and good cheekbones (the things that she had mistakenly thought

34

would keep ageing at bay) but her eyes were from Mike's side: wide-set, almond-shaped, hazel-coloured and topped by thick brows. Three tiny studs decorated her right earlobe. Her granddaughter knelt on the floor beside Jock and, as her bangles slid down her arm, stroked his head. 'What do you want?' She couldn't have sounded less interested.

'Don't speak to me like that. We've got something to ask you.'

'I'm busy.' Charlie turned over her shiny pink phone in her hand, glancing at its face.

'We heard. Put your phone down. Please!' Helen visibly exercised every ounce of self-control. 'This won't take long, I promise. You know I'm going away on Monday?'

'Yeah.' Charlie put her phone face down on the coffee table.

'Keisha's mum's called to say they can't have you to stay after all.'

Charlie bent over Jock so they couldn't see her face. 'So what? I can stay here on my own. I'm nearly fifteen.'

'I don't think so. Not after the suspension and the party.' Helen's hands were tightly clasped in front of her.

'The party wasn't my fault. I told you. Lucy invited those boys from the high school.' She kissed the top of Jock's nose.

What party? What boys? What else hadn't Helen told Isla?

'That's not what her parents say.'

Charlie's shoulders hunched, as she closed her eyes. 'Whatever.'

Helen glanced at Isla as if to say, *See what I have to deal with.* 'So we've had a great idea.'

We?

Isla watched them both – the two people she loved most in the world, however hard they sometimes made it – wishing she could knock some sense into them.

'I don't want to go with you. You'll be working all the time.' Charlie looked up and Isla saw the longing in her eyes that contradicted her words swiftly extinguished.

But Helen was gazing into the mirror over the mantelpiece and missed her daughter's need altogether. She tucked a stray piece of hair behind her ear, adjusted one of the invitation cards.

Isla spoke. 'Perhaps . . .'

But Helen wasn't going to give her the chance to backtrack. She sailed straight over her. 'Granny's going on a driving holiday for the next couple of weeks, and she says you can go with her. Isn't that great?' Couldn't she hear how desperate she sounded?

Charlie looked up and pushed her hair back over her shoulders. 'Me? Go with Granny? Are you serious? You're not even going to be away for two weeks.'

'She'll put you on the train home before next weekend. We'll sort it out.'

'Yes,' Isla heard herself say, while trying to ignore how appalled Charlie sounded. 'Would you like to? Though you'll have to put up with Jock. His farts can be vicious. And Betty can be temperamental at times. My car,' she explained to their puzzled faces.

A suspicion of a smile on Charlie's face disappeared as

quickly as it came. 'What about the end of term parties? I've got to be here for them.' She turned to her mother. Each of them was as adamant as the other. Isla felt powerless, knowing any interference by her would only make things worse.

Helen shook her head. 'No more parties.'

'Mum! I *have* to be there.' Charlie's eyes glistened with unshed tears.

'There'll be plenty of other parties later,' offered Isla only to be quelled by such a look of disdain that she suddenly wished she could retract the invitation. But it was too late.

'After the last one?' said Helen. 'I don't think so. And I'm not sure the other parents will want you there either. Not after . . .'

'I told you that wasn't me.'

'But they think it was and that's enough.'

'That's so unfair.'

'That's the way of the world. Sometimes people don't believe us, and sometimes we have to do things we don't want to.'

'You don't.' Charlie ran her finger down Jock's nose.

'Oh, believe me, I do. And anyway, I'm nearly forty, not fourteen. I've suffered for the privilege of doing what I want. But the point is I can't leave you here and Dad's away filming till August so this really is the only way.'

'Finished?' Charlie stood to face them. 'I do love you, Gran—'

'Thanks.' Isla floated on a tide of grandmotherly love for a moment. 'The feeling's mutual.'

Charlie's hand was on the door handle. 'But I've got so much to do here. Mum doesn't get it.'

'I understand. No hard feelings.' A glimmer of hope surfaced. Perhaps she would be travelling alone after all.

'Thanks.' Charlie left the room and they heard her heavy tread on the stairs. In moments, the music had started again, every bit as loud as before.

'See how difficult she is?' Helen flopped into a nearby chair.

'Honestly? I see a lonely, confused, unhappy teenager. Not so different from the way you were. Don't you remember what it was like?' Isla did, only too well – work and motherhood: a perpetual and exhausting round of negotiations to avoid confrontation in which neither side understood the other or had time to try.

'Don't go all sentimental on me. I'll spend time with her when I'm back – I promise. But right now, I've got to persuade her to go with you.' She straightened her white T-shirt, picking at a teeny stain. 'Parties! For Christ's sake.'

'What else has happened that you haven't told me?'

'Nothing major.' She waved a hand to dismiss the whole thing. 'Mike and I were away for the night. Charlie invited some friends over here. More people turned up than she was expecting. That's all.'

'And?'

'Oh, not much. A bit of damage and one of them got carted off to A and E because they'd drunk too much.'

'That sounds quite a lot to me.' But Helen was playing the

whole thing down so as not to put her off the idea of taking
Charlie with her. She knew her daughter well.

'No. Trust me.' Helen closed the subject. 'Anyway I'll get
her to see sense.'

'I'm not taking her hostage. That won't work.'

'She'll agree. I'll make sure she does.'

A bribe of some item of new clothing had always worked
with Helen when she was that age.

'So . . . What are we doing tomorrow?' Helen asked. The
subject was closed.

As they discussed the exhibitions Isla might visit while
in London, the shops she might go to, what she could bring
home for supper, she began to relax again. Perhaps taking
Charlie wouldn't be so bad.

She thought of her granddaughter, defiant, yet underneath
so vulnerable; of Helen bent on advancing her career. She
thought of herself, and how she had struggled to push herself
along her chosen path as a museum curator while Helen was
growing up. Her employers had been so considerate, tolerat-
ing her bringing her daughter into work, or her taking time
off to look after her. The world Helen had chosen for herself
was much more cut-throat.

She would wait to see what Charlie decided. But, deep
down, she knew how Helen would turn the tables in the three
days before Isla left. It wasn't as if she hadn't had practice.

6

Paris, 1954

May had only been in Paris for an hour or so and was already infected by the unfamiliar and thrilling energy of the city. This was nothing like home. Dunfermline was miles away. But standing on the doorstep of her new home, her nerves returned. How would she and the Dubois family get on? Would this diminutive woman who had answered the door be a hard taskmaster? How was she going to make friends? How was she going to make herself understood? Would her schoolgirl French be enough to begin with? She followed Madame Dubois inside, clutching the handle of her suitcase.

What had seemed like a brave, bold decision to come to France now seemed the height of foolhardiness and fraught with pitfalls. Her lack of fluency in French being the first.

'Oh, you'll soon pick it up,' her father had said. 'Be speaking like a native before you know where you are. The Dubois said they'd fix you up with lessons. Then you can come home and work as a translator or something worthwhile. Aunt Jess

40

will fix you up in London.' She was his spinster sister who did something mysterious in the War Office.

Her mother had been less certain. 'But she'll be alone in a city of strangers, Frank. I'm not sure it's such a good idea.'

'Moira, stop that nonsense. She'll be back before you know it.'

That did it. Anything to escape her mother who liked having her oldest daughter at home where she could call on her whenever she was needed. To have any freedom, May had to get away, even if it meant leaving her dear younger sister Aggie behind. A meeting between her father and a French business associate had led to her being offered the post of caring for the six-year-old child of an acquaintance of his. The job would give her some money and a roof over her head while she improved her language skills and found her way round a new city. She had jumped at the opportunity. She didn't know much more about children than she knew French, but how hard could they be? And Paris! To think of it! On Pathé news reels in the cinema she had seen dizzying footage of men painting the Eiffel Tower without safety harnesses, shots of the city lit up at night, busy streets full of cars and people, elegant tree-lined boulevards, street cafés, the fashion houses. And now here she was.

The apartment seemed spacious and comfortable, with high ceilings and furniture that was neat and tidy, though had perhaps seen better days. Madame chattered away but May couldn't keep up with what she was saying. Her room was at the very top of the house where the servants from all the other flats would once have slept – a *'chambre de bonne'*, Madame explained. The room was small and the bed was pushed against the wall with a side table and a light beside it. The curtains at the narrow window were patterned with oatmeal-coloured bees and laurel wreaths on a white background. Outside she could see the spring sunshine and the tops of the trees in the park opposite.

It didn't take long to realise, however, that her charge, Emile, would prefer her not to be there. The first clue was the marbles laid out on the floor. She had spotted them in time to avoid slipping and breaking a leg. The second was a piece of rancid cheese hidden behind her bedside cabinet. They were the sort of pranks that May would have played herself as a child, and she couldn't help smiling when Emile's back was turned.

Soon after her arrival, May was in the nursery, wondering how she could jolly it up. There was no sign of Emile. A shiny rocking horse sat motionless in the window, looking out towards the trees on the other side of the road. On top of the heavy chest of drawers sat three string puppets – a clown with red hair, Pinocchio and a growling wolf in checked trousers – heads lolling, their blue eyes in fixed stares, rictus smiles. She touched Pinocchio's nose with a fingertip. In a corner, she found a one-armed teddy left on a chair, a little blanket strewn roughly over him. She stepped over the railway track that ran round half of the room, the trains on it stationary.

A sudden noise made her spin round, hand on her heart, as a clockwork soldier marched across the floor towards her, banging his drum. *Rat a tat. Rat a tat.* She snatched him up.

'You scared me.'

From behind the heavy wooden door came a muffled sound that she pretended not to hear.

'But we could be friends, as I can't see any children here. Where do you live?' She spotted a toy fort in the corner opposite the abandoned teddy. 'Will you fit in here? No?'

'He lives here.' Emile raced into the room to point at the mahogany armoire, one of his knee-length socks down round his ankle.

'Where have you been hiding?' She pretended surprise so he laughed. 'I thought we might go out.' She spoke in her best very basic French as she pulled open the armoire door to find four shelves neatly stacked with toys in boxes. Remembering she was only to speak English with him, she repeated herself very slowly in her mother tongue, her hand itching to ruffle his hair that was combed so flat on either side of his parting.

'*Oui*. We go to the park?' His eyes lit up.

'Of course.' If she kept the English simple, they might even get on. Her stomach was churning as it had since the moment she arrived.

They couldn't possibly get lost going across the road to the park on the other side. She took the navy jacket that her mother had insisted she bring especially, although she was aware of how unfashionable it was, bought for the long cold Scottish winters. Emile took a model sailing boat, and together they headed down the stone stairs and out of the front door onto the street.

'Emile! Stay with me,' she said as they crossed the road. The spring sunshine filled the air with promise, and the trees were misted green with new leaves. When they reached the gate, she stopped for a moment to stare back at their building again. Goodness, how ... well, how elegantly the Parisians lived. Seven storeys of imposing cream stone with elaborate narrow wrought-iron balconies on each of the four principal floors, decorative stone scrolls supporting each one. Paris was nothing like her home town of Dunfermline, dominated by the great abbey on the hill, but it didn't matter. She was already intoxicated by Paris and to discover somewhere as beautiful as this so soon was a blessing.

Emile was running ahead of her. She ran after him, glad of the sensible flats her mother had insisted she pack. 'Come back,' she yelled, aware it wouldn't make a jot of difference. Fortunately the model boat slowed him down, so she soon caught up with him.

'We won't come here again, if you run away,' she said, knowing full well they would come here as often as she could.

Emile was taking them down a long avenue flanked by trees, past women with prams, other children playing ball, people walking dogs. Through the trees, she saw a group of men throwing heavy-looking silvery balls in some sort of game that required all their concentration and a lot of stand-ing around. Three children sat astride donkeys that were being walked down the path. In front of them, the avenue led to a vast open area of ornamental gardens and gravelled paths, with statues around a large pond, and presided over by an imposing palace with a decorative clock marking the centre of its façade. May had never seen anything like it. While Emile ran over to join the other children sailing their boats in the pond, she approached a girl about her own age, sitting in one of a pair of seats. She could sit here, take in the scene while keeping an eye on her charge.

'Is this taken?' Her French was careful.

'No. It's yours.' The voice was as English as May was Scottish. 'You must be looking after one of the horrors too?' Below the hair that made her look a little like Marilyn Monroe, her eyes were friendly and shone with her enjoyment of life, at the same time inviting May's confidence. 'Well, aren't they?' She raised a hand to her flyaway blond curls as she shook her head in mock despair.

May laughed. 'Mine is, rather.' She pointed out Emile who was trying to right his capsized boat. A flock of little boys were crowded round offering advice.

The other girl grinned, and just like that, May was on the way to making her first friend. Wendy was from Bournemouth and was working for a family who lived on the opposite side of the Gardens, looking after a little boy called Amaury. Within minutes, Wendy was pointing out the regulars to her.

'That old woman in black always walks her dogs at this time and sits on that seat. If anyone else takes it, she moves them on.' She looked around. 'Now, you see those two?' A tousle-headed young man was passionately kissing a woman as if they were alone in the park. 'One of them's married to someone else. You can tell by the way she keeps looking around her as if she's worried they'll be seen. That man there always sits alone, waiting for someone who never comes.' He wasn't old but he looked as if he had the cares of the world on his shoulders. 'And those boys must be students at the Sorbonne.' She waved with her fingertips at a group of young men with satchels. One of them returned the wave before another looked their way, said something and they all laughed.

She smiled back. 'You'll get to know them all.'

May was entranced. By sitting here and watching, she could tell the French were different. The women had a style that the good burghers of Edinburgh and Dunfermline couldn't dream of. A flower in a lapel, a piece of ribbon, the angle of a hat, the heel of a shoe – a single stylish detail could make all the difference. She took note and vowed to try it for herself.

A boy ran over, clutching a ball. 'Can we go? I'm hungry.'

'How good your English is already, Amaury. Of course.' Wendy stood, wiping her hands on the skirt of her dress. 'Perhaps I'll see you tomorrow? Same time?'

Perhaps she would.

7

Norfolk, 2019

'So where are we actually going?' Charlie straightened up in her seat and took out her earphones. This was the first time she'd expressed any interest in their journey, so Isla felt a little encouraged.

'Norfolk,' she replied. 'It's a long way round, but I haven't seen my best friend for months and I miss her. I want to talk to her.'

'Can't you do that on the phone?' Charlie turned hers in her hand.

'Of course. But it's never the same as face to face. When Mum died, stuff happened that I want to tell her about.' Mary was the only person Isla wanted to tell the full story. She had explained the bare outlines over the phone but there was plenty more for them to chew over.

'You can tell me if you like.'

Isla laughed, surprised. 'Would you be interested?'

'Why don't you try?' She wound the cable around her phone then popped it in her backpack by her feet. 'Go on.'

She hadn't thought of telling Charlie the reason for the Norfolk detour, but why shouldn't she know? They were going to be together for a long time. They turned off the M11 onto the A11 towards Newmarket and she began to explain how the row over selling Braemore escalated, the things they had said.

'So Morag and I haven't spoken to Lorna since. Although she's still on about selling, if not the house itself, then some of the land. Apparently she talked to the solicitor about it and he's spoken to Morag, who's incensed. I've no idea why Lorna's so set on this, but nothing can be done till we've got probate.'

Charlie bent forward and retrieved her phone. 'Actually, you know what, Gran? It sounds pretty playground to me.'

'Oh.' Isla was taken aback by the put-down. 'You think so?'

'Yeah. Sounds like everything blew up out of control but you should be able to patch it up. It's just a question of saying something.' Her attention was turning to whatever was on her screen, her thumbs moving at speed over it.

'Well, yes, I suppose so.' Charlie was more mature than Isla had given her credit for. Her solution was the obvious one, but even so it didn't seem that easy. She had deliberately skated over being left out of May's will. She'd save that for Mary, the one person she could trust not to judge, the one person whose opinion she relied on.

The rest of the journey they travelled in near silence, the only sounds being the tinny music that occasionally leaked from Charlie's earphones accompanied by a gentle snore and a constant stream of pings from her phone.

Eventually they arrived on the outskirts of Sheringham, and turned into the driveway of a very modern house. She parked by a white gabled garage. 'You have arrived at your destination,' pronounced the satnav. Isla had not been here before and the house was not one she would ever have imagined for Mary. Gabled wings extended on either side of the plate-glass front door: the left one entirely glass-fronted so she could see right through the sitting room to the garden at the back; the right one had two narrow windows, one on top of the other. Very *Grand Designs* and nothing like the messy Victorian terrace they had left behind them in Camden.

'Wow!' Beside her, Charlie was coming to life again, having been out cold for the last half hour. 'Is this where your friend lives?' Her hand tightened on her phone as if it was a body part she was frightened of losing. Anxiety overtook Isla's excitement.

'Looks like it.' She got out of Betty and crunched across the gravel to the front door. Although she could hear the chime inside, no one came.

'How do you know her anyway?'

'We met at a school fête when Helen and Gaby, her daughter, were eight. They lived right round the corner from us in Camden and we've been friends ever since.'

'Oh.' She obviously wasn't tremendously impressed. 'Long time.'

'Maybe they're in the garden.' They went round to the back of the house where a large paved area contained an arrangement of outdoor sofas all set at angles to one another that were interrupted by square tubs containing box bushes. To one side, in a glass-sided wooden shed, there was, quite definitely, a gym. There was no one to be seen. Could this really be Mary and George's house? In London they had lived more like Isla, fighting off the tide of children's belongings and, by the time their children had left home, just accepting things the way they were. But they must have been pining for this contemporary pared-down lifestyle all along. How unlike Isla who had moved to her pretty house in Oxford's Jericho and taken all her slovenly housekeeping habits with her.

'Mary said there was a key under the big pot ... in case she wasn't here.'

They watched Jock go straight up to the first sofa. He sniffed at it then cocked his leg and peed against it.

'Jock! Oh my God! You can't do that.'

Charlie burst out laughing. 'Here.' She unrolled a coiled hose by the house and gave the end to Isla. She went back to the tap. 'Ready?'

Isla nodded. 'Yes.'

The water shot out with such force that the sofa and Isla were drenched.

'Shit! Sorry.' Charlie looked as if she was expecting a ticking off, eyes half shut, face set, shoulders hunched.

But as Isla stepped out of the puddle they'd created, she

couldn't help laughing as she wrung the water from her skirt. 'Great start!'

Charlie visibly relaxed. Maybe her grandmother wasn't that bad.

They found the key and let themselves in. Charlie stood just inside the front door with her hands on her hips, looking round. 'Where can their hub be? They must have WiFi, mustn't they?'

'God knows. I suppose so.'

They heard a car parking outside, the slamming of two doors, footsteps and the handle of the door.

Mary hadn't changed. Her greying short hair was swept back off her face, accentuating her features. She looked cool in cream trousers and flat twinkly sandals with a deep-pink patterned Indian kurta over the top. Isla hugged her friend as a Border terrier tore past them towards Jock.

'Toby!' Mary warned as she broke away from Isla. 'It's so good to see you. It's been too long. Let me show you your rooms first and then you can make yourselves at home. It's such a gorgeous day.'

Isla took in the vast open-plan downstairs area with plate-glass windows running along the back wall past living room, dining area and kitchen. It was white and light-filled, with one deep pink wall in the kitchen. There were prints on the walls that Isla didn't recognise from London and, in corners, were impossibly healthy-looking plants in ceramic containers. It was all like something out of a magazine – gorgeous to look at but with no personality at all. Anyone could live here.

Mary put her arm round Isla. 'We've got so much to catch up on.'

'You said it.' This was just what Isla had been looking forward to. She had no doubt that Mary would cut through to the heart of her problems and tell her what she thought.

Charlie didn't come down from her room immediately so Mary sat Isla down on one of the garden sofas with a white wine then raised her own glass. 'Cheers. First of all, tell me how you got saddled with Charlie.'

Isla looked up towards Charlie's bedroom window which, despite the ferocious summer heat, remained firmly shut. 'Don't say "saddled", that makes me feel awful, even if it is true.' She briefly explained what had happened. 'It's hard for Helen and Mike. I suppose that's the curse of the freelance life,' she said, trying to find an excuse for what she could only describe as their benign neglect of Charlie. 'No time or too much time, so Charlie gets a raw deal.'

'Still, on the positive side, it's nice you'll get to know her.'

'Honestly? It's like being with a creature from another planet. I can never tell whether she's going to talk to me or go all sullen. And the phone! She's never off the bloody thing.'

'My grandchildren are exactly the same. It's oxygen to them: without a phone they'll die.'

'But she must have a weak spot, and once I've found that I'll worm my way in.'

Mary laughed. 'I hope so for your sake. Or it's going to

be a long old week.' She stretched out her legs. 'Anyway ...'
She sipped her drink. 'I was sorry to hear about your mum.'

'Thanks. But you don't know the half of it.'

'Tell me then.' She sat back and listened as Isla began to
explain exactly what had happened that night at Braemore.
She left nothing out. When she finished she picked up her
drink and waited for Mary's reaction. Her friend was staring
at her, astonished.

'My God! That's extraordinary. But why?'

'That's what I keep asking myself. I thought I could accept
it but the implications just niggle away at me. I want to find
out why. At the least, I want the three of us to be on speaking
terms again.'

'Then be the one to break the ice. The longer this goes
on, the harder it will be.'

'That's what I'm trying to do.' But she was glad to have
Mary's approval.

'But for your mother to do this ... it's unimaginable. Did
she always treat you differently?'

'Not at all. She was a great mum. When we were little, it
was all picnics on the beach, games in the garden, smoothing over squabbles, helping with homework and bedtime
stories – that sort of thing. 'She gave me my first five Wade
Whimsies one Christmas. One of them was a corgi and I
called it Elizabeth after the Queen.' She laughed. Her collection of small porcelain animal figures, initiated by that gift,
was now in Fernleith Museum of Childhood, the museum
she ran. 'No, she adored us. But as we all got older, she

seemed to become more introverted, less tolerant. Especially when it came to me.'

'I wonder why. Did something trigger that?'

'Not that I can remember. But once I was a teenager, I could never do anything right. Skirt too short, make-up too heavy, rude, ungrateful – you know.'

Mary nodded. 'Isn't that the way, though?'

'My God! I had some epic rows with Helen over exactly the same sort of stuff, but this was different. I never stopped loving Helen but I wonder if Mum ever loved me at all. I guess her will proves she didn't. That's what it felt like at the time. I always ended up tiptoeing round her, never understanding why she was so impatient with me. In the end, we drifted apart. It was easier than having a confrontation, although I wish we had now. I only went back home when I had to, largely to see Dad and then, after he died, of course I wanted to go on seeing Aggie who then moved into Braemore with Mum. When I did come up, Mum and I gave each other a wide berth. I didn't behave well.'

Regret and sadness silenced her.

'What about Morag and Lorna?' Mary was intrigued. 'You mean she wasn't the same with them?'

Isla recovered herself. 'She was more tolerant with them.'

Odd memories had flashed into her mind over the past weeks, prompted by what had happened. Her first intimation something was wrong had been bad enough. She had been fourteen.

'You were such a mistake!' May had shouted it in

54

frustration during an argument over the length of a skirt Isla had chosen to wear to a school party. That must have been when the first corner of the sticking plaster that kept them together began to be ripped away.

Afterwards, May had been apologetic. 'I should never have said such a thing. You know I didn't mean it.' But words like those could never be forgotten. The arms that had hugged Isla were stiff, and Isla had refused to yield to them. Being the oldest and a mistake had obviously been enough for her to merit different treatment. But what kind of mother would divide her children like that, she asked herself. How little she had known her. And now she never would know her better.

'That's terrible.' Mary shook her head. 'What a family!' Hers was close knit and, as a result, she thought everyone else's should share that same sort of love.

'I'm going to stay with Morag and Lorna on my way north. I want to sort this mess out as best I can. They're not speaking, although Lorna's asked the lawyer if they can put some of the land up for sale. She won't give up, even though they haven't got probate and Aggie has the final say. I don't know why it's so important to her.'

'Perhaps she needs the money.'

'Andrew's got plenty.' Isla had wondered more than once if that was why her sister had married him. Her marriage to a successful lawyer from a local family had fast-tracked Lorna through Edinburgh society. She had never needed to work and she led as sybaritic a lifestyle as any Edinburgh housewife might want.

Mary looked puzzled. 'Bang goes that theory. What would your mother say?'

'She'd probably enjoy it.' Isla lowered her hand to Jock who had come outside to see what was going on. 'Once we got older, divide and rule became Mum's method of parenting.'

'She's been outstandingly successful then.' The sun glinted on Mary's glass as she lifted it to her mouth. 'Why though?'

'God knows. I've gone over and over what I can remember. Maybe it was simply that she had her favourites and I wasn't one of them. Maybe it was that Scottish Presbyterian streak that frowned on my longing for independence and leaving home to study drama in London.' She shook her head.

'Except it obviously began before that. I only met her recently at Helen and Mike's wedding, but I remember how she kept at a distance from everyone. I tried to talk to her but she didn't seem interested.'

'Par for the course. I was so used to it, I didn't even notice. Sometimes I wonder if marrying Dad stopped her from having some other life that she wanted. But they got married so young, what could that have been? I don't remember her talking about anything much before that.'

'First child syndrome. That's probably what it was. You're like the lab rat that has everything tested on them. The next ones have it much easier.'

Isla considered the idea. 'Maybe.'

'Have you ever talked to Lorna and Morag about it?'

'I tried once or twice but never got anywhere. They just said I was making too much of it, especially Lorna.'

'You should definitely have it out with them. If you don't get to the bottom of it now, you never will.'

But Isla found confrontation less easy than her friend.

The sound of a car pulling up on the other side of the house stopped their conversation.

Mary slipped on her sandals and jumped to her feet. 'That'll be George.'

Toby and Jock trotted off round the corner of the house to investigate.

Minutes later, George appeared from the kitchen, shirt sleeves rolled up, a bottle of beer in his hand. A stocky man, his head like a brown boiled egg, and a smile that sent wrinkles chasing across his tanned face. 'Isla! So great to see you. As beautiful as ever.' He kissed her cheek. 'What about this weather? Isn't it the best reason in the world to have moved here? Big skies, sea air. And a day spent "at work" on a golf course.'

He sat down beside her, after dropping a kiss onto Mary's forehead.

'I hear you've been having your difficulties.'

'Mary told you?' She didn't like the idea of them discussing her behind her back. She'd always believed her chats with Mary were confidential.

Sorry, mouthed her friend.

'You have my sympathies.' George swigged his beer. 'My family's as dysfunctional as they come. My father didn't speak to his brother for years so all the cousins are completely estranged. Still. What you don't know, you don't miss.'

'Actually, that's not terribly helpful.' Mary nudged him to shut up. 'Why don't you have a shower before supper.'

'Why not indeed.' He smiled at her then looked at Isla. 'Mine is only to obey.'

'Idiot!' Mary punched his arm.

Isla didn't know another couple like these two. Where others existed in a state of cold warfare, buckled under the strain or survived in resigned affection, they seemed as much in love as they had ever been. She looked on them with some bemusement, wishing she had it in her to give as much to someone as they gave each other. When it came to relationships, she had always held herself back, a strategy she had developed as a deliberate precaution so that she wouldn't get hurt. The shell she had developed to protect herself against her mother's slights had been fortified after Ian left her. She didn't want to be hurt like that again. As for her relationships since then and where they had gone wrong, the answer was always the same. She was always the one saying goodbye and returning to her solitary existence, which she relished until the next relationship came along. Even Keith had left in the end. They had eleven years together, although he always kept his own home. Somewhere he could escape to and see his children. This arrangement had seemed to suit them at the time but in the end he found what she couldn't give him, that one hundred per cent commitment, with someone else. She acknowledged her failing – if that's what it was – but couldn't help herself. Self-preservation at all costs. However, now she had met Tony, those barriers were breaking down. Maybe this time . . .

8

To Isla's relief, Mary had laid on company for an otherwise extremely bored Charlie. She and George had moved to Norfolk to be near their daughter Gaby and twin grand-daughters who were about Charlie's age and also came with phones attached, looking, with their long hair and skimpy dresses, as if they belonged to the same tribe. After an awkward start while the girls sized each other up, reluctant to be thrown by their grandparents into the same group, they accepted Charlie, and she them. As a result, both trips to the beach, both picnics and a barbecue were a pleasure as the teenagers detached themselves from the adults, leaving them to relax. Isla watched as Charlie, Leila and Sammy shared earbuds, singing along to the same songs, sharing whatever was on their phones, posing for selfies. Occasionally when it got too hot, the three of them would leap to their feet and run, long-limbed and free, hair blown by the wind or knotted up high, into the sea to cool down, shouting at each other and laughing. Isla was delighted to see Charlie enjoying herself. But when she had to engage with Isla, she reverted to disinterest and monosyllables at worst.

For two days, they all relaxed together. With Gaby and George and the girls, Isla and Mary found they didn't have as much time on their own as Isla had hoped they would. It wasn't until their last night, when Charlie had been swept off by the others to have a fish and chip supper in Sheringham and George was inside, preparing some work for the coming week, that Mary and Isla found themselves alone again.

Outside, it was still warm, the last of the sun casting a rosy glow across the sky. A couple of candles flickered on the table in front of them. The scent of jasmine and roses drifted on the night air. Mary had curled up on the sofa, her legs tucked underneath her, glass of rosé in hand. She looked relaxed and untroubled – sun drunk. 'This is the life. It's going to be another scorcher tomorrow.'

'What a sunset.' Isla looked up. The vastness of the Norfolk sky emphasised what a teeny speck they were on the planet.

'Isn't it fantastic? I'm so glad we moved here. No regrets.' Mary took a sip of her wine, thoughtful. 'So, I've been thinking about May. Just leaving you a picture doesn't make sense at all. What's it like?'

'It's of three angels and used to hang in Dad's study until he died and Mum relegated it to the attic. When I was a kid, we'd look at it together and he'd always say, "You're my little angel, Isla."' She felt a pang of sadness at the memory.

'Sweet. Do you think that's why she thought it was special?'

'God knows. In fact … hang on.' Isla went inside to bring out her bag. From her wallet, she took out a folded piece of paper fragile with age. 'I got it reframed just before

I left, and the framers found this behind the backboard.' She opened it carefully. 'Another note. I don't suppose it's anything.' She passed it to Mary who was already reaching for her reading specs.

She peered at the scratchy, curlicued writing. 'It's in French. *Mon cher . . .*' She hesitated. '*Pour ton anniversaire.*'

'For your birthday,' translated Isla.

'I know! *Je t'aime de tout mon coeur, pour toujours. Gros bisous. Céleste.* I love you with all my heart, for ever. Kisses. My A-level French comes up trumps at last. How romantic. Who's Céleste?'

'No idea. It must have been in there for years.' Isla refolded it with care, trying not to tear along the folds.

'Do you think it's written to your dad?'

Isla laughed at the thought. 'No! Mum and Dad married when they were in their early twenties and never looked at anyone else.'

'As far as you know.'

'True. But this is in French and Dad didn't speak anything but Scottish.'

'As far as you know.'

'Also true. But as far as I know neither of them ever went to France. They certainly never mentioned going there. If he had, he must have been so young.'

'Youth doesn't stop you falling in love.' Mary raised an eyebrow. 'George and I got together when we were nineteen, amazing as it may seem. And look at you and Ian.'

'Yeah, but we're talking about Dad.' A kind and

decent man but who hadn't a romantic bone in his body. Anniversaries went unnoticed, birthdays forgotten. She didn't remember him ever buying May flowers.

'He must have had a life before you though.' Mary was turning the letter in her fingers. 'Céleste. Mmm. Interesting.'

'Stop it! Wouldn't we know if he had?'

'Not necessarily.' Mary's eyes gleamed. 'Children don't know half of what goes on in their parents' lives.'

'But this must date back much longer ago than that.' Isla tucked the note back in her wallet.

'Show Morag and Lorna. Just in case they know something you don't.'

'You're the only other person who knows about this. I haven't even told Tony.' His name slipped out without her thinking. What would he make of her, a woman whose mother didn't want to know her? Damaged goods. Run, as fast as you can. She wouldn't risk that. Not yet.

'Who?'

She hadn't meant to keep Tony a secret from Mary, but she worried that talking about him might jinx things. Although, she reminded herself, she had told Ian. The more people who knew about the relationship, the more real it became. Up till now, they had existed in a private bubble that no one knew about, and they had been quite happy there.

'Don't be so coy,' Mary prompted. 'You'll have to tell me in the end. Have you been on that dating app again?'

'Never again.' Isla took a breath. 'I met him having coffee at the Ashmolean.'

'Really?' Mary looked at her, disbelieving.

'I'd gone there for the Jeff Koons exhibition – not for me, as it turned out. Afterwards, I went up to the restaurant for a quick coffee. He asked if he could share my table.'

'Nice move. They say galleries are meant to be the best places to get picked up.'

'It's never happened to me before and God knows I've tried!' Isla laughed. 'Remember that bad patch after Ian when I was so scared of a future on my own?' Those early days after he had left had been so empty that Isla would trail round the National Gallery or the V&A while Helen was over at a friend's, not really seeing the pictures and collections she loved so much but wondering what she would do with herself. She gave a small shake of her head to clear those memories. 'Anyway, we got chatting . . .'

'What about? And what does he look like? I want to know everything.' Mary actually rubbed her hands together. 'Have you got a picture?'

'He's taller than me, slim.' She left out the slight pot belly. 'Quite good-looking if you don't mind a receding hairline! And he's got a sweet, slightly wonky smile.' She pulled out her phone and scrolled through the photos. 'There.'

Mary snatched it from her and blew up the picture to get a better look at his face. 'Mmm. Nice.'

Isla smiled. He was. 'And what we talked about? I honestly don't remember – whatever he'd just seen in the museum, probably. The weather. Nothing momentous.' She was too embarrassed to admit to the way she was immediately drawn to him as he asked about her job and listened attentively as she told him. He had been genuinely interested, whereas others often dismissed a Museum of Childhood as something frivolous or irrelevant. 'When I got up to go back to work, he asked for my number.' She remembered how his hand had shaken as he passed over his phone for her to key it in. That had endeared him to her.

'And then?'

'He texted me that night to say how much he'd enjoyed meeting me, that he didn't make a habit of approaching strange women in restaurants but he'd like to see me again. I left it for a couple of days—'

Mary sighed as if there was no hope for her.

'I didn't want to seem too keen,' Isla justified herself. She couldn't confess even to Mary how difficult she found making any kind of move. 'And then I texted him back. We met for lunch and . . .'

Mary shifted position so she was leaning forward not to miss a word. 'And you haven't looked back?'

'Well, I wouldn't say that but . . .'

'But you do like him?' At least she didn't clap again.

'Yes, yes I do. But with my track record . . . I'm nervous.'

'For heavens' sake. You've just been unlucky.'

'For thirty odd years?'

'Yes, well.' For once, Mary didn't have an argument. '*Very* unlucky then. So tell me about him. What does he do?'

'He ran a gîte in France for the last ten years but when his wife left him he had to sell up.' He had shown her pictures of a group of beautiful stone buildings bathed in sunshine, centred round a sparkling blue pool, surrounded by fields and woodland. The place looked idyllic. 'With all the uncertainty of Brexit, he decided to come back here and start something new, so he's looking into all sorts of possibilities, renewing the contacts he had before he left the country.' That's what he had told her.

'So where's he living?'

'With friends outside Kidlington. Apparently they've got a self-contained one-bed flat over some stables where he's staying for the moment.'

'Apparently? You haven't been there then?'

Isla felt herself blushing. 'No. He stays at mine. It's much easier. He hasn't got any work to go to in the mornings and I have, so it makes sense.'

She had been shocked at the speed with which their relationship had developed. Despite her reservations about committing herself again, she found herself enjoying his company – his cooking too. He liked nothing better than rustling up meals in her kitchen, using up what was in her cupboards, going out to buy more. He had been a good listener when she needed one, but he was an entertaining and knowledgeable talker too. He made her laugh. As hard as she might resist she found herself falling for him. If she didn't take a chance or two in her mid-sixties, she reasoned, it would soon be too late. After all, if Ian still could, then so could she.

'When did all this happen?'

'A few months ago.' The date February the 12th was

imprinted on her memory, just five weeks before her mother died. Isla took a sip of her wine, then looked towards the bottom of the garden where the twilight was deepening.

'What?!' Mary pushed herself forward in her seat so she was almost on her feet. 'All that time and you didn't think to tell me?'

'If I'd seen you . . . over the phone seemed to be making too much of it.'

'Oh, come on. But you do like him?'

'He's lovely, very kind. We have a good time together.' But was that enough?

Now Mary was looking dubious. 'You don't seem very sure. Are you happy, at least?'

Isla thought for a moment. Was she happy? What was happy? Getting used to someone else in the home that she had made for herself was hard. Her house in Walton Street wasn't big but it was just right for her. She had got used to her independence, her freedom, her habits that she hadn't realised were habits until Tony teased her about flossing her teeth in the morning while boiling the kettle for her first cup of tea, putting the milk on the teabag before she poured in the hot water, hanging her washing over the bath and leaving her shoes littering the hall. Initially she had been annoyed but she had made a conscious effort not to let it get to her and over the past weeks, her habits had begun to change. After all, what she got in exchange was companionship and the warmth of another body in her bed, that intimacy that she had been without for so long, the touch of skin on skin.

And sex! She had given up the on the idea of ever having it again but she had been surprised by the ease with which they slipped into such an unexpected and regular shared pleasure. After the initial awkwardness, she soon discovered she wasn't too old for it after all.

Mary cleared her throat. 'So are you?'

In the twilight, her friend was almost a silhouette across the other side of the table. The candles guttered so the light came from the moon and stars.

'I think so.'

'I know you don't like to go overboard, but that doesn't sound good, even for you.'

Isla laughed. 'It came out wrong, that's all. He's a great guy who looks after me and that takes a bit of getting used to. I'm so used to fending for myself.'

'Is he going to move in?'

'He's staying at the house while I'm away. He offered to keep an eye on it, water the garden – so it seemed sensible. I haven't thought much beyond that.'

Of course she had. But she hadn't come to any conclusion about how she would like the affair to progress.

'Life's short,' Mary said with a nod to acknowledge the cliché. 'You might as well get on with it before it's too late.'

'It's not what I want. I love my life and I'm not ready to change yet. We hardly know each other. But he has been incredibly supportive over Mum's death. I was a mess when I got back from the funeral. He makes a mean hot toddy and he looked after me.'

'So he knows about your legacy? The painting?'

Isla shook her head. 'No. It sounds so melodramatic. Without saying anything, I've let him think I've inherited a chunk of mum's estate. He thinks I was devastated by her death, that we didn't get on and I want to know why, and that the three of us have fallen out. I suppose I'll have to tell him eventually but right now I don't want anyone to know except you. I don't want people, least of all Tony, asking questions and wondering what's wrong with me or what I must have done to deserve it.'

Mary leaned forward. 'You didn't do anything. I'm sure.'

'But you don't know that, and neither do I.'

9

Paris, 1954

May held out her Gauloise for a light. What would her parents say if they could see her now? It had taken time to get used to the cigarette's strong taste that caught at the back of her throat but she and Wendy had persevered. As she had with her French. Already she could make herself understood to most people and could understand the simplest of rapid conversations and was racing through the novels of the fashionable writer, Colette.

Only a few weeks into her stay and she was already quite at home in the city. The cellar *boîte* or nightclub where they were was small, hot and packed with people; it felt as though sweat were dripping from the low ceiling. She couldn't hear a word of what was being said over the music and the voices. She was there with Wendy, Max and Sam, two American boys who were studying at the Sorbonne and whom Wendy had met in their local *tabac*. May's friendship with Wendy had blossomed since their first meeting in the park and the two young women went everywhere together. Wendy was like May in many ways but braver, more outgoing. Max and Sam were quite different. They were brash, confident and with plenty of money to splash about. May had heard these lucky Americans who came to study at the Sorbonne were known as 'Amerluks'. There was a shine and flamboyance about them that she had never seen on any boys she'd met at home in Scotland. They had style. She was fascinated by them, drawn to them like a moth to a flame.

Max flicked his lighter and they cupped hands as she inhaled. '*Merci.*' She blew a cloud of smoke above his head. Quite the *Parisienne.*

Butterflies stormed her stomach as he gazed into her eyes. 'My pleasure.' He was so close, they were almost kissing. Then he pulled back, leaving her uncertain. Did he like her or not? She watched him turn to say something to Sam, then throw back his head and laugh so the light caught the contours of his face. She resisted the urge to reach out to touch them.

She took his proffered hand with a shiver and followed him onto the dance floor. Wendy was already there with Sam. The steps May had practised at home in her bedroom in Scotland didn't seem right for here so she followed her friend's example and soon picked up the rhythm, dancing until they could barely stand.

Without Wendy her time in Paris would have been very different. The two of them explored the city together. She had marvelled at the curiously shaped domes of the Sacré Coeur in Montmartre, climbing to the top of the largest before exploring the streets round the back of the church, dallying to watch the street artists at work, chatting over a coffee or an ice cream. They wandered through the chaotic food market of Les Halles, people-watched from one of the cafés, bought flowers on the Quai des Fleurs, watched the fishermen on the banks and in the little boats on the Seine, stared up at the grotesque gargoyles peering down from the heights of Notre Dame, and had been filled with awe by its cavernous interior. And now, excitingly, they had made friends with Max and Sam, and they were seeing another side to the city. The four of them spent time in the street cafés, bars, and nightclubs, lingered in the grand public parks, visited the art on show in the Louvre and the Musée du Jeu de Paume, and went to the cinema where they had seen *L'Air de Paris* and, along with all the other women in the cinema, May had fallen in love with Jean Gabin, the star.

How wonderful everything was. During her dreich Dunfermline schooldays, May had never imagined she would be pitched into . . . this life, this colour, this excitement. Like Dorothy in *The Wizard of Oz* she had gone through a door that took her from a faded black-and-white film strip into a world of blazing technicolour.

'You wanna see the Eiffel Tower on Saturday?' Max was leaning towards her, shouting so she could hear. She melted under his gaze. Blue eyes, square-jawed, slick blond hair. His smile touched her heart.

'I think so.' She felt breathless with excitement, although

aware she should not seem too keen. She didn't want to give him the wrong idea about the sort of girl she was.

'What?' His hand was holding her arm, pulling her towards him. 'I cain't hear ya.'

She nodded, as her insides melted. 'Yes.'

Of course she did. The Tower dominated the Paris sky-line but so far she had been nowhere near it. When she told Wendy about his invitation on their way home, her friend clapped her hands. 'A date. I knew he liked you. I knew it!'

May shook her head. 'No. He's just being nice.' But the way her stomach somersaulted again told her something else was happening. This was another side to Parisian life that she had only heard about.

Madame Dubois had proved to be a kind employer who had soon made May feel at home. She rarely saw Monsieur who left the house for work early and often returned late. What Madame did with herself during the day was some-thing of a mystery. She was out a lot – seeing friends, Isla guessed – but had found time to take Isla round the neighbourhood, showing her the local *pâtisserie*, the *pharma-cie* – where she had been mystified by their bemused reaction when she told them she was hot, only to discover that '*Je suis chaud*' meant she was feeling sexy (the mortification!) – the *tabac* for postcards and the nearest funny yellow post box. Everything she saw was so different, such fun. As long as she fulfilled the terms of their agreement and looked after her son, Madame didn't seem to mind what May got up to out of hours, provided she told her where she was going and when she would be home. As long as she and Emile spoke English every day and spent their allotted time together, they were left to their own devices. When she turned his bed back in an apple pie and he ripped the sheet, he found it hilarious and a friendship began to form, cemented by the card tricks she had learned as a child. They had become regulars at the Jardin du Luxembourg or the 'Luco' as she had learned to call it. As spring became summer, the park had got busier and she had got to know other girls like her, employed to look after other women's children or learn French, but Wendy and she were closest, especially now that Max and Sam were on the scene.

On her evenings off, never once had Monsieur or Madame Dubois raised an eyebrow at the mention of a nightclub or café, whereas her own parents would have had fifty fits. She could only imagine her employers were too caught up in their own worlds to worry about what went on in hers. Late one afternoon she had heard a man's laugh coming from the master bedroom long after the two-hour lunchbreak when everywhere in Paris seemed to shut down. She knew Monsieur Dubois was out. And if he wasn't at home, or in his office, where was he then, she wondered.

When she mentioned it to Wendy, her friend tossed her blond hair and laughed. 'What? You don't know?'

'What?'

'The French way ... *cinq à sept*.' This wasn't the first time Wendy had been astonished by May's naiveté.

'What are you talking about?' May had no idea.

Wendy proceeded to enlighten her. 'No one turns a hair

at a man calling on a woman on their way home from work, never mind if one of them is married. Lucky Madame,' she said. 'A husband and a lover in one day. Monsieur Dubois was probably doing the same thing.'

Isla's eyes were opened. 'Would you . . . ?'

Wendy roared with laughter. 'You are funny. Of course not. Although I wouldn't say no to Sam if he asked.'

Would she say no to Max, May wondered. She was quite taken with him. He was attentive, funny and handsome. Being with him set all sorts of sensations racing through her that she hadn't experienced before but that she enjoyed, so she tried to find excuses to be with him, and he didn't seem to mind.

It seemed an age until Saturday came. May met Max outside the Odéon metro station on the Boulevard Saint-Germain. May was wearing the new floral waisted shirt dress she had bought with Wendy's approval in the fabulous Galleries Lafayette, cinched at the waist with her red belt. Her only shoes were the sensible flats her mother had insisted on her bringing but her finances didn't run to a new pair of shoes as well. She had tried to tame her short curls into something less bouncy, more elegant, and failed.

'You look lovely,' he said, and kissed her cheek.

May's pulse was set racing by the compliment and by his familiarity.

'You look nice too.' She appreciated that he had made an effort: beige slacks, an open-necked short-sleeved white shirt, tan loafers. He pushed his hair back off his face, showing the small red birthmark on his forehead.

'I've never been on the Metro.' She tried to hide her apprehension. Wendy had scared her with stories of thefts and attacks.

He took both her hands. 'Come with me . . . I'm going to lure you into the depths.' He grinned. 'It's very dangerous, but I'll protect you.'

Was he teasing?

'We're so cool,' he said as they descended the steps. May was nervous, given what she had heard about the dangers lurking in subterranean Paris, but Max negotiated their route with ease, chatting all the way, calming her nerves, and they emerged unscathed at the Champ de Mars. '*Et voilà.*' He spread his hands like a showman as if he'd magicked the tower from nowhere. He bent over and whispered. 'Didn't I say I'd protect you?'

His breath was on her cheek and their heads were almost touching.

They took the Quai Branly and turned up into Avenue Gustave Eiffel until they stood right under the tower itself. Up close, it was like a giant Meccano model rearing into the sky, much taller than she had ever imagined. The iron latticework was painted a reddish brown, presenting an extraordinary feat of engineering. May was lost for words.

Max grabbed her hand. 'And now, hold on to your hat. We're going up it.'

'We are?' How could they possibly? But she was following him, thrilling with excitement, up the steps to the ticket office. While he bought the tickets for the lift, she bought a postcard for her parents and another for Aggie from the selection that festooned the window of the souvenir shop to the right of the entrance. She would write them when she got back to the quiet of her room.

'Did you know Eiffel built a secret apartment for himself at the very top?' Max was back, clutching two tickets.

'Are we going right up there?' Her palms were sweaty.

'We'll see.' He took her hand again and led the way to the lift, not giving her the chance to change her mind.

Nothing in May's life yet could match the experience of being in that lift cabin. She stared out of its partially louvred windows as they rose steadily, first one floor, then the second, higher and higher above the city. When the lift shuddered to a halt, they got out and peered over the railing at the microscopic people scurrying below them. May gazed over the panorama of the city laid out at their feet, quite overwhelmed. Masses of grey rooftops were divided by the network of streets, interrupted in one direction by the glass roof of the Gare St Lazare and the green copper roof of the Madeleine. Windows glinted in the sun and, on the ground, the traffic moved about like ants racing from one burrow to another.

'There's Notre Dame,' said Max pointing in its direction.

'Where, where?' She followed the direction of his pointing finger. 'The heart of Paris,' she said happily. They took over one of the telescopes from a couple who were leaving and went on identifying highlights of the city to each other – the Palais de Chaillot, Sacré Coeur, L'Opera, the *bateaux mouches* on the Seine, the Arc de Triomphe, Les Invalides – until they had named everything they recognised.

They stood close together, May barely breathing from excitement. Max put his arm around her shoulders and pulled her even closer. She relaxed into his embrace. Her day was complete ... her week was complete ... her life was complete. She had never known anyone like him. Forget the boys from Scotland. They had none of Max's swagger and energy. They didn't know about places like this.

'Souvenirs!' A man appeared up the steps with a trayful of miniature Eiffel Towers.

'M'sieur.' Max went over and bought one. 'For you,' he said, presenting it to May with a flourish. 'For a wonderful morning.'

May took it and tucked it in her bag as if it was most precious thing she had ever been given.

After that day, they spent as much time together as they could. May would count down the hours until she next saw him, her mind only half on her French lessons, watching out for him when she was in the Luco with Emile. Whenever she wasn't working or at her French classes she would meet him, sometimes alone and sometimes with Wendy and Sam. They wandered through Paris, exploring. Thanks to the German Occupation, the city itself had not been decimated by war and was coming back to life with determination. They dawdled by the *bouquinistes*, the second-hand booksellers on the left bank, rummaging through the books and prints. Max's favourite bookshop was Le Mistral on the Rue de la Bûcherie where they would spend hours, poring over the books while Max spotted notable visiting writers. This was the hub of Bohemian Paris, and she was part of it.

'One day, my books will be on these shelves,' he'd say with longing. May would squeeze his hand in support.

They exclaimed over the puppies and kittens in the animal market where small caged birds of every colour sat on perches waiting to be taken home and hung in apartment windows. They sat in street cafés taking hours over a single cup of coffee, talking, talking and even kissing. They learned everything about each other and bit by bit May found herself falling in love.

She listened to Max's stories of his happy childhood in Wisconsin, how he came to Paris with his brother Walt who had gone home months earlier, homesick and unable to pick up the lingo. But Max stayed where he was, obsessed with his dream of becoming a writer, of hanging out at Café de Flore, the Brasserie Lipp and Les Deux Magots with the notable writers of the day, of being internationally recognised for his talent. Sometimes he would read out an excerpt from his writing which she would admire extravagantly without quite understanding what he was trying to say. There were plenty of philosophical meanderings embedded in prose full of metaphor and words May had not come across before.

One evening they were in a café, eating *oeufs en cocotte*, when Max took her hand across the table. May waited for him to speak.

'I thought we might go to Brittany for a few days, get out of the city.' He raised his eyebrows, questioning.

Just the two of them! Her immediate reaction was excitement, but then a note of caution kicked in as her mother's warnings about boys echoed in her head. 'Oh, I don't know,' she said. 'I'd have to ask Madame.' There was nowhere she'd like to go more and Madame was bound to let her have a couple of days off.

'Not just us,' he added. 'I was going to ask Sam and Wendy to come along. You girls can look after each other.'

She laughed. 'I think we can look after ourselves.' The idea of some time out of the city, alone with the others was thrilling.

So a few weekends later, Max drove her with Wendy and Sam to Brittany in the green Renault 4CV he borrowed from a friend. Where they went, on the south coast, was a paradise apparently untouched by the war with small white-sanded rocky coves sheltered by pine trees, the turquoise water crystal clear lapping on sandy beaches.

They took two rooms, one for Wendy and May and one for the boys, in a local family-run hotel that was modest in its decoration but warm in its welcome. Immediately May knew they would have a good time. And they did. Their days were spent exploring the region, lying on the sun-kissed beaches or strolling along coastal paths with only the occasional heron or cormorant for company. May felt thoroughly relaxed, loving this time with Max. Every day seemed to bring them closer. She never wanted their time there to end.

On their last night, they had a simple supper of *truite au bleu* and potatoes accompanied by deep red burgundy wine.

'You girls have made all the difference to this summer,' said Max.

'We try,' said Wendy, looking pleased.

May said nothing but enjoyed the warmth his words gave her. Max touched her arm, making her shiver with delight. 'You have.'

'As you have to ours.' She kissed his cheek.

'A souvenir,' he said, as he peeled the label off the wine bottle, kissed it and gave it to her.

At that moment, it seemed the most romantic gesture in the world.

It wasn't long before Wendy and Sam turned in. 'The sea air's done for me,' said Sam with a nod to Wendy.

'I've drunk too much, and I want to enjoy our last day tomorrow.' Her voice slurred slightly.

When they reached the door of the small *salon*, Wendy turned and winked at May. But May was so engrossed in her conversation with Max, she didn't stop to think what it might mean. 'I'll be up in a minute,' she said and turned her attention back to Max, who was elaborating on how he wanted to buck the plans his father had for him to go home to work in the motor trade. 'My dad's built up the business from scratch, and now wants Walt and me to take it over. But I'm going to stay in Paris. I'm sending some pieces I've written about the city home to a local newspaper. If they publish them, it might make my father understand how serious I am about this.'

'Can I read them?' His excitement was infectious, and she

felt dull by comparison. All she had was her father's ambition for her, which mainly involved getting her off his hands. Marriage or a job she didn't want in London. What she wanted was to stay in Paris with Max. Now she had met him everything was changing. He had brought a draught of life-enhancing air into her sealed-up world. Even if she didn't quite grasp what he was writing about, with him anything was possible.

'When we get back, maybe.' He yawned.

She suspected he realised she didn't appreciate his work as much as he'd like. When they got back to Paris, she would try harder.

'We should call it a day.' He got to his feet and held out his hand to pull her up. Her head spun as she stood, making her realise she had drunk too much. They tiptoed up the stairs, giggling, trying not to wake anyone. When they got to the landing, they shared a lingering kiss good night before going to their separate rooms. She felt the heat of his touch as his hand moved under her shirt and up her back. His body was hard against hers, pressing her back into the wall. She had never experienced anything like the electricity sparking between them. She knew she shouldn't let things go too far but she was losing herself to what was happening to her, heady with desire. As she paused for breath, her mother's words flew into her head. '*Boys only want one thing, May. If you give it to them, it only ends in trouble.*'

She made herself pull back from him.

'What's wrong?' He stepped back, sounding anxious.

'I shouldn't,' she insisted, her face burning. 'I must go to bed.' But all she wanted was to fall back into his arms and kiss him again. She looked up at him, drowning in his stare, took a step towards him. '*May* . . .' Her mother was back.

Her hand shaking, May put the key in the lock and tried to turn it but the door stayed firmly shut. She tried again, wishing she could fling herself through, then realised the door must be locked from the inside. She heard a stifled laugh that sounded like Wendy's. And only then the penny dropped. Wendy and Sam were inside. Together. And they weren't going to answer her frantic tapping.

'Looks like we have no choice.' Max was standing on the other side of the corridor, the door to his and Sam's room open. He smile was inviting, knowing, his head tipped on one side.

'I suppose not.' This was not how she had imagined the weekend would turn out. How stupidly innocent she had been. But how much she wanted to go with him. She walked towards him and followed him into the boys' room, her heart thumping.

Max turned on the bedside lights as May looked around her. The room was identical to hers and Wendy's: white walls, pretty floral curtains, a pine chest of drawers, hangers on the hooks on the back of the doors. There was nowhere else to sleep apart from the bed or the floor. What should she do? Aside from waking the other residents by trying to get in her own room again but more forcefully, nothing. As she moved towards Max, she heard her mother's disapproving snort but she took no notice.

'Sit down.' Max was patting the bed beside him, looking at her with such longing that she felt herself weaken. 'I just want to hold you.'

She did as he said, watching his hand as it ran up her thigh, under her skirt, closing her eyes as she experienced a longing like nothing she'd known before.

'I won't do anything you don't want me to, I promise.'

Safe with his arms around her, she kissed him back, giving herself up to the sensations that were thrumming through her. Even if she tried, she couldn't resist. After all, she loved him. He loved her. She would prove her mother wrong. Max would look after her now. Her future was secure.

10

Leicestershire, 2019

As Isla and Charlie reached the M1, a foul smell filled the car.

'Oh God, no! What's that?' Charlie picked a bud out of her ear so Isla could hear the tinny strains of whatever music she was listening to. She held her nose with her other hand. 'It's like rotting cabbage but much worse.'

'I'm afraid it's Jock,' admitted Isla, winding down her window to let out some air and the fumes and noise of the traffic in. 'I did warn you.'

'Jock!' Charlie turned round in her seat to confront the innocent old dog. 'That stinks.'

'It's a hazard of the trip.' Isla concentrated as they overtook a couple of lorries in the slow lane.

'I wish we had a dog.' This was Charlie's first stab at conversation since they had left Mary and George's. As soon they had said their goodbyes and were under way, she'd gone straight back to sleep, her head thudding occasionally against the window. 'Even one that farts would be good.'

Isla had decided to let Charlie take the lead. She was happy driving in silence or with the radio on. Making the next few days a success was her responsibility so, turning down the radio – *You and Yours*, again – she leaped on Charlie's opener. 'What kind would you have?'

The earbud dangled round her chin. 'I don't know. Something medium sized – a cockerpoo like my friend Molly's. He's so sweet.'

'We know a gorgeous golden one – Barney. Don't we, Jock? We meet him in the park most mornings. He's the sweetest thing.'

'I'd get a black one and call her Nancy. Mum won't let us have one though.' She put in her earbud and began scrolling down her phone. 'Too much of a tie.'

Their brief connection was almost over.

'What are you listening to?' Isla raised her voice so she could be heard.

'Billie Eilish. She's deadass.' She sang a few lines.

'Nice,' said Isla, though they sounded bleak. 'You go on. It's a long drive, and I've got the radio.' She remembered those endless drives to Scotland in Christmas traffic to visit her parents, fighting over the radio stations with Helen, being subjected to an ear-battering from radio stations she'd never heard of until she couldn't stand it any longer.

'That's so old-school, Gran. Got any podcasts?'

'Never got the hang of them. Radio 4's good enough for me.'

'You should try them. I'll show you another time.' In went the earbud. Conversation over. Isla glanced at her granddaughter, noting her nail varnish, a blue so dark it was almost black, chipped on one finger. Across her forehead and down the side of her face ran a rash of pimples, more visible now she hadn't had time to put on any make-up. Isla turned her attention back to the road, upped the volume on the radio and listened with increasing despondency to the Brexit-dominated news, punctuated by occasional pings from Charlie's phone.

'Why are you stopping?' Charlie looked up as they turned off the motorway into the service station.

'Jock needs a walk and I might get a coffee. Coming? You don't have to.'

'No. I'm coming.' Charlie grabbed her black backpack and got out of the car, phone in hand. Isla wondered if surgical removal of phones was a thing these days. 'I'll get something to eat in there.' She nodded towards the services building.

'Okay. I'll meet you in there?'

As Isla walked Jock around the scrubby patch of grass reserved for dogs and foolhardy picnickers, she thought about where they were headed. She had been relieved that Morag, whose touch-paper could be quick to light, had been quite relaxed when she called to tell her of her change of plans.

'The more the merrier. At least you've *got* a grandchild! I'll be interested to see what that's like. The last time I saw her she was about ten.'

The thought crossed Isla's mind that Morag might be relieved not to have any grandchildren when she met

Charlie, but she put it to one side as she returned to the car, gave Jock a drink and put him in the back.

A year earlier, Morag had married Louise, her long-term partner. To be able to commit to one another publicly as wife and wife in front of all their friends was cause for a wild and eccentric celebration at their home of which Isla had loved being part. Lorna, however, had been noticeably absent. 'She was invited but she cancelled at the last minute because she wasn't feeling well. Or so she said.' They both knew the score. Lorna had distanced herself from her sister for some time to give the most feeble of excuses for missing a day that meant so much to Morag and Louise. She hadn't hidden her discomfort when Morag came out. By then Morag was studying to be a vet at Birmingham University, far enough from home to be able to live with her then girlfriend without any backlash from her parents. As it turned out, Lorna was the one who found it hardest to accept. Somewhere deep in her Presbyterian soul, having a sister who was a lesbian rankled. She and May had both been cool in their acceptance of Morag's sexuality, whereas Isla and their father had celebrated with her.

'Be proud of who you are,' he had said, surprising them all. 'Be happy. That's all I want for you.'

May had said nothing, just given a tight smile of congratulation. Not that she disapproved, but she hadn't their father's generosity of spirit. She was embarrassed by something she didn't really understand, and worried about what her friends would think, that they might judge her in some way. Lorna didn't have that excuse.

'In this day and age too. As if,' Morag had said, disbelieving and disappointed.

May's legacy had been the greatest test of the sisters' relationship yet. No apologies or friendly words had been exchanged since. When Isla had eventually phoned the other two to suggest she stay with them and to explain why, the reception had been lukewarm at best.

'Hasn't everything been said that needs to be?' said Morag. 'But I understand you need to find out about Mum so ... If I can help, I will. When do you want to come?'

Lorna didn't bother to mince her words. 'I thought I'd made it clear that I didn't want any more to do with either of you.'

'Oh Lorna, come on. Don't be such a drama queen. Just because we disagree over the future of the house, that doesn't mean we should break up the family.'

'Why not?'

'Because we're all we've got left.'

There was a moment of silence.

'Well, okay then, if you must,' said Lorna. 'I'm not sure we've got anything to say but, okay, come before Aggie's party.'

Isla was nervous about seeing both of them, but ... this was in her hands. Having Charlie with her when she saw Morag might make things easier.

And then there was Aunt Aggie. What wasn't she saying? As far as Isla could gather, their aunt was already making a new life for herself, her friends gathering round to support her. But when she called, Aggie was always busy or about to go out, never with time to chat. At least the sisters didn't have to worry about her. However, Isla was determined to get her to talk about her childhood. If anyone could bring May to life for her, Aggie would.

The inside of the service station was a blur of noise and brightness, a mecca to consumerism. She wandered from Costa where she bought a flat white and a croissant to WHSmith to MacDonalds, looking out for Charlie. There were plenty of other almost identically dressed teenagers but not the one that belonged to her. She found a seat, wondering where Charlie could have got to. Suppose she'd hitched a lift to the nearest train station where she could slip back to London and her friends? As her imagination let loose, she looked up to see her granddaughter coming towards her. Those black jeans were so tight they looked sprayed on, that crop top extremely brief. As Isla watched, she saw two young guys nudge each other, say something and stare at Charlie. Every curve in her body was neatly outlined. Isla wanted to call the men out but, without embarrassing Charlie, how could she?

'Haven't you got one of these?' Charlie sat opposite her oblivious to the minor stir she was creating, holding out her black reusable cup. 'You should, Gran.'

'I only go to coffee shops when I'm driving. And, this is a paper cup. So I'll recycle.' At least she could show her granddaughter she was doing something towards saving the planet. At least she was aware.

'That's one-use plastic.' Charlie was disapproving. 'Honestly, you should get one of these, made from recycled coffee cups. It's important.'

Isla was pleased to see her so passionate about something. 'Okay,' she said. 'If I give you the money, perhaps you could get me one like that.'

'Sure, I will.' Charlie opened her backpack and took out an apple. 'Want one?'

'I won't, thanks.' Isla pushed the croissant flakes around on her plate, suddenly self-conscious about her laissez-faire attitude towards the planet and her diet. Despite all her good intentions since watching David Attenborough's *Blue Planet*, she hadn't made any additional efforts to do her bit beyond the usual recycling when she remembered. Now she asked herself why not. When she was young, she had forced Rachel Carson's *Silent Spring* on the whole family, begging them to read it, and for a brief while considered herself an environmentalist. What had happened? Her youthful drive to change the world had lapsed long ago, to her shame. But perhaps she and Charlie did have something in common after all.

'Listen.' This moment seemed as good as any. 'I know you wouldn't be here by choice, but let's try to make it work for both our sakes.'

'Yeah, 'kay.' Charlie was only half-listening as she busily thumbed a message to someone.

Isla longed to scream, '*Put that bloody phone down and listen to me.*' Instead she plumped for a more strategic approach. 'Helen told me why you're not at school.'

'Yeah, that.' But she wasn't taking the bait.

'If you want to talk about it, what you're feeling . . . I'd be happy to listen.' If she treated her like an adult perhaps she'd behave like one.

Charlie smiled at her screen. 'It's okay. I'm fine.' She didn't even look up.

'Okay. I'll meet you at the car then.' As she went to the Ladies, Isla wondered why she didn't feel as in control of the situation as she should. Was it Charlie's unnerving unpredictability? She was so full of surprises, Isla didn't know what to expect next.

11

Paris, 1954

'Pregnant?!' Wendy shouted the word, then looked around the surrounding tables to see if anyone had overheard. She and May were sitting outside their favourite café, Au Bon Coin, waiting for one of the white-shirted waiters to bring them their Coca Colas, when May broke the news. 'You can't be!'

Despite May having made the most momentous of announcements, life continued on around them as if nothing had happened. The people sitting nearby carried on chatting with the waiters moving through the tables, balancing glasses of beer, cups of coffee on their trays.

May couldn't stop the tears. 'I must be.' She lowered her voice and leaned across the table. 'I've missed the curse twice now. And my bosom . . .' She put her hand on the front of her tailored white shirt where her breasts were tingling.

'Twice! Why didn't you say anything before? Since when?' Wendy's alarm was making May feel more anxious than she already was.

'Since Brittany.' She watched understanding dawn on Wendy's face and, as it did, the reality of the situation was driven harder home. 'I didn't think anything of it until now. I've never been particularly regular.' But she knew enough to recognise some of the signs.

'Have you told Max?'

May shook her head, miserable.

'It is Max?'

She was shocked. 'Of course! You don't think . . .'

'No I didn't really, but you'll have to tell him. Sooner rather than later.'

May couldn't imagine how she would begin to do that. The summer had been so perfect until now. This would mark the end of everything. Never had she imagined that she would be able to find such happiness with one other person. And Max – so handsome, so funny, so clever, so loving. Every day, she counted down the hours till they met again. At night she lay in bed conjuring up his kisses, what he had said to her, what they had done together. The thrill she felt being with him was tempered by a great sense of security. These were their salad days and she didn't want to ruin them with this.

'Didn't he use a *préservatif?*' Wendy was shocked that he might not have. 'I always make sure Sam does.'

'I didn't know. I can't remember. And anyway it doesn't matter now.' She didn't tell Wendy that she'd been sick two mornings running, and had seen Madame Dubois giving her a suspicious glance when she came out of the bathroom.

'*Comment ça va?*' Her touch on May's shoulder was light but reassuring.

For a moment, May was tempted to tell her everything, but then realised that would mean the end of her job, the end of her and Max, her return to Scotland and the shame that would greet her there. No, this was something she'd have to sort out on her own. 'I'm absolutely fine,' she said briskly. 'We're going to the zoo with Amaury and Wendy today. The boys want to see the elephants.'

Madame smiled. 'You are so good to him, my dear. But you're sure you're well enough? You look pale.'

'Really, I'm fine. Thank you.' Despite the nausea rising in her throat, she managed to get herself back to her room.

No more was said.

Confessing to Wendy had made the situation that much more real. How could she have got herself into this position when her mother had warned her about men so often? And just when she was so happy and everything was going so well. She couldn't go home. She couldn't tell her parents. They would kick her out. And their anger . . . she shuddered to think about it.

'You must tell him immediately. He'll do the right thing.' Wendy was very sure. 'He loves you. He and Sam are decent boys. He wouldn't abandon you to . . . well, what would happen to you? He knows the implications. When are you seeing him again?'

'Tonight.' She turned her coffee cup in its saucer. The right thing. Marriage. But Max was not in Paris to find a wife. He was there to fall in love, to be a writer, to experience all the exhilarating romance that Paris had to offer. She was part of that scenario, not there to tie him down with a squalling baby. He wouldn't want this. In her heart, May knew this was the truth. But if he loved her as much as she loved him, perhaps Wendy was right – she had to cling on to that small hope.

'You must tell him then.' Wendy was quite definite, certain this was the answer.

'That's what you'd do, because you want to marry Sam.'

Wendy tossed her head so her curls bounced. 'So? Don't you want to marry Max?'

Of course she did. 'Max isn't Sam. Max loves his freedom. He loves Paris.'

'He loves you.'

'Does he?' Did he love her enough? She would have to wait and see.

That night, she waited till Emile had gone to sleep and she was free to go out. She tried to tame the short fringe she had cut recently and put on a little rouge and the orangey red lipstick Max had said he liked. Her peach floral dress was tight-bodied and full-skirted and her new shoes had a little heel to make her taller. She opened the door to the salon where Madame Dubois was sitting doing her petit-point. She was humming to one of her jazz records on the gramophone. She looked up as May came into the room. 'Ah, you look adorable. That dress suits you well.'

'Thank you, Madame. I'm going to meet Max at the

Brasserie Bleu, near the Café de Flore.' Being just around the corner from such a literary landmark was as close as Max would allow them to go in the evening, feeling he had to earn his literary spurs first. They would walk slowly past, looking to see if he could spot any of the literary giants who frequented the place. Once he was sure he recognised Jean Paul Sartre and Simone de Beauvoir as they went in to meet friends. He didn't stop talking about them all night. The Brasserie Bleu was close enough to feel part of the scene without actually being part of it.

She felt Madame's X-ray gaze on her. 'Have you anything you'd like to talk to me about?'

May froze, put a hand on her stomach. Madame had guessed. She couldn't have. 'No,' she said firmly. 'Nothing else.'

Max would know what to do. That was enough. Friends of his must have found themselves in the family way and found a way out. Nobody else need know.

12

Derbyshire, 2019

As they eventually left the motorway and began to climb into the Derbyshire Peaks, Isla's grip relaxed on the wheel. As they were early, she chose the longer route, that took them up the A515 and then up towards Monyash. Under the big blue sky, the landscape was sublime, stretching away on either side of the road, field after field separated by grey stone walls, punctuated by the very occasional farmhouse and outbuildings, stands of trees and of course grazing animals. She had to admit to herself that she was also putting off the moment of arrival. She was nervous about seeing Morag again, the first time since that night. The village of Monyash was pretty in the sunshine, clustered around its village green but Isla couldn't help imagining how bleak it must be mid-winter. Then they were through and back in the lush countryside and her spirits lifted. 'Isn't this wonderful?'

But Charlie was sitting as she had been for almost all the journey since their stop, still bent over that tiny screen, thumbs working overtime, humming snatches of music. 'Mmm?'

'Look out of the window. We're not on the motorway anymore.' She rapped her fingers on the steering wheel.

'You sound just like Mum.' But she did stop what she was doing and looked up for a moment.

Isla ignored the intended insult. 'What are you doing?'

'TikTok.' She laughed at whatever she was watching. 'Look at these two dancing. They're wicked.'

There was a flash of pink phone in the periphery of Isla's vision.

'I can't see while I'm driving. What is it?'

She sighed. 'Short films. They're funny.'

'Show me later when we're out of the car.' Isla was curious about whatever had such a fierce grip on her granddaughter. 'We're nearly there now.'

'Don't they live in a town?' Alarm crept into Charlie's voice.

'No, but not far from one. Don't judge too soon. You may like it.' Though she thought it was unlikely.

'Do they have any pets?' Charlie was scrolling down her screen again. Please don't let her miss something.

'Dogs, cats, pigs, chickens. You'll see in a minute.' She felt Charlie perk up beside her.

There was a series of pings in quick succession.

'Can't you turn those off? They're driving me crazy.'

This phone addiction was too much. But how she would have hated to be parcelled off with her own grandmother instead of finishing school and hanging out with her mates, Isla corrected herself. But whose fault was that?

'I wonder how Mum's getting on.'

The satnav chose that moment to announce they had arrived at their destination. Isla pulled into the turning for a field gate. There wasn't a house in sight. Jock sat up, anticipating the freedom that came at the end of a journey. On the other side of the fence a couple of cows looked up at them with huge liquid eyes, blinked, then returned to the grass.

'Why are we stopping?'

'This doesn't look right.' She couldn't see any landmarks she recognised. 'Bloody satnav. Mind you, I came from a different direction last time.'

'Did you put the right postcode in? Mum got it wrong once and we ended up miles from where we were going.' Despairing of the inadequacies of the older generations, Charlie damned Isla with faint amusement.

'Yes, of course I did.' Isla was certain she had been quite precise. However, she keyed in the postcode again, checking it against her own phone and the satnav sprang to life. 'Continue along the . . .'

'See,' said Charlie, with a small but smug smile.

'Anyone could have made that mistake.' Isla defended herself, annoyed that she had.

Not far from Bakewell, Isla recognised the turning to the house at last. She got Charlie to get out to open the gate to a long straight driveway flanked by trees. The drive dipped over the brow of a hill and swept round to the right. In front of them was a solid sandstone house. They rattled over a cattle grid and turned through a wide gateway into a farm-yard. Straight ahead of them was the house and to their left some stables where a couple of horses observed their arrival, ears pricked. On the brick walls of the outhouses opposite were hanging baskets of red geraniums.

From nowhere, a black-and-white sheepdog rushed at them barking, followed by a less energetic golden retriever.

'There's your answer,' said Isla.

Morag opened the front door, an apron with the words 'Domestic Goddess' covering her jeans and loose shirt. She looked as apprehensive as Isla felt. Nonetheless, Isla forced a smile. She could do this.

Morag raised her hand in greeting as a Jack Russell darted out between her legs.

As soon as the car door was open, they were immediately overwhelmed by the dogs, jumping, sniffing, licking, bark-ing, tails beating against their legs.

'Stay down,' yelled Morag from where she stood. 'Come.'

They immediately ran back towards her.

Isla let Jock out to join the pack. He hesitated, poked his grizzled nose out of the door, considered the situation for a second, then jumped out. After circling each other and giving a good sniff, the four of them dashed off together, whirling about, barking.

'Journey all right?' Morag crossed the yard, Birkenstocks slapping against her soles. She and Isla hesitated then hugged.

'Fine.' Isla felt some of the tension in her drain away. It was going to be all right. 'It's good to see you.'

'And you.' Morag smiled. 'And you must be Charlie.'

Charlie was standing on the other side of the car, watching the dogs. She nodded as she lifted her phone for a photo of them. 'Yes.' Then a pouting selfie with them in the background. She laughed as the smallest dog turned too tight a circle and fell over.

'That's Titch, Shep and the other one's Red. But come inside first and I'll show you round and you can meet the troops. Lou's out with the horses – Bonny foaled a couple of days ago – but she'll be back soon.'

With a look that amounted to interest, Charlie opened Betty's back door and pulled their bags from the seat. 'You've got a foal here?'

'Yep. You can see him in a minute.' Morag took them into the wide flagstoned hall and straight upstairs to a less spartan carpeted landing. Leaving Charlie to get used to her room with instructions to 'come down in five minutes', Isla followed her sister to the back of the house to be shown into hers.

'Sorry about the mess. We use it as a bit of a dumping ground although I've done my best to tidy it.'

Isla eyed the teetering pile of cardboard boxes in one corner, the books piled on the dressing table.

'I can hear Mum now. Remember how she was always going on at you and me to tidy our rooms. Lorna's was always so bloody immaculate. Don't you think that was weird?

'What was weird?'

'The way she was always different from us. Tidy, organised, all that. Remember when she left all her stuff piled neatly on the beach and . . .'

'. . . that dog came and peed on it.' They laughed at one of their favourite family stories.

'You both look alike though.' As a child Isla had loved the fact that she looked so different from her sisters.

'Yeah. You lucked out with Dad's genes. I'd love to have had red hair.'

'Titian, actually!'

They laughed together again at one of their father's oldest protests.

The ice between them was definitely thawing.

Now she looked, Isla could see scuff marks everywhere, dust on the surfaces. Whatever Morag said, her sisters' and her own approaches to housekeeping had always been very different. In contrast to Morag, Lorna was indeed obsessively tidy whereas Isla fell somewhere in the middle, falling short of both OCD and total slovenliness. She stepped round a stack of pictures leaning again the wall. 'It's lovely here. Who cares about a few boxes when you've got that view.' From the window she could see nothing but fields, cows sheltering in the shade of trees, ducklings in the duck pond. 'And thanks for being kind to Charlie. It's all a bit difficult.'

'Who in their right mind would take a teenager on holiday with them?'

'Pressure from Helen – she's got the chance of a big writing job so had to go to the States.'

'You never could refuse her.' Morag grinned. 'Look, I don't know what your plans are but we thought Charlie might go to the surgery for a day with Lou. Give her something to do, and then we can talk. And we must.' An urgent note had entered her voice.

'I want to talk. I thought I'd come to accept what Mum did but I really haven't.'

'I can't say I'm surprised. I can't stop thinking about it either.'

'I must get to the bottom of why she left me that picture and nothing else. We must be able to find out more about her. I want to know who she was and what she was going to say in the rest of that note she never finished. *Dear Isla*, she said . . .'

'You've left it a bit late! You should have had those conversations before she died.' Morag paused, realising she had been too blunt. 'Sorry, but I honestly don't know how I can help . . .' She tapped her temple as if a light bulb had gone on. 'Unless there's something in that hatbox I took away when I was last there.'

'What hatbox?' Isla's interest was immediately piqued.

Morag looked uncomfortable. 'After you'd gone, Aggie said I could take some of Mum's old clothes for our local fête – Louise and I have been given the bloody jumble stall *again*. I was looking through them and found the hatbox at the back of the wardrobe. It's full of odd bits and pieces but I thought it looked interesting. I've been meaning to go through it, but haven't got round to it yet.'

'We could do it together.' Isla was excited. Might it hold a few answers to her many questions? At least it was something.

'Of course we could. I put it in in the loft with all my other rainy day projects that never get done.'

'Could we look now?' Perhaps something in there might help her.

Morag shrugged. 'Sure. Hang on.' Outside the bedroom, she took a pole hook leaning against the wall and used it to open the loft door so a ladder extended down to them. 'Just like Jacob's!' She laughed as she climbed up it.

Isla heard her say, 'Here it is,' just before she descended, carrying an old-fashioned black-and-white striped hatbox from Adairs, the family store, tied with a wide faded red ribbon. 'So this is what I've got. Let's take it downstairs. I'll make us a cup of tea and then we can unpack it.'

'What's that?' Charlie came out of her room.

Isla explained as they went downstairs together. In the living room, they waited for Morag to make the tea.

'Sit down, Gran. You're like a tiger, pacing up and down like that.' The pink phone provided enough distraction for Charlie.

Isla avoided a pile of *Horse and Hound* before almost tripping over an old saddle that had been left on the floor behind a chair.

At last Morag returned, put the tray on the fraying ottoman, kicking a pair of trainers underneath it as she did so. Once the mugs were filled and handed round, and Isla was safely sitting down, Morag undid the ribbon that held the lid of the hatbox in place. 'Here goes.'

13

'Look at this.' Isla ran her finger over the lid of the hatbox where something was handwritten in ink that had faded with time. '*Paris.*' She lifted it off and peered inside. She was confronted by a jumble of things that must have sat in there for years.

'I wish you'd told me you had this.'

'But you haven't been talking to each other,' Charlie pointed out. 'So why would she?'

'Exactly. Thanks, Charlie.' Morag gave her an appreciative smile. 'Why would I? And I am now. To be honest, I didn't think anything looked particularly important.'

Charlie picked out a small metal model of the Eiffel Tower and held it up. 'I've got one like this. I got it when Mum took me to Paris for a long weekend. We went right to the top. It was awesome.'

'Paris. Did you know she'd been there?' Morag sat back and let the other two rummage.

Isla picked out a Walters Palm Toffee tin that rattled as she pulled it out. 'No, definitely not.' Charlie was leaning over her as she prised off the lid, breathing down her neck.

The tin was full of buttons, some loose and some fixed in sets to cards.

'Wow! These are like really cool vintage buttons.' Charlie took the tin from her. 'You could vamp up some of your old stuff by swapping them over.'

'I don't want to vamp anything up, thanks.' Isla reclaimed the tin and ran her fingers through its contents. 'Mark you, these are gorgeous.' She picked out a set of six multi-faceted jet glass buttons that gleamed in the light.

'You could put three each on the shoulders of that black jumper you've got. It would make a difference.'

'Maybe.'

'Can I have them if you don't want them?' Charlie's attention was moving on to a small scarred leather box. She clicked open the lid to find it lined with dark blue velvet and containing a pair of tiny scissors with blades fashioned like a bird's beak on one side, and on the other, three slim implements, two with mother-of-pearl handles. 'Wow! Are these for sewing?'

'Must be.' Morag took them from her and held them up to the light. 'If she mended a tear you could barely see it. And that's hard. She taught all of us to knit too. Not that I ever got the hang of it.'

'Here's a menu. Look. *Foie de veau. Cotelettes. Steak frites.*' The card was browning at the edges and had a couple of splotches of food or wine on it. '*Le Notre Dame*,' she read.

'So she must have been to Paris. By why never mention it?' Isla's eye ran down the entire menu. 'You'd have thought

107

when I went on that school trip there she'd have said something instead of trying to persuade me not to go. Do you remember? She'd go, 'That nasty French food' or 'I've heard they can't make tea at all.' Dad talked her round and she was furious. I never understood. Once Ian and I asked her to come with us for a long weekend and she refused.'

'I've no wish to cross the channel.' The refusal rang in Isla's ears.

'And a beret!' Morag took out a faded black beret and put it on at an angle. '*Tres chic, non?*'

'Definitely *non*,' said Isla, reaching out for it. 'It smells of onions.'

'You're imagining it.' Morag waved it under her nose, then passed it over.

'And a string puppet – but the strings are all tangled.' Charlie pulled it out so it dangled in front of them. 'Look! Pinocchio.' She laid it on the table to see if she could straighten it out. 'Why would she have kept a child's puppet?'

'And a box made of shells. I remember seeing these in Brittany.' Isla opened it to find the rolled-up label from a wine bottle. She tried to unfurl it but it was stiff with age.

'And postcards.' Isla shuffled the little collection into a neat pile. 'Let's see. Some of them aren't written on, like this one of the Eiffel Tower, but here ... *Madame has been very kind, and I'm getting on better with Emile now. We live opposite the Jardin du Luxembourg – look it up on a map. Paris is beautiful. Love, M.*' She held the card up to the light so that she could read the postmark. 'Nineteen fifty something. So now we know she was definitely there.'

'But why didn't she talk about it? Why keep it secret?'

'If it was only a short time, maybe she just forgot. How much can you remember about your misspent youth?' Morag picked up another card. 'Look. Sacré Coeur. *Aggie! I wish you could meet Max. He's a dreamboat. Don't tell Mummy and Daddy.*'

'I'd remember something as special as being in Paris must have been in the nineteen fifties. The war hadn't been over long, and she was a young woman. It must have been eye-opening. And who's Max?'

'You'll have to ask Aunt Aggie. You're bound to get something from her – if she'll spill.'

'She's been so cagey when I've tried to ask her anything over the phone. She just plays deaf or makes an excuse. Maybe it'll be different face to face.'

'But before you get there, we need to talk about Braemore.' Morag rolled the red ribbon round her fingers.

'Oh, God. Is there anything left to say? I'm more interested in all this, and finding out more about Mum.' Isla pointed at the hatbox. 'And why the will.'

'Where are you?' Louise's voice came from the kitchen, interrupting them.

'In here,' Morag yelled back.

Louise appeared, looking worn out, but still smiling and carrying a mug of tea. Her denim dungarees were dirty, there were smears of what might be blood on her arms, and her hair was escaping from a loose bun. 'God! I need this!

Long day, but the foal's fine except she doesn't have a name. You can come and see her, if you like.' She looked at Charlie who was still poking about in the hatbox. She stopped with a photo in her hand, not realising she was being spoken to. 'Is this her?'

'Would you like to, Charlie?' Isla prompted, impatient.

'Oh, me? Yeah.' For a moment, Charlie looked as if she was going say more but turned back to the photo. 'Yeah, of course.'

'We thought you might like to come to the practice or even come on my rounds.' Lou sat down with a sigh of exhaustion.

'Really?' Charlie looked up as enthusiasm broke through her signature indifference.

'Thank you,' said Isla on her behalf, glaring at her as if that would instil some semblance of manners.

Charlie frowned back. 'Yeah, thanks. I really would.' She held the photo out to Morag, who took it.

'That's Mum all right. Look. Who's she with? She looks like a young Marilyn Monroe.'

'Don't they look happy? Look at the way she's gazing at the person behind the camera.'

'Max? Another question for Aggie.'

'Back in a minute.' Charlie left the room, her phone in her hand.

'What were you going to say about Braemore?' Isla didn't miss the glance exchanged between the other two women. 'What?'

'It's Lorna. She's been leaning on Aggie to sell the place.'

Morag punched a cushion and put it behind her. 'It's completely out of order.'

'Even if that's true, what can I do about it?'

'Aggie told me. She was upset. Apparently there's a developer who wants the paddocks. He's made a substantial offer subject to probate. Lorna wants her to accept. She can go on living in Braemore.'

'It's got nothing to do with me now,' said Isla firmly, despite feeling sadness their family home had become such a bone of contention. But May had made sure that was the case. Had she known a developer was sniffing around? 'Why do you mind so much, anyway?'

'Because it's our home. I know it's sentimental but I can't bear to think of it ruined or sold off. And because we don't know what Aggie will do in her will. You may inherit part of it then.'

Isla laughed. 'I don't think so.' She remembered their mother sitting in a deckchair next to their father on the stone terrace at Braemore, slim in a striped dress, hair held back off her face with a scarf, head thrown back as she laughed. 'Just think, David. One day we won't be here and the girls will have all this. Imagine that.' What had happened to change her mind?

'Whatever Mum's done, Braemore's still part of you. You grew up there, for God's sake. Our family home's about to be parcelled off piecemeal if Lorna has her way. Imagine it with two or three des res right beside it. She must have notified the developer herself.'

'But you don't have any proof,' Louise reminded her.

'I don't need proof. I know her. What's she up to? Isla, you're the only one who can stop her.'

'Me?' Isla put the photo of May and her friend back into the box.

'Who else?'

'She must need the money. But what for? Andrew's loaded.' Apart from his lucrative position in one of the top Edinburgh law firms, as an only child he had inherited plenty when his parents died. Lorna had never lacked in that department.

'But you must care about Aggie. You're the one she's closest to and she's being bullied into something she doesn't want and that's not right. You can help her stand up to Lorna.'

'She's on my conscience but when I've called her she never wants to talk.' Since May's will it was as if Aggie had distanced herself from her. Isla had read that as her being uncomfortable about being left Isla's share of the estate. Yet she never said so. This wasn't like her at all. Isla knew and loved Aggie like a second mother so she was baffled and hurt.

Before she had moved in with May, Aggie had lived in a large Edinburgh flat overlooking the Meadows, gloriously independent, and impossibly glamorous, working at the Lyric Theatre. For Isla, the flat had been the most wonderful retreat from family disagreements, and Aggie always gave her the warmest welcome. The flat was stuffed with things she had accumulated from her time working in the theatre: theatrical posters adorned the walls, programmes of the many shows she had seen or been involved with were piled up on the bookshelves. They would sit in front of the fire and toast marshmallows, or eat drop scones dripping with butter, while Aggie regaled her with stories from the days when, as a young woman, she had run away to London where her Aunt Jess had introduced her to a stage manager who had given Aggie her first job.

'Those were the happiest days of my life,' she'd say, looking dreamy. 'Far from home, in a job that I loved. We did everything then, finding the props, painting the set, prompting the actors – whatever was needed. Once, when I ...' And off she'd go into one of her rambling reminiscences about one actor or another whom she'd worked with. So very different from her sister, May, who, as far as Isla knew, had a much more staid youth that she seemed to prefer to forget about.

'Actually I asked Aggie about Mum, too.' Morag interrupted her thoughts. 'You're not the only one who wants an explanation.'

Isla was immediately alert. 'And?'

'And nothing.' Morag shrugged as in apology. 'She dived off down a tangent about not giving the right prompt to Alec Guinness.'

'Oh, that old one.' They shared a complicit grin – Aggie's theatrical anecdotes had all been heard many times over. 'But she must know something about the Paris connection. We now know Mum was there. And there's the picture and its note. There must be a connection.' That felt to Isla like a valuable nugget of information, although she had no idea why.

'Not necessarily.'

'But it seems likely.' Isla's head was befuddled with the few facts she knew about her mother's early life. And now Paris. The answer she was looking for must lie in there somewhere. 'So that was before she met Dad?'

'Didn't they meet at a party in Edinburgh? But you'll have to catch Aggie after a couple of gins and quiz her when her guard's down.'

'Have you ever seen a picture of their wedding?' Where other friends' parents paraded the happiest day of their lives in their living rooms, Isla couldn't remember ever seeing one of her parents'.

'She had a tiny black and white one of them at Gretna.'

'They went there? Why? I'd have thought they'd have had a really fancy affair, given he was an Adair.'

'Dad was a dark horse, more romantic that we gave him credit for, maybe?' But it was obvious Morag didn't believe that any more than Isla did.

'But none of this explains why Mum left me out.' She disliked this feeling of resentment.

'I did ask Donaldson about that.'

'You spoke to the lawyer too? Why didn't I think of that?' When initially trying so hard to push her mother from her mind, she had failed to cover all the bases. And May had refused to let her go.

'I thought Mum might have said something to him.'

'And?' Isla leaned forward. Had Morag been holding back the answer all along?

'Client confidentiality blah blah, but he did say that he'd pointed out to her that she had missed you out, asking her if it was deliberate. Apparently she simply said, yes it was and it was too late to explain.'

'What the hell does that mean? Why too late? To explain what?'

'I don't know. But it's just like the note you found in her bedroom.'

'Did he say anything else?'

Morag shook her head. 'I'm afraid not. After that it was just a brick wall.'

'I will find out why.' Isla clasped her hands together. 'I will.'

'I know. And I'll do whatever you ask to help.'

14

That night Morag and Isla didn't have much chance to talk again about May or Braemore. They all ate in the kitchen, which was large and lived in, the hub of the house, complete with cream Aga and a Welsh dresser full of china and bits of post and fliers for local events. In the centre was a big oak table. Before the meal, Isla had helped clear the remains of the last meal, and shopping that hadn't been put away. At one end there was a fireplace flanked by two tatty armchairs, one of them occupied by one of the stable cats.

Their conversation almost exclusively revolved around the animals, largely for Charlie's benefit. The ploy had worked. There was a new light in the girl's eyes. She had taken photos of everything she'd seen on the farm but most of the new leggy brown foal with knee-length white socks and a white blaze. She had watched, enraptured as it balanced on its spindly legs and fed greedily. When she suggested the name Echo, Louise had leaped on it. 'That's perfect. That's it.' Charlie was over the moon the name had stuck. In the barn they found a litter of kittens born a couple of months earlier: adorable black-and-white bundles of fluff that skittered about, avoiding human contact. Eventually Louise caught one on top of a hay bale and gave it to Charlie who cradled it as if she'd never let it go.

'Can you take a picture of us,' she said, holding out her phone. 'Her heart's beating a million miles a minute.' She stroked the little head with a finger while Isla clicked away for her.

By the time supper was over, Isla was exhausted and happy to leave the heavy conversation till the following day.

Alone at last, she decided to call Aggie again. It was late enough for her aunt to think it might be an emergency, so she might answer. And sure enough . . .

'Aunt Aggie!'

'My God, hen. What's happened? It's ten thirty.'

'Nothing at all. Don't worry. I just want to ask you about Mum.'

There was a hush from the other end of the line, so she ploughed on.

'I'm at Morag's. That hatbox she took was full of stuff from a trip Mum must have made to Paris years ago. Was she sent there to be finished? There must be a connection with the picture she left me? Because I found a note in the back of it, written in French. What do you know?'

'Och, it's so long ago, dear.'

This was typical prevarication.

'Can you remember where she and Dad met?'

'It's *so* long ago. But yes, she went to Paris when she was about twenty I think. I've got a few of her postcards somewhere.'

'There are some in the box.'

'Are there?' She sounded flustered. 'I must have given them back to her then. Did I tell you that I found the letters Michael Caine wrote to me? He was such a dear. He . . .'

'Show me when I see you next week.' If she didn't cut the story off now, they'd be on the phone for hours. 'What was Mum doing in Paris?'

'She looked after a little boy. I don't remember his name.'

Isla could almost hear the cogs whirring in her brain.

'Who was Max?'

'Yes, there was an American boy. Was that his name?'

'Did he and Mum have an affair?'

Isla sensed Aggie had started to play for time so repeated the question.

'Och, heaven knows, dear. It's too long ago, and it's very late.'

'I'm sorry. I should have waited.' Isla brought the conversation to a close, feeling that she had taken a step forward. An American boy. Why would Aggie remember him if he weren't significant? But significant how exactly? The layers were being peeled away from her mother's life but she still had no inkling of what she would find at its heart.

The one other person she was dying to talk to was Tony. He might be interested in the little she'd found out about May. However, she must remember she hadn't told him about being left out of the will, just about the argument and her longing to know her mother better.

'I was just going to bed,' he said. 'But all's well here. You mustn't worry.'

'I'm not.' Not quite true. She missed her home. 'I just wanted to hear your voice.'

'And now you have, what are you going to do?' He laughed softly.

'Sleep better.'

'Then I'm glad you called, because now I will too. Is everything all right?'

'I'm unpicking stuff, bit by bit. We've found a hatbox full of mementoes from a trip she made to Paris in the Fifties. I'll tell you more when I see you. What have you been doing?'

'Trying to progress some of the irons I have in the fire, and it looks as if one of them just might be about to come off.'

'That's great.' She was pleased for him. Having a job would give him a security she knew he hadn't felt since his return to the UK. 'What is it?'

'I'm not telling you yet because I don't want to jinx it. But I think you'll be excited. I am. And then I'll be able to pay you back what I owe.'

'I don't want you to worry about that.'

'But I do. I've kept an exact tally.'

Which was more than Isla had done. But she trusted him.

They talked for a little while, but when she finally turned out her light, she didn't sleep better at all. She couldn't help thinking about Braemore. Why had May divided it the way she had, and why was Lorna so desperate to persuade them to sell? Morag was right. Even though she wasn't part of the decision, Isla hated the idea of her family home being sold

off in lots until all the family history that gave it its character had gone.

She thought of her sisters. As they grew up, their differences had of course become more pronounced. Morag's
devotion to animals had never wavered in all that time.
When she was about seven, she set up her own vet's practice
in the old potting shed where she held all sorts of injured
birds and animals that she found in the fields until they were
better. The death count had been high. There was a small pet
cemetery at the end of the garden where there were frequent
funerals with Morag as the chief mourner.

As the youngest, Lorna had always wanted to be the boss.
Things weren't right unless they were done her way. To
begin with, Isla and Morag had fallen in with her because
she was the youngest and it was easier to take the least line
of resistance. Until the day Pluto, a pigeon with an injured
wing escaped Morag's surgery to be caught and killed
by the cat.

'You let him out on purpose!' Morag was screaming, tears
pouring down her face.

'I didn't.' Lorna was dismissive.

But Isla had seen her lift the catch to the cage and walk
away, leaving it open, not five minutes after Morag had
drunk the last of the homemade lemonade so there was none
for her sisters. Lorna's revenge could be swift and cruel.

They stopped being such pushovers after that but often
when they stood their ground, May would step in and protect
her youngest daughter. Lorna had grown up used to getting

what she wanted so Isla knew she wouldn't give up easily when there was something in her way.

As for Isla ... the geeky one, obsessed with her collections – birds' eggs, pressed flowers, sea shells – happy to be alone sorting them out, labelling them, organising them in the architect's plan chest her father had found for her, keeping out of arguments when they flared up between the other two.

'Goody goody,' her younger sisters would taunt as they ganged up against her when she preferred to go off on her own rather than join in some prank they had dreamed up. The dynamics between the three of them became increasingly complex and changeable as allegiances shifted. And she had been the ugly duckling – ginger hair, freckles and big teeth – who transformed into a model (short-lived as it was) and actress (ditto).

Isla's concentration on her return to Braemore was prompting so much: had their childhood really been as idyllic as she had told Mary? Or was she giving it a more positive spin than it deserved? Now she remembered May's inexplicable mood swings, even when they were little, which led to her father's long-suffering silences and retreats to his study. He was the one who had always been even-handed in his kindness to his children: the way he'd slip them a forbidden sweet, bring them treats back from his occasional business trips away, always ready with a kind word when he was at home.

When she was eight, he taught Isla to tell the time, then gave her a watch for Christmas.

'You can't give her a watch,' May protested. 'What about Lorna and Morag?'

'They can't tell the time.' A cloud of smoke puffed from his mouth towards the ceiling. 'When they can . . .'

Isla had swelled with pride at her achievement.

'That's not the point. I'll keep this until then.' May put the watch in her apron pocket and, despite her father's protest, didn't return it. Isla had run to her bedroom in tears, but not even that had softened her mother's heart; May remained true to her word.

All their adventures had taken place in the extensive garden where, in the summer holidays, they would put on plays on top of the mound in the south-west corner. Their long-suffering parents and friends would be attentive and enthusiastic audiences, sitting on old deckchairs or rugs on the lawn. Lorna was always the director and star of their plays. Isla was always cast in the male roles because of her height and ran around being the dogsbody subject to Lorna's whim. 'Find me a dog lead.' 'Find me a blue pillowcase.' Once she'd asked Isla to steal a scarf from the neighbours' washing line. 'I must have it for Juliet. She's got hundreds of them. She'll never notice.' But of course she did and Isla took the blame. She didn't mind then. That was how it was. She wanted to be loved by her sisters and if her doing that made Lorna happy, then so be it.

What had happened to the three of them?

As they grew up, their father seemed to withdraw even further into himself while their mother responded by being even more short-tempered. If her irritation wasn't directed at him, it was Isla who bore the brunt of it.

'*Don't think you're going out looking like that.*' How many times had she said that? '*Go and change.*'

'*Is that make-up?*' she'd ask, leaning in close to check. '*Wash it off immediately. You look too tarty.*'

'*Doing your hair like that doesn't suit you.*'

Their father would step in with '*May, don't you think you're being a little harsh,*' then back off as she snapped back at him:

'*I think I know what's best for her.*'

But the damage was done.

Her protective shell had started to thicken so that her mother could not hurt her. Since then she had been able to withdraw into it when she needed to. When Ian left her. When she and Keith split up. When Helen left home and didn't always return her calls. But not this time. May had excelled herself.

She smiled at the image of herself as a tortoise. When things got too much, she withdrew into her carapace where nothing could hurt her. Nothing, it turned out, except her mother.

15

Louise and Charlie returned from their morning at the veterinary practice together, with Charlie full of what she had seen.

'There was a dog who'd swallowed so many stones. I saw the X-ray and Lou's going to have to operate.'

Louise laughed. 'Morton brought in one of his sheepdogs,' she explained to Morag who was ladling out bowls of home-made vegetable soup. 'He'd no idea what was troubling it, but it was obvious when I palpated her, though I X-rayed her to be sure.'

'And there was a really fat guinea pig who turned out to be pregnant. And a cat with a cut ear from a fight. Then we went to see a cow ... Can we go and see Echo?'

Isla exchanged a smile with her sister over Charlie's head. Seeing Charlie like this completely vindicated her decision to bring her on the trip. She couldn't wait to tell Helen.

'Of course. I want to check on them anyway. Let's have some soup, then we'll go.' Louise sat at the kitchen table, where she cut several slices of bread then handed them round.

'I thought we could go to Haddon Hall this afternoon,' said Isla, setting herself the impossible task of making it sound as exciting as the morning's adventure.

Her granddaughter didn't raise her head from her phone. 'Charlie!'

She looked up. 'Yeah?'

'Shall we go to Haddon Hall this afternoon? It's a stately home – a manor house.'

Charlie's face conveyed exactly how little she thought of that idea. She looked back at her phone, her hair falling like curtains around her face.

'I thought you might be interested as you're doing History.' That was more off-putting still. 'I've wanted to go for ages.'

'Why don't you try the Monsal Trail? You could take the dogs with you.' Lou pulled her hair back into a stubby curl of a ponytail.

Charlie perked up. 'Can we? I'd rather.'

'Sure.' Isla was disappointed to have her plan derailed but would prefer they did something they both might enjoy.

'You can take the four-by-four, then you'll have room for them all.'

Isla took a deep breath. *Calm*, she said to herself. *Stay calm. You can pull this week back into shape. You just need to find the right moment.* 'Then that's what we'll do.'

After lunch she and Charlie set off together with the dogs piled into the back of the car. But by the time she had navigated the unfamiliar vehicle through Bakewell and up to the disused station building, the atmosphere in the car had turned decidedly wintery. Something on Charlie's phone seemed to have plunged her into a gloom.

'What's the problem?' Isla tried to sound as casual and disinterested as possible.

'Nothing. Just a stupid message . . .' Her words trailed off into an indistinguishable mumble.

'Saying?' Isla knew enough about online bullying to be concerned. If that was what this was, she would have to involve Helen.

'Nothing.'

'I bet they didn't spend the day with a vet.'

The eye-roll she caught told her exactly what they might think of that.

'Of course they didn't.' How could one fourteen-year-old load so much disdain into a sentence? 'They're in London hanging out together. No one cares what I'm doing.'

'Have they said that?' Isla glanced at Charlie, whose chin was wobbling. 'Oh, Charlie.' She quickly put her hand on her leg. 'Don't take any notice of them.' So easy to say. 'This is much better.' Isla pulled the car into a space, aware that it wasn't better at all. 'Come on.'

She remembered Helen, home from school in floods of tears after two girls she considered friends had thrown stones at her. The detail was hazy now but she had fought tooth and nail for her daughter (despite being begged not to), visiting the parents and the school until she was finally believed, the ringleader was expelled and the bullying ended. She would do the same for Charlie if need be.

When released, the dogs leaped out of the back, excited by the prospect of a walk. Charlie remained in her seat, hunched over her phone, messaging someone somewhere. Isla wanted to help but didn't want to interfere and drive her further away.

When Charlie eventually clambered out, looking glum, Isla longed to give her a hug. She took a step towards her, almost getting bowled over by Jock and Red in the process. Seeing the excitement of the dogs switched something in Charlie and she chased after them.

Titch, Shep and Red knew exactly where they were going and darted down the side of the pretty Victorian station building.

'Are you sure this is right?' Charlie shouted over her shoulder as she followed them to the back of the building where a wide path replaced the old railway line.

Isla caught her up, inhaling the sharp smell of cow parsley frothing in the hedgerows. 'Looks like it.' She was wondering how she could get Charlie to talk about what was troubling her.

As they walked, Charlie kicked at stones on the track for Titch to race after. 'Louise told me there's a dog show tomorrow. Can we go?'

'Yes – on one condition. I'd like us to be honest with each other.' They were walking side by side with no eye contact to deflect the conversation.

'What do you mean? Now what have I done?' Charlie was immediately on her guard.

'Nothing at all. I just think we should have some rules for the next few days.'

'Rules.' The word was muttered.

'Yes, rules.' Isla felt a new determination to make their relationship work. 'So I'm going to be straight with you. Neither of us expected to be in this situation, and I get that you'd far rather be with your friends at home. But you rather screwed that up for yourself, didn't you?'

'It wasn't my fault.' Charlie kicked a stone onto the verge, sending Titch racing after it.

'Once is one thing. But twice?'

'Why won't anyone believe me?' Her sense of injustice was heartfelt and almost convincing. Helen used to use exactly the same tone.

'Listen. I'm not sitting in judgement. That's for Helen and Mike, if anybody. But, my point is, we didn't exactly choose to be on holiday together—'

'You don't want me any more than they do.'

Isla was appalled. 'But of course I do and so do they. But I'd like us to enjoy the next couple of days. Or at least to do our best.'

'I enjoyed going with Lou,' Charlie said defensively.

'I saw that and I'm glad, but that's not being with me. So I've been thinking . . .' They stopped for a family wobbling by on their bikes. 'Jock! Come!' The old Lab came back immediately on command, the other three dogs in his wake. Isla and Charlie grabbed their collars and stepped back onto the overgrown verge as they waited for them to pass.

Charlie was silent, obviously expecting some ultimatum that she would have to endure.

'Okay,' said Isla once they were on the move again. 'Here are my rules. For everything I want to do that you don't, we'll do something that you want to do, that I don't.'

Charlie looked up, her eyes brighter. 'So like I get to do some of what I want? Really?'

'Yes, but we have to be honest with each other. Right?' Optimism flared inside Isla. Perhaps, when awake in the small hours, she had hit on something.

'Right. So we *can* go to the dog show?'

'Exactly. Now I don't particularly want to go to that but ... if you come to Haddon Hall, then yes, we'll go. You never know, we might surprise ourselves and enjoy them both.'

Charlie's scepticism was probably healthy.

'And ... my other rule.' This was the one that Isla was more nervous about. 'You don't bring your phone to the table when we're eating.' A step too far?

'What?!' Charlie hovered between disbelief and outrage.

Her face was such a picture, Isla had to stop herself from laughing. As she suspected.

'But someone might text me.'

'I'm sure they can wait half an hour for a reply.' Probably not true, but fair. 'I don't think it's a lot to ask.'

There was silence as they carried on walking, the path taking them under an old road bridge, Isla anxious she had just made things worse between them.

Finally Charlie spoke. 'So I can make some rules too?'

'Of course.' Why not? 'Like what?'

'I'm thinking. I'll tell you soon.'

'All right. So while you think, why don't you tell me what happened at school?' At that point, the trees on the left of them cleared to reveal meadows running up to the dark green of a forest.

'Okay, that's rule number one. Not to sound like Mum.'

Isla laughed. 'Fair enough. Even though I'd like to know.'

'Even though. But I'll tell you this time.' She pulled at a piece of long grass, then bent down to pat Titch and give him a treat from her pocket. 'Like, my friend Emily had a house party when her mum and dad went away to their country place. Her brother was there, and he didn't mind. Someone brought some weed – but because I was there, I got reported to the school too. Somebody's mum actually complained. The one with the weed was expelled and the rest of us were suspended. And Mum's furious. Fucking unfair.'

'Charlie!'

The girl wagged a finger at her. 'First rule broken again. You sound just like Mum. What's the fine?'

Isla laughed. 'He who breaks the rule gets the next treat. Want an ice cream?'

They had reached an old station building, Hassop Station read the sign, that had been requisitioned as a thriving café and shop so, in agreement, they tied the dogs to a railing and went inside. From then on the walk was a pleasure. After

Charlie's confidence, Isla found herself opening up too in response to Charlie's questions.

'I don't really understand why you think your mum being in Paris has anything to do with her will. I mean, she was young then.'

'I know. It's just a hunch born from the fact she left me a picture with a note in French attached. I can't help feeling that it all connects somehow.'

'Seems a bit of a stretch, if you ask me.'

'Maybe. But it's all I've got at the moment.'

They walked a long way, through another abandoned station, past picnic spots, houses with people chatting in gardens, and through a long dirty, damp tunnel that opened up to a stunning view from a long viaduct over uninterrupted rolling countryside. By the time they eventually returned to the car, a truce had definitely been brokered.

However, within moments of shutting the passenger door, Charlie's phone was out and she was back in her own world. There was nothing Isla could say without breaking the new rules. She was determined to stick to her side of the deal.

16

To Isla's surprise, Charlie stuck to her side of their bargain by not producing her phone at supper and joined in the conversation without scowling whenever Isla spoke. Morag and Louise were good at drawing Charlie out of herself and, perhaps key, treating her like an equal.

'Have you got a boyfriend, Charlie?' Louise didn't look up from her plate as she asked. Isla would never have dared.

Charlie blushed. 'No.'

'Early days, I guess. You will, if your grandmother's anything to go by.' Morag inclined her head towards Isla.

'Hang on. That's a bit of an exaggeration.' Isla's cheeks were burning.

But Charlie's interest had been snagged. She put down her knife and fork and looked at her. 'What do you mean?'

'Your grandmother was a tearaway when she was young.' Morag grinned, deliberately taunting her sister, daring her to shut her up.

'Must you?' Isla could have throttled her.

'Were you?' Charlie asked with absolute incredulity.

'Not so much.' She glared at Morag, not wanting to

elaborate, then paused – wasn't that exactly what her own mother had done? May had doctored her past, as far as her children were concerned, so that it was as if her life before them had barely happened.

'Let's just say she enjoyed herself, then.' Morag crossed her arms over her chest, and leaned back, satisfied that she'd put the cat smack dab among the pigeons.

Isla placed her knife and fork carefully on her plate, exactly side by side. 'I didn't do anything anyone else wasn't doing at drama school in the seventies.' They had been good times, even though they had seen the end of her ambition.

'You wanted to be an actor? I never knew that.' Now Charlie was interested.

Isla gave in. 'I did. Aggie gave me the bug.'

'She was in lots of school plays,' encouraged Morag.

'Yes, but once I got to college, I realised being good at school wasn't good enough. There were people there who were much more talented than me. But I kept going because I didn't know what else to do.'

'And because of Robbie,' prompted Morag.

'Oh, for heaven's sake.' Isla hadn't thought of Robbie Jennings for years, the first boy she slept with who came out soon afterwards. At the time, it hadn't been much of a boost to her morale and it made her the butt of many a joke.

'And then she met your grandfather.'

'I'm sure Charlie's not really interested.' Those days seemed so long ago now, but she could remember the burst of excitement when she first saw Ian, his long hair overlapping the collar of the black velvet cape he always wore: ridiculously theatrical from the start.

'I am,' her granddaughter protested.

'I've got Mum's old albums and I'm pretty sure there's a photo of both of you in it.' Morag got up and went off to find it.

'Talking of men. Are you seeing anyone at the moment?' Lou was looking at her, interested. As was Charlie.

Isla could feel herself blushing again. 'We-ell . . .'

'You are?' Morag could barely contain herself as she returned to the table with a fat photo album with faded blue covers. 'At last. Is he a keeper this time?'

'You're making me sound like some sort of . . . I don't know what.' Couldn't the others see she was uncomfortable talking about this in front of Charlie?

'Don't be daft.' Morag took absolutely no notice of her most basilisk stare. 'Well, is he?'

'I don't know.' She gave in. 'He's nice. I'm . . . well, yeah . . .'

'Nicer than Grandad?' Charlie couldn't take her eyes off Isla.

Morag hugged her. 'There aren't many men nicer than Ian. He just wasn't great husband material.'

'Why not?'

Oh God.

'Well, I'm hardly the one to tell you.' She smiled across the table at Louise. 'But I daresay Isla can.'

'This is a daft conversation.' Isla attempted to put an end to it.

'No it's not,' Charlie protested. 'I want to know.'

Isla remembered again May's frustrating reticence about her own past. '*Not now, darling. Not interesting.*' Or '*You don't want to know.*' '*I can't remember.*' She'd brush any questions away like irritating flies.

Isla didn't want to be that woman. If Charlie was interested, Isla should tell her. 'He was a better actor than me and got a chance to go to Hollywood.' She decided to edit out Anna Frank for now, the actor who had travelled ahead of him and sent urgent messages home saying how much she missed him, and telling him about the opportunities her agent had assured her awaited him. He had left a couple of her letters in their letter rack where Isla found them. At that point, their relationship was on its last legs, thanks to his apparent indifference towards their life as a family. His career came first. His decision to go to LA had been the final straw. All the letters had done was confirm what she already knew: she and Helen were better off without him. But she didn't want Charlie to think the worst of him.

'Helen was about ten then so we decided that she and I would stay here while he explored the possibilities. By then I'd changed direction and had a job in a local auction house that I loved much more than acting. The plan was for us to join him when he was ready.' She ignored Morag's raised eyebrow in response to what she knew was untrue. 'But it didn't work out for him so in the end he came back. By then, we'd grown apart and decided the best thing for all three of us was to stay friends but live separately. I wasn't an actor anymore and didn't think that raggle-taggle gypsy life would be the best thing for Helen.'

'And it worked out very well.' Morag gave her support at last. 'Look!' She held out the open album. 'There they are in *Midsummer Night's Dream.*'

'Let me see.' Charlie stretched out her hand for the book. 'Wow! Is this really you, Gran?'

Isla looked at the image of herself, ethereal and pretty, her red hair tamed by a circlet of flowers. 'I had to buy those wretched flowers from the market every morning and weave that crown myself.' She enjoyed the memory. In the photo, her hand was extended to Robbie, her Oberon, dark and tousled, his narrowed eyes focused slightly over her shoulder. She remembered that performance precisely. Afterwards they had gone to the pub where she saw him out the back kissing Anton Speight who had played the King. Two beautiful young men who no one had realised were gay. She wondered what had become of them.

'And that's Ian,' Morag chimed in, interrupting Isla's train of thought.

'Let me see?' Charlie's finger hovered over the page until it landed on her grandfather, as glorious a youth then as the rest of them, on his knees in front of Isla and Robbie.

'Mustardseed,' Isla said. 'Those fairy costumes were terrible. Ian's tights were so small the crotch was practically at his knees, so he spent half the performance yanking them up.'

Charlie laughed. 'And this?'

She could remember as if it was yesterday. 'Noel Coward's

Hay Fever in our last year. We'd just taken the curtain call and were leaving the stage when Ian called me back and proposed to me in front of the whole cast. I didn't even know Mum had this photo.' Not only had, but put it in an album as if she was proud of her.

'That's so romantic.' Louise helped herself to another spoonful of summer pudding. 'Better than a wine bar after a day of lambing.' She and Morag exchanged a smile.

'Weren't you embarrassed?' Charlie was entranced.

'Mortified. But I was so thrilled too.' She could still remember that feeling of sick anticipation as Ian dropped to one knee and she realised what was happening. As the whole cast and crew stood waiting for her reply, she dismissed any doubts. She was in love: head over heels with a man who adored her, and continued to until Helen was ten. If he had affairs before Anna Frank, she had simply closed her eyes to what she didn't want to know, until she couldn't any longer.

'Here's the wedding.' Morag flicked forward a few pages until she found it. Isla realised she was enjoying herself, looking back. She hadn't seen these photos for years.

'Gran! What *are* you wearing?'

'That's very of its time, I'll have you know. Biba was the cool place to shop.' She and Bea, her friend and witness, had found the dress, after spending the early part of the day dressed up as Trolls in Olympia, selling kitchen equipment on a job some ad agency had found for them. Ian had been touring with a production of *Boeing-Boeing* so the two of them had gone home via Kensington High Street. Bea had shepherded her into Biba's when she admitted she hadn't thought what she might wear at her own wedding. 'If this isn't an excuse to dress up, then nothing is.' After they'd found the dress, they went to Kensington Market for henna. In the photo, her hair was at its reddest. Ian had dug out a dark green velvet smoking jacket from the company's wardrobe and looked the most dashing she had ever seen him. They had been so happy that day, celebrating after their registry office wedding with six friends in Camden Lock, collapsing back at their flat that evening where they stayed in bed for the next couple of days, making nothing but coffee, toast and love.

'Are they your mum and dad?' Charlie pointed at the man and woman standing on either side of them. He was smartly suited, looking at Isla with such pride in his eyes. May wore a small hat like a shell covering her neat chignon so her face, staring straight at the camera, was visible. Her expression suggested she would rather the photos were over.

'Is that real fur?'

'They all wore them then.' Isla looked at the mink stole her mother wore whenever she could, a trophy for being the wife of the owner of Adairs department store. May had made a big thing of wearing it that day even though the September weather was mild. She had clutched it round her as if it was Harry Potter's cloak of invisibility, hiding her button-up dress with the full skirt. Isla hadn't thought about it in that way before. Perhaps May hadn't been stand-offish and difficult with Mary at all but shy, embarrassed by being on show. Perhaps there was a side to her that Isla had never even tried to understand but that she might at least get to know better now.

'Have you still got your dress?' Charlie sounded hopeful.

'I gave it to a friend once I'd had Helen and couldn't fit into it anymore.'

'Grandad's hair!' She ran her finger over the photo.

The dark curls touching his collar made him look very different to the Ian of today.

'Here's one of you pregnant.' Morag had flipped forward through time to a photo of Isla, at eight months, doing yoga in the garden of Braemore. That had been a disastrous visit, when May had stayed in her room for much of it so Isla had spent most of her time at Aggie's flat, wondering how she could make things right with her mother. Her father had reassured her that May had a migraine, that it was nothing personal. But deep down Isla sensed it was more than that. For some reason her mother didn't want to see her pregnant, happy.

'And look at this of Mum with Helen.' They were posing stiffly in front of the camera together, May on her knees reaching out for the ball her granddaughter offered her. They were in the garden of Braemore. The look of joy on her mother's face as she looked at Helen was something Isla had quite forgotten. So it hadn't always been as consistently difficult as she remembered. She had buried the good memories somewhere beneath the bad.

'That's enough.' Isla took the album and snapped it shut. 'We've all got the general idea.' But she would look at more when she was alone in her bedroom to remind herself of what she had been through to get to where she was. 'I didn't even know you had this.'

'We did talk about it when we were at Braemore and agreed I'd keep the albums until either of you wanted them. So I have.'

'What's this one?' Charlie had taken the other album and opened it.

'Ancient history,' said Morag. 'That's us in Sandgreen.' The tiny black and white picture was of three small girls climbing over their laughing mother. 'You must have been about eight,' she said to Isla. 'Oh look, here's Mum and me.' She pointed at a photo of May holding a chubby beaming baby.

'What happened to us?' Isla couldn't help asking the question again.

'You grew up,' said Charlie.

The two sisters laughed.

'We did that all right. Oh, look at us with Lorna.' They were standing in their elasticated nylon swimsuits beside an enormous sandcastle, every one of its towers decorated with shells and draped with seaweed. Isla and Morag had their spades in the air, triumphant, while Lorna put the last tower in place, grinning manically at the camera.

'And here's the cottage.'

'You stayed there?' Charlie stared at the ramshackle wooden hut with a covered verandah. 'It looks tiny.'

'Big enough. And it was right on the beach. I'm going to stay there next week, just to see how it's changed.'

'Wish I could come with you,' said Morag. 'But duty keeps me here.'

'Talking of which, I'm going to check on Echo. Want to come?' Louise pushed back her chair.

'I'll stay here.' Charlie was on her feet but Isla could see her hand had travelled to her jeans pocket containing her phone. She'd done well this evening. 'Can I watch *Love Island*?'

Isla called for Jock and headed to the back door with Louise, leaving Morag to show Charlie how to work the TV.

17

Paris, 1954

May was fizzing with nerves as she made her way to meet
Max at the Brasserie Bleu. She was glad to find there weren't
many people there that night. The mirrors behind the red
leatherette banquettes made the room look much bigger.
Vases of flowers and chipped figurines decorated the shelf
that ran between the mirror and the top of the banquette.
Max was already there when she arrived, his back to the
centre of the room, a glass of red wine and some crusty bread
in front of him.

His reflection in the mirror was thoughtful. She felt the
usual flutter of butterflies in her stomach when she saw him.
The contours of his face were as familiar to her now as those of
her own. She knew the exact blue of his eyes, the small mole
just under his jawline, the scar by his right ear that he earned
in a scooter accident. She knew all of him. As she passed the
cheese trolley, she raised her hand to her mouth, almost gag-
ging. Usually she loved the smell but tonight it made her sick.

Not even when she had said her goodbyes to her Aunt Jess

at Victoria Station, about to board the boat-train to come to
Paris all on her own, had she felt as nervous as she did now.
Max turned and watched as she slipped between the tables
and slid along the padded seat to sit opposite him, straightening the skirt of her dress so it wouldn't crease too much.

'You look wonderful tonight. I ordered wine.' Max looked
nervous too, as if he had a premonition of what she was about
to tell him.

A waiter filled her glass on cue.

'Could I have some water?' The last thing she wanted was
the smell or taste of wine.

He poured some for her, concentrating on the task in
hand, giving her time to study the face she had got to know
so well, the blond hair swept to either side of his parting,
the eyes that would look up at her from under his lashes
in a way that made her go weak at the knees. Today they
seemed darker than usual, as if they were harbouring something serious.

'We need to talk.'

'We need to talk.'

After saying the same thing at exactly the same time, they
looked surprised then laughed, embarrassed.

He reached across the white tablecloth and took her hand.
'I'm sorry.' He turned her hand over and gently traced the
lines on her palm.

She breathed out. It was going to be all right.

'You first,' he said with a little squeeze of her fingers.

'No, you. I insist.' That way, she could pretend nothing

had changed for just a little bit longer. She could continue to exist in what was about to be the past. Once she had her turn, everything would be different.

'If you insist, I can't refuse.' He almost smiled, before looking down at the table. With his free hand he manoeuvred the breadcrumbs spilled on the white tablecloth into a neat little pile. 'This is hard. I wasn't expecting to feel this way.' He paused.

Her hopes spiralled upwards. A proposal would solve everything.

But was that the solution she wanted? A life with him. Yes, it was. She had no doubts on that score. And what choice did she have? She took a sip of water to calm her stomach, as her thoughts spun out of control.

'I'm so glad we met and you know how crazy I am about you.' He cleared his throat as he put his hand in his jacket pocket.

Her heart was beating as fast as if she had run from one side of Paris to the other without stopping. Could he not hear it banging against her ribs?

'I'll never forget the past few months.'

'Nor me.' She allowed herself the two words, not trusting her voice to stay steady for any more.

'And I don't want it to end.' At last he looked up at her, his eyes quite steady as he mastered his feelings. She turned her hand over and clasped his, her heart pounding faster than she thought possible.

This was the moment.

Had he chosen the ring himself? What would he have chosen?

She knew exactly how she would reply.

He withdrew his hand from his pocket. And with it – a pack of Gauloises. 'But I've been given no choice. After everything I've said about staying here, about being a writer here and nowhere else, I know this'll come as a surprise but ... I'm going back home.'

She felt as if she'd been kicked in the stomach. 'America?' The world stuck on her tongue.

He nodded, unable to look at her now. 'I'm sorry,' he said again.

'When?' she managed. Her thoughts were tumbling over themselves too quickly for her to be able to make sense of them.

'Tomorrow.'

'Tomorrow!' She gasped and took the cigarette he offered her, knocking another couple out onto the table. She left him to pick them up. 'But why ... I don't understand.'

'Dad wrote to me a month ago. If I'm not on that flight, he's cutting off my allowance. I have no choice.'

'You've known for all that time and never said anything to me?' Disbelief, anger and upset raged inside her. 'Didn't you think you owed me that?' Had he known when they were in Brittany? He couldn't have.

A couple on the next table turned to see the source of the raised voices. May waved away the waiter who was hovering behind Max with their omelettes and frites.

'I couldn't.' He looked straight at her, unrepentant. 'I'm sorry. There's a girl I left behind. June's her name. When I left, I said I'd be back and she and my parents have expectations.'

'What about your writing?'

He shrugged. 'That was just a lark. Kids' stuff. I've always known deep down I'd never make it. Sometimes you gotta give up on your dreams.'

'But what about me? I thought you loved me ...' What about her and Max – her dream?

'I do. I did. But everything's changed. You must be able to see that. We had fun, I know we did. But that's all it was, wasn't it. A bit of fun.' He blew a plume of smoke over her head, giving a smile that was encouraging her to agree.

'But I think I'm pregnant.' The words rushed out of her.

For a moment, she watched his face change – not to the concern she had hoped for, but to shock and anger.

'What?!' He pulled his hand away, ran it through his hair. 'Are you sure?'

'I haven't seen a doctor yet but I'm sure as I can be.' Surely this would change his mind.

'You can't be. I was very careful.' He looked at her with an expression she hadn't seen before: disdain; dislike; fear. 'If this is a way to trap me into staying, it won't work.'

She looked around the brasserie, at the mirrors, the glistening glasses, the white drapery that she so loved then back at him. 'I could come with ...' She remembered June.

'With me?' He finished her sentence for her as if astonished she would suggest such a thing. He gave a short laugh. 'That wouldn't work in a million years. Like I say, it's been fun but it's over now. I'm leaving come what may.'

'And me?'

'That's up to you, sweetheart.' He looked down, unable to meet her eye.

She pushed her chair back, scraping it on the floor tiles. 'I should go.' She dug her nails into the palm of her hand, the pain stopping her from crying. She would not let him see how upset she was. She had only one person to think about now. Only one future.

A glimmer of regret crossed his face. 'Don't go.'

For a second she was tempted to stay where she was. Then everything he had said came roaring back to her and she remembered how she had been duped. 'What is there to stay for?' She took a handkerchief from her bag and blew her nose. 'I'd never have believed you could be so heartless. I thought we loved each other. What a fool I've been.'

He flinched as if she had slapped him. 'I'll write.'

'Don't. I won't read it.'

At once, she saw Max for what he was: a spoilt rich American boy with a romantic vision that meant nothing. He was all talk. As soon as his dad crooked his finger, he went running. And he had a girl waiting for him back home in Wisconsin. June. Good luck to her.

Somehow she found unexpected strength at the heart of the crushing misery that left her almost breathless, otherwise she would never have been able to get home. She walked

back to the apartment on auto-pilot, oblivious to her surroundings, trying to make sense of what had just happened.
Getting in the family way was her fault. It wasn't as if she
hadn't been warned. Getting drunk and trusting Max had
been her downfall.

She had no idea what she was going to do about the baby
or where she would go for help, but several things were clear
to her. Now she had seen Max's true colours, she did not
want him or his money. She was better than that. Equally, she
couldn't go home and face her parents' disappointment, or
the attendant local scandal. She would have to stay in Paris.
She would have to find a way of dealing with the baby. She
would have to find a way of saving herself because no one
else was going to.

18

Derbyshire, 2019

When Charlie eventually surfaced the following morning, she was as disengaged as she had ever been. Phone held in front of her mouth, she was involved in an animated conversation. She lounged against the kitchen units, once or twice catching Isla's eye then looking away.

'That last coupling. I didn't think she'd drop him . . . Yeah. No, he's fit but she's . . .'

Isla stopped listening. Instead, she shunted cereal, toast (cold) and jam across the table, hoping that Charlie would remember their meal-time deal. Eventually the call ended and Charlie came and sat down with all the energy of someone who had just completed a marathon.

'So!' Isla tried to be breezy but ended up sounding like a school teacher. 'Haddon Hall. Ready?'

Charlie pulled the cereal towards her, then reached for her phone. Several narrow silver bangles and a fabric wristband that Isla hadn't noticed before slid down her arm.

'Rules,' she reminded her. She bit back a comment on

Charlie's denim shorts, so short that the pockets hung down her thighs from the inside and her bum could almost be seen from behind.

'Fuck's sake.' Charlie spoke under her breath but with such irritability that Isla didn't need to hear the words to understand the sentiment. Nonetheless the phone disappeared into a pocket.

'Tea?' Isla said as if there was nothing wrong.

'Please.' Charlie began to spread honey on a piece of toast. They didn't speak for a few minutes while Charlie ate that then helped herself to another. Then she broke the silence. 'Gran, have you really got a boyfriend?'

'Well, yes.' Charlie's curiosity made her feel uncomfortable.

'Why isn't he here with you then?' She bit into the last piece of toast with a crunch.

'He's not that interested in me and my issues with Mum, and anyway he's got his own stuff to do. He is coming up this weekend though.' She felt herself blushing.

'Is he?' Now Charlie was really interested. 'When? Will I meet him?'

'He's arriving at Preston when I put you on the train home. I'm not sure which happens first, so maybe.' She hadn't anticipated introducing him to the family so soon.

'Oh.' A ping made her take out her phone and flick at its side before putting it away again. 'What's he like?'

'Tall. Kind. Funny, sometimes.'

And he's woken me from my determinedly single state, reminded me what life can be like.

But Charlie had already lost interest. 'Can we go to the dog show first?'

Isla couldn't help smiling. 'No. We'll go to Haddon Hall while it's quiet. Then we'll spend the afternoon at the show. There you are. One each.'

'You'll like the dog show.' But she wasn't going to insist. 'And you might like the Hall. Let's go.'

'Give me a chance.' Charlie picked up her tea, a frown so deeply etched on her forehead, Isla couldn't help but smile.

Much later than planned, they were walking over a small hump-backed bridge on the path leading to the Hall. Charlie sat on the low wall, held her phone at arm's length and pouted towards the lens. 'Insta,' she said, by way of explanation.

Isla understood but as someone who had managed to get through life without using any more social media than Facebook sporadically, she didn't really see the point. 'You'll have to show me how it works,' she said. She was interested in Charlie's and her friends' secret world.

'Later.' Click. Thumbs.

They crossed the uneven courtyard and went through a front door surrounded by rambling roses. Inside, the house was cool and dark. They wandered through the Tudor kitchens, envying the vast fireplaces and touching the cool stone surfaces. 'I'd rather have an Aga,' was Charlie's opinion.

Back in the banqueting hall, Isla pointed at an iron manacle and lock attached to the wall. 'Look at this! If you drank too much or too little you'd be locked here and have drink poured down inside your sleeve.'

Charlie adjusted her ponytail, unimpressed.

As they wandered through the rooms, Isla sensed Charlie's interest as she stopped to look at the dogs painted on the ceiling in the parlour, the wonky glass in the long gallery, the plaster relief of Orpheus taming the animals in the bedroom. She was careful not to go on too much, remembering the tedium of being dragged round the occasional stately home by her parents. But Charlie listened to what she did say. When they reached the terraced gardens, she left her grand-daughter sitting on the grass mooning over her phone, while she mooched around, seeing what ideas she could pinch for her own garden, inspired by the huge blousy poppies, old-fashioned roses she hadn't seen before, the wild flower borders and the mixing and matching of colour and plants.

'Almost done.' Isla came and sat down beside her grand-daughter. Bees buzzed in the lavender behind them. 'Imagine what it must have been like living here.' Below them were the water meadows, a stream crossed by a picturesque arched stone bridge; behind them, a wood.

Charlie was staring at the cover of the guidebook. 'Weird.'

They sat for a bit until Isla got to her feet. 'We should make a move. A quick look at the chapel, then we're done.'

With a sigh that expressed her extreme suffering, Charlie followed her. In the tiny chapel, Isla couldn't resist laying her hand on an exquisite effigy of a young boy at rest. The marble was chilly to the touch.

'Who is he?' Charlie, who had been standing at the door of the chapel (escape route), came to stand beside her.

'He died when he was nine,' read Isla. 'His mother was an amateur sculptor who was so grief-stricken she spent the next thirty years making this. Imagine.'

'Mum would never do anything like that.' That note of vulnerability had crept back beneath the don't-care veneer.

Isla put an arm round her. 'She might, you know.'

'She'd never get her scripts written if she did.' Charlie spoke with resignation and resentment as she shrugged Isla off.

The brief moment of togetherness was over.

'I wonder how she's getting on.'

'What if they want her to go and live in the States some of the time?' Charlie turned her phone over and over.

'They won't.' This wasn't something Isla had even considered. 'She belongs here with you and Mike.'

'He's never here though.'

'That's a cameraman's job for you. It's not because he wants to be away from home.' Couldn't Helen see how much their frequent absences upset their daughter? Should Isla blame herself? She had tried so hard to be different from her own mother, to be as present and loving as she could be to her own daughter, and now Helen seemed to be reverting to May's ways. But trying to discuss it wouldn't help, she knew that from experience. 'I'm sure she wouldn't agree to that. She's got too much that she loves at home. Including you.'

'Okay.' She didn't sound convinced.

'Time for the dog show. You want to take Jock?'

Charlie brightened. 'Of course.'

'Then we'd better go back and get him.'

Every possible breed of dog had been gathered at the show-ground. Spirited springers pulled at their leads, lean lurchers looked into the distance, Labradors sniffed around the waste bins, hopeful. Isla spotted a pair of shaggy Spinones – her favourites – drool trailing from their mouths.

'Gran, look!' Charlie pointed at a basset hound whose long belly almost scraped the ground. She laughed before her attention was taken by a group of handsome English and Irish setters.

The sun shone on tents busy with people out for a good afternoon. The beer tents were doing a roaring trade while queues snaked away from the food vans. The atmosphere was buzzy, loud with chatter and the sound of a brass band. Announcements were made over a couple of tannoy systems that no one seemed to take much notice of.

There were stalls selling everything a pet could need, dog-food stalls, dog charities reeling people in for their money. The smell of fried food and the sweetness of candyfloss wafted across the ground.

'Look at those foot-long hot dogs! They look wicked.'

So, armed with one each, they planted themselves at the edge of one of the show rings. They watched dogs retrieving things, terrier racing and a gun-dog scurry, dogs competing over hurdles, in agility tests and show classes. Charlie loved it, pointing out the different dogs, cheering them on, taking photos.

Isla was quite happy half-watching what was going on in the ring and half daydreaming, to the extent that she didn't notice Jock edge closer and then pounce . . .

'Jock! That's my lunch!'

Too late. The sausage had gone. Charlie laughed and laughed.

Grateful to him in a way, Isla pulled out her own phone and photographed an elegant black greyhound that had just won the fastest recall competition. Charlie reached for it. 'You could put that on Instagram. Look.' Thumbs flying and few minutes later, Isla had an Instagram account and had posted three photos and followed four people. Morag, to her surprise, was one of them. Ian was another. Helen another. And Di, her next-door neighbour.

'You'll soon have loads more.' Charlie was confident as she returned to her phone. 'I said I'd show you.'

'Do I really want loads?' Isla thought she probably didn't but perhaps she'd post a few more pictures and see what happened. She sat and scrolled through Ian's feed, curious to see what he posted. Always theatre-related, often self-regarding, there were pictures of him at work and of posters of the shows he been to and recommended. She 'liked' one or two of them as Charlie had showed her. During a break between events, she did what she'd vowed she wouldn't and switched to her emails.

Mum! I'm sorry not to have been in touch more. Phone calls are hard because of the time difference. How are

155

you and Charlie getting on? Hope she's not too much
trouble. And have you got to the bottom of Granny's
will yet? I've been thinking about her a lot, trying to
understand, but I don't feel I ever really got to know her.
I guess we lived too far away. LA is extraordinary – not
somewhere I'd choose to be exactly, but the meetings I've
had have been really promising. More soon. Hxx

What did she mean, *more soon*? She was due back in a
couple of days. Among her other emails, Isla noticed one
from the museum but ignored it. She had promised herself
she would only check work emails in the evening when she
was alone. She clicked out of the app and turned to Charlie.
She had seen couples in restaurants sitting together in silence,
each absorbed by their own screen. That was just what she
and Charlie had been doing. Isla put hers away.

When she was a child, the family was made to sit at the
table and talk. Whether they liked it or not.

'You first, Isla. What have you done today?' Her father
would peer over the top of his spectacles and listen, not
allowing interruptions.

They would talk about what they'd done, what was going
on in the world, what the news was from their friends. Their
father would probe for more information – '*Do you think men
should land on the moon?*' – always interested, always prising
out what he wanted to hear: '*Can you imagine being able to see
who you're speaking to at the other end of the phone?*' '*Do you think
that was the right thing to do?*' May would listen too but could

never tolerate a conversation that went on too long – so she would hasten the meal on when she'd had enough. '*David! Really!*' Isla could hear the sound of those fingers tapping against the table top even now.

Her phone pinged with a text. She fished the phone back out of her pocket. Ian.

> Stalking me now?! What next?

She couldn't help smiling.

> Seriously, I was thinking about Aggie's party when I saw you follow me on Insta and that decided me. The idiots passed me over for a part and I'd love to see the old girl again so I will go. I thought I could come up a couple of days before and meet you? Then I could spend a bit of time with Charlie. Give you a break.

A break! He'd never offered to help her before. He must be at a very loose end. No job. No fourth wife. But he was another one who thought her holiday could be interrupted at will? Did no one think she might actually want to be on her own? She typed back without a second thought.

> Charlie going home from Preston on Friday so won't be here. Not sure where I'll be after that

Not true.

I'll see you in Edinburgh. Your first ex-wife

Huh!

She looked up. Charlie was staring at a pair of dogs with long white dreadlocks and thumbing something into her phone. 'Komondors,' she said authoritatively.

'They must be boiling.' Isla patted Jock. 'You're lucky, old boy.'

The dog was panting noisily, so Isla got the bottle of water and bowl out of her shoulder bag for him.

Charlie was as relaxed as Isla had seen her, her hair tied back in a ponytail so Isla could see her face. She reminded Isla of the way Helen would sit, rapt, in front of the show when she'd take her to the theatre.

'What?' And all at once, she was that glowering teenager again, challenging Isla with a glare.

'Nothing.'

'You were staring at me.'

'I wasn't.' She hadn't meant to. 'I was thinking about the next few days and what we're going to do.'

What *were* they going to do? Those couple of stately homes and gardens en route that she'd been looking forward to exploring were clearly off the menu now. She fingered the National Trust card in her pocket.

'You could put me on a train home. Ellie says I can stay with her.' Charlie nodded at her phone. So that's what she'd been doing: gathering support. So not everyone was against her. That at least was something.

'Can you imagine what Helen would say if I did that?'

Charlie raised an eyebrow in acknowledgment of the hell that would be raised. Isla would be accused of taking over, not respecting Helen's decisions, interfering. Helen was sensitive about her potential inadequacies as a parent and, as a result, defended her decisions to the hilt.

'Have we had enough?' She'd kill for a shower and a cup of tea.

'I guess.' Charlie looked around her before getting to her feet. 'And I suppose I do want to see if you get to the bottom of everything.'

'That makes it sound very serious.'

'But it is, isn't it? To you, at least.'

'Yes, you're right. It is.'

On their way back to the car, Charlie walked a couple of steps behind Isla as if she'd rather not be seen with her. Isla was okay with that. If Charlie preferred to keep her distance for a bit, so be it.

19

That evening, Morag and Louise drove them to see the well dressings in Youlgrave.

'You'll like this,' encouraged Louise.

'Yeah?' said Charlie as she made crossing the car park look like a gargantuan effort.

In the shade of one of the church buttresses, they found their first well dressing. Flower petals, eggshell, straw, coffee beans and other natural materials had been pressed into clay to make a picture the size of a large door.

'This is extraordinary,' Isla said, leaning as close as she could to appreciate the intricacy of the work. Charlie had been leaning over the barrier too before straightening up.

'It's all about the destruction of the rainforest,' she said, as if they couldn't possibly have understood. 'I saw a documentary about this. They're clearing forests to plant palm-oil plantations so the natural habitat of the orangutans is destroyed and they have nowhere to go.'

They all stared at her.

'They use palm oil in all these products.' She pointed at the petal illustrations framing the main image. 'But look what happens to the wildlife. See. "We are made of the leaves of one tree."' She read the words running around the image of a human hand shaking an ape's.

Isla felt proud her granddaughter knew about the situation and, more importantly, cared.

'Are there any more?' Charlie was already walking towards the gate into the main street.

The three women exchanged glances. They had expected her to submit to the expedition unwillingly. Instead, the four of them walked the length of the picturesque main street together, admiring each well dressing in turn.

'Read this, Gran!' Charlie called to Isla who was watching Jock greet a sheepdog. 'Look! This is important. It even mentions Greta's speech. Did you hear it?'

'Well, not all but I know the gist,' she said, ashamed by the way she'd dismissed the Swedish schoolgirl and climate and environmental activist, Greta Thunberg. But if she had made Charlie and her friends take responsibility for the environment, perhaps Isla should have paid more attention, given them more credit. After all, they weren't so dissimilar. In 1982, she and a group of friends had travelled to Greenham Common in a Transit van to join women from all over the world who linked arms round the airbase's perimeter fence that December. Ian had dismissed the women's protest as a waste of time, which had made her all the more determined to add her voice to the rest.

'Freedom,' she whispered, repeating the rallying cry. 'I protested too, in my day,' she said in answer to Charlie's puzzled expression. 'Then we were terrified by the prospect of nuclear war. Thousands of women camped around an airbase to protest against the storage of nuclear missiles, some of them for months, and in really difficult conditions. I just went up for a couple of days. Ian was so bloody awkward about my going as it was.'

'And did it work?'

'In all sorts of ways.' She remembered the mud, the cold, the smell of wood fires and food, the lights, the police, the women, and the extraordinary feeling of camaraderie found in a common purpose. Yes, everyone should act on their own beliefs to make the world a better place.

Charlie had already wandered off – a protest that had happened in the mists of time didn't much interest her. This did. Isla dragged Jock over to where she stood by a sign beside the final well dressing that was propped up outside the door of a Methodist chapel.

'This one's about climate change. Look! All these things are what we should be doing. Insulating houses, using green electricity, eating food grown locally. Read it.' She took a photo of the explanation and then a few selfies in front of the dressing that illustrated the progress of the earth from its creation to its destruction by mankind. At the bottom, spelled out in red petals was a line from the Book of Malachi: 'For the day cometh that shall burn like an oven.'

'When we get back, I'll play Greta's speech for you.' Charlie ran out of the churchyard after Jock.

Isla stared after her. She was a girl full of surprises.

They found a table outside the Bulls Head and tethered the dogs to it while Morag went inside to buy a round. Isla adjusted the parasol so they were in the shade. Around them, the tables were busy with sun-soaked people topping off their Saturday. Cheeks were flushed, limbs tanned, everyone enjoying themselves. They had only been there for a few minutes when Louise's bleeper went. She took out her phone to call the surgery, listened and hung up.

'Sounds like John Barker's prize dairy cow might have ketosis – selective anorexia and a reduction in milk yield.' She looked at Morag for her agreement. 'I'm on call so I'd better go see. I'm sorry to break up the party.'

Morag knocked back her shandy, resigned. 'I'm used to it. And yes, you're probably right.'

When they got home, Louise took off in the 4x4, saying they should eat without her. 'I've no idea how long this will take.'

'When I was working full time as well, we scarcely saw each other,' said Morag as she and Isla started preparing a vegetable lasagne at the kitchen table.

'What's it like being a vet?' Charlie looked up from chopping the courgettes. Morag had caught her just as she was heading to her room and roped her in.

'Bloody hard work,' said Morag. 'But satisfying. Do you fancy it?' She passed a couple of aubergines to Isla.

'Maybe.' Charlie pulled at a strand of hair, examining it for split ends.

'Well, you've got time to think about what you want to

do,' Morag picked up cheerfully. 'You should be enjoying yourself now.'

'I would be if I was at home.' She looked thoroughly fed up.

'Charlie!' Just when things seemed to be going so well.

'I know what you mean.' Morag stepped in. 'I wouldn't want to be stuck up here with us when I could be celebrating the end of term with my mates. What are they up to?'

'End of term parties, chilling, you know.' Charlie glanced downwards, pushing the sliced courgettes into a pile, the knife scraping on the board.

And Isla did know. The draw of being with your tribe, people of the same age with the same likes and dislikes who spoke the same language. That was what had grounded her in a world where she had yet to find her real place. During those shifting sands of adolescence, things changed so quickly. She remembered that too. Even she in her restricted Scottish upbringing where pubs didn't even open on a Sunday and closed at ten at night, when there was nowhere to go except home and her parents didn't encourage friends. And during the day - no shopping centre, no Starbucks or Costa, few charity shops, and definitely no make-up for a fourteen-year-old, at least not in front of the parents.

'*Isla!*' She heard her mother's voice. '*Wash your face! You're not going out like that.*'

The past was very definitely a different country.

'Do you remember when you answered that ad in the *Evening News* to be a model?' Morag's question came out of the blue.

'Did I?'

'Yes! You must remember.' She was impatient. 'You and Bryony were asked along to a hotel room somewhere to be "seen".' She gave the word inverted commas with her fingers. 'You told them you were eighteen.'

Something clicked in Isla's memory. She pictured the hotel's dim foyer, the bedroom where they had their photos taken. Just a 'cameraman' and a 'director' suggesting they undo just one more button. The whole thing had been horribly sleazy but at the same time exciting as a whole new future was dangled in front of them.

'Oh my God! I'd totally forgotten that. I was so full of it when I went home and Mum was absolutely furious. That's what made her try to sabotage me going on the school trip to Paris but Dad said I should go.'

'He was always soft on you.'

'Paris again,' said Charlie. 'It's a bit of a theme.'

'She was so down on me after that.' It was as if Isla's memory was clearing at last. That had been a turning point in her relationship with her mother. Although thwarted that first time, Isla had determined from that moment to leave home when she could, and May's attitude towards her had hardened as she put one small obstacle after another in her way. A particular scene clarified in her mind. May was in the living room of Braemore, standing by the fireplace, shouting at their father. They didn't know Isla was outside the half-open door listening. *'We're not going to tell her why. It's the French in her that makes her think she can do what she wants.'*

Then blank. But what did it mean and why was Isla remembering it now? She strained to remember what happened next, but nothing came.

'Do you remember her saying I had French in me?'

'You wish!' Morag laughed. 'No. Now you're imagining things.'

And perhaps she was.

'Where's that photo album?' Charlie asked, having finished the job she'd been asked to do.

'In the living room. Help yourself.' Morag pointed the way with a wooden spoon before returning it to her white sauce.

Charlie opened the album on the kitchen table. Little square black-and-white photos of the three sisters in the park with their parents, and a small white dog. 'Is that you?'

Isla went over to take a look. 'Yes, with Snowy. Snappy little thing that he was. Mum was the only one of us he liked.'

'Because she fed him.' Morag put the tray of vegetables in the oven to roast.

Charlie was running a finger round the photos on that page. 'Is this her?' She pointed out their mother, sitting with a ramrod straight back. Her hair was wavy, swept back off her still lean face and she was wearing a button-through shirtdress with a wide lapel. 'Great dress.'

'Mmm. She took care about how she looked but she never had Aunt Aggie's pizzazz.'

'She looks serious.'

'Dad was the fun one.'

'You're making her sound terrible,' said Morag.

'Okay, I take it back. She could be funny and loving but I remember the bad times better. That must say something.'

'About you, maybe. She'd take us to the theatre for special treats that Aggie organised. That's why you got so stage-struck. That's why she liked Ian so much. Your grandfather was a real ham and a charmer, Charlie. Mum fell for it completely.'

'But she had such a short temper if we got things wrong. Dad was much easier.' Isla nodded as Charlie pointed to a photo of a gentle-looking man with a moustache, his mouth in a contented smile, pipe in hand.

'You were always his favourite. And that infuriated her.' Morag took a bottle of wine from the fridge. 'I think it's time? You were the oldest of course. Can you pass me the corkscrew from that drawer?'

'I'd have liked a brother or sister.' Charlie went to the fridge and helped herself to a can of Coke.

'That's only because you haven't got one. But honestly – being the baby is a breeze because everyone dotes on you.' She shot a glance at Isla. 'Being the oldest is too because you're the boss and get all the privileges first, but if you're in the middle like me, it's hard. We fell in and out all the time.'

'Excuse me while I get my violin,' Isla mimed playing while the other two laughed.

'But now – Lorna hasn't spoken to us for months. She's as stubborn as they come.' Morag absolved herself from blame.

'Gran told me that you were too.' Charlie opened the can so the Coke foamed over the top.

Morag focused on opening the packet of pasta. 'Oh, did she?'

'Don't start,' Isla warned, wishing she could throttle Charlie. 'I was just as bad.' Except she hadn't been. Who was the one trying to build bridges?

'Sorry.' Charlie took the hint and quickly turned the next page of the album. 'Is this Sandgreen again?'

Isla went to look over her shoulder. 'Yes. Even Mum relaxed while we were there.' She pictured her in a swimsuit stretched out in a deck chair, gin and tonic on the little picnic table beside her, with their father wearing his holiday short-sleeved shirt and shorts. Sometimes they'd pore over the crossword together, something they never did at home. Sometimes they played cards. The three of them were probably down on the beach, playing with summer friends, building dams, climbing rocks, shrimping or hunting for shells. 'That's Lorna in that red swimsuit. She only wore it once.'

'Because when she came out of the sea, the top sagged right down.'

'And Jan's brother, Tommy, who Lorna liked, saw everything on offer.'

'She was mortified and couldn't look at him again.'

Charlie was grinning, either at the story itself or the pleasure the two women had in telling it. 'How awful. I'd have died.'

'What about you, Charlie. D'you fancy anyone?' Morag asked, raising her glass of wine. 'Someone at school? Was he at the famous party?' she added, forgetting she was under strict instructions not to mention it.

'No.' Charlie looked up sharply. First at Morag in surprise, then at Isla as the truth of her betrayal sank in. She blushed as her eyes filled with tears. 'Did you have to tell her?'

'Only because she asked why you came on holiday with me. I couldn't lie.'

'Why not?' She spoke as if it was the most natural thing in the world and she couldn't understand why Isla wouldn't. 'Anyway it's none of your business.' Charlie was gripping the album, her knuckles white.

'Keep your hair on. I only asked.' Morag reached out to Charlie who snatched her arm away. 'If you don't want to talk about it, that's fine.'

'For God's sake, leave me alone.' She jumped up and ran out of the room. They heard her run upstairs and the slam of her bedroom door.

'Sorry,' said Morag, grimacing.

'I'll go up.' Isla reluctantly got to her feet. She had thought her days of negotiating with a recalcitrant teenager were long over and the last thing she wanted to do was to repeat them. At the same time she had some sympathy with Charlie.

'Don't.' Morag poured them both another drink. 'Let her stew. There was no need for that. She could quite easily have headed me off.'

'She's only fourteen, remember.'

'True. The clothes and the make-up make me forget. You should get her to turn it down.'

'Not my job.'

Isla's phone broke into their conversation. Ian's name came up on her screen, so she took the call. 'Hello.'

'No need to sound so wary. It's only me.'

'I know it's you, but why?' She could see Morag's interest was piqued although she was disguising it by focusing on her preparations with more energy than before. 'What do you want?'

'That's not very nice. Perhaps I just want to hear your dulcet tones.'

'Ian . . .' A warning note.

Morag looked up, intrigued.

'Okay. I know you said don't come but a holiday in Scotland will be like old times.'

'I don't know where you've got this idea from but we're not going to holiday in Scotland together.' There was only one way to deal with him: firmly. 'We're going to see each other at Aggie's. Get the train to Edinburgh and I'll see you there.'

'Perhaps I could come up sooner, just to see Charlie.'

'Ian, no. I told you, I'm putting her on the train on Friday. After that I have plans and I'm afraid there's no room for you in them. They're complicated enough as it is. I'll see you in Edinburgh.' She knew from experience that if she didn't firmly nip the idea in the bud, he'd sweet-talk her round.

'Well, don't blame me for trying.' At the same time, defeat was something he took in his stride.

When Isla ended the call, Morag put her hands on her hips. 'Well done.'

'He can be so maddening. I'll never be rid of him. But I don't want him botching up the holiday too.'

And yet, she wasn't sure she wanted to be rid of him. She rather liked still being his first port of call in a storm. She felt a deep affection for her ex-husband that would never go away, she knew that now.

20

The breeze brought the musky fragrance of the Rambling Rector rose outside the window into the bedroom. Idling on her iPad, Isla went to check her work emails. Her Oxford home and the job of managing the Fernleith Museum of Childhood had given her the security and happiness she wanted. Thinking of the museum transported her to a happy place, surrounded by reminders of her own and other people's childhoods when the future was full of hope and possibilities.

As she ran through her emails, there was one from Heather, her deputy manager at the Museum reassuring her that everything was running smoothly.

> I've had a letter from a woman who's got two Käthe Kruse dolls she wants to donate. Apparently they need a little repair but they're from the Twenties. Amazing. I've made an appointment for her to see you when you're back.'

Isla felt that same flicker of excitement that always ignited when something particularly special was brought to the museum. She knew the dolls Heather was talking about, first made by a German woman who wanted to create a doll that was as naturalistic as possible instead of the stiff porcelain models that were common then. If they were in reasonable condition, they would definitely add range to their doll collection. That was a meeting to look forward to.

After that, Heather's email touched on a few minor business matters, nothing that needed Isla's intervention. As she read on, her phone rang again. Helen. Just two days to go.

'Hey, Mum. How's it going?' She could hear an excitement in Helen's voice that must mean good news.

'Good. We . . .' She stretched out on her bed, preparing to run through their day, wanting to reassure her daughter there was nothing — at least not much — to worry about. Perhaps she should talk about her worries about the online bullying, even though Charlie hadn't mentioned it again.

But Helen had other plans for the conversation. 'I only got the job!'

'Oh my God! You didn't? Well done.' How proud she felt of her.

'They loved what I'd done and they've asked . . .' She paused.

Isla could tell she wasn't going to like what was coming next.

'They've asked me if I'd stay on for another week so that I can meet the team involved in the production. I couldn't say no.'

And now she could guess what it was.

'So ...'

And she didn't have to think too hard about her reply.

'I was just wondering if you could you keep Charlie with you? I know it's asking a lot ...'

Yes, it was.

'I can't. I'm sorry, but I've got a friend coming up to join me when I put Charlie on the train.' How much was she looking forward to seeing Tony? She didn't want anything to spoil their weekend together. Although her journey was beginning to yield its frustrating results, time with him would mean she could switch off and relax, the highlight of her time away.

'Who?' Helen was immediately curious.

Isla hesitated. She would prefer not to introduce Tony into their lives over the phone. 'No one you know. Someone I met recently.'

'Mum! Not a man?' She didn't wait for a reply. 'Oh my God, how exciting. You never said anything. Who is he? Do you like him?' This wasn't the suspicious question of a jealous daughter but one full of hope. Helen had long ago realised that the idiosyncrasies of her father made him such an impossible partner. All she wanted was for Isla to find happiness with someone.

'Yes, I do.'

'But do you really like him?'

Isla paused before she answered. 'Yes. Really.' But was 'like' what she meant?

'That's so great. I'm pleased. When can I meet him?

You haven't even told me his name. How long have you known him?'

Isla laughed, delighted by her daughter's enthusiasm. 'Well, you'd better get back here so you can.' Then she related the story of their chance meeting in the Ashmolean and what had happened since.

'He's staying in your house while you're away?' At last a note of doubt crept in. 'Are you sure that's wise? After all, you haven't known him that long.'

Isla smiled as their roles reversed and Helen was the one worrying about her for once. 'But I do know him,' she said. 'Don't worry. The house is much better with someone in it.'

'And what about Granny? How's that going? Have you found out anything?'

'I feel as though I'm close to something. I'm hoping that Janet, Lorna and Aggie will help more. I know she worked in Paris before she met Dad.'

'And you think that might be a connection with the picture?'

'Perhaps. But it doesn't explain who Céleste is, or even if Mum knew her. And why leave the thing to me? If she was trying to give me a message, it's a bloody opaque one.' Then she remembered that flash of memory she had. *It's the French in her.* What could that have meant?

'You'll get there, I'm sure.' Isla heard a bell ringing in the background. 'Look, I've got to go. So you will take Charlie?' It was as if the intervening conversation hadn't happened.

'No, I can't,' she repeated. 'You'll have to ask one of your friends,' Isla pushed back. Helen shouldn't expect to get her own way every time.

'We've been through this.' Helen was more abrupt, her bubble of American excitement burst, her interest in her mother's love life suspended.

'Charlie mentioned she could go to Ellie's.'

'She said. But when I checked, it was the first her mother had heard of it. And she said they've got a friend staying. No one can, or they're about to go on holiday or they don't want her, and Mike's not back from filming till the week after. You know that.'

Once again, Helen was putting her in an impossible position. Of course Isla could continue to refuse. Of course she could insist that she have the holiday she had planned. But what about Charlie? Helen had waited for a break like this one for years. Who was she to spoil it? Yet these few days were meant to be just her and Tony. But really, how much did it matter when they had the rest of their lives ahead of them?

However much she liked the secrecy, the feeling of their affair being something so special to the two of them, the family had to meet Tony some time. Although she liked the idea of keeping Tony to herself, she also liked the idea of showing him off, of seeing how much everyone else would like him too. Perhaps she should simply bow to the inevitable. He would understand that she had no choice.

In her ear, Helen was going over again why this job was so important to her, how long she had waited for such an opportunity and couldn't stuff it up now. Surely Isla could understand how much it meant to her.

And Isla could.

When their conversation was over, Helen was mollified and Isla annoyed with herself, partly for giving in again but more because she wanted to look forward to spending time with her granddaughter without resenting it. How could a fourteen-year-old make her feel so conflicted?

Anyway, she had agreed, so she would have to make the best of it. At least Helen was telling Charlie while she broke the news to Tony.

In the background she could hear music, people talking. 'Where are you?'

'A bar with friends. Can I call you back?'

'Another pint?' asked a woman's voice.

She looked at her watch. Ten thirty.

She wanted to tell him then so he had time to get used to the idea. 'It's not really urgent but ...' She tried to sound as relaxed as possible. 'I just wanted to let you know that it looks as if Charlie will still be here when you arrive after all.'

She could hear someone near him laughing loudly, but from him there was silence.

'Tony?'

'I thought you were putting her on a train.' He sounded puzzled. 'What's happened?' She pictured him rubbing a finger under his left eye, something he did when pondering the implications of a decision.

She explained quickly what had happened but she could

tell she only had half his attention. 'Of course I'd rather there was just the two of us . . .'

'I'm sure it'll be fine. I've got to go.' He lowered his voice. 'I'm with friends discussing the business opportunity I told you about.'

'And?'

'It's just a dinner that's gone on but I'm hopeful . . . Listen, we'll speak tomorrow. But I'm sure everything will be fine. I'd like to meet her.'

How lucky she was. She had to love him for taking the disruption of their first holiday together with such equanimity. She'd call the hotel first thing to see if they could find them another room. And if they couldn't? She'd just have to find them somewhere else. But it wouldn't be the same. This was the place that he had chosen.

At least she and Helen had a relationship that allowed them to be open with one another. Helen could ask. She could say no. Even if it didn't take much to change her mind when it came to Charlie. Helen knew that her daughter was Isla's weak spot. Isla's thoughts went to May again. If only they had been able to talk. How different their relationship might have been. She felt a sudden pang of grief that almost winded her. What had she done wrong? What had she done to make her mother turn against her?

Without thinking she googled 'Paris in the Fifties' and clicked on Images. A black-and-white world presented itself that looked so very different from her own. A man planting a kiss on the cheek of a smiling woman. A stall selling fruit in a street market with another woman being passionately kissed. Scruffy children playing in the streets. Two nuns with a pushcart of provisions. Ruined buildings and deserted streets. Vintage cars. Models posed in elegant tailored suits on street corners, on stairs or in front of cafés. Isla remembered May, typically Scottish, without an ounce of the romance and glamour she saw in the photos. As far as Isla knew her, she had been an ordinary housewife focused on her family and her home. Occasionally she'd dress up a bit but not with the willowy elegance of the women Isla saw on her phone. She found it hard to imagine May in this lost world. How on earth would she have fitted in to somewhere so different from the Scotland where Isla and her sisters had been brought up?

21

Paris, 1954

Alone and pregnant in Paris. The inner strength May had found when she learned Max was leaving and realised he was not the man she had thought had mutated into grief and disappointment. They washed over her when least expected. She hadn't heard from him again. Wendy had told her that he had left Paris for good as he said he was going to, returning home to Wisconsin to his girl and good job prospects. He hadn't sent her a message, a note; nothing. But she, of course, was not all Max had left behind him. He had left her with a problem that she didn't know how to begin to solve.

When she was with Emile, she had to pretend there was nothing wrong. Similarly in her French classes, she sat at her usual desk, slipping away at the end so she didn't have to engage with anyone. She avoided Mme Dubois by going to her room whenever she had any free time. There, she sat for hours on the edge of her bed staring at the bee-patterned curtains. Outside, the late summer sun shone but she barely noticed. All she could focus on was her terror of what the future held in store for her, her devastation over losing Max and her shame and distress over her predicament.

She had always imagined that one day she would be married with a family of her own. She wanted her own children more than anything but not like this, alone in a strange city. She had pictured herself at home in Scotland after her adventures, marrying a Scotsman and having her children then – two girls, she thought she'd like.

Abortion was illegal – she had heard dire warnings about backstreet abortionists and women who didn't survive to tell the tale, her mother had made sure of that – but keeping the baby was an impossibility. How would she manage on her own? If she went home for help, her parents would disown her, her father sad his plans for her hadn't worked out, disappointed in her, her mother furious. If she had the baby, how would she live? She wouldn't have enough money to rent an apartment of her own, however small. How would she eat? How would the baby thrive? No! It was impossible.

Wendy was little help, wanting to ask advice from everyone they knew but May stopped her. The shame was too great. She didn't want to be the object of disgust or pity. She needed someone in whom she could confide and trust without the whole world knowing her misfortune. These thoughts played round and round her head, paralysing her. And all the while, time was ticking by, making the need for decision all the greater. Unless Max were to return and rescue her. But as time went past, that thinnest sliver of hope receded.

Not long after Max's departure, Madame Dubois cornered May in the nursery when she was putting everything back in its place while Emile was in school. Madame was a stickler for tidiness so as soon as her son left the apartment, May was under strict instructions to tidy everything away. She couldn't leave the apartment for her classes until the job was done.

Madame stood in the doorway for a minute or two, watching May at work, her eyes burning holes in May's back. Eventually she said, 'May, *ma chérie*. I think we must talk.'

'About?' May was immediately on the defensive. If Madame sacked her, what would she do? Where would she go?

Wendy had made it clear she couldn't help. 'Madame Fougère doesn't like me having anyone round to the apartment so you certainly couldn't stay. None of them do. You know that. Perhaps I could help you with some money towards your fare home.' Even she seemed to be washing her hands of May, which made her feel more alone.

May would have to go home. But she couldn't.

'About your condition.' Madame still had her eyes on May but her expression was kind. She raised her hand to the bow at the neck of her silk shirt.

May tried to look completely innocent. 'What do you mean?' She had wondered if Madame had guessed, but then persuaded herself she couldn't have when nothing was said.

Mme Dubois came in to sit in the nursery chair, hitching up her black pencil skirt a fraction. There was a rustle of nylon as she crossed her legs. 'Come. I'm a woman and I notice these things. I have heard your sickness and seen you not eating. I think you may be *enceinte*. Am I wrong?' She smoothed her dark hair, tied back tightly in a ballerina's bun at the nape of her neck.

May shook her head, as tears streamed down her cheeks unchecked. What was the point in denying it now? At the same time she felt a tremendous sense of release that her secret was out. Now she would have to confront the fact head-on and make a decision, for good or for bad.

Madame handed her a lacy handkerchief that she pulled from her sleeve, hardly enough to mop the tears or for May to blow her nose. But the relief at being able to confess was as enormous as the dread of what would follow the confession.

'I am right then.' Madame's angular face softened. 'And who is the father?'

May tried to drive the picture of Max from her head. But her longing for him would not let him go. She pictured him in the Brasserie Bleu where they last met, at the top of the Eiffel Tower and lying in bed in Brittany, that smile playing on his lips. She knew every inch of him and would never forget them. She would never find someone like him again. 'An American boy. But he's gone back home, ordered by his father. We won't see each other again. He has a girl who's been waiting for him. He didn't tell me.' She broke down again at the memory of his betrayal of her trust.

'Pff! Les Américains!' She pursed her lips in disgust. 'And the baby? You want to keep him?' Madame was nothing if not direct. She sat bolt upright, her expression thoughtful as she waited to hear what May had to say.

'If I do, perhaps Max will come back . . .' Her voice faded.

'Bah!' Madame threw her hands in the air, exploding that dream. 'I ask you again. You want to keep him?'

'How can I?' May started sobbing again, as Madame produced a second handkerchief from a pocket.

'Then you must let me help you. I know this is not what you want but we have to act now or it will be too late.' Madame brushed her hands together as if everything was decided, before she got up to go.

For May, the next few days blurred together as she tried to keep going as normal while Madame consulted a friend of the family, a private doctor, and arranged for her to have the procedure. 'You must say nothing about this to anyone, *ma chérie*. Because this procedure is illegal *en France* and anyone caught is punished severely. But Bernard will do it for us, and I will pay him.'

'But why?' May asked at last. 'Why are you taking this risk for me?' Despite a deep-seated longing to keep the baby, her first child, this was the only route open to her unless she wanted to throw herself to the winds of fortune. Of the two options open to her, that would require the sort of bravery she didn't have.

Madame clasped her hands in her lap, careful not to wrinkle her chiffon blouse or her skirt. Her head was tipped to one side, her beady gaze fixed on May. 'Because I was young once and I also made a mistake, like you. Someone helped me then, so I know your situation. I know how scared you feel. I know how scared of your parents, too. And, if I am truthful, I feel we are to blame when they trusted you to us. Perhaps we should have looked after you better in return for your excellent care of Emile. So I will look after you now.'

'How will I ever be able to repay you?' The hurdles that lay ahead of May seemed insurmountable.

'There is no need.' Madame shrugged. 'You have been so good with our little boy.' This was the first time she had paid May such compliments and, despite the gravity of the situation, May glowed with pleasure.

'I like being here.' She choked out the words. 'I'm very fond of Emile.'

'And you will continue to be here. We will keep our arrangement. I will tell everyone you have the food poisoning for a few days, and then you will start again.' Madame hesitated as she deliberated on what she was going to say next. 'It is not a crime to love a man, you know. But you must be more careful in the future.'

Only a fortnight after Max had gone for good, so had the baby. Apart from the doctor, the only people who would ever know of its existence were May, Madame and Wendy. The whole episode was over. The procedure had been swift. Madame had escorted May to the doctor's office. He had reminded her of detective Poirot, immaculately suited with a distinctive moustache. He was brisk and matter-of-fact, showed her to the anteroom where he would conduct the procedure with a nurse (his wife) in attendance. Although May felt ashamed and foolish, lying in front of him, he had not judged her, just got on with what he had agreed to do.

Her immediate relief was enormous. The results of her terrible lapse in judgement had been dealt with. She was free.

Except she wasn't. Other feelings began to creep in, breaking down her barriers until they were holding her tight. Grief. Guilt. Anxiety.

What had she done?

Madame was kind and let her do only as much work as she could, nothing for the first few days, but May was keen to get back to Emile and her language course. She believed keeping busy would help her forget. But how could she? She had lost the only man she had ever loved as well as the only thing that bound her to him. The baby was the one thing she would have loved unconditionally if it had had a chance in the world. Although she did her best to put on a brave face, Max and his baby haunted her wherever she went, whatever she did. She thought of writing to him but had no address. Not to tell him what had happened but to see if there was the slightest chance he might return to her. That they might have a future together after all. Then she would change her mind, relieved she would never have to see him again. What might have been was the thought that travelled with her and coloured her every waking moment. Even Wendy and Sam couldn't lift her spirits. And they tried.

'Come for coffee with us. One of those croissants you like so much.' Wendy tried to jolly May out of her mood, but the last thing she wanted was the companionship and laughter of the gang. She wasn't ready.

Being with them only reminded her of what she had lost.

Instead she took to going to the Luco on her own. Turning off the main paths, she discovered smaller areas where she could often be alone. She found sitting studying a statue, or just staring through the branches of the trees to the sky was restful and gave her time to order her thoughts. She wrestled with what she had lost and where she would go when she went back home. It was all very well staying in Paris, but she didn't belong there. The magic had been lost. Occasionally she would look up and Max would be walking towards her, grinning, his hand raised in greeting. Her heart would beat faster until a second look always proved she had mistaken someone else for him.

One day she was sitting by the baroque Fontaine de Medici, staring at the grotto with its statue of Polyphemus, about to launch a stone at his rival Acis who lay below him with Galatea, his lover. In front of them stretched a long channel of water enjoyed by the ducks that were paddling about in it, two of them quacking and squabbling over a piece of bread.

'May I take this chair?'

May hadn't noticed the young man in a black beret with his hand on the back of the chair beside hers. He spoke French with a curious accent that suggested he was a foreigner too.

'Of course.' She moved hers along to give him more space.

'Thank you.' A folded newspaper sticking out of his jacket pocket fell to the ground as he sat down.

They bent to retrieve it at the same time, nearly knocking

heads as they did so. They faced each other and laughed. She guessed he was a little older than her, good-looking in his own way with a crop of dishevelled tawny-red hair, dark-framed spectacles and a friendly face. His dark blue shirt was done up to the collar under a rumpled grey V-neck sweater. His trousers looked worn, with a paint stain on the right thigh.

'You're English?' she asked, pointing at the copy of *The Times* in his hand.

'Scottish, if you don't mind.' The sadness of his smile was reflected in his eyes.

'I don't at all. I'm from Dunfermline myself.'

'Really?! You're the first person I've met from home.' The way he said 'home' struck a chord with her, simultaneously wistful and dismissive. He carried with him an air of sadness or regret, she couldn't tell which. May wondered what his story could possibly be.

'I'm looking after a wee boy here, and I'm taking French lessons. I live over there.' She pointed in the vague direction of the apartment.

'Oh, yes?' He held out his hand for her to shake.

His palm was firm in hers, his fingers short and neat.

'David Adair. I work here – in import-export. Not very interesting at all. I came here thinking life would be very different. I had such dreams and plans and . . . well, it is different but not in the way I'd hoped. Not at all.' He opened up his newspaper and folded it back on itself so he could read it more easily. Their conversation was over.

'Of course.' She accepted the matter was closed. Apart

from their home country they would have little in common. Besides, she had no wish to start talking to someone she had never met. Especially not a man. She was nowhere near ready for that yet. She went back to her thoughts, trying to tune him out despite the rustle of his turning pages.

Eventually he got up to leave. 'Goodbye,' he said with a little bow, then straightened his beret. 'Perhaps we'll see each other again.'

'Perhaps,' she said. But she didn't think so. Being entangled with Max had taught her all she needed to know about men for the time being. For once, her mother had been entirely right. She would keep her distance and distrust them until she knew them well. But hadn't she thought she knew Max better than anyone?

A couple of days later, she told Wendy about the encounter. She had finally given in to her friend's insistence that they should meet, so they did after her classes, before they were due to pick the boys up from school. Wendy chattered on as May stirred the sugar cubes into her *café allongée*, listening to everything Wendy had done and seen.

'And you'll never believe what she said next . . .'

How much she enjoyed Wendy's company and her excitable interest in life. How short-sighted she had been to forego it for so long.

'You see.' Wendy nodded when she had listened to what May had to say. 'You'll soon make new friends. Come out with us tomorrow, do. We're going to a Vietnamese restaurant Sam has found near the Boule Saint-Michel.'

'No, I . . .' She stopped. The realisation hit her like a bolt of lightning. Wendy was right to encourage her and she was wrong to refuse every time. Eventually Wendy would stop asking, and who could blame her. Nobody wanted to hang out with a misery. If anything would get her through this dreadful time, it would be her friends. She couldn't mope for ever and life had to go on. Even if she were battered by her experience, her eyes had been opened. Nobody else need know what she had gone through. She would pick herself up and try harder. She was lucky to have a friend who cared. 'Yes,' she said. 'Yes, I'd like that.'

22

Lancashire, 2019

It was late in the afternoon when Isla pulled into the service station on the M61. Charlie unplugged herself from her phone and looked about her as if she'd just woken up to the world.

'Where are we?'

'We've just passed Bolton, so we've still got a way to go.'

'So why've you stopped?' Charlie held back a yawn, her teeth chattering.

'Jock needs a pee, and I need to stretch my legs.' Isla opened the car door, her knees stiff as she swung her legs out, a slight ache in her lower back. When had her body started objecting so vigorously to her treatment of it? She dreaded returning to the tyranny of the pilates class schedule even though she and Jock walked round Parker's Piece every day, rain or shine.

A steady hum and whoosh of traffic came from the motorway.

She let Jock out of the back, grabbing his collar as he jumped past her with a groan, and clipping on his lead. She stretched her arms to the sky, then bent side to side with Charlie watching her from inside the car.

'Coming?' Isla raised her voice and pointed towards an expanse of grass. Charlie shook her head and plugged in one then the other earbud, nodding her head to a beat.

'That's fine by me,' Isla said out loud. 'Come on, boy. We'll do once round the field.'

Once they got there, she let him off the lead so he could sniff out a good spot. Without Charlie there to overhear, Isla got out her phone. She needed to warn Lorna that Charlie was coming with her. She was not a woman who liked surprises. And yet it was Isla who was surprised by the equanimity with which Lorna greeted the news.

'It'll be fun to see her. It's been ages.' She was in danger of sounding friendly but she altered her tone just in time. 'I gather you've been asking Aggie about Mum and Dad.'

'She told you?'

'I was round the other day, helping her clear up more of Mum's stuff.'

And what else? Isla wondered, but this wasn't the best moment to bring up the sale of the house. They'd only argue. No. For once she would be more diplomatic.

'Yes. I'm trying to find out the story behind the picture she left me. I'll explain when I see you. Did you find anything unexpected?'

'Only Dad's old passports, stuffed in the bottom drawer of the desk. I don't remember them travelling at all but the earliest one showed he'd been to France.'

'Really?' Isla's heartbeat quickened. This was too much of a coincidence.

'Yes, he was there in 1953. Aggie took them before I could look at anything else.'

The year before May had sent those postcards home.

'Jock!' Isla yelled, suddenly aware he was about to go under the fence next to the road. 'I'll have to go. He's about to get killed. More when I see you.' She cut her sister off and ran over to grab Jock's collar just before he escaped and ran in front of a lorry. What had she been thinking of?

By the time she got back to Betty, Isla felt much better and full of new resolves. From now on she wouldn't object to Charlie constantly charging her phone so she could listen to her music, while Isla's battery was left at six per cent. Nor would she complain about the unidentifiable snatches of song that Charlie sang, forgetting she wasn't alone. She wouldn't complain again about the endless ping of notifications. And she would resist the temptation to reach out to still Charlie's hands that rapped out the beat of whatever she was listening to. No, she would listen to Radio 2, 3 or 4 on her own and keep driving. They could try talking another time. She was going to channel every ounce of zen calm she possessed. Travelling with Charlie reminded of her own teen car journeys with her parents when her mother refused to let them listen to Radio 1 as she and her sisters sat crushed on the back seat on the way to the Scottish borders. Denied the option, they would nudge and pinch each other until a fight broke out, and their mother rounded on them over whatever classical piece she was listening to, yelling at them to Be Quiet and Sit Still.

Isla turned the key in the ignition but the only response was a click: not a sound from the engine. Nor on the second and third attempts. She banged the heel of her hand on the steering wheel. 'Damn! Betty, you can't do this to me.'

'What's wrong?'

'No idea. Not my strong point.' How could Betty let her down now, in an anonymous motorway car park, miles from their cheap hotel in Preston? Outside her house was one thing, but here . . . With her elbows on the wheel, she put her head in her hands.

'You're not crying?' Charlie's concern was muddled with mild alarm.

Isla looked up. 'Of course I'm not. I'm wondering what the hell to do.'

'Gran!'

'That's hardly swearing,' she sat up. 'And if it is, you ain't heard nothing yet. I'll try the petrol station and see if someone can help. You stay with Jock.'

It was no surprise to discover there were no mechanics on hand. Walking back, she noticed the motel was 'closed for refurbishment'. Her heart sank.

When she got back to the car park, Charlie was not in the car and Betty's bonnet was up. *Charlie!* She ran the last little bit only to find her granddaughter peering over a strange man's shoulder into the engine.

'Charlie?'

'What? He was standing by the car so I asked if he could help.'

The man straightened up, wiping his hands together. He was in his thirties, at a guess, with a broad smile that tipped into a grimace as he shook his head. 'I can't help, I'm afraid. I think it might be your starter motor.'

'I don't even know what that means.'

'The garage, I guess.' He shrugged, his shoulders muscular. Oh God, they were stranded. They should have left earlier. 'Is there one nearby?'

'I'm not from round here.' He tucked his shirt into the back of his dark blue shorts. 'But the petrol station should know.'

'Or we can google,' added Charlie, holding out her phone, confident. With Isla's backing and occasional interference, she took command of the situation and a taxi soon turned up to take them from the car park to the Dragon and Maid, a pleasant-looking mock-Tudor pub in the nearest village.

When the manager heard their predicament he called the owner of the local garage, 'an old mate', who agreed to collect the car key and then pick up Betty first thing in the morning as a special favour and of course at a special price. On top of that, Isla would have to pay whatever additional parking charges would be levied overnight.

'We're busy tonight,' he said. 'Them refurbishing the motel has done us a good turn.' Eventually he handed Isla a key and the WiFi code and issued instructions that took them up the stairs, along a crooked corridor to a door at the end, which Isla unlocked. Inside was a double bed, a chest of drawers on which perched a TV and its controls, and a chair and side table.

They looked at each other.

'There's only one bed.' Charlie dumped her backpack on it, then threw herself beside it.

'I'll go and say we need another room.' No way was Isla sharing a bed with Charlie. She dumped Jock's bed that she'd lugged from the car in a corner.

'It's this or nothing,' Isla announced on her return. 'We're going to have to make the most of it.' She did her best not to sound as doomed as she felt.

There were scuff marks on the pale grey walls, and the green furnishings had seen better days but at least the place seemed clean. An uncomfy looking chair by the window overlooked the busy pub garden. Isla opened the window to let out the musty beery smell, only to be knocked back by the smell of roasting meat on the barbecue right underneath them. All the tables in the garden were occupied, glasses clinking and cigarette smoke in the wind, and screaming kids tore around the play area.

Charlie propped herself up on one elbow, challenging her. 'Now what?'

'Good question. We don't want to eat for another couple of hours – do we? – and I didn't see anywhere to go in the village. It's just the one main street. We could go for a walk or read?'

Charlie was filming Jock as he circled round on his bed before lying down. 'I don't think so.'

'Why not?' They weren't going anywhere, had no one to dress up for. 'We've got to do something. Got any suggestions?' Isla could think of nothing she would like more than to lie on her bed and read. Quietly. On her own. A waft of spit-roast pork drifted into the room. 'What are you doing?'

'TikTok.' As if that explained everything. Again.

'Let me see.'

Reluctantly Charlie sat up, making room for Isla, holding the phone so they could both see a girl dancing. That gave way to two girls lying on their backs juggling footballs in time to the music. And then, someone failing to get their dog to dance with them. All accompanied by tinny electronic music. *Er, why?* They all seemed utterly pointless to her. 'I think it's a young person's thing.'

'Mmm.' Charlie didn't care.

Silence fell as Isla made two cups of tea, put one on Charlie's bedside table and took the other to hers. Just as she had opened her book, Charlie put down her phone. 'I could do your make-up. I could make you look really nice. I sometimes do Mum's and she's stolen loads of my ideas.'

'Really?' But the quiet longing she heard made Isla take notice.

'We could do each other's.' But Charlie was giving up now, expecting rejection.

'Okay.' Isla took up the challenge. 'Show me what you can do.' Her book could wait.

'Do you mean it?'

'Yes! Go for it.' She had make-up remover. What had she to lose?

Sitting in the chair, Isla waited while Charlie emptied a ridiculously oversized make-up bag onto the bed and sorted out the bits she was going to use. 'I need to like pin back your hair but I can't find my grips.' She rummaged through her kit.

'Shower cap?' Isla went into the wet room where there was a basket of shower gel and shampoo that included one. She opened the box and put it on before sitting back down, feeling naked and vulnerable, in front of Charlie's considered half-smile.

'Primer first.' She picked up a tube and squirted some onto the back of her hand.

'You won't overdo it, will you? I usually go straight for the foundation.' Although she was pleased to see Charlie so absorbed.

'Gran! Let me do it my way.' She started patting the primer onto Isla's face. 'If you don't like it, you can wipe it off after.'

'Okay, I give in.' There was no point in talking about what she had learned about make-up when she did that brief stint of modelling to pay her way. How May had hated her doing that. When Isla thought her mother would be proud of her resourcefulness in earning her own money, she had been furious.

'Parading yourself about like that. You can do better for your-self than that.' Her dislike of this development in Isla's life whipped down the phone line. *'Why can't you be like Morag*

and have a proper career?' How proud she had been of Morag and her vocation. By the time it came to Lorna, secretarial work and a decent marriage was good enough. As Isla remembered that conversation, she also remembered how May had subsequently dialled down her affection again from lukewarm to cool after that. They never recovered. But why not?

'Where's your make-up? I might be able to use some of it.'

Isla jumped back to the present and extricated her embarrassingly grubby make-up bag and tipped its contents onto the bed.

'That's it?'

'I don't need much.' Isla defended her minimal regime.

'I'll use this.' Charlie picked the fancy foundation that cost an eye-watering sum, bought on a whim after reading an article in one of the Sunday supplements. 'I saw Kylie Jenner using it. The vlogger,' she added quickly, certain the explanation would be needed. 'One of the Kardashians.'

'I know,' said Isla. 'I'm not in the Dark Ages. I know what's going on.'

There was a snort from behind her head. 'Yeah?'

'Yeah, actually.' Isla relaxed and let Charlie do her thing.

'I'm going to mix these two foundations together.'

'Two? Really?'

'Gran!' That came with a warning note. 'But you could look after your skin better. Don't you have any moisturiser apart from this?' She discarded Isla's tub of Nivea onto the bed.

'It's always worked for me.'

'Mmm. Since those Dark Ages!' Charlie laughed. 'Now for some concealer.'

There was a stippling sensation under Isla's eyes and she caught the smell of chocolate on Charlie's breath. What Isla had thought would take ten minutes turned into more than half an hour of explanation and preparation and reapplication as her brows were pencilled and gelled, her eyelids subjected to a range of browns and terracottas. Having someone else's fingers moving over her face – smoothing, patting, tapping – was pleasantly soothing. She shut her eyes and let her get on with it, listening to the explanations with half an ear.

At one point, she opened her eyes to see Charlie coming at her with a tiny medieval instrument of torture.

'Eyelash curlers. They make the difference.' She snapped them together.

Isla pulled back her head to avoid them but they were clamped close to her right eyelid anyway. 'Ow!' Then the left.

Charlie stood back and studied her work so far.

'Can I see?' Isla interrupted the humming. 'Is there a mirror?'

'Not yet. Let me finish first.' She picked up a brush and powder. 'Contouring.'

Isla shut her eyes, feeling one brush after another buffing over her cheeks, the stroke of mascara, a pencil drawing the outline of her lips, and finally the gloss of lipstick.

Charlie pulled off the shower cap and fluffed up Isla's hair with her fingers. 'Cool.' She sounded pleased. 'Go and look.'

'Okay, I'm ready.' Deep breath. In the mirror over the basin, someone who was her, and yet wasn't, stared back. 'Charlie! This is amazing. I've never looked better.' Instead of the caterpillar brows, glowing cheekbones and exaggerated lips she had dreaded was a subtle enhancing of her features, that made her look younger, less tired. She was entranced, captivated by her granddaughter's sensitivity. 'Where did you learn to do this?'

Charlie shrugged, looking down at the floor. 'Online. You can learn like everything there.'

'Well, you're bloody good at it.'

'Your turn, then.' She waited for Isla to get out of the seat.

Isla had forgotten that part of the deal. 'Are you sure? I won't be anything like as good as this.'

But Charlie was already in the chair, shower cap on. 'You can try. Make sure you get rid of my freckles.'

'Let me do it my way.' Isla repeated Charlie's words while she stared at the bewildering array of cosmetics in front of her, wondering where to start. 'If you don't like it, you can always take it off.'

They grinned at each other.

Isla quickly realised her own way of doing things wasn't going to be enough so began poking through Charlie's kit.

'Come on,' said her granddaughter, concentrating on the photos scrolling down her screen. 'Look at this.' She stopped at a photo of a girl about her age – but who knew? 'See. It's all about the eyes and lips.'

'Give me a chance,' said Isla, settling on the primer Charlie had used on her. Seemed like the right place to start. 'What are you doing now?' she asked, as Charlie took another selfie.

'Streaks.' As if that explained everything. Charlie stopped as Isla began to apply the primer.

'Which are?' Isla's attention was focused on several foundations, wondering which to plump for. However, she looked up in time to see Charlie's eyes do that familiar roll towards the ceiling.

'You post a photo every day to a friend and they have to post one back . . .' She stopped speaking as her thumbs moved over the screen, '. . . for as long as you can.'

'And if you stop?'

'You might lose a friend.'

'That's a bit extreme, isn't it?' What a mystifyingly daft waste of time.

Charlie shrugged. 'Look.' She held out her phone. 'See that number – fifty-two? That's how many days Tilly and I have been going.' She spoke with such a sense of achievement.

As a teenager, Isla remembered she'd been equally obsessed but with her collections. She'd given up the child-hood pressed flowers and birds' eggs for her precious egg cups and snow globes and Wade Whimsies, those little porcelain animals. Ordering and adding to her collections gave her another way of passing those tedious hours of being a teenager when you're too old to stay in and too young to go out.

Charlie had the same pale skin as Helen, with an identical light scatter of freckles over the bridge of her nose. With some judicious highlighting, Isla could make it look narrower. 'Look up if you want me to do this.'

Charlie rested her head back in the chair, holding her phone high up in front of her where she could see it. The silence of concentration was punctuated by the sound of the camera's shutter.

'Charlie!' Isla forced her arm down to her lap. 'I can't do it with your arm in the way.'

'Oh, okay.' She gave in and closed her eyes.

Isla worked fast, repeating what she thought Charlie might have done, digging out the glitter eye-shadow, drawing in her eyebrows until they could pass for Frida Kahlo's. Perhaps a bit much but that was the look – no? She was working with a combination of dredged-up knowledge from her far-off modelling days and what she had picked up in the back of Sunday colour supplements.

'Open your eyes.' She picked out a mascara wand.

Charlie flinched as the wand just missed her eyeball. 'You're gonna blind me!'

'No I'm not.' Isla went at her again, less confident than the first time. Eventually her work was done. 'Right! Sit up.' She took a step back, ready to admire. 'Oh!' The look she'd achieved was a bit more heavy-handed than she'd intended.

Charlie leaped out of the chair and into the bathroom. 'Gran! That's terrible. Look at the flicks!'

'It's not that bad.' But Isla began to laugh, watching Charlie leaning forward examining her work closely. 'I tried.'

'What have you done to my nose?'

Isla went to stand in the doorway.

'I can't go for supper like this.' Charlie reached for her sponge bag and her cleanser. 'My eyebrows!' Now she was laughing. 'You should go online and see how to do it.'

'Maybe I will. But it's difficult doing it for someone else.' She felt she had to justify her failure.

'For you I mean. You look great like that. You just need some practice.'

She was right. Isla wasn't remotely embarrassed to be going down for supper looking as she did. In fact she thought she might smarten up to go with it. While Charlie removed and redid Isla's attempts at a makeover, Isla changed into her cropped grey linen trousers, a plain white shirt and sandals.

'You look cool,' was Charlie's verdict.

'As do you.' She was not going to be embarrassed by the shortness of Charlie's skirt. If she was relaxed in it, then Isla would be too.

They left the room a shambles, locked the door, and went down to supper.

23

Isla hadn't slept as badly since her brief affair with Chris, a history academic a little older than her, who had snored like a trumpeting elephant all night. The few times he stopped, he rocked the bed violently as he got in and out on his way to the bathroom and back. She had vowed there and then never again to sleep with a man with incipient prostate problems, however much that might limit her options at her age. Jock had kept up a steady snuffling punctuated with loud whimpers when he got close to the rabbits in his dreams. That, combined with Charlie's constant thrashing about on the other side of the bed, kept Isla dozing in fits and starts until someone started moving the bins and clearing up under their window. From then on there was no hope of sleep. But, at least she finally got a chance to read her book.

By the time she got to the garage that was tucked up a turning at the end of the main street, they had collected her car from the service station and the overalled mechanic was already working on it. 'Paul at the pub said you needed it urgently so here we go. It shouldn't take too long.'

She nodded. She wasn't going to think what she and

Charlie would have done if they'd been stranded here for days, waiting for the delivery of a spare part. There was only so much make-up they could apply. But now they would make it to Preston in time to meet Tony's train. The thought of him lifted her heart.

While the car was fixed, she took Jock round a couple of fields, through a small wood where the sun dappled through the branches, and over a brook babbling back towards the village. A perfect summer morning. While Charlie still slept – there was no reason to bully her out of bed that morning – Isla took advantage of the opportunity to be alone. The previous night's breakthrough had lasted for a few hours, through a supper of overcooked spit-roast pork and stale rolls, until something on her phone disturbed Charlie again. She wouldn't say what but rolled onto her side, with her back to Isla, and didn't talk again before she went to sleep. They had arrived back at square one without even trying.

What was Charlie going to make of Tony? Isla was determined not to make a big deal of introducing them to each other. She tried to see him as Charlie might. Would he like her? Of course he would – he was a kind man and would put up with her granddaughter's moods. More than anything she wanted them to get along.

She called to Jock, who stopped nosing round a rabbit burrow and trotted up to her, nudging her pocket for a treat. 'Food! Is that all you think about?' She tossed a half biscuit in the air that he caught with a practised snap.

And Lorna? Seeing her would be tricky. But she was

glad to be going there. Lorna wouldn't have agreed to her staying unless she wanted to put things right between them. But what if Lorna had an ulterior motive: something Isla wouldn't put past her. The big issue was obviously the future of Braemore. Could Lorna be hoping Isla would persuade Aggie to sell her share? They all knew that if Aggie would listen to anyone, it was her. If Aggie agreed to the sale, Morag would have to cave in and go along with it. Isla was puzzled. Why would Lorna imagine that she would want to be part of this ongoing fight after May disinherited her? Even Lorna must be able to understand Isla's reluctance to be involved.

But Lorna had always loved their family home and until now, out of all of them, had the most romantic view of its past. She couldn't possibly want to see the paddocks give way to a few modern new-builds that would crowd the old house and destroy its character. The more Isla thought about it, the more puzzling it was.

She picked up a stick and threw it for Jock who ambled off in its direction, going more to please her than himself. When he reached the stick, he sniffed at it, then turned away.

'Oh, come on, Jock! Haven't you learned anything?'

She would quiz Lorna about May, and that's what she was looking forward to most. As the youngest, Lorna had always had the place closest to her mother's heart. When Morag and Isla came back from doing something together, they'd find Lorna and May bent over something – a cake they were baking or a piece of tapestry or knitting – laughing together. Isla had always envied them the closeness that she had lost.

But Lorna had always been volatile, quick to defend herself against her older sisters for any perceived slight. Any divide between them had been driven by her certainty that they looked down on her. But the other two remembered things differently.

Once Isla had left home, the other two became close again but then Lorna had got off with Jimmy, Morag's then boyfriend. And the balance shifted. Morag found out thanks to a friend who spotted the two of them in the back row of the Dominion cinema: far enough from home to assume they wouldn't be seen. Lorna had no defence. Her bond with Morag was severely damaged although Morag was eventually glad to have been shown what an untrustworthy bastard Jimmy was. That was confirmed when a year later, he dumped Lorna cruelly. But the damage had been done.

Families.

Had May really said there was some French in Isla? She rather liked the idea that they might have French ancestry somewhere and that she was the one who had inherited a gene or two? May had almost eradicated her own youth as soon as she met David. That's at least how it seemed. As far as her children were concerned, marrying their father was where she began. Unlike Muff and Puff, their other grandparents, May's parents Nana and Grandpa were kept at arm's length, easy enough to do when her father died and her mother moved to Inverness. But as far as Isla knew, they were Scottish through and through.

If there was a French connection somewhere, no one had ever mentioned it to her. As she took the sun-dappled path through the wood, Isla smiled at the thought of a couple as ordinary as her parents having some sort of secret exotic family history. It was so unlikely. But Aggie must know.

And the picture? Where did that fit in? Perhaps it had been passed down generations of the Adair family and no one knew. Could Céleste be a relative? Or someone known to one? Perhaps when Isla got home, she would take it to an auction house and see if someone could tell her something about the painter.

'Jock! Come.' She called him away from truffling in a rabbit hole. He trotted up to her then went off his own way again, sniffing his way through the woods.

Soon, she and Charlie would be on the road again.

'Are we nearly there yet?' The question was followed by an agonised sigh as Charlie pulled out her earbuds and dropped them on her lap.

'No.' Isla's grip tightened on the wheel. Since Charlie had eventually got up, she had been venomous, jumping down Isla's throat at the slightest opportunity – if she spoke at all. She opened the glove compartment and helped herself to one of the packs of Polos that Isla kept there.

'Yes, I would like one, please.' Isla kept her eyes on the road but she could hear the discontented grunt, the click of the compartment door and the tear of paper. A hand appeared in her peripheral vision with a white sweet in its palm. She took it with her left hand. 'Thanks.'

She was aware of Charlie shifting in her seat, rearranging

her legs around the backpack she would not be parted from. Perhaps she should try again.

'So what happened last night?'

'What?' She clearly resented the question.

'Last night on your phone. You seemed upset.'

'Nothing.' A flash of pink caught Isla's attention as Charlie picked up the phone again.

Well, two could play at that game. Isla concentrated on pulling out to overtake a lorry, knowing that if she pursued the matter, she would get nowhere.

'Did you know horses can sleep lying down and standing up?'

What?!

Isla gave her a sidelong glance.

Charlie was staring out of the window.

'Useful,' she replied, wrong-footed by the sudden change in mood.

'Did you know they have around two hundred and five bones in their skeleton? How many do we have?'

As quickly as it had disappeared the previous evening, the sun was coming out after the storm.

'No idea.' Isla barely dared speak in case it went in again.

'Two hundred and six. Yet we're a completely different shape. Weird, no?'

'I suppose so. I've never thought about it. But now you say it . . .'

'Did you know a snail can sleep for three years and a slug has four noses?'

'Where are you getting all this stuff from? No, I didn't know that.'

'I've just been reading it online.' She was putting in her earbuds again.

That was the last of the conversation until they reached Preston station. While Isla drove, Charlie slept or entertained herself, occasionally breaking out into snatches of song, responding to the notification alerts. Isla found a space in the car park at the bottom of the hill beside the station. As she switched off the ignition, Charlie sat straight in her seat and stuffed her phone in her backpack.

Walking back up to the station entrance, Charlie spotted the TK Maxx store in the shopping centre opposite. 'Can we go there?' She held out Jock's lead for Isla to take. 'Just quickly.'

Isla checked her watch. 'We haven't time. We'll go once we've met Tony. I'm sure he won't mind.'

'Why don't I go while you meet him?'

Two young men walking past turned to stare at her. She had been so keen to get away that Isla hadn't registered what Charlie was wearing that morning but now she looked, she realised that her top was barely decent. And the shorts. And the make-up.

'No. We might lose each other.' She could see the shutter coming down. 'Imagine what Helen would say.' But her attempt at humour fell flat. Her granddaughter was sulking.

They went through a side entrance, Charlie keeping her distance, her flip-flops slapping the tarmac. Isla looked at the

Arrivals screen to check the train was on time. They crossed the covered bridge and down the steps into the station.

'I suppose I can't even buy a KitKat on my own?'

'Don't be silly. Of course you can.' Isla was inured to the Charlie eye-roll now. She waited while she went into WHSmith, watching as a mother with a toddler stared at her a moment longer than necessary.

'Isla!'

She'd recognise that voice anywhere. She turned to see Tony walking towards her, a broad smile on his face. She couldn't remember being this pleased to see someone in a long time: her knees felt as though they might give way. He looked as if he'd stepped away from the Riviera, a loose white collarless shirt, its sleeves rolled up, tucked into stone-coloured chinos, sunglasses hiding his eyes that she knew were smiling. He was carrying a large black holdall that he dumped on the ground when he reached her.

'At last.' She caught a whiff of his familiar aftershave as he wrapped her in a tight hug. How good it felt to be back in his arms. Just as she tilted her head back for a kiss, he pulled away. 'Ah! You must be Charlie.'

'Mm hm.' Her mouth was too full of KitKat for her to be able to speak but at least she shook the hand he offered. Isla could see her weighing him up, wondering who was this man in her grandmother's life. But that reserve wouldn't last.

'I can see the resemblance.'

'I don't think so,' retorted Charlie, having swallowed her mouthful.

'Oh!' He was taken aback by her hostility. 'And Jock.' He reached down to give the old dog a pat but a low growl made him withdraw his hand from Jock's head as if he'd been burned.

'Jock! Stop that!' Isla flicked him with the end of the lead. 'What's the matter with you?'

Charlie took the lead from her and walked back towards the car with the dog trotting meekly beside her.

'I'm not sure that was the best start.' He pushed his greying hair back over his ears.

'Don't take any notice. She'll come round.' She put her arm through his. 'I'm glad you're here.'

At the car, he held out his hand for the key. 'I'll drive.'

She flicked open the boot for his bag. 'No, it's fine. Really.'

He took the key from her. 'Let me. Country roads. You can ride pillion.' He laughed. 'And you.' He faced Charlie. 'I'm afraid you'll have to get in the back with the cases.'

'But I—'

'Don't fuss, Charlie. We'll swap next time.' Isla didn't want any difficulties. All she wanted was for them to have an enjoyable few days together. Each of them could at least try.

Looking daggers at them both, Charlie flung her backpack into the back seat and climbed in after it. She put her fingers through the grille behind her to tickle Jock's ear. He grunted a welcome.

'Seatbelt,' said Tony.

Isla glanced at him as he adjusted the mirror, surprised by his tone. He winked at her. She got out the Polos and turned to offer one to Charlie. The look she received in return was withering. She ignored it.

'Got the directions?' Tony turned the key in the ignition and drove towards the main road while Isla got Google Maps on her phone. 'I hope this place is good.'

'Well, they were very helpful in getting an extra room for Charlie. And it looks beautiful.' She sat back in her seat, trying to relax. These few days were not going to go wrong – whatever it took.

24

Soon after they left the city outskirts, they found themselves in wild countryside, driving through narrow lanes, drystone walls dividing sheep-strewn fields that swelled to distant fells and pine woods. Tony was relaxed – Isla could tell by his grip on the wheel, finger tapping – and began to talk about what he'd been doing while she had been away.

'I've been giving the old place a going over.'

'Old place? That's my home you're talking about.'

'I'm teasing.' He patted her thigh. 'Just trying to help. '

But she didn't want his or anyone's help. Her home was exactly how she liked it.

'I feel sick.' The words from the back seat were muffled by Charlie's hand over her mouth.

'Can't you hang on for a few minutes? We're nearly there.' Tony glanced in the rear-view mirror at her.

'No, I really do.'

Isla turned to see Charlie ashen-faced, bending forward over her knees.

'Tony! Stop the car!'

'Where? There's no—'

'Just stop!'

As he swerved into the entrance to a field, Isla leaped out before they came to a standstill. She was opening Charlie's door just as the girl lurched forward and vomited into the cup holders between the two front seats. Tony pulled back his hand from the gearstick, but not quite quickly enough.

'Christ!' He held it out as if it was contaminated.

Isla took Charlie's arm to guide her out of the car. 'There might be some tissues in the glove compartment.' Standing on the dried rutted earth, Charlie bent over, retching while Isla held her hair off her face, her other hand on her back.

She could hear the click and slam of the glove compartment being opened and shut.

'Can't find them.' He got out and bent to wipe his hand on the grass verge. 'Ouch! Oh God! I've been stung by a bloody wasp!' He was shaking his hand up and down. 'Jesus!'

By this time, Charlie had recovered herself, although she was still ashen-faced. 'That always happens if I'm in the back. I tried to tell you ...'

'But I didn't listen. I'm so sorry, love.' She had been too bound up in welcoming Tony and trying to ensure his enjoyment to remember her priorities. 'You can ride in the front from now on.' This was not how she'd envisaged things, squished in the back of the car with a couple of suitcases and Jock's meaty breath drifting over her shoulder. 'Let me see your finger.' Tony was clutching his hand and swearing under his breath. 'You okay?' she asked over the hot roof of the car.

'Just. Couldn't she have hung on?'

His finger must be agony, making him snap like that. 'Being sick isn't something you can wait for.'

'I'm sorry. Of course not.' He hopped round in a circle, his face screwed up in pain, shaking his hand. 'Can you drive the rest of the way? This really hurts.'

They swapped sides and all got back into the car that now reeked of sick.

'There must be a tissue somewhere?' Tony had to bend double to climb in the back.

Jock barked once.

'Jock! Stop it! I don't know what's got into him.' She rummaged in her bag and produced a small packet containing a single tissue. She made an ineffectual stab at wiping the vomit from the cup holder.

The rest of their short journey was completed in silence, punctuated by short gasps of pain from the back seat, with the windows open as wide as they would go. Charlie held her hair over one shoulder so Isla could see the colour returning to her face.

Eventually, they arrived at a wide stone manor house set back from the road behind a small green, its mullioned windows gleaming in the sun. On a whitewashed wall at one end, a sign read The Inn at Whitewell. Above the white studded porticoed door that was open in welcome, a Union Jack had wrapped itself round a flagpole. To the right of it, a climbing hydrangea smothered the stone wall.

'It's gorgeous. However did you find it?' she asked. It was

more than a step above her and Charlie's previous night's accommodation. She had a momentary wobble about the hit her bank account was about to take but that was the deal – he chose, her treat.

'Friends,' he answered. 'And Google. I wanted somewhere special for us.'

And it would be. Their first holiday together.

Their first holiday together with Charlie.

She turned in her seat to see him leaning away from Jock, hand over his nose.

'What are you feeding him?' He pulled a face. 'Can we get out? Please?'

'Oh God! Child locks. Sorry.' She jumped out to open his door.

As they approached the Inn, Tony walked a few steps ahead, carrying their bags. Isla half-ran to catch up with him. 'I know it hasn't been the best start . . .' she began.

'Things can only get better.'

'You'll get used to Charlie.'

'I'm sure I will.' Although he didn't sound sure at all.

They went down an unevenly flagstoned corridor to the reception which they found in an extremely well-stocked wine shop. Surrounded by antique furniture, paintings, animal heads, the vibe was definitely relaxed country house. A couple of dogs wandered out of the bar, then went back in again. The place was busy with the sound of loud chatter: walkers, fishermen, judging by the rods propped by the wall, and those just enjoying themselves. Isla immediately felt at home there. They were soon in possession of their keys and being shown down a warren of corridors and stairs until they reached their room.

A four-poster bed took up the most part, the same pretty chintz on the bedspread, tester and curtains. A huge mirror dominated the wall over a small desk and chair. The bathroom was all black marble, the height of modern chic. Isla threw herself on the bed, knocking the floral cushions to one side.

'I could stay here all weekend and never leave the room.'

Tony laughed at her pleasure as he sat on the sofa at the end of the bed. 'Just look at this view.'

'Except there's Jock to walk – and Charlie, of course.' A last-minute cancellation had meant Charlie had an attic room which she had insisted on being taken to on her own.

The view from the window was across fields, grazed by cows, lit by brilliant sunshine. The woods to the left led up to a distant farm with the swell of a hill behind it. It was impossibly bucolic and so much greener than she'd imagined, like the background of a Stubbs painting. A fire was laid in the fireplace – all it needed was the flick of a match.

Tony came to lie down beside her. He touched her cheek. She could feel his breath on her face, smell the Polo he'd eaten in the car. She pushed herself up. 'I'd better go and check on Charlie.'

He sighed, resigned, stepping back to sink into the sofa. 'If you must. I'll be here.' He swung round, kicked off his shoes and put his feet up.

'You sound like some matinée idol,' she said. 'I will be back.' She felt odd about having sex with Jock in the room.

'You'd better be.'

Along the corridors, stopping to look at some of the many pictures, with Jock at her heels, she tapped on Charlie's door. 'You all right in there?'

The door opened and she walked into similar but different luxury. Charlie's room was tiny but every bit as comfortable as Isla's, although the view was over the lane outside.

'Look at the bathroom!' As clean and modern as theirs.

'Wow!' Looking at her granddaughter's face, Isla was pleased she could give her the treat. She sent up a thanks to whoever had made the last-minute cancellation.

They sat on the bed together, Charlie stroking the red brocade bedspread.

'Just one thing – there's no phone signal!' she said as if announcing a national disaster, throwing her phone on the pillow.

'But at least there's WiFi.'

Charlie grunted.

'I know this is a bit difficult for you.'

Charlie looked up sharply. 'No. I'm fine.'

'But I think you and Tony will get on.'

'He doesn't like me.' Said with such finality.

'He does. He was just shocked when you were sick on him.'

Charlie's eyes flashed. 'He should've stopped sooner.'

'Yes, he should. I agree. But come for a walk with us now – it's beautiful out there. You can get to know him better.' As she spoke, she could see it was hopeless. Charlie had made up her mind. This would take time. Possibly more than they had.

Her granddaughter shook her head. 'Nah. You're all right. I'll stay here.'

'But what will you do?'

'Have a coffee.' She nodded towards the Nespresso machine. 'Watch TV. Message my friends. Look after Jock.'

'I thought Jock might come with us. He needs the exercise.'

'Oh, please. He's happy here.'

Jock was lying at the side of the bed as if he had been born there.

'Okay. He can walk tomorrow.' She would love a chance to be alone with Tony as they had originally planned. 'If you're sure. We'll meet you downstairs for supper at seven thirty?'

'I'm sure.'

Persuaded Charlie was happier in her room, Isla returned to her room and Tony. Having lost Jock to her granddaughter, she had lost her inhibitions too.

'I said we were going for a walk but . . .'

He pulled her down on the bed beside him, her insides melting as she rolled into his arms.

They didn't get outside until sometime later. The heat of the day was less intense when they eventually set off, having been given directions by the hotel. They walked round the side of the old parish church beside the Inn and followed the footpath signs to a long chain of stepping stones over the river. Laughing as they jumped from one to the next, they then turned right to follow the river past the Inn, raised high on the opposite bank. They passed cows grazing contentedly until they reached a simple bench overlooking the water where a pair of ducks were dabbling.

'Let's sit here.' Tony took her hand. 'Isn't this perfect? Remind me where you're going next. I wish I could come with you.'

'No, you don't! First, Charlie will be with me. And second, I'm seeing Janet, my old school friend, next and together we'd bore you rigid. And then we're off to stay with my youngest sister.'

'You haven't given up then?' Tony had been unimpressed by her sleuthing skills when she'd updated him with her slow progress.

'If anything I'm more determined. I'm sure I'm getting closer to Mum and who she was.'

'Why don't you think the note in the picture was written to your father?'

Isla burst out laughing. 'To Dad?! If you knew him, you'd never suggest that. He was the most unromantic soul.'

'Maybe to you, his daughter. But suppose someone gave him the picture. Could have been before he met May.'

'No.' Isla was quite certain. 'They'd have said. Anyway he didn't speak French. The paper was so fragile that I'm sure it dates back before him.'

'Well, if you're sure.' He let an ant run along a piece of grass all the way onto his finger before he squashed it.

She shook her head. 'I'm not sure of anything.'

Standing up, he held out both hands and pulled her up. As they took in their glorious surroundings, his arm fitted round her waist. 'But you're glad we came here?'

'Yes, that I'm sure of.' Her arm wound round him and she kissed his cheek. She hadn't felt as comfortable with a man in a long, long time.

Back at the hotel, they showered and changed before finding themselves a table on the sunny terrace at the back of the hotel looking straight across the river to the fields beyond.

'Gin and tonic?' Tony called over a waiter to take their order.

'I wonder why she left you that particular picture then. One picture and your share of everything else.' Tony took a handful of peanuts and tossed them into his mouth. 'I never thought I'd end up with a wealthy woman!'

'You haven't.' She would have to tell him. 'I haven't given you the whole story.' At least this felt the right time. 'I'm not wealthy at all. She didn't leave me anything else.' There. She'd said it. Now everything between them was in the open, and she felt better.

'What, nothing?' He picked bits of broken peanut from between his front teeth with a finger nail and ate them.

'Nothing. I don't know why. That's what I'm really trying to find out.'

'Why didn't you tell me?'

'Because I was embarrassed. Because I imagined you'd

223

think there must be something wrong with me. Perhaps that was stupid.'

'It was. I'm glad you've told me now.' He studied the ceiling as if he was thinking of something else. 'I've never come across someone doing that before. How cruel. But if you've found out she was in France. And the note inside is in French ...'

'Yes, but briefly and she was there before she met Dad. The picture could have belonged to anyone before them.'

'You know that?'

'No.' Isla sipped her drink, then smiled. 'What is this? The Spanish Inquisition.'

'I'm just trying to help. You don't seem to have got very far.'

'I'm further than I was when I started.' She raised her glass. 'Cheers. To past loves.'

'And to present ones.' He clinked his glass against hers. 'Talking of which, where's that moody granddaughter of yours.'

'Charlie, you mean.' Isla felt protective of her. 'She doesn't want to be here any more than you want her to be, so be nice.'

He threw his hands in the air, denying the charge.

'I'll go in and find her.'

He looked disappointed. As Isla went inside, she resolved not to rise to any teasing. She stopped to examine a huge stuffed pike in a case, its glazed eyes staring ahead, its jaw open. She took her purse from her bag and pulled out the note to read again. 'Who were you, Céleste? And who did you love?' she asked under her breath. 'Did they love you back? I hope so.'

There was no reply from Charlie's room so Isla went back downstairs. Walking through the bar, an elderly black Lab like Jock caught her eye. But he wasn't the only one there. Then she realised the object of his adoration was Charlie who was perched on a bar stool beside a couple of young guys wearing shorts and polo shirts. They were identical, dark-haired, big-mouthed, sporty-looking. Charlie was wearing one of her shortest and prettiest dresses, and she had plaited the sides of her hair and tied them at the back of her head. As usual, her make-up was flawless.

'Charlie! I was wondering where you'd got to.'

Jock's tail wagged furiously as he snuffled into her hand.

'Are you joining us?' Oh God! She sounded like an overenthusiastic cheerleader. 'We had a lovely walk.' Dial it down, Isla.

'Fuck's sake.' Words heard quite clearly despite the crowded room.

'Hi.' Isla addressed the two men, failing to dial it down in any way. 'I'm Charlie's grandmother, Isla.'

If it was possible to hear an eye-roll, she was sure she did.

One of them put out his hand and shook hers. 'Ellis and . . .' he pointed at his twin, 'Peter Booth. We're staying here too. We met Charlie outside.'

'Saved her life, you mean,' said Peter.

'I would have seen it,' said Charlie, indignant. 'He came round the corner too fast.'

'You were nearly run over?!' Helen would never forgive her if she found out. What was she even doing out there?

'Only a cyclist,' said Ellis, dismissive.

'I'd taken Jock out.' Her lower lip rolled over. 'I was only trying to help.'

Isla swallowed. She should have insisted on taking Jock with her.

'Anyway no one was hurt so we came here for a drink.' Peter nodded towards the two bottles of Sol and one of J2O lined up on the bar. At least Charlie had stuck to something soft.

'Thank you for saving her then,' said Isla, pretending a calm she didn't feel, as she untied Jock's lead from the bar stool. 'Are you joining Tony and me now we're back?'

'You're all right.' said Charlie. 'I've got an orange juice going here.'

'You could take it with you,' Peter pointed out. 'We're joining our folks.' He gestured towards what looked like a private room. 'Silver wedding anniversary. No escape. Perhaps see you later.'

Isla could have kissed him, despite the three of them laughing as if they shared a secret joke involving their unquestionable superiority over their elders. Isla led Jock towards the terrace, trusting Charlie would follow them, not turning to see her expression. She didn't have to work hard to imagine that.

25

Throughout supper, Charlie barely spoke. She managed to order a selection of vegetables but beyond that her conversation didn't extend beyond infrequent and monosyllabic. Apparently she was thinking of becoming vegetarian. Tony was little better. Being in Charlie's presence seemed to silence him so Isla found herself gabbling, desperately trying to fill the silences and lighten the mood as she described their visit to Morag's, the animals, Haddon Hall, the dog show, anything that popped into her mind. Charlie didn't join in as Isla had hoped she might, not even to laugh at Isla's jokes against herself, and Tony seemed barely interested, only occasionally interrupting with an 'Mmm', or an 'Ah ha'. As the evening went on, and she helped herself to one then another glass of wine, her anger intensified. Charlie she could just about tolerate, giving her licence for being another bloody-minded teenager. But Tony! Despite getting off to a bad start, he had no excuse.

As Isla filleted her fish, she was aware of Charlie watching Tony tucking into his roast rack of saltmarsh lamb as if she was watching a cannibal consume his victim. At the same time she picked at her plate of vegetables. Eventually Isla could bear it no longer.

'If neither of you are going to make an effort, then I think I'll go to bed and have a nightcap in the room. I hoped you'd both be better than this.' She stood up, pulling at her dress that was sticking to her legs in the heat, disappointed that everything was going so badly.

Tony caught her hand. 'Don't be daft. We're all just tired. Aren't we, Charlie?' He waited for her to lift her head, eyes glassy with tears before they flicked back to her lap.

'Yup.'

Isla immediately felt terrible. Perhaps she was expecting too much of Charlie. As she watched her, concerned, she realised that Charlie's attention was a little too intent on her knees.

'Are you on your phone?'

As her granddaughter's right hand moved from her lap into her pocket there was an unmistakeable flash of pink as she shook her head. 'No.'

'What did we agree?' Anger boiled up inside Isla.

'Whatever,' Charlie mumbled so Isla could barely hear.

'Has something happened?' Isla had no way into the world Charlie inhabited. Without her help she couldn't begin to help navigate her through. 'Oh, come on, Charlie. Just try. That's all I ask.' It was as if Tony wasn't there, despite the fact that she could feel his hand squeeze her thigh as she sat down again. His apology and reassurance he was there for her. She couldn't leave Charlie like this. 'What's happened?'

'Nothing.' She speared the last carrot and put it in her mouth. She heaved a huge sigh as if it was the end of the world.

Realising she wasn't going to get anywhere if she pursued it at that moment, Isla changed the subject. 'What about pudding? What if we all make an effort?'

'Done!' said Tony. 'I'm sorry but I was thinking about something else altogether. But shall we share some cheese? And have a glass of port?'

Charlie sniffed but roused herself enough to order raspberry and elderflower ice cream.

'So ...' said Tony as if about to announce something momentous. They looked at him, expectant, Isla grateful at last that she could call on him to rescue a situation and that he'd respond, however reluctantly.

'What's on the agenda for tomorrow?'

Was that really the best he could offer? Charlie gave a long sigh and examined the ceiling as if she'd rather be anywhere else but sitting at the same table as them.

'If the weather's like this, we could take a picnic and go for a long walk.' He knocked back the last of his wine.

'I'm sure there's something else we could do, if you don't like the idea.' Remembering the hell of long walks with her parents, she turned to Charlie, hoping to encourage a flicker of interest. 'Would you like another drink?'

'But I thought that's what you ...' Tony drummed his fingers once on the table's edge.

'It's very hot,' said Charlie at last. At last she was trying although her eyes were only on Isla, never Tony. 'How long's long?'

'Forecast says it's going to be cooler tomorrow,' said Tony. 'So we could ask the hotel for a picnic. We can take it slow.'

'Gran?' Charlie ignored him, just glanced towards the bar. But the twins didn't reappear.

'Let's decide in the morning.' How was she going to broker peace between these two?

After supper, they went straight to their rooms. Tony went ahead of Isla while she said goodnight to Charlie. 'Are you okay? You looked so upset.'

Charlie shook her head. 'All my friends are at a party tonight. And they've all been to a film I wanted to see. And a couple of them have joked about me being on holiday with my grandmother. How lame it is.'

'Really?' Isla was incensed. 'What the hell do they know? I happen to be the best company any girl could wish for. Tell them that!'

That earned her a watery grin.

But there was nothing worse than missing out, especially when you didn't want to be where you were.

'Don't worry. We'll try and find something that we *all* want to do tomorrow.'

'Doesn't matter. He doesn't want me tagging along.'

'Charlie! I told you before: he does. You've just got to make more of an effort.'

'What about him? Do you really like him, Gran?'

They stared at each other for a moment, Isla controlling

her temper. Charlie took her key from her dress pocket and turned it in her hands. 'Just asking.'

'I don't know why you don't stay off social media if it gets you so upset.' Isla bent forward to kiss her on the cheek, although Charlie turned away so she missed.

As quickly, she relented and kissed her back. 'Night, Gran. It'll be okay.'

And then she had gone.

'Just us, at last.' Tony began to brush his teeth.

Isla couldn't help reflecting there was something inherently unsexy about a middle-aged man getting ready for bed. What with his teeth, his feet and the normal washing and hair titivating, he took longer than Isla. Not that he was particularly vain, but he seemed to have a lot to deal with.

She stood behind him, looking at his reflection over his shoulder, waiting for the familiar flip of her insides, but it didn't come. With a touch on his shoulder, she turned him round to face her. There it was. 'I know she's difficult but it would be great if you could try a bit harder. For me.' Though she shouldn't have to say so.

His brow furrowed. 'I'm sorry. I thought I was. Just not used to teenage girls, I guess.' The words were mangled round his toothbrush. 'And what's with all the make-up and the skirts? She looks like a Russian prostitute.' He spat into the basin and rinsed his mouth.

She slapped his arm. 'No, she does not. She looks like a confused fourteen-year-old. She wants to be treated like an adult although she's still a child.' Isla opened the minibar and got out a miniature of brandy. 'Don't tell me you haven't met one before.'

'Not one like her.' He threw off his clothes onto the chair under the open window, put on a T-shirt over his boxers and climbed into bed with the TV remote. 'Shall we find a film?' He began to flick through channels. 'But yes, okay, point taken. I'll do my best.'

'Thank you. I know it's not what we planned but we can still enjoy ourselves. You haven't been much better so far, and you haven't even got youth on your side as an excuse.' She sipped her brandy and shut her eyes as she felt its burn in her throat. When she next looked, Tony was shaking with laughter.

'What's so bloody funny?'

'You. You are. Oh, come here.' He threw back the sheet. 'Don't let's spoil things, and I will try. Promise.'

Isla began to undress, feeling the warm night air on her skin. Through the open window, she heard an owl. 'Did you hear that?'

'What?'

'Hearing an owl hoot at night is meant to be an omen of bad luck.'

'Oh God! I've fetched up with a witch woman.' He mimed a scream then laughed.

'Shut up, you idiot.' Isla got into her side of the bed and rolled into his outstretched arm. With her head on his chest, she could hear the beating of his heart. 'It's just a superstition.

Wouldn't you have liked a grandchild?' The side of his face she could see was non-committal. 'You must have some family somewhere.'

He wiped his brow with the back of his hand. 'No. I know what you must be thinking but I've told you – my parents are long dead and I don't have siblings or cousins. There was only me.'

'But you were married.'

'Twice, but never had children of my own.' There wasn't a trace of self-pity in his voice. He was simply presenting the facts. 'Most of my friends had children but we drifted apart because we had less and less in common. Eileen and I tried but it wasn't meant to be. So teenagers are entirely alien creatures to me.' He smiled before kissing her forehead.

'What happened to her?' Both of them brought so much history to this new relationship and she was desperate to burrow into his and find out as much as she could about him. She wanted to know him better than anyone. 'The woman who wanted to have children with you.'

'Eileen? We went our separate ways years ago.' He shut that subject down. 'Then I married Angie when I was in my forties but it was too late for children then. We moved to France for a new start seven or eight years ago. We bought an existing gîte but then she preferred our French builder to me, it turned out. When they moved to the Gironde together, I carried on the gîte alone but, as you know, it all got too much and I was worried about Brexit, so I sold up and now I'm back here to start yet again.'

He continued to present the facts without a trace of emotion. Isla wondered how much hurt he was hiding and squeezed his hand. 'I'm sorry.'

'Don't be. You need a woman's touch in that sort of business.'

'Oh, please! Tell me you're not that unreconstructed. But I love you all the same.' She froze.

The L-word.

Her tongue had been loosened by the brandy.

'You're not so bad yourself.' To her relief, he skated over it.

But the word had come from somewhere. Did she love him? Was that really what she felt for this dear man whom she had only known for a few months? This was not the youthful passion she had felt with Ian, nor the tentative abandonment she had experienced with Keith. This was something else altogether that made her feel safe, cared for. But was it love?

Tony turned off his bedside light and rolled over to face her, his hands moving over her body, touching, caressing, his lips soft against hers.

Instead of questioning her feelings any further – what was the point? – she gave herself up to the moment.

When they woke in the morning, the heatwave was over. Torrential rain fell from an unforgiving sky the colour of a donkey's belly. Isla looked out of the window at the plants on the terrace being battered under the onslaught, rain bouncing off the paving stones, while beyond the river cattle huddled together under a spreading tree, waiting for respite.

A walk was out of the question.

Charlie didn't come down for breakfast and Isla didn't wake her. Jock would do that when he was hungry or desperate to go out. He wouldn't let her ignore him. Instead she and Tony indulged in a delicious breakfast – muesli and poached haddock for her while Tony went for the full English. He had hesitated.

'Oh go on, have it,' Isla encouraged him. 'It's on me, remember.'

'Well, in that case ... and we're away. Who cares about carbs today,' he said, patting his stomach.

Eventually when they were halfway through a game of backgammon, Charlie appeared. Isla noticed Tony register the ripped jeans that were barely held together by fabric. She waited for him to comment but instead he said, 'Morning, Charlie! Dreadful weather, so the walk's off. Can we get you something to eat? The sausages are especially good.' He was trying.

Charlie pulled at the fat single plait that fell over her right shoulder. 'I don't eat meat. I told you.'

'Ah, of course.' Undeterred, Tony went on to recommend the rest of the menu while Charlie played with Jock's ears, not responding.

'I think they may have stopped serving,' Isla interjected gently. 'And Jock should go out. I'll give him a quick walk down the lane.'

'I'll go with you.' Tony and Charlie spoke at exactly the same time.

'No. You stay here. I won't be long.' Perhaps throwing them together might work.

'I'm coming.' Tony pushed back the chair, catching the backgammon board with his jacket so all the pieces jumped onto the floor. 'Damn!'

'Toast's fine,' said Charlie.

Isla grabbed her rain poncho from behind her, took the lead from her granddaughter's hand and made a swift exit, grabbing an umbrella from the stand at the front door. She hadn't got far before she heard steps behind her. She turned to find Tony running towards her, hunched under his own umbrella.

'You needn't have taken off quite so fast.' He hopped over a puddle, taking care not to splash his brown suede shoes.

'For Jock's sake,' she said. 'He was desperate.'

'Doesn't look like it's going to clear up any time soon.' He hesitated, clearly torn between keeping her company and ruining his shoes. The shoes won.

'I'll see you in a minute.' Rain deluged onto her umbrella. Behind the hotel wall a marquee was ready for a wedding – poor souls, on a day like this. She stepped over the low wall onto a path that ran beside the road, careful not to trip over the exposed tree roots until they reached what looked like the remains of an old bridge. Isla looked across the river then turned around.

'That's enough, old boy. The weather's too grim to go on. Maybe the other two will be talking to each other by now.'

When she got back, Charlie was at the table surrounded by the remains of her breakfast. 'They took pity on me.' She finished the last mouthful of toast.

Tony was nowhere to be seen.

'Are we staying here for the day?' She sounded so hopeful that Isla was tempted to leave her in her room with her TV and phone. At the same time, she didn't want her to feel any more unloved or neglected than she already did.

'Why don't we go to Clitheroe. And have lunch? And shop?' She spoke just as Tony joined them, having changed his shoes, she noticed. His and Charlie's faces told her exactly what they thought of that idea.

'Why can't we just relax here?' he asked. 'We don't have to go rushing around in search of entertainment. There's everything we could possibly need.'

At last Charlie looked as if she approved of something he had said. 'Great. I'll be in my room, if that's okay, Gran. There's something I've been dying to do.' She got up to leave them. 'Come on, Jock.'

The dog looked up at his name and, with a wag of the tail, followed her out of the room.

'Cupboard love,' said Isla, remembering the open biscuit packet in Charlie's room.

'But it's love,' he said. 'Over here.' He led her to an empty sofa. 'I'm so glad I've found you,' he said, moving the cushions to make room for her. They picked up the papers, discarding a couple of fishing magazines, and started leafing through them, quite at ease with each other. There was no need to fill the silence with conversation. Eventually Tony spoke. 'Actually,' he began. 'There is something I'd like to talk to you about.'

'Sounds ominous.' She hoped she hadn't gone too far the night before.

He laughed. 'No, no. I've just had an email. Remember I was having that meeting the other evening when you called? Well, it worked. I've been asked to go into business with an ex-colleague. We worked together at GSK and I got in touch with him when I got back from France, on the off-chance.'

'I knew you'd find something soon.' She felt excited, vindicated. 'What is it? A small hotel, something like the gîte? Where?' She stopped. If he moved to the other end of the country, what would that mean for their relationship?

He put up both hands to protect himself against the flood of questions. 'God, no. I'm done with the hospitality business. This is much more exciting, and different. And worthwhile. He's developing an eco-alternative to supermarket packaging.'

She looked at him in disbelief. 'Do you know anything about that?'

He smiled. 'Not much but, believe it or not, he wants me for my business brain. We'll be taking over a small sustainable packaging company. Don has done this before very successfully. Listen.' He went on to explain the work they did, using seaweed and algae among other things to produce degradable food packaging. 'This is transformational. I can show you their existing website.'

'But why you?' She couldn't imagine what Don thought Tony would bring to the business.

'Are you doubting me?' His disappointment was clear.

'Of course not. It's just that I didn't know you had that sort of background.' Hadn't he led her to believe that that he had lived a much more hand-to-mouth existence?

'Surely I told you that when Angie and I went to France I gave up a good job – if by good you mean well-paid – in the food packaging industry?'

'No, you didn't.' She'd remember that.

'Angie persuaded me that we'd have a much better lifestyle if we gave up everything and moved to France. I guess *she* did.'

'But you're back on your feet now.' Isla couldn't help thinking how much this new job might impress Charlie.

'Yes, I am.' He gave a wide smile. 'I simply can't believe this has happened.'

'This is great news. I'm so pleased.' She really was. Although he never said, she could sense how despondent he'd been as he tried to find work. This would make all the difference.

'There's just one catch . . .' He took her hand and counted off her fingertips one by one, thoughtful.

'What is it?' Surely nothing would spoil things for him now, just as he was finding his feet again.

'He wants me to invest in the company – obviously, if I'm to be a proactive part in it and so that I get my full due. Obviously the return should be substantial, otherwise I wouldn't be thinking of it. My problem is that my savings are tied up in an investment account so I've got to get a loan and/or drum up some other investors because he needs the money now so that he can speed things forward. So that's what I'll be doing next week while you're up north: raising funds.'

Neither of them spoke as she digested all this. She had never seen him so animated. This venture obviously meant everything to him and was restoring his self-worth after months of job-hunting. 'But I don't understand why he needs your investment so urgently.'

'It's a bit of luck, in fact. He had a business partner who's had to step aside because he's been diagnosed with oesopha-geal cancer. Nasty.' He pulled a face. 'So Don's been looking for someone to step in for a couple of months and I've come along just in time. If the deal's going to happen, he needs to sign everything off fast, because these people are getting itchy feet and will look for someone else if he doesn't.'

'It does sound a fantastic venture. Worthwhile.' She didn't have enough of a business head to understand the ins and outs of an investment partnership but presumably, if you liked the sound of something it made sense to snap it up. That was why she and Heather made such a good team at the museum. Heather complimented her and took care of the book-keeping while she curated the collections and dreamed up the children's events.

'It really is, and I'm convinced we can develop what's already there and really make a go of it.'

How could he switch from gîte-owner to planet-saver so quickly? The swift change of direction brought home to her how little she knew him.

'But how will you raise the money?'

He rubbed his hands together. 'I've got a couple of ideas, and I'm sure that anyone who looks at the figures will want a piece of the action too – frankly, they'd be a fool not to – so I'm not too anxious.'

Isla thought of her own savings that sat waiting for her eventual retirement, put aside to pay off her mortgage and for the travelling she wanted to do. Not too far off now. If May had left her a share of her estate she would have much more financial security for her future – just as Tony had imagined she had. So swelling the pot by some astute investment would be to her advantage. But he was talking about approaching his business associates, not people like her.

'How much are you looking for?'

'Just twenty grand in the first instance. That could be a personal loan to me but if anyone wants to invest in the business, and I think they will ... Don will be over the moon. He knows I can do this. Look, let me show you the website at least.'

He was back with his laptop almost before she had time to register him leaving the room. As he fired it up, went to the website and started to explain their plans, his enthusiasm was contagious. As he talked, she could feel the possibilities thrumming through her veins too. 'This is amazing.'

His face was alight when he looked at her. 'You really think so?'

'Absolutely.'

'Your believing in it too means everything.'

'Why wouldn't I? In fact perhaps I could loan you the money or make an investment?'

'You'd do that? But that's not what I meant at all.' He put the laptop on the table and she could see his eyes were bright. 'I owe you so much already. I couldn't ask you ...'

The few times she had lent him cash when he needed to go to the cash point, or paid for a meal didn't concern her. Once this job was up and running, he'd pay her back. 'That's different. And you're not asking me, I'm offering.'

He looked thoughtful. 'No, no. I can't let you do that. It's too much of a risk.'

'But you've just spent ages showing me how risk averse it is. I need to make some money over the next few years, and I'd like to be involved in it with you.' And how Charlie would approve. This was a way of doing her bit to better the world as well as being the gateway to a new future for both her and Tony. 'I want to do this.'

'You don't want me to try my other leads first?' She could hear the hope in his voice.

'No. I've made up my mind. I'll transfer the money straight away. That shouldn't be a problem. Who to?' This would make up for her mother leaving her nothing. Not that she had been relying on that, but he was giving her a helping hand.

'Why don't you transfer to me and I'll make the investment arrangements for you. I'll tell Don. He'll be delighted. And you must meet him soon.'

He leaned forward and kissed her. In the background she

heard a whoop from the doorway. He pulled away. 'Thank you. I really wasn't expecting you to do this. But you won't regret it, I promise.'

'I'd better not,' she said, feeling a warm bubble of happiness burst inside her.

26

When Charlie eventually came down to the bar, Isla stared at her, shocked. The ends of her hair were dyed a deep purple that faded upwards to the level of her chin.

'Like it?' Charlie twisted her head from side to side so the full extent of her handiwork could be appreciated.

'Actually, I do.' She came round to it quickly. It was fun. 'I wouldn't do it myself though.'

Charlie laughed. 'If only. I've been dying to do this for ages but Mum always said no.'

Isla's heart sank a little bit. 'So what makes now different?'

'You're not as strict as she is.'

Did that made her feel better or worse?

'Anyway, I can always wash it out or cut it off.' She passed over her phone. 'Will you take my photo, Gran.'

'Again?'

'Yes. I want Alice and Tilly to see the hair and where I am.' She tipped her head to one side and pouted.

'That really doesn't suit you.' Isla waited for her to choose another expression.

'You're sounding like Mum again. Rule broken.' She was triumphant. 'What's the forfeit? Anyway I like it. Look!'

'Backgammon?' Isla had taught her to play on a family holiday a couple of years earlier.

Charlie looked out of the window where the rain had slowed to a steady drizzle. 'There's nothing else to do.' As they settled down to the game, with cups of tea and slices of sponge cake (the forfeit) sandwiched together with lashings of cream and jam (photo taken of that too) Isla said, 'I must tell you what I've done. I think you'll be pleased.'

More than anything she wanted Charlie's approval of her involvement in this new company and by extension, of Tony.

But as she explained, and watched Charlie's expression change to one of astonishment, she began to wonder what the hell she had just committed herself to.

She could hear her family: judge and jury.

May. *'You hardly know the man. I hope you're not making a terrible mistake.'*

Her father. *'If that's what you want to do, I'll support you but . . .'*

Morag. *'Shouldn't you at least have someone do some background research before committing.'*

Lorna. *'Oh, Isla. Is this wise?'*

Had she been too rash? She didn't care. She wanted to support Tony, and this was a perfect opportunity. And she needed to build a nest egg for her old age – this gave her the chance. Yes, she had made a quick decision, but what was life about if you didn't throw in a bit of spontaneity and risk every now and then? She was excited about seeing Tony do well and watching the business develop. She couldn't wait to meet Don and hear more about it.

'Gran! That sounds a bit mad to me.' Charlie grimaced. 'Maybe in a good way.'

'But why? I thought you'd be the first to think it was a good idea.' She was disappointed not to have the eco-warrior's support. She jumped her black checker a two and then six, to take one of Charlie's white ones off the board.

'Well, the idea sounds good.' She retaliated by blocking Isla's exit from her side.

'Well then?' Isla threw badly so one of the dice bounced out of the box.

Charlie scrambled to pick it up. 'Whatever. I heard Tony talking when you were getting ready for lunch. He said he would have the "table, etcetera"' – she bracketed the words with her fingers – 'picked up on Tuesday, and he gave your address. Are you moving?'

Isla frowned then laughed. 'You must have misheard.'

'But you live there.' She threw and moved again. The game was moving too fast for Isla's liking.

'But so does he at the moment.' She felt herself blushing, wondering what Charlie might be thinking about her. 'He must be getting rid of some of the clutter he brought with him.' She wasn't proud of the welcome she had given the few belongings he had brought from his place, but her house was small and was . . . well, hers. If he had got the message and was doing something about it, then good for him. She liked him all the more for it.

'Even the painting you got from Braemore?'

Isla stopped shaking the dice. 'Charlie, stop it!'

Charlie looked dubious. 'If you say so.'

Charlie moved her last checker into her home section. 'Well, I hope he's not getting rid of it then.'

'Stop it!' Isla's throw failed to get her last piece out of her starting quadrant. 'Why are you so determined to think the worst of him?'

'I'm not.' She shook the dice hard. 'I just know what I heard. There.' A double six cleared her side of the board. 'Best of three?'

'All right.' Rising to Charlie's bait would only make things worse.

'Can anyone join in?' Tony had snuck up behind them without either of them noticing. He put his hands on Isla's shoulder, his fingers reaching round her throat, pressing on her collarbone.

'I wish you wouldn't creep up on me like that.' She smiled up at him.

He noticed Charlie's hair. 'What *have* you done?'

'Don't you like it?' said Isla.

'Not much.'

Isla could have killed him. Again, why couldn't he try? 'I do. It's pretty.'

'I'm going back upstairs. I want to see what Tilly's been up to.' Charlie left the table.

'You don't have to . . .' Isla didn't want her to go.

'I know. But I like it there.'

'And I like it when she's there too,' said Tony softly once she had gone. 'I like having you to myself.'

'We've got plenty of time. Did you have to be so tactless?'

'Sorry. But honestly. She looks awful.'

'She's young. Give her a chance. You'll never guess what she's got into her head now.' Isla laid out the checkers for a new game.

'What?' His finger traced down the length of her hand.

'She's convinced you're selling some of my furniture.' The idea was so ridiculous, she couldn't help laughing.

The finger stopped. 'Where on earth did she get that idea?'

'She overheard you on the phone.'

His hand went to his eyebrow, smoothing it. 'When? Isla, this has got to stop.'

'While I was getting ready for lunch.'

His face cleared. 'Oh that! She's got completely the wrong end of the stick, of course. Now I'll have to tell you. I was going to surprise you by having your oak table restored.'

'You don't need to do that.' She loved her table with all its scratches and dents from long use. 'I like it having history.'

'Just as well she overheard me then.' He clicked his fingers. 'There's time to cancel. I'll do that now.'

She watched him leave the bar, simultaneously finding a number and putting his phone to his ear.

When he returned, he was smiling. 'All done. They were fine about it. But I'm disappointed because that was my treat after all you've been through. Now Don's come through, I can afford to treat you.'

'No need,' she said. 'You've done more than enough.'

'I'll think of something else then. But right now, I'm going to thrash you at this.' He sat in front of the backgammon board. 'And then, if it ever stops raining, we'll go for a walk.'

The rest of their stay passed relatively peaceably. Tony and Charlie kept their distance and Isla didn't try to change that. She was resigned to the fact that they weren't going to find a common ground. Whatever Tony did or said, Charlie was ready to find fault. Not that she said much, but a raise of the eyebrow, a click of the tongue was enough.

The weather improved until they were back in their summer clothes, wishing for the respite of rain again. On Sunday, it was too hot to do anything much. Neither Tony nor Isla wanted to explore, they were quite happy where they were and Charlie seemed to have adapted to it too, especially when the twins offered to take her fishing for a couple of hours. They came back empty-handed but Charlie was beaming. Isla caught her taking a selfie beside the cabinet containing the dead-eyed perch. She just smiled.

On their final night, she and Tony were in bed when she said, 'I'd love to stay for longer. Just a day would do.'

They lay facing each other, each with their head propped on their elbow.

'I've got to get back to see Don.'

His reply disappointed her but she shrugged it off. 'Of course, you have. The money should be transferred to you by then. You'll let me know how it goes?'

Suddenly his arms were round her and he was showering

her with kisses. She felt as if she were in her twenties again, giddy with love.

'That's so generous of you, my love. I'm so thrilled we're in this together.'

My love.

'And you've got work of your own to do.' He pulled away from her as he reminded her.

She sighed. This weekend had almost taken her mind off her family dilemmas. But she was as determined as ever to get to the bottom of things. 'If only I could find the key to it all. There must be one.'

Isla finished loading Betty while Charlie lolled by the front passenger door and Tony took the wheel. The smell of sick was still strong but Charlie pulled an atomiser from her bag and sprayed through the door into the interior. 'That's better.'

'God! What *is* that?' Tony waved a hand in front of his nose.

'It is quite strong.' Isla felt the atmosphere change.

'Bare Vanilla,' said Charlie, clearly irritated that they didn't like it. 'Body mist from Victoria's Secret.' The way she said it suggested the scent was most desirable.

'Well, I wish it had missed my body.' Tony coughed, and wound down his window. 'Isla, get in or I'll miss my train.'

'It's not that bad,' she said, trying to diffuse things.

'See what it's like inside the car.' He put Betty into reverse. 'Get in. I'll make it easier for you.'

As he began to reverse, Charlie was half in and half out.

'Hey! Hang on.' She jumped back, knocking her head on the doorframe. As she stumbled, she slammed shut the door so it didn't hit the neighbouring car. At the same time, she dropped her phone and Betty's front tyre rolled slowly back over it. There was a crack.

'Nooo!'

The wail was loud enough to make Tony brake suddenly.

'Back up some more!' Isla yelled, having seen the whole thing. Charlie was close to tears.

'What's happened?' Tony leaned out of the window.

As Isla explained, Charlie was on her hands and knees, waiting as Tony reversed until she could pick up her phone, her face disbelieving.

'Okay?' Isla asked.

'Of course it's not okay!' Charlie shouted, white with anger. 'He's just driven over it! Look!' She held the phone out to Isla.

Isla could see the face was crazed with cracks. 'Can you use it?'

'No! Of course not!'

'Not the end of the world.' Tony got out and came round to look. 'You can get the screen replaced. Easy.'

She took a step back, her face puce with fury. 'Where?' She looked around her. 'Over there?' She gestured towards the other side of the green. 'Oh! There doesn't seem to be a repair shop. Can you see one?'

'That's enough!' he snapped. 'I'm sorry but it was an accident. I wasn't the one who dropped it.'

'No. But you drove right over it.' Charlie's face was red, her eyes bright with tears.

'Calm down.' He put his hands up, defending himself. 'It'll be good for you not to rely on it for a bit.'

Isla wanted to punch him. He knew exactly how much the phone meant to Charlie. 'I'm sure we'll find somewhere in Preston,' she said. She put her arm round Charlie's shoulders, feeling her shaking. 'We'll get it sorted, don't worry.' How could he let her down like this?

'Can you please get into the car,' Tony was standing by the driver's door, looking at his watch. His fingers rapped against the roof with impatience.

The look Isla and Charlie exchanged spoke volumes. This would be over soon.

Isla wound down her window in the hope that the lingering smell of Bare Vanilla and sick would disperse. Tony followed suit.

Neither Tony nor Charlie uttered a word on the way to the station. Isla's 'Take it easy' as he tore down the country lanes was ignored. She understood he was upset but killing them all wouldn't speed things up.

Charlie sat pressed against her door as if she couldn't get far enough away from him. Any possible rapprochement between the two of them had been forgotten. The countryside flashed past in a blur, too fast for them to appreciate it, and they were soon back in the outskirts of Preston.

At the station, Tony jumped out of the car, grabbed his bag from the back seat, and ran ahead of Isla as if he couldn't wait to get away. Charlie and Jock stayed behind. When Isla caught up with him, he was checking his watch against the departures board. 'Thank God, it's ten minutes late. I'm sorry, darling,' he said to Isla.

'Well, I'm sorry it hasn't been quite the weekend we planned.' She didn't point out that he could always have taken another train.

'I'm just tense about a meeting this afternoon. I was frightened I'd miss it.' As if he'd read her mind. 'I'll make it up to Charlie somehow.'

With some relief, Isla saw the train pull in alongside them.

He picked up his bag and was opening the train door when she touched his arm, wanting that reconnection before he left. He turned to look at her with an expression she didn't recognise, almost as if he didn't know her. Within a moment, it transformed to the face of the man she knew and loved.

'It wasn't all bad,' he said with a grin.

'No it wasn't.' She slipped her arm around his waist. 'And we'll do it again.' Everything would be all right. She would make that effort.

They kissed quickly, and she was reminded of how when things did go well with him, they went very well indeed.

He climbed onto the train just before the whistle went and, with a long sigh, the train began to inch forwards, gathering speed. Tony leaned out of the window waving till they left the station.

When Isla got back to the car, Charlie was smiling. 'Can we go now?'

'Yep. Next stop, Scotland.'

'Next stop, phone repair,' Charlie corrected her. 'Please.'

'Of course. How could I forget!' Isla was surprised to feel a weight had lifted from her, as if all was well with the world again. At least when she and Charlie were alone together she was beginning to know where she stood.

The two of them had a coffee in Fishergate while a repair shop replaced the phone's screen. Charlie was thrilled to be back in a Caffè Nero, sitting on a battered brown leather sofa with a cappuccino in her own cup, delighted with more loyalty stamps, watching people passing by the big plate glass windows beside them. Without no phone for distraction, she had to talk to Isla.

'Favourite bit of the weekend?' Isla organised the drinks and slices of cake on the small round table, and began the game that she and Helen had always played on the way home from a holiday.

'Being in my room with the TV and Jock. We watched almost all of *Sex Education* on Netflix,' she said as if it was something to be proud of. She tasted her gingerbread latte and a satisfied smile crossed her face.

'God knows what your mother would say.' Perhaps Isla should have laid down some viewing rules. She knew Helen was quite strict about what Charlie watched. But how did she even keep track? Oh for heaven's sake! They were on holiday. Charlie was happy. What did it matter?

'Oh, I told her.'

'You've spoken?' Isla hadn't even rung Helen again. Her mind had been elsewhere.

'She emailed. She got the gig and she's been meeting all these people.' Charlie didn't sound too happy as she stirred sugar into her coffee. 'She loves Hollywood!'

'But that's good isn't it? In fact that's absolutely brilliant. Good for her.'

'I guess, except she'll be there all the time.'

'No she won't. She'll work from home and may have to go over to visit every now and then.' Isla had no idea what she was talking about but wanted to lift Charlie's spirits. 'And if she does, you can always come and stay with me, work in the museum and earn some money.'

Charlie brightened. 'Really?'

'Why not? You could work on the desk, I'm sure. And worst bit of holiday so far?' She was going to play the game to the end. 'The car breaking down was mine.'

'Being sick in the car.' She picked up her cup. 'And Tony.' She looked down as she spoke so Isla only just heard her.

'Why?' Her irritation threatened to bubble over. 'He's a lovely man. If you'd made more of an effort you might have found that out for yourself.'

Charlie looked doubtful. 'If you say so. I did try.'

'I wish you'd tried harder. I like him. He makes me happy, and that should be enough for you.'

'I don't trust him.' Her latte gave her a milky moustache which she wiped off. 'There.'

Her forthrightness was shocking and hurtful.

'Well, you should. You overheard a conversation, added two and two to make five. He was planning a surprise for me which admittedly I'd have hated so, thanks to you, I was able to stop it in time. Apart from that, he had to put up with a lot from you this weekend. Not least you being sick on him.' She banged her cup back on its saucer.

There was a shocked silence. Then they both began to laugh, quietly at first until they were laughing their heads off.

27

Paris, 1954

As winter embraced the city of Paris, fewer people came
to the Luco. But the mothers and nannies still appeared
with their charges wrapped up in coats, hats and gloves.
Occasionally a carer would push a wheelchair containing a
well-wrapped patient to get the benefit of the biting fresh
air. The trees stretched their skeleton fingers towards the
sky while, beneath them, the flowerbeds looked bleak and
empty. Wendy and May were still regulars there, often
meeting other friends that they'd made together. After so
many months, Emile and Amaury, Wendy's boy, had become
good friends too and would happily race around together,
inventing games, hiding from their nannies. Wendy and
May would wander through the different areas of the park,
hunting for the boys while catching up on each other's news.
Wendy was a constant source of chatter, always ready with a
bit of gossip about someone, or to talk about her relationship
with Sam that was going from strength to strength.

'He says he loves me.' She clasped her hands together as if

she were the subject of a pre-Raphaelite painting. 'He even suggested I go to America with him. Imagine.'

May felt a sickening pang of envy. If only Max had said that to her, everything might have been so different. 'I wonder what Max is doing now.'

Wendy tossed her curls. 'Don't think about him anymore. He's not worth it.' This was a typical reaction. She was a young woman who only existed in the here and now, an incurable optimist. The past was to be forgotten. She had dismissed Max as soon as the pregnancy was dealt with and clearly thought May should too.

But it wasn't that easy for May. Despite all that had happened, Max still haunted her dreams. In the world of her imagination, he changed his mind, returned to France only to sweep her and their baby off to a fantasy America, where their future was rose-tinted. There, Max was a successful writer after all and they lived in a white clapboard house where she looked after their perfect family of two children. They'd exist in a world of Hollywood films, Coca Cola, jiving to Bill Haley and the Comets, eating steaks and peach cobbler – all the things she had heard about.

However, one lunchtime, between the end of her language class and the time she had to collect Emile from school, May went into the park alone to prepare herself for her charge's boundless energy. That afternoon, they were going to the Parc Zoologique, Emile's reward for tidying his own room. He was desperate to see the Asian elephants again. In the meantime, walking cleared her head, helped her think, and made a neat transition between one part of her life and the other. She valued having that time during which she could reflect on what had happened to her and what she would do next. So far, no amount of thinking had solved the problem. She would be staying with the Dubois till spring, when her year would be up, but she had nothing lined up for afterwards. Her parents were expecting her home, expecting to send her to London and Aunt Jess but Paris had cast its spell on her. She didn't want to leave the city and the friends she had made there just yet.

Although she had taken back her life and made new friends among her fellow students, none of them were as close to her as Wendy. She had deliberately held herself in reserve, keeping away from any deep friendships and particularly approaches from any man she met since Max had so badly burned her. She studied other people as if she was from another planet, trying to work out what made them behave the way they did. She watched lovers embracing in the Luco. How did they know when to trust one another? Perhaps they didn't. Perhaps you couldn't expect that from a relationship. She couldn't imagine ever trusting anyone again. She even doubted Wendy sometimes. After all, if she had told May her plan had been to sleep with Sam that night in Brittany, May might have been more careful about going with them. But it was possible that Wendy hadn't planned anything but been spontaneous in response to her feelings. That was at least how she had explained it when May pressed her for an answer.

As she approached the formal gardens and the boating

lake in front of the grand Palais itself, she recalled her first visit there. How innocent she had been then, how hungry for life and excitement. She would never have dreamed of all the things that had happened to her since: falling in love with this dazzling city; falling in love with Max; and then how everything that brought her such happiness had crashed down round her. What a different, more cautious person she had become as a result.

The day was crisp and blue. She waved at Camille, a fellow student in her French class. They sat on one of the stone seats, flinching at the cold underneath them. As they talked about their last assignment, May's eye was caught by a man sitting a little way along from them. He sat staring into space, his beret at that particular French angle, the lower part of his face covered by his navy-blue muffler. The man with the newspaper. She would recognise that hair with that beret anywhere.

Camille noticed her looking at him. 'I've seen him here before. He comes here alone and always looks so sad. I bet he's not much fun.'

She was right. He did look miserable. When he glanced in their direction May raised her hand in a little wave. She imagined he was wondering who she was and then remembering their previous brief encounter: the first Scottish person he had met in Paris. He saw May, recognised her and, to her surprise, turned his head away.

'You know him?' Camille was eager for gossip.

'Not really. I met him here once before.' As she explained, she stole surreptitious glances at him, wondering what his story was, what had brought him here, why he was always alone. She liked the fact that they were both from Scotland. In a foreign city, that felt like a bond.

After that she spotted him another couple of times, always alone, sitting on the same bench, giving off the same sense of misery. She always headed in the opposite direction, curious but intimidated, and not wanting to be sucked in. The third time, he had his hand on the handle of a pram, pushing it back and forth, back and forth. Without stopping to think, she went over to him.

'We met, do you remember? I'm from Dunfermline.'

'Of course.' He gave her a bleak smile. 'I remember.'

'Is this is your baby?' As she leaned over the pram, an unbearable sensation of loss weighed her down. The tiny baby stared up at her, wrapped up so that only its delicate rosebud mouth, perfect teeny nose, and plump cheeks showed. Its eyes were clamped shut asleep. This was what she had given up. This was what she had killed. All the emotion she had kept battened down since the abortion came hurtling to the surface.

'Oh.' The word emerged in a breath.

She yearned for the baby she would never have, mourning its loss all over again.

'Eloise,' he said, oblivious to the emotions churning through her.

'She's beautiful.' She wanted to ask why he was alone with her. Why wasn't he at work? Where was her mother? 'How old is she?' she said instead.

He smiled. 'Five weeks. Five long weeks. Her mother doesn't want to know.' He looked surprised that he'd said so much, and shook his head, despairing.

This time May was not going to let him get away so easily. 'She'll come round.' She knew from the other girls that some women found becoming a mother more than they could handle. Without children of their own, they had observed the mothers of their charges and had become instant experts in the subject. But, like so many things, bonding with your child was often just a question of time. However, she couldn't believe that any woman wouldn't fall head over heels in love with a baby like this. She couldn't help wondering what her own baby would have looked like. Would she (she somehow knew it was a girl) have had her dark hair? Or would she have had Max's patrician blond good looks? Her hand went to her heart.

'I hope so.' He looked doubtful. He held out his hand. 'I'm David Adair.'

'I remember.' She recovered herself, removed her glove and shook hands. 'May Campbell.'

And that's how they left it.

As she walked away, she felt a sob choke her. A baby, a perfect baby. She clenched her fists so tightly that her nails dug into her palms. What was she thinking? What had she done?

A few days later it was too cold to sit, so May joined David in his walk round the park. She walked beside him, peering down at Eloise who slept all the way round, aware that they must look like a married couple, like the family that could have been hers if Max hadn't shipped out. Meeting David and Eloise had deepened her sense of loss and developed it into a longing for something to fill the void inside her. She and David passed the time reminiscing about Scotland: about the fireworks in Edinburgh on New Year's Eve that she had seen the year before she came to Paris. He had been in the crowd too. About going to Portobello Beach in the summer. They had both been in the crowds lining Prince's Street when the newly crowned Queen and Prince Philip made their state visit to the city and travelled in a coach to St Giles in 1953. They talked about walking in the hills, debated the merits of haggis, and he told her of the disappointment he shared with her father in Scotland's dismal performance in the Five Nations Championship the year before. Being with him was like being at home. Talking with him gave her a sense of belonging and an inkling of homesickness that she hadn't felt for a long time. When Eloise cried, he allowed her to take her from the pram and soothe her, making her heartache worse.

'Put your hand here.' He put his on hers and moved it to support Eloise's head.

Eloise looked up at her. May's heart was lost in that moment.

Once they went to a café, where they sat inside, lulled by the smells of coffee and hot chocolate. They shared a mille-feuille, laughing as her attempt to cut it in half ended in its creamy destruction, with pastry flakes all over the table. When Eloise woke up, David passed her to May so she could soothe her while he finished his drink. But she didn't want to give her back. The warm curl of the baby's body, the smell of the top of her head, tiny fingers clutching and unclutching, her constantly mobile face. May was fascinated by her, thrilled to be able to give her a bottle, taken aback by how strongly her own body responded.

'Your wife must adore her now.'

How could anyone not? She hadn't asked about his wife since her first meeting with Eloise. Neither had he mentioned her, although she was a constant presence shadowing their walks.

He shook his head as Eloise hung on to one of his fingers with all five of hers. 'I'm afraid not. She didn't want to have her in the first place, but I was so sure that once she saw her, she'd come round. I thought every woman loved their own baby unconditionally. But I was terribly wrong. What she wants is her life back as it was before.' He sounded so hopeless.

'Why was it so special?' It was impossible to imagine a life that was too full to include Eloise.

'She's a fashion model.' He spoke as if that explained everything.

'I don't understand.' As May spoke, Eloise began to cry, quietly at first then, resisting any attempt to comfort her, growing louder.

'Perhaps we should go.' David looked apologetic. 'This sort of thing doesn't make me any friends. Perhaps I'll tell you another time.'

May respected his reserve. After all, he was not unlike her.

Their meetings soon became a regular thing. At lunch-times, she would meet him and walk or take shelter in the warmth of the café, depending on the weather. They sat on a green banquette in a corner between the counter and the window, savouring the smell of coffee, trying out the different pastries on offer. They never stayed together long because of Eloise and because David had to get her back to the nanny and to work while his wife had gone to the south of France on a protracted modelling job. Bit by bit, he began to talk about himself and what brought him to Paris. At last the story of his 'marriage' found its way into the open.

'I fell in love with Céleste the moment I saw her.' May sensed his relief as he began to unburden himself to her. 'I remember her walking into the room at a house party outside Edinburgh one weekend. None of us had seen anything like her. The French would say "*mignonne*". We were introduced and we didn't stop talking all night. My friends were as astonished as I was that she felt the same way. I suppose we were an unlikely match but at the time you don't think about that. She would say I'm set in my ways, though she didn't think so then. And she's a free spirit who tilts at life. I loved that about her.' He stopped. 'You don't mind me telling you all this?'

She put his hand on his. 'Quite the contrary. I want you to.'

He looked down at their hands, leaving them for a moment before moving his away. 'I proposed to her two months later. I was so certain.'

May was astonished. 'But that's so quick. I'm sorry, I

shouldn't have said that.' But what he was telling her was like a story from one of the women's magazines that Wendy was sent from home.

'But I was so sure we were a perfect match. And she was too. I proposed on Arthur's Seat after we'd climbed up there at dawn: the best place to see the city.' He smiled at the memory. 'And she said yes.'

'Did you marry straight away?' May was rapt, enchanted by the romance of it all.

'No. She hated Scotland. I wanted us to marry in St Giles, where my parents and sister had married, but she'd none of it.' He crossed his legs and started rocking the pram. 'She'd only marry me if I came back with her to Paris where she belonged.'

'There are worse places.' She had seen plenty of churches, so much prettier than the dour cathedral of Edinburgh, that she could imagine getting married in.

He gave a rueful smile. 'True. And I thought it would work, that I'd get a job through one of my father's contacts, and we'd live happily here. But I gave up everything, including the family business – you know Adairs, the big department store on Prince's Street? My younger brother's in line to be manager now instead of me, even though his ambition was to be a lawyer. I grew up knowing that's what I'd do and now I've forfeited all that.' His pain was obvious as he stopped and stared at his lap.

'So you came here,' she prompted. 'What then?'

'To begin with, it was better than I could have dreamed of.

We had our flat, each other. Nothing else really mattered. I got this job and Céleste picked up the threads of her old life. Everything boded well. But if she was a fish out of water in Scotland, so I'm a fish out of water here.'

'What do you mean? You've got the beret.' She tried to joke him out of his sadness.

'I don't fit in to her world. They're actors, models, artists – people of the night. I like walking the fields, listening to the skylarks, managing the business. It was only months before I knew it was a terrible mistake.' His voice dropped. 'And so did she.'

In the café, over coffee and a madeleine each while Eloise slept, he told her what happened next. 'We were on the brink of going our separate ways. I felt desperately sad but would have gone back home without much harm done to anyone else – just my hurt pride and loss of face. But then she told me she was pregnant.' He paused to peer in the pram and adjust Eloise's blanket. 'I couldn't have been happier. I hoped, no, I believed the baby would bring us together again, and I believed she thought that too. In fact it's been quite the reverse. For her, nothing's changed. She wants the life she had before Eloise was born; she'll have it. You already wouldn't guess that she'd just had a baby. We'll never marry now.'

At last he had told her the truth.

'I'm sorry. That's such a sad story.' What was there to say? Both of them had made wrong choices that had affected their lives irreparably. She couldn't help being reminded of

Max. Perhaps this is what would have happened to them if he had stayed. Once the baby was born, he'd have realised his mistake and disappeared. Perhaps she had a lucky escape after all.

'And Eloise?'

He put his head in his hands. 'I don't know.'

'Céleste's family?'

'She doesn't see them. They disapprove of her and seem to have disowned her. She hasn't even told them about Eloise. I'm not sure what's going to happen but we'll muddle through. Perhaps she'll come round.' But he didn't sound convinced.

The next time they met, David was distraught, unshaven, his face grey with anguish. He began to speak before she had a chance to sit down. 'Céleste isn't coming home. She's moved in with the photographer, Jean-Luc.' He shook his head. 'I simply can't believe it.'

May was appalled to see a tear run down his cheek, then another. She had never seen a man cry before. She reached out her hand then withdrew it, worried it might be seen as too forward, yet she ached to comfort him. Instead she waited, speechless, for more.

'And Simone, our nanny, won't work without another woman in the apartment so she's left too.' He shook his head as if unable to process what was happening to him. 'As if she couldn't trust me. I've only ever wanted one woman – Céleste – but it's too late.'

'Is she taking Eloise?' An unexpected sense of panic

engulfed her as May realised how much their meetings meant to her.

'No.' He groaned. 'She wants me to have her. But how can I?'

May was shocked. How could she have left Eloise, such a good and beautiful baby? May couldn't understand how any woman could have so little heart. How could she have abandoned such a gentle, loving man for another life? And what about Eloise? A man couldn't bring up a baby on his own.

'I could help out,' she said before she had even thought what she was going to say next.

He looked at her. Gratitude and astonishment chased across his face.

'Perhaps Madame would let me while Emile's in school. I could skip my French classes.' Her French was more than passable now, so what did that matter anyway?

'You'd do that?' He looked at her as if she was an angel sent to save him. 'It needn't be for long, just till I get back on my feet and sort things out.'

She wanted to help him. The idea of doing something for someone in need made her feel better about herself immediately. This was unquestionably the right thing for her to do. She was sure Madame would understand.

'I would,' she said, never more certain of anything.

And so it was arranged.

28

Galloway, 2019

'Grandmothers! Who'd ever have thought it?' Isla's old schoolfriend Janet raised her glass towards the horizon. 'Cheers! She seems a nice girl though. You should meet mine – such a prima donna. And the make-up!'

'Don't I know?' said Isla, raising hers in tandem, looking across the wide beach to where Charlie was throwing a ball for Jock who ambled after it but then left it where it was. They had spent the afternoon exploring, Isla trying to enthuse a monosyllabic Charlie into collecting the tiny cornet-shaped shells found on the little shell-covered beach she remembered from her childhood. She had decided to ignore any mood swings Charlie threw at her and just press on regardless, her rulebook thrown out the window. If Charlie didn't like it – too bad.

Janet had driven over in the late afternoon. She had put on weight since they had last met but was as agile clambering over the rocks as ever. Her eyes shone from a lined face that showed how much time she spent outside. Her hair had not seen a hairdresser for ages and was scraped back and held in place by kirby grips. Seeing her again, the time fell away as it does with good friends.

'God, but this takes me back.' Janet's gesture included the vast bay where the tide had pulled the sea right back towards the horizon, leaving a vast expanse of rippled sand. Runnels of sea water sparkled in the evening sun, among them thousands of coiled lugworm casts, with the Murray Isles silhouetted in the distance – all was just as it had all been for years. Sailing boats covered in tarpaulins were pulled to the back of the beach where they rested on their trailers. Over to their right, the river Fleet was a silver ribbon gleaming as it flowed out to sea past Mossyard and Cardoness on the opposite side of the estuary. Everything was as Isla remembered, and yet not the same at all. The campsite had expanded and changed. The green caravans of her memory had been replaced by much larger static homes and luxury wooden cabins that lined up along the sea front. There were tarmacked roads and careful landscaping. The pleasant modesty of her youth had gone upmarket – sign of the times.

'Even the diving platform's gone.'

Her father had taught them to dive from the rickety wooden diving platform that must have succumbed to the elements years earlier. Shivering up there, watching the sea swirl around them had always been thrilling as they'd egged each other on to jump in. May would encourage them to go swimming even in the rain. How many summers must they have spent racing up and down the beach, learning to sail, shrimping in rockpools, building sandcastles and dams? Life was so simple then, when they had all got on and played together.

'And how different is this?' Isla turned back to the neat grey clapboard house with plate glass windows that gave a wonderful view of the shore, just the other side of the low brick wall. When she had last been here, there were no palm trees, no terrace, no manicured lawn, just scrubby grass. 'I wonder when they knocked down the old house. I can't remember it clearly at all.'

'It was just a holiday home, basic and battered round the edges. In fact your parents always seemed a bit too smart for it.'

This was the second evening they'd spent together. Janet had got rid of her husband a decade earlier when she realised that life was better and easier lived alone. She bought a pretty aqua-coloured cottage in Kirkcudbright's High Street, made friends there and spent much of her time painting and going on long walks with Ferdie, her golden retriever. 'He's the only company I need in my life.'

Isla couldn't imagine such a pared-down existence for herself, while envying it too. They had been best friends since Janet whispered her two prompts in the school play and saved Isla from making a complete fool of herself. After that their friendship had never faltered. Their parents had become friends too, and Janet's would take the next-door cottage on the beach for shared summer holidays. Her dad, a choleric-faced lawyer, would take them out in his Wayfarer, teaching them all to sail – and capsize, the best fun. In the evening they often ate together. When the kids went down to the beach in the dark, the parents would sit on one verandah or the other, often wrapped in blankets, watching out for them and chatting.

'You said you wanted to talk about May.'

'Yes, I do. I desperately want to know what motivated her, made her who she became. You're my oldest friend. Maybe you remember something I don't.'

'We were scared of your mum, you know. She could be awfully stern.'

'Were you?' Her image of her parents on holiday was benign. Her father was in his swimming shorts, smoking his pipe, showing them how to cook and eat the shrimps they'd caught. Her mother had a cigarette in hand, a sleeveless white shirt tucked into a skirt gathered at the waist, her hair rolled into a French pleat, sometimes a little headscarf fluttering round it. Perhaps she was a bit more carefully dressed than the other mums, but they weren't married to the MD of Adairs.

At Sandgreen she remembered a more carefree, more loving side to them – towards each other and their three girls. Each year May would insist they all dress up and go to the Cally Pally, the grand hotel in the woods behind the campsite for afternoon tea. They'd be given a table by the window of the huge dining room and she would order scones and cakes till they were stuffed. Other times they'd go to Kirkcudbright where their father would buy them fish 'n' chips – something they were never allowed at home. May's favourite thing was the apple pie from the baker in Gatehouse that she'd eat cold with lumps of Scottish cheddar. In the evenings, the mood became more competitive when David would get out the Monopoly or cards. Isla always tried to avoid getting paired with May who got so cross if she played a bad move.

'She must have learned that intimidating air in Paris.'

Isla put down her glass. 'How do you know she went to Paris? Did I tell you?'

'Didn't they meet there? I'm sure that's what Mum told us. We thought that was so glamorous and romantic. But you should know. Another?' She gathered up their two glasses.

'I always thought they met in Edinburgh. Morag thinks so too. But Lorna told me Dad was in France the year before Mum was there.'

Janet shrugged. 'I don't know.' She got up and poured them another couple of drinks. 'She was elegant though, wasn't she?'

'I suppose so. And of course I've got Aggie to ask.' But would their aunt even remember? Or be prepared to? However unlikely it seemed, Paris had cropped up too many times not to be significant. But if that was the case, why hadn't either of her parents ever mentioned it?

'Look, I found this.' Janet pulled a tartan-covered photo album out of her bag and opened it.

Isla spun it round so they could look at it together. 'Morag got out the old family snaps too. Oh my God. I'd forgotten you had these.' Janet and Bill had come to London for her and Ian's wedding.

'Shame you split up. He was a great guy.' Janet sipped her drink, ice clinking. 'Look at him. Greek god-like.'

'I know, but he was impossible ... I still see him, you know.' She looked again. It was true. He was once impossibly handsome too.

'Isn't that hard, after all this time?'

'Not at all. He's Helen's dad after all, and we've both moved on.'

'Have you?' Janet gave her a look.

'Of course.' She was aware that when she thought of Ian, it was with a special sort of affection very different from her feelings for Tony. 'You know what they say – you never forget your first love.'

'Why are you blushing?' Janet teased.

Isla batted her away like an annoying fly. 'That was years ago. We're friends, that's it. We've had to be for Helen's sake. And I've got Tony now.'

By the time Janet left, it was too late to call Morag to tell her what she had said about their parents' meeting. Instead, Isla made herself and Charlie a hot chocolate and they lay on her double bed and watched a film on her laptop. Charlie had come in just before supper and presented her with a small collection of cornet shells. 'For your collection.' Isla was touched. Now, giddy from too much gin, tingling from the sun on her skin, happy at being back where she once belonged, Isla plumped up the pillows, added some cushions and away they went, only pausing it briefly in the middle to get some biscuits. She went along with Charlie's choice. She'd never heard of *Pitch Perfect* but was soon sucked into the story. She laughed, she cried (almost) and she was amazed to hear Charlie sing every single number in the film, quietly at first then with increasing power until she was belting out the final song.

'You really can sing,' said Isla when the film was over.

Charlie emerged from the bubble that she'd entered once the music had started and looked embarrassed. 'Was I too loud? Did I spoil it? Mum's always telling me to shush when we do this.' She reached for another Hob Nob.

'Not a bit. Is this what you do with Helen?' She liked the idea of the two of them having girly evenings together.

'We used to. But she's like too busy at the mo with Dad being away so much and stuff.'

'She and I did too but we'd be on the sofa, toasting marsh-mallows in the fire.' Those were happy times, just the two of them, no dramas. 'But your singing . . . Are you in a band or a choir or something? You should be.'

'I was in the school choir once, but I didn't like all that religious shit they sang. So now I sing in my bedroom or with my best friend, Alice.' She took another biscuit. 'Shall we watch today's episode of *Love Island* on catch-up?'

'It's nearly midnight,' Isla pointed out, then saw Charlie's face cloud over. 'But we're on holiday, so what the hell? We're not meeting Janet till lunchtime. Switch it on.'

Charlie laughed. 'God, Gran. You're so old-school.'

Within minutes, they had been transported from the Scottish borders to an exotic sun-kissed villa peopled by impossibly beautiful young men and women with perfect bodies and perfect smiles. Charlie gave a running commentary as it went along about who was who and who they had or hadn't been coupled with. Isla found it hard to follow or be really interested but she did her best.

A jab in her arm woke her up.

'When did you go to sleep?' Charlie accused her. 'Did you miss the bit when—'

'I wasn't asleep. I was just resting my eyes. I heard everything that was going on.'

'Yeah, right!'

'Truly.'

Charlie grinned as she got off the bed. 'See you in the morning, then!' Isla was left to sweep the biscuit crumbs off her bed, but feeling once again that a small corner had been turned.

The next morning, she was on the phone to Morag before she was out of bed. 'Janet says her parents told her Mum and Dad met in Paris.' Outside, it was a beautiful day with blue sky, fluffs of cloud, seagulls shrieking over an incoming tide.

'I never knew that.'

'Could they, do you think? I talked to Lorna and she—'

'Why?'

'To tell her Charlie was coming with me. That's all. No, we didn't talk about Braemore – I thought that was better left till we're face-to-face. But she and Aggie found Dad's old passports. He was in France the year before Mum was. Isn't that odd?'

'How long for?'

'She didn't say – were you stamped back in when you came home? I don't know – but apparently that's what Janet's mother told her. They thought having been in Paris was what made Mum so different – as if the Parisian style had rubbed off on her. I can't believe we didn't know.'

'I don't buy that. That was being Mrs Adair, wasn't it? She had to look smart. '

Isla was frustrated by her memories being so patchy. Perhaps that was because she'd left home as soon as she could and never gave her parents a thought until she went home on a duty visit. They had been unhappy when she had applied to drama college in London. But she wasn't one of the stay-at-home tribe, and had been encouraged by Honor, one of her best friends, who had her heart set on independence too. They had set off on their big adventure together and never looked back. May accepted her decision reluctantly, pacified by the knowledge that Honor's grandparents lived in London. Not that they ever saw them. When she did go home, Isla bent over backwards to be the sort of daughter May wanted but however much she tried, it was never quite enough. The barrier between them calcified and became the status quo.

She remembered how protective of Helen she had been when she reached the same age. Protective but ineffective.

Helen had inherited the same strong will and if Isla said no, her daughter just did whatever it was anyway without telling. And it looked like Charlie had inherited it too.

When they met Janet in Gatehouse, she and her dog, Ferdie, were standing by her car in the small car park at the end of the High Street. Beside her were two freezer bags and a picnic basket.

'What are we doing?' asked Isla. 'I would have brought something.'

'You'll see,' said Janet, piling into Betty, not minding the back seat and Jock at all. Ferdie leaped in beside her. 'It's a Magical Mystery Tour. You've brought your swimming things?'

A nod from Isla and a grunt from Charlie.

'Then just follow instructions.'

Even Charlie, who had had to be dragged out of bed to get there on time, brightened up. However, by the time they'd driven out of the town and were heading east she was fast asleep again.

'Meet my exciting travelling companion,' joked Isla, with a nod in Charlie's direction. She caught Janet's eye in the rear-view mirror.

Charlie opened one eye. 'Keep your eyes on the road,' she said. And shut it again.

'Where are we going?' Isla asked. They had driven back through the town, turning off the main road onto a narrow lane, belted Galloway cows and black-faced sheep grazing in the fields behind the drystone walls.

'Wait and see. Somewhere perfect for a day like this.' Indeed it was another day of clear skies and sunshine. They passed a couple of working farms and several modest white-washed houses, holiday homes perhaps, brilliant under the sun. In the far distance the land rose towards the hazy blue hills beyond. As Janet pulled into a passing place to wait until an oncoming tractor had gone by, Charlie woke up.

'Where are we going?' She looked out of the window. No shops. No cafés. She clutched onto her lifeline, her phone, and grabbed her earbuds.

'You'll see.' Janet winked.

Eventually they came to a wood where there was a lay-by with room for a couple of cars. They got out, letting the dogs run ahead into the wood as they gathered up the picnic things. Charlie clutched her backpack close to her. A short walk took them through the close-knit pine trees, illumi-nated by shafts of sunshine, with the sound of running water not far away and the crunch of cones and needles beneath their feet, the smell of pine resin. Isla and Janet carried the picnic, forging ahead together towards the sound. Charlie stomped behind them, staring at the ground, having been given the task of carrying the picnic rug that trailed on the ground behind her. Her feelings about the expedition were perfectly clear.

'If only she'd make more of an effort,' hissed Isla.

'Ach, nonsense. She'll come round.' Janet raised an arm to show the way. 'Just over here.'

And there before them was a clearing in the trees where

a burn flowed over a waterfall into a pool of clear peaty-coloured water. Janet laid out their picnic on a couple of flat rocks by the waterfall, putting their drinks into a plastic bag that she hung into the pool to keep cool. She took the rug from Charlie and spread it in the shade on a bed of pine needles. 'There.'

Charlie and Jock dropped onto it as if it had been put there just for them while Ferdie went off exploring.

'But first . . .' Janet lifted her T-shirt over her head and unzipped her trousers to reveal a red and blue swimsuit. 'Anyone else coming in? It's fabulous, I promise you.'

'Really?' Isla hesitated, but it looked so inviting. 'You'd better be right. Charlie? Coming in?'

'No way.' Her forehead glistened with sweat as she peeled a strand of hair off it.

'Remember our rules? Try it.' Isla changed behind a nearby bush. How good it was to be out of her sticky clothes, feeling the air on her skin. She put her toes in the water. 'Christ!' She withdrew her foot smartish. 'It's icy.'

'Once you're in, it's great.' Janet raised her arm and splashed her.

Isla could hear Charlie laughing behind her. 'Go on, Gran.'

'You can laugh. I don't see you trying to get in. I'll probably have a coronary.' She scooped up a handful of the clear brown water and walked back to her granddaughter, dripping all the way.

'No! Don't.' Charlie shrieked. 'No! My phone!' She was about to stand up and run but Isla was too quick. She opened her almost empty hands and the remaining water splashed onto Charlie's face.

'Okay! Okay! I'll try.' She was laughing as she put her phone in her trusty backpack and took off her shorts. 'I hate you.'

'My work here is done.' Isla ran back to the pool and this time plunged in without waiting to be splashed by Janet again. The initial shock of the cold paralysed her for a moment, as icy needles pricked all over her body. Then, after a minute or two, once she realised she could just touch the bottom, that the current wasn't strong enough to whisk her away, she regained the feeling in her body. Beside her, Janet was floating on her back, so she rolled over to do the same, feeling the sun on her face as she squinted through the branches above her head to the cornflower-coloured sky.

All at once there was a massive splash. Water cascaded over them both. They both upended, gasping for breath, the perfect moment over. She turned to see Charlie, swimming the few strokes between them, a grin splitting her face.

'Gotcha!'

29

Back at Sandgreen, Janet and Charlie took Jock for a walk in the Cally Woods behind the site. Isla decided to return a missed call from Lorna. She quite hoped that her sister might be phoning to cancel their arrangement. If she did, they could stay on longer. And if not at the campsite, Janet would be bound to put them up for a couple of days. Isla wanted to explore more, rediscovering this part of the world that meant so much to her. She hadn't even been into the Murray Arms in Gatehouse where once upon a time she and her sisters would be left sitting on a bench outside, with packets of crisps and blue paper twists of salt and glasses of pop while their parents drank indoors.

Sitting just inside the French windows with the whole beach spread before her gave her a deep-seated feeling of contentment. The sound of the waves, shouts from the beach as boats were hauled across the sand or over a game of rounders in progress, and seagulls flying by – this was so timeless, transporting her back to her childhood. The smell of sausages on a barbecue and the sweet smell of new-mown grass floated on the air. With a glass of lemonade at her side, she got out her phone and readied herself.

'Lorna, it's me, Isla, returning your call.'

'You've taken your time.' Why did she have to be so rude?

'I'm sorry. I've been so busy, and I thought we'd talk when I get to yours.'

'But I'd hoped we'd talk about Braemore before that.'

'There's nothing to say, is there? You two and Aggie own it. I don't.'

'I know that of course. But I need you to talk to Aggie for me.' As had crossed Isla's mind, this is what Lorna had been building up to.

'What about?' As if she didn't know what was coming.

'A developer wants to buy the fields at the back of the house. It's a fantastic deal and it means Aggie can stay where she is for the time being.'

'Where did the deal come from? Who told him the paddocks might be up for sale?' Morag must have been right.

'I met him and happened to mention it. He was immediately interested. Keeps on getting in touch with me.'

'I bet he does.'

'Meaning?' She was on the back foot now.

'You know perfectly well. But Aggie would be living in a building site. I'm sure that's not what Mum would have wanted.'

'She thinks it might be a good idea but she's undecided. We've talked about it a lot.'

'A good idea for who? You? Anyway, why tell me? It's got nothing to do with me anymore.'

'I thought you might tip the balance for me. Once she says yes, Morag will have to.'

'What?' Isla could barely believe what she'd just heard. Her sister had no shame.

'It's just . . .'

'I know what it is, but I don't understand why. Why are you so keen to sell now? Can't you wait?'

'No. No I can't.' She sounded angry and upset. 'I knew you'd side with—'

Isla broke in. 'Before one of us says something we regret, let's row back a bit. We were all upset last time, perhaps me most of all, and we all said things that would have been better left unsaid.' She gathered all her powers of diplomacy. 'We should be patching things up now, not making things worse. So . . .' She paused so they could rewind and start again. 'We're looking forward to being with you at three-ish tomorrow. Is that okay?'

'You're right of course.' That was the closest Lorna would ever come to an apology. 'Yes, I'm looking forward to seeing you.' She paused. 'Really, I am.'

'Can we talk about Mum, too?' All that childhood hurt from never being the favoured one rolled back towards her. She wrapped her free arm round her middle as if it would protect her.

'I'll have a think. And I want to hear all about this guy you've met.' She was sounding more like the sister Isla wanted now.

'How do you know about him?' She was sure she hadn't mentioned Tony to her.

'Ian told me. He's still got a soft spot for you, you know.'

If there was a soft spot anywhere, it was the one Lorna held for Ian.

'Don't even go there.' Isla laughed. 'When did you talk to him?'

'He phoned.'

Isla's hackles quivered. 'Why?'

'To see if he could stay before Aggie's party, so he's arriving tomorrow too.'

'Oh God! I asked him not to.' She heard herself sounding like a spoiled child. 'What's wrong with an Airbnb?'

'I suggested it. I thought it might be fun.'

Fun!

Isla could hear Lorna was aware she had done something her sister wouldn't like. 'I know you're still friends ...' She had always found it something of a mystery that Ian had kept in touch with Lorna. 'And that's great.' No, it wasn't. 'But he and I aren't part of that.'

'I thought it would be like old times.' A pleading note entered her voice.

No, she didn't. She was simply stirring the pot. Nothing had changed.

'Except we're not married anymore. So it won't be.'

When she ended the call, Isla sat with the phone in her lap, pondering. What was Ian playing at? He may have remained friends with her family – irritating in itself – but he had no right to insinuate himself into her holiday at the last minute. Did he do that to his other wives? On the spur of the moment, she called him.

'Isla . . . to what do I owe the honour? Are you all right?'

She could tell he knew he'd done something wrong. She tried to rein in her irritation. 'Lorna says you're coming to stay tomorrow.'

'Yes, last-minute plan. Morag told me you and Charlie were going to be there and I thought it would be a good place to stay for Aggie's birthday.'

'But I said, don't come. I thought you'd stay in an Airbnb and turn up for the party. Full stop.' Now she sounded peevish. 'Do you do this with all your ex-wives? Especially when you know Lorna and I have got stuff to work out between us.'

'Of course I don't. I don't get on with them. And I have enough of Airbnb's when I'm on tour. And . . .' He took a breath. 'Maybe I can help bridge the breach for you.'

'Bridge the breach? What are you even talking about?!'

They started laughing. Their shared sense of the ridiculous had nudged them through the best of times and the worst of times. Maybe it would be a good thing to have him there smoothing the way. At best he might make things easier between her and Lorna and, at worst, she'd have him to lean on, and it would be nice for him and Charlie to hang out too.

'Where are you, anyway?'

'Sandgreen.'

'Ah, beauteous spot of childhood hols. Memory heaven. See – my presence will only make things better.'

'Idiot!' She dismissed him, giving up the fight. Whatever she said wouldn't make the slightest bit of difference.

Before calling Tony, she took a deep breath of sea air and walked outside the cottage, stretching her arms out to the side, enjoying the warmth of the sun on her face as she looked to the sky. This really was God's own country – in this weather, nowhere was more beautiful. You could take your French Alps, your Cornish Riviera, your Welsh mountains – but for her, nothing beat this sort of balm to the soul. Returning to her seat, she made her final call. She had no second thoughts about helping Tony and letting him organise the details. In doing so, she may have helped herself. They were in this together.

When he picked up, she could hear voices in the background and pictured him in her kitchen, Roberts radio on the side, windows open to the garden. At the far end, her vegetable patch was planted out and would soon be coming into its own. She hoped he hadn't forgotten to mow the grass.

'Where are you?' He sounded agitated, as if he was too busy to speak for long.

She described the view to him, at the same time realising that she was glad to be alone here. He wouldn't have appreciated how much it meant to her. 'How're things at home?'

'Nothing much to report.' Surely he could do better than that. He knew how much her home meant to her.

There was a bang in the background, and a voice. 'Where's the screwdriver?'

'Who's that? Have you got people there?'

'Just a mate. It's a different surprise. They'll be gone soon.'

There was another bang in the background. 'Keep the noise down,' he yelled.

His laugh made her happy, as did the knowledge her support was giving him renewed confidence and the chance to do something that he believed in. And that she believed in too. Although she was uneasy about the sort of surprise he might be preparing that involved noise and a screwdriver. 'What are they doing?'

'Wait and see.'

'Are you missing me?'

'Of course. But we're managing.' She told him about their day and how Charlie was coming out of her shell at last. She didn't add that his departure had made things much easier.

'You don't think the worse of me?' The anxiety that her confession might have changed his opinion of her still nagged away at her.

'You poor thing. Of course not.'

She heard her doorbell in the background.

'I'd better get that.'

'Who is it?' He hadn't introduced her to any of his friends since they had been together.

'A friend come to help. Must go.' And he cut her off.

Isla held out her phone, staring at it. *What the hell?* She immediately redialled. But her call went straight through to voicemail.

'What are you up to?' she said out loud. But what was the point? A gentle ripple of unease ran through her. Surprises made her nervous. Telling herself not to be stupid, she went outside again. Making the most of the short time she had left alone, she reclined the old-fashioned stripy deckchair as far as it would go, lay back and closed her eyes. Why was she so protective of her own home? The answer was not hard to find. She had waited a long time before having somewhere all to herself and, since she had moved to Oxford and begun curating Fernleith Museum, she had entered a new phase of her life that she had come to treasure. She had her dream job, her ideal home. And in Tony, perhaps she had found her perfect partner. But, but, but . . . Something still stopped her. She wished he had made more effort with Charlie. A prerequisite of loving her had to be loving her granddaughter, however difficult that might be at times.

That night, she and Charlie sat at the table playing rummy. The night air was balmy and a slice of moon hung above the glittering sea. In the campsite, lights were on in most of the cabins and caravans, or on the tables outside. Someone nearby had a radio on. Cooking smells carried across the park. Shouts and laughter came from a bunch of people having a barbecue on the beach. Isla had lost two games to Charlie and was in danger of losing a third, yet again picking up a card that failed to improve her hand, when Charlie interrupted their concentration.

'Gran.' She paused as if she was about to say something important.

'Mmm,' Isla looked up from her hand. The last few days had been enough to change Charlie's appearance. Gone was the unhappy peaky child Isla had brought from London. In front of her was a lightly tanned, more relaxed teenager who even looked as if she might be enjoying herself.

'I really like it here.'

'Me too. So many memories.'

'You're lucky you had Morag and Lorna here.'

'Is that the only child speaking?' she teased.

Charlie smiled. 'I was only thinking . . .'

'It wasn't always that great, believe you me. Lorna once pushed me off the diving board when the tide was going out, and I broke my ankle. I spent the rest of the holiday in plaster, watching everyone playing on the beach. And once Morag and I climbed that rock.' She pointed down the beach towards a rock that stuck up out of the crowd. 'It doesn't look much now, but at the time it seemed huge. I don't know how we got to the top but once we were up, we couldn't get down and the tide was coming in. I told Morag we were going to drown and she believed me. Mum and Dad were furious having to come and rescue us in the middle of a game of cards, and then barred me from the beach for a day because I'd scared Morag so much.'

Charlie listened entranced as Isla told her more. After a while, she sat back in her chair, cards face down on the table. 'All the same, I still wish I'd had a brother or sister.'

Isla had often wondered how Helen and Mike, with such busy schedules, would have managed another child, but nature had made the decision for them. After years of trying for a second, Helen had been distraught, despairing. Isla often wondered if that was why she channelled so much of herself into her work, when she could have given more to Charlie – a constant reminder of what she couldn't repeat. Grief and resentment made unhappy bedfellows.

'But you're a very special only one.'

'I'm in the way.'

Isla was appalled. 'You must never think that. Your mum and dad adore you.'

'If they did, I wouldn't be here with you.' She shrugged, as if she was used to it.

'It's just unfortunate that their schedules clashed this time, that's all. But you've got me and you've got friends.'

'They don't like me either.' She pulled out her phone and held it in the air as proof.

'That's not true.'

'My streaks have been broken, and my so-called best friend Alice has ghosted me. She's stopped replying,' she explained. 'They don't mind that I'm not there. They don't miss me.'

Even fifty years on, Isla could remember the agonies that went with the highs and lows of friendship, what it was like to be part of a gang one moment, then ostracised the next.

'Often people are too busy living in the present and just don't think,' she said. 'As soon as you go back, you'll pal up again.'

'I don't think so. They're bitches.'

'Charlie!'

'They are. They were only my friends because they thought I could get them stuff.'

'What stuff? I'm sure that's not true.'

'You know that party?' She put her cards face down on the table to pick at a cuticle until a bead of blood appeared at the base of her nail.

'Don't do that,' Isla said, made aware from the glare she received that she was sounding like Helen again. 'Which one?'

'I didn't tell the truth.'

Isla sat quite still, unsure what to say. She put her cards face down on the table, stared out to sea so she didn't catch Charlie's eye and waited to see what would come next.

'I did take some weed to that party. I wasn't the only one.' Her sniff alerted Isla to her crying. She found a tissue in her pocket and passed it over. 'I wanted to impress two girls in the year above. And I did, or I would have if Clara's mum hadn't come in. You're not angry, are you?' She glanced up and then looked away as she blew her nose.

Anger didn't seem the right reaction. 'Not at all.' Anger, if there was any, was for Helen to have, although Isla was shocked and puzzled. 'But where did you get it?'

'That's easy. A couple of girls who left last year meet us in the park after school and bring us what we want.' The scrappy area round the corner from the school that was used by dog walkers, drug-dealers and desperate mothers – Isla remembered Helen once pointing it out to her. Charlie's face closed up as if she realised she had said too much. 'You won't say anything, will you?'

'Why are you telling me now?'

'Because I don't want you to think I'm a liar.' Her voice was so soft Isla could hardly hear her.

'But I didn't think you were before.' Helen would go ballistic if she found out. She had defended Charlie to everyone and anyone who would listen, confident that her daughter would never break the rules, be one of *those* girls. By telling Isla, Charlie had presented her with a dilemma – should she tell Helen or keep Charlie's secret? Her loyalties were to both of them. Charlie had opened up to her at last and that was important. Isla wanted to keep her trust, becoming someone she could turn to: the sort of person Aggie had been for her. At the same time, Helen's trust was so important too. Because Isla had brought her up on her own, with Ian's interference, their relationship was particularly strong and precious. But perhaps there was a way she could be useful to them both without damaging anything – she just had to find it.

'Yes, you did. About Tony.' Charlie interrupted her musing.

'Don't be daft. I asked him about that. You misunderstood. That's quite different.' What Charlie was telling her was far more important.

'Maybe.' But she didn't sound convinced.

'I'm not going to discuss it again. More important is what I'm going to do about you.'

'You won't tell?' She sounded alarmed.

'I don't know . . .' Isla saw Charlie gripping the edge of her seat so the whites of her knuckles showed. 'So when you get back home, are you going to get into it again?'

'Maybe.' She shifted in her seat, avoiding Isla's eye.

'Why don't you leave it until you're older?' Oh God! Was that the wrong thing to say? 'When your exams are over. When you've left home.' No, she was encouraging her not putting her off.

Charlie picked up her cards. 'Whatever. But you mustn't tell Mum.'

'Charlie, how can I not say something? Unless you tell her.' She looked horrified. 'I couldn't. She'd go mental. I shouldn't have told you.' She threw her cards across the room.

Isla stood up. 'She'll go mental if she finds out you told me and I kept it to myself.' Or perhaps she would be glad if Isla tried to help Charlie. After all, their relationship would continue beyond these couple of weeks and perhaps she could be more constructive when they got home. This was a result they hadn't foreseen. 'Telling the truth can be a good thing.'

'Not this time.' Charlie went outside.

Isla followed her. 'We'll work this out. I promise. You want me to trust you. Well, that cuts both ways, and I prom-ise I won't do anything without telling you first.'

Charlie turned to face her. 'Promise?'

'I promise.' Exactly how easy was that promise going to be to keep? Why could children make one's life so bloody difficult?

30

Paris, 1955

'Are you serious?' Wendy's eyes were wide with disbelief. 'A baby. A father who's been abandoned. You'll be working all hours. We'll never see you.' She twirled in front of the shop mirror, considering the spotted blue jacket she was thinking about buying. 'Do you really think this suits me?'

'Yes, it does.' May wondered whether Wendy ever thought about anything deeply. 'I'm just going to help him out until he decides what to do. And you will see me. I'm only going to be there while Emile's at school.'

'But you'll be exhausted.' She put her hand on her hip and pouted towards the mirror. Sometimes the way she skittered over the surface of important things could be quite irritating. 'I'm not sure about the colour. I think I'll leave it.'

However, Wendy's prediction was spot on. Within a week of beginning work with David, May had found out just how demanding a baby could be and she was on her knees. Where David lived was very different from the

Dubois' apartment. Instead of the faded but elegant grandeur where neatness was paramount and nothing was out of place, his was a cosy bohemian flat in a tall, dilapidated building in a little cobbled side street just off Saint Germain. On the ground floor was a pâtisserie that sent the smell of baking up into the apartment at all hours, driving May to distraction. The apartment itself was chaotic. Chairs were covered with baby clothes, books lay everywhere, the washing up was barely done. Céleste's clothes trailed out of the wardrobe, and May found bits and pieces of her make-up left in the bathroom cupboard. There was one painting of three angels that hung at the end of the bed, draped with David's ties and a scarf that must be Céleste's. Sometimes she sat on the bed staring at it, lost in appreciation of the limited palette of blues and greys, wondering how they owned such a beautiful thing.

She did her best to organise things so David could run his life more smoothly, sorting out Eloise's room so everything was in its place, finding a laundry where things could be washed on a regular basis. Looking after Eloise meant that she barely had time to sit down, never mind eat. If she wasn't attending to her immediate needs, she was washing baby clothes and nappies, ironing, sterilising bottles and making up feeds. It was non-stop.

But it was worth it. Every gummy smile had her beaming back at Eloise. Holding her, rocking her, soothing her, feeding her gave her greater fulfilment than she would have ever imagined possible. But Eloise was also a constant reminder of what she had lost, often making her wonder whether Max was making plans for his own family with June. As far as May was concerned, however much she might yearn for it, that side of her life was over. Connecting with someone else in the same way she had with Max seemed unimaginable. Instead she would make the most of what she had and, at the moment, that was this adorable baby.

Sometimes, just before she left to collect Emile, she would stay to have a baguette and cheese for late lunch with David. They would swap Eloise between them, taking it in turns to hold her as she screwed up her face and wailed inconsolably or charmed them with her gurgles and smiles.

As Christmas overtook the city, she found herself looking for little gifts for Eloise, certain the child's mother wouldn't. They hadn't heard from her once. A little pair of bootees. A rattle. A tiny knitted hat. She even bought David a pair of gloves. Was that too presumptuous? No, he would think it entertaining.

May found herself enjoying being with David more and more. What had started as a working relationship and friendship became something much more precious as they began to confide in each other. He was the first person she had met in some time whom she felt she could trust. They had so much in common. They were Scottish, they had both fallen in love with the wrong person; they had both been badly hurt; they loved French food; they admired the Impressionists and loved wandering the streets of Paris. And of course they both adored Eloise. But there were differences too. David thought the Eiffel Tower was a monstrosity. She liked washing in hot water.

One day, David was describing how much Céleste hated being pregnant and how sad that had made him. 'All I wanted was for us to be a family. Her, me and the baby. I would have done anything to make her happy. But I couldn't change her mind.'

'But having an abortion might not have made her happy either. I should know.' And suddenly she found herself telling him why.

David didn't bat an eyelid but listened, intent on her story, reaching out to put his hand on hers. The first time he had touched her.

'I'm so sorry.'

Leaving her hand in his, she felt tears on her cheeks. 'Thank you.' He didn't think the worst of her.

While she had gone through her ordeal, she had never dreamed of talking to anyone about it. It was a matter of shame, sadness and regret that she didn't want to share. All three emotions had stayed with her, digging in their claws. Madame had helped with her recovery but they never spoke about Max again or what the loss of the baby really meant to her. Madame offered practical help and a respect for her privacy: no more. After all they were employer and employee, not dear friends. Wendy, her closest friend, had expected her to bounce back from the abortion as if nothing had happened. That's what *she* would do. She wouldn't allow anything to spoil her time in the city.

May tried to explain to her. 'But I feel so confused. Although I couldn't have done anything else, I can't stop myself feeling sad.'

'Really? Still?' Wendy didn't understand. 'But you'll get over that. You must come to the little club that Sam and I found round the back of the Sorbonne. The drinks are deliciously cheap. He says ...' And she'd be off, prattling about Sam, with zero interest in how May's body was full of yearning for something lost. Or she would gossip about what the other girls were up to or what they might do themselves. For her, life had to be one long round of uninterrupted enjoyment.

Which was why May was hardly surprised when Wendy broke the news that she was going back to America with Sam. 'There's nothing for me back home in England but Boston, Massachusetts ... that's different. It's a land of opportunity. That's what they say.' Her eyes shone, her curls bounced. 'Just imagine, our children will have American accents!'

'But it's so far away,' was May's feeble objection.

'Exactly. But it's new and exciting and Sam's family are longing to meet me.' She held out her left hand so May could see the amethyst solitaire that sparkled on her finger.

May grabbed it. 'You're engaged! This is gorgeous.'

'Sam chose it himself. He said the colour went with my eyes! We'll be married in Massachusetts.' She looked wistful. 'How I wish you could be there. You could help me with my dress and be my matron of honour.'

Neither of them spoke as they thought of what might have been.

Then Wendy brightened. 'But I'll send you photos.'

Her excitement was infectious, and May suppressed her thoughts of how life could have been for her and Max, if only they had both been braver. But she couldn't help envying Wendy's situation. Marriage seemed such a secure and enviable alternative to facing the world alone.

In David, May had found a soulmate, someone with whom she could share anything that was on her mind. He was a wonderful listener, kind and considerate, and, in return, she listened to him. She was intrigued by the sound of his family. There was just him and his brother Donald. She knew their department store. She remembered as a child being mesmerised by how money was sent shooting round the store in tubes suspended between counter and cashier. Favourite was the haberdashery counter where she had bought ribbons and buttons. Their shared background helped them understand each other so well. And of course they had Eloise in common now. Despite her frustrations in trying to get the angry little bundle to sleep or to stop crying, May felt she had been given a purpose at last. Just when she was on the point of giving everything up and going home, she had been given a second chance.

Céleste had abandoned her little family completely. David hadn't heard from her for weeks. At least May could give Eloise some love that, if not motherly, was the next best thing. Poor little scrap.

Constantly rocking her in her arms, burping her on her shoulder, changing her nappies were chores made bearable by those blue eyes that gazed up at her, trusting, reliant. May's ambitions to go to London and find herself work as a translator faded away altogether as she devoted herself to the welfare of two beings who needed her most.

31

Edinburgh, 2019

Lorna had lost weight since they were last together. She looked anxious, brittle, her smile barely reaching her eyes as Isla hugged her, shocked to finding herself embracing a bag of bones. Lorna's resistance was barbed with tension.

'Oh Jock! I forgot he was coming too.' Lorna pulled away as he came up, tail wagging, to say hello. He looked up, expectant, but she ignored him.

'He comes almost everywhere with me. You know that.' Isla tickled his grizzled muzzle.

'I'd forgotten. Could he sleep in the garage?'

'Of course not. When I'm away, he sleeps where I sleep, or where Charlie does.'

'I don't like animals in the house, but if he must.' Lorna looked as though she was waiting for Isla to back down.

However, she didn't. Some things were sacrosanct.

As they followed her into the house, Andrew emerged from the living room to meet them in the hall. His welcome was warmer than his wife's, although Isla suspected that might be down to the amount of alcohol he had clearly taken on board at lunchtime, judging by the smell of it on his breath. His complexion was redder than ever, his nose more swollen, his eyes sunk into the flesh of his face. His belly prevented them getting close enough to kiss hello.

'Isla! Too long! And you must be Charlie. Last saw you when you were yay high.' As he put a hand out to show her, he staggered forward a couple of steps.

Lorna reached out to steady him. 'Why don't you have a nap this afternoon?' she suggested through teeth so gritted, Isla could almost hear them grinding together.

'A nap?' he roared. 'Don't be ridiculous, woman. I'm just doing up my flies ready for tomorrow.' He looked around at them through glassy eyes, a smile hovering on his lips. 'Fishing competition,' he explained to Isla, then started laughing.

Lorna's eyes were closed as if she'd heard the joke a thousand times. Charlie's were wide open with astonishment as Andrew grasped the end of the banisters for support before tucking in his paisley cravat with his free hand. Some of his lunch had stained the front of his shirt. He picked at it ineffectually then lurched back through the door he had entered from, leaving the three women speechless.

'See what I have to put up with?' said Lorna sharply, but Isla didn't miss the sadness there too. The grandfather clock in the corner whirred before striking three. 'Tea, I think. Let's go in the kitchen.'

The kitchen, like the rest of the house was a testament

to organisation and control. Everything was in its place. Not an overlooked crumb, not a stray wooden spoon, piece of cutlery, open tin or even the day's post messed up the pristine quartz surfaces, so clean a surgeon could operate on them without qualm. On the walls, painted a soft relaxing green, open shelves held ordered piles of white plates of different shapes and sizes, jars arranged in order of ascending height, and a bookshelf laden with the latest cookery books arranged by colour. Charlie and Isla perched on the bar stools tucked into the central island while Lorna started filling the kettle and getting what she needed from the shelves. Every move she made showed Isla how tense and unhappy she was.

What had happened to her? As the baby of the family, she had been more sunny than difficult, more loved than not. Now, she seemed like the loneliest of souls rattling around this house having lost Andrew to the bottle and her children to their own lives. 'Are you okay?'

She spun round from the kettle. 'What do you mean? Of course.' She tucked her pink T-shirt into the waistband of her jeans.

'You seem a bit jumpy.'

'I just get scratchy when he drinks too much in the day.'

Of course. Appearances mattered, and nothing would prompt an admission that things were anything other than they should be. But Isla could tell there was something else her sister wasn't saying. She tried another tack. 'How are the kids?'

'They're good. At least as far as I can tell on WhatsApp. I didn't think Canada would suit Jamie but that logging company's just promoted him, and Lesley and the kids seem to be enjoying themselves there.' Her eyes had lit up at mention of her family. 'And Beth's got her hands full with the business but it's doing so well. Who knew that making bespoke pyjamas would become such a thing? Tea, Charlie?' She seemed to deflate in front of Isla's eyes.

'Yes, please.'

'Shall we go into town afterwards?' Isla suggested. 'I thought we could get our nails done. For Aggie's party.' Doing something together might cheer up Lorna.

Charlie turned her palms upwards, bending her fingers to examine her nails. 'Really?' This was the first time she had sounded positive about anything Isla had said since the previous day. An uneasy truce had existed between them as Isla digested Charlie's confession and Charlie regretted making it.

'Yep. Do you want to come, Lorna? It'd be fun.' She deliberately repeated Lorna's word from their last conversation. She was also aware of wanting to butter up her sister so they could talk openly.

'I had mine done just the other day. I'll tell you where to go, though.' She drummed her perfect peachy nails on the counter. 'And I've supper to get ready. Ian should be here soon.'

All the more reason for them to get out of the house. And while they were out, Isla would think of the right way to approach Lorna about what lay behind her desperation to sell the paddocks.

By the time they got to the nail bar in Morningside, it was five o'clock. As soon as they got in there, Charlie's phone was put on charge, her face relaxed and she was busy catching up with whatever she had missed. Not that it seemed to improve her general mood much.

'So, what colour?' Isla passed her a swatch of coloured nails.

Charlie brightened as she flicked through them, stopping at an edgy deep green. 'This one, *Things I've Seen in Abergreen.* You should try this one. *Purple with a Purpose.* It'd go with your skirt. Or *Do You Have This Colour in Stockholm*?' She pointed out an icy blue–violet.

'Who thinks up these names? I love them but the colours are a bit much for me.' Isla flicked back towards the safety of neutrals.

'Noo! They'd look great on you. Those are sooo boring.' Charlie took the swatches back again.

She was right. They were.

'Look, what about this. *Significant Other Colour.*' She picked a shimmery pink lilac. 'Different but a kind of a statement. Go on. Dare to be different.'

Isla balanced the nail shape on hers, turning her hand this way and that. What the hell? 'Okay. I'll go with this.' The colour was nothing like any she had worn before and didn't go with her red shirt but Charlie's triumphant smile made that worthwhile.

As the nail technicians got to work, Charlie had to

put down her phone. 'I've had a message from Alice.' She sounded pleased.

'Good.' Isla kept her eyes closed. 'All good?'

'Her mother confiscated her phone for two days because . . . Imagine.' She was outraged, but Isla could imagine only too well. And sympathised.

'So you weren't ghosted at all?' And apparently not bullied either.

'No. Shame about the streaks though. We'll just have to start again. Look.'

Isla opened her eyes to see Charlie taking a photo of her nails. 'Before and after,' she said with a grin. Isla smiled back. She was resigned to her granddaughter's changeable moods. She was even beginning to rather like them.

The outing was a success. Isla was pleased with her nails, despite noticing Lorna's raised eyebrow when she saw the colour. She just had time to take Jock into the wooded public park not far from the house. Charlie came too. They walked through the woods by the Braid Burn, sun filtering through the trees and across the path, until they reached the gothic eighteenth-century house at its heart before turning back. Now the heat of the day was waning, runners were out, other dog walkers too. Jock trotted along, sniffing and wagging, happy to be out and about. Isla began to look forward to the gin and tonic Andrew would make as soon as they got back.

'So! The wanderers return.' Ian's voice was the first thing to greet them as they walked through the door. 'Hello, my darlings.' He came into the hall with Lorna at his heel, looking more cheerful than she had done since they arrived. 'Come here, my favourite granddaughter.' He swept Charlie into a bear hug.

'Your only granddaughter,' she pointed out as she wriggled free.

'And all the better for that.' He released her and turned to Isla, putting his hands on her shoulders and kissing each cheek.

'I did say don't come.' But his ease was a welcome alternative to the others' tension. 'Sorry. It's nice to see you again.'

'Ah well, things change.' He winked at Charlie. 'And I did say I wouldn't miss Aggie's eighty-fifth. Of course I'm here.'

'Anyone for a drink?' Andrew shambled out of the living room. 'Sun's definitely over the yardarm.'

'I'll take a G 'n' T into the kitchen to help Lorna,' said Isla, who could see her sister was heading in that direction.

'No sooner said than done. I'll bring it to you. Ian? Charlie?'

The two women were left alone in the kitchen. Lorna had three cookery books out on the counter with all the ingredients for each recipe on plates or in pots arranged around each one. 'Could you?' she asked, pointing out the dessert. 'It's only a question of grating a bit of chocolate and whipping some cream while I mix all this together for the fish curry.'

'Fancy,' said Isla, pulling out a bar stool and getting to grips with the recipe.

'I try.' Lorna smiled at her as Andrew came in with their

drinks. As he put Isla's down he tripped, spilling the drink over the cookery book.

'For Christ's sake, Andrew!' Lorna's mood changed. 'Can't you do anything right?'

'Jesus, woman! It's only a book. I can make another drink.' He shuffled towards the door.

'That's about all you can do,' she muttered under her breath, but the way he hunched his shoulders as if he'd been hit showed he had heard.

'What the hell's going on? He didn't deserve that.'

Lorna's knife clattered against a bowl. 'He did! He deserves it all. His drinking's gone from bad to impossible since he took early "enforced" retirement. *He's* impossible. I can't even bear being in the same room with him anymore.'

Isla had never heard Lorna say a bad word about Andrew before, however provoked. 'Can't you do something about it?' The possibilities ran through her head. AA. Counselling. Rehab.

'Why do you think I've been trying to get Morag and Aggie to agree to sell the land?' Her face was white.

'I've no idea. What do you mean?' To Isla's concern, Lorna brushed away a tear. Crying was not something she did.

'I didn't want anyone to know. I need the money so that I can leave him.'

'You're leaving Andrew?!' Isla was astonished. This was a bold or desperate step.

'As soon as I can afford to.' A look of desperation crossed her face.

'But you're entitled to half his money. Surely you don't need more.'

'Yes I do.' She almost screamed the words in the frustration of not being understood. 'He may seem the most convivial man in the world, but he's tight as hell. I have everything I want but I have to account for every penny. If he knew I was planning anything, he'd make it impossible. I've got to have my own funds, just to get going.'

'Jesus, Lorna. Why didn't you say? I'd have lent you the money.' Except now she'd invested it with Don and Tony.

'Because I feel a failure. I didn't want the two of you lording it over me.'

'A failure? Look at me – the woman with more failed relationships under my belt than hot dinners. And an ex-husband. I can't talk. If you'd said something, we wouldn't have fallen out. We could have tried to work something out together.'

'We'd probably have fallen out about something else.'

'Maybe.' There was a grain of truth in that. 'But now you've told me, what are we going to do?'

'I need you to persuade Aggie.'

'I can't. Morag will kill me. Besides, even though I've no interest in the place anymore, I think it's the wrong thing to do.'

'I can't stand living like this any longer. Please. I'm begging you.' Lorna's eyes met Isla's. First one then another tear rolled down her cheek. 'You must understand. You're divorced and it was the right decision for you. Wasn't it?'

Isla had never seen her sister like this. Normally Lorna was completely in control.

'This is a bit different. Ian was having affairs, and we were younger. At the beginning it was hard but for Helen's sake, I had to make it work. And he left me, remember?' That said, she couldn't imagine her life without him in it somewhere. 'But it's worked out in the end.'

Lorna leaned forward so her elbows were on the work surface, her head on her hands. 'I'm scared.' She looked around at the house. 'Where will I end up? My life's going to change out of all recognition.'

'But not necessarily for the worse. Look at me. I love living on my own.' Except she did feel lonely sometimes, she did miss the companionship and touch of someone else. She wasn't like Janet who had become entirely self-sufficient, and that's why she had let Tony in.

'I don't want all my friends talking about us and speculating.'

'They're probably doing that anyway if today's anything to go by. You're both obviously unhappy.'

'Think about Mum and Dad. They weren't really happy in the end. I wonder if they ever had been. But they stuck together – till death did them part.'

'But look what it did. She became so angry. Times have changed, and people are more understanding, less judge-mental now.'

'You still have to be able to support yourself. If only I'd had a career instead of being a housewife.' She sighed. 'Although I've been good at that.'

'Need a hand?' Ian stuck his head round the door.

'We're talking about marriage.' Isla thought that might be enough to drive him away. That and the desperation on Lorna's face.

'Ah. I'm something of an expert at that.' He came in, brandishing his drink.

'But not necessarily in the best way,' she said. 'I'm not sure we need your advice.'

'We were talking about Mum and Dad's,' said Lorna, presumably nervous Isla would give something away.

'Ah. A Paris romance has much to answer for.' Another theatrical gesture with an arm flung out to the side.

'What do you mean?' Isla was puzzled.

'That's where they met, isn't it?'

'Is it?'

'I'm sure that's what she once told me.'

'That's what Janet said. But you never said anything to me.'

'You and I were barely speaking then, and we rarely saw each other. Besides she asked me not to.'

'Why? What else did she say?' Isla's hunger for information made her push Lorna's problem to one side. Why hadn't she thought of asking Ian? Although May had liked him, Isla hadn't imagined them exchanging confidences.

'Nothing much. Why? Is it important?'

'It might be. You know I'm trying to find out more about her.'

'As far as I can remember, David gave her a look and she clammed up straight away. I remember feeling there was something more she wanted to say but when I asked her again, she just said she'd been a nanny and had met David while she was there. "Nothing more interesting than that," she said.'

'Did she tell you when they got married?' Isla sensed she was inching towards something.

'She did indeed. She was sure her parents wouldn't approve so they tied the knot in Gretna on their way back home. Dead romantic, no?'

'Can't imagine it, but yes, I suppose so.' Although the notion of her parents being young and in love didn't tally with the resigned and often loveless couple she had known. But it was another piece in the jigsaw.

'Why did she tell you and not us?' Lorna was looking interested.

'I must have been up doing a show. God knows what it was.' He looked thoughtful for a moment. 'But it's the old charm offensive. Always works.'

Isla raised her eyebrows to show what she thought of that. But why would May have asked him not to mention that she and David met in Paris? Why did where they met matter so much? And why had they told their children that they met in Edinburgh? Both versions couldn't be true.

'Aggie must know the whole story,' he added. 'If you're so keen to know, why don't you ask her?'

'That's just what I'm going to do.'

32

Paris, 1955

May had imagined that David would make a decision about his future far sooner than he did. Instead the three of them forged their own routine that seemed to satisfy each of their needs. When May arrived in the morning, having dropped Emile at school, David handed Eloise over and dashed off to work. Somehow he had persuaded his compassionate employers to retain him part-time, perhaps because they both knew it wouldn't be forever. Madame had taken to picking up Emile from school, so May was able to stay on until a little later.

Airmail letters arrived regularly from Wendy, written in a hard-to-read scrawl on tissue-thin airmail paper. She was busy getting to know her new family and arranging her wedding.

We're marrying in the sweetest wooden church and the reception will be at his parents' place. I so wish you could see my dress - his mother's sewn it up for me. If only you could be here ...

She never mentioned Max, never said if she had seen him or if he was invited. But he and Sam had been such good friends, it was hard to imagine he would not be there. With June, his girlfriend. May couldn't help wondering whether Max ever thought of her in the way she still thought of him as she lay in her bed at the Dubois', imagining his hands on her, feeling the intensity of his kisses, yearning to return them. Or had he been able to forget her? Despite knowing she would never see him again, she couldn't shake off the memories.

And then David dropped his own bombshell. One morning, he returned from work, left his briefcase at the door of his bedroom that doubled as his office and came into the kitchen where May was putting out carrot soup, a baguette and some smelly blue cheese she had bought in the street market onto the scarred wooden table. 'I've made a decision at last.'

She looked up. 'About?'

'I've been in touch with my father who says there's still a place for me at Adairs if I want it. My brother's cockahoop that he might not have to work there after all.'

Him too?! Fathers and their sons. He was going to leave her, taking Eloise with him. Her hand rose to her chest as her heart constricted. She could not credit history repeating itself, ensuring she lost two more people who had become so dear to her. 'But what about your job here?'

That was the question she asked but others were shrieking in her head. *What about Eloise? What about me?*

'The job was never going to work out once Eloise came along and Céleste left. They've been generous given my circumstances, but I can't take advantage of them for any longer. Besides, their patience is running out. I need to go home. I can't bring up Eloise alone here. At home I'll be able to get the right sort of help . . . And what will happen to you when you go home, as I know you will?' He took her hand. 'Please don't look so sad.'

The prospect of starting all over again was devastating, even though she knew how selfish she was being. He was doing what he believed was the best thing for his daughter, making sure that she was brought up to have a life. Of course he had Eloise's best interests at heart.

But what would she do? She would have to leave Paris now, but the thought of home . . . she wouldn't think of it. She sat down and ran her finger round the stain a saucer had left.

'I don't know. I'm going to miss you both so much.' Her throat tightened.

He closed his fingers round hers again as he sat too. 'That's what I was hoping you'd say. You see, I'd like you to come back with us.'

'What do you mean?' He knew going back to Scotland would only ever be a stopgap for her before she headed south to London and the unknown. An unknown she didn't have the confidence to face alone now. She had come bravely to Paris but she didn't trust herself anymore.

He smiled. 'Yes, that's what I said. I'd like you to go back with me . . . but as my wife.'

'Your wife?' May looked at him, dumbfounded. This was the last thing she had expected. By coming to Paris she'd thrown her cards and her future into the air but this . . . Her relationship with David had developed into a special friendship but the passion she had experienced with Max had been notably absent, and she had been glad of that. She hadn't been ready to replace him. No. David was her good friend whom she was pleased to help. No more than that. Or at least that's what she had thought until then.

'Please.' He got on one knee and took both her hands. 'We make a good pair and Eloise adores you. You complete us.'

She felt her cheeks burning as she looked down at him. 'Get up, please,' she said. 'You don't need to do this.'

What was she thinking? What was he? Was this a love-match for him or a marriage of convenience? She hoped the former but was scared it might be the latter, although she couldn't believe he was capable of something so cold-hearted. That wouldn't fit with the man she had come to know.

'But I do. Perhaps I should have seen sooner that Céleste and I were quite wrong for each other . . . We wanted such different things from life. I was stupidly swept away when I should have waited until I met someone like you: someone who's grounded, kind and loving, and with interests we can share.'

May saw a shadow of something pass across his eyes. Longing? Regret? Relief? 'But if we get married . . .' She could hardly believe she had said that. 'What about Eloise?'

She could imagine the scandal when they arrived home.

The small-town gossip machine would go into overdrive. *Another woman's baby! Have you heard? May Campbell's bringing up another woman's daughter! Where's the real mother? What did May get up to while she was in Paris? Did she steal him from the mother? Is it really hers? Are you going to the wedding?* This wasn't the way she had envisaged going home at all, or indeed the way she wanted to go there.

'I'm just imagining the reception we'd get.' Her family would be mortified or angry, or both. She couldn't go through with it.

'My family will adore you. You needn't worry about them.' Still on his knee, he clasped her hands tighter.

Would Max's family have adored her? The thought flashed through her mind unbidden. She pictured Wendy preparing for her wedding. How much easier it was for her — just her and Sam. But this was very different. Did she love David? Wasn't that a must for a happy marriage? But what was love? The extraordinary head-over-heels madness that she had felt for Max might not be there with David, but there was so much else that was. He was kind too, thoughtful, a wonderful father in terrible circumstances. He might not be as exciting a catch as Max but he was steady, reliable, the best of friends.

Would her family adore him? They probably would. And they, especially her mother, would be impressed that she was marrying into the Adair family. Her idea of a shopping expedition in Edinburgh always took in a visit to the department store, and David's parents were like local celebrities. Her mother would love being associated with them and being one up on her friends.

But Eloise.

Her existence was more difficult to explain away. If it was anyone but May, her mother would be in the frontline of those gossipmongers, surmising, muckraking, enjoying any misfortune visited on someone else's family. May couldn't have that. Eloise had done nothing to deserve the sort of attention she would attract in the small-minded community May was from.

'You've taken me by surprise.' She didn't want to explain all the reactions that were tumbling through her head until she had resolved them.

'Then think about it.' He got to his feet and took a seat at the table. 'I don't want to push you into doing something you'd regret. Some people might think it's too sudden but I don't care. They don't know how well we've got to know each other and I can't think of having a life without you now.' The blush that raced over his cheeks touched her, as she recognised the truth in what he said. Even if they were on the rebound from their separate relationships, they were both benefitting from this one in so many ways. The three of them made each other happy: they completed each other. Could May bring up another woman's child? In that moment, she had never been more certain of anything.

'I don't need to think about marrying you. Of course I will.'

The look on his face as he heard those last four words made everything worthwhile. He loved her, all right. He wanted to be with her for the rest of his life. And she wanted to be with him. Of course she did. It made sense. He leaned forward and kissed her. The feeling of his lips on hers for the first time ignited something in her as she lost herself in his embrace. And yet . . . and yet . . . something was missing but she brushed that thought to one side. They didn't know each other in that way yet. All it needed was a little time. They were brought back to the present by the sound of Eloise waking and playing in her cot. May extricated herself from his arms. 'I'll get her. But before we say anything to anyone else, we must talk about Céleste and Eloise.'

'Must we?' For a moment he looked downcast. 'I know you're right. I don't think we'll have any trouble from Céleste. Look how she's behaving. Her career is what matters to her. That and Jean-Luc. She's not interested in Eloise. I suspect she'll be relieved to see the back of us.'

Brave words. But would she? Taking the decision out of Céleste's hands might backfire when what she had given up was thrown into focus. When something was unobtainable, that's when it became more desirable. If she came back to reclaim Eloise as hers, May didn't think she could bear it. Once Céleste saw her daughter again who was almost sitting now and charmed everyone who set eyes on her, surely she would want her back. May couldn't stop that happening.

A hungry Eloise put paid to any more serious thought before May had to leave to collect Emile.

That night, May lay still wide awake at two in the morning, hearing the ormolu clock on the table outside her room strike the hour, while the lamplight outside leached into the room through the gap in her curtains, making silhouettes of everything in there, as if she were in a macabre fairy tale. She had replayed her last conversation with David over and over again, making herself both excited and anxious. In retrospect, perhaps it was odd that she hadn't considered something like this happening but she had never thought of David in a romantic way. At least not until now. Until that kiss. A future that she had never envisaged or asked for had opened up in front of her.

In exchange for her dreams of a life with Max or an independent life on her own she was gaining something far more precious. She would be married to David. They would love each other and she would have security, comfort and the family she had dreamed of, just a little sooner than she had imagined. Her only very real concern was how Eloise would fit into all of this without being hurt.

There was no escaping the fact that Eloise was another woman's child. Céleste had as much right to be involved with her daughter's life as Eloise had to be with her natural mother. Whatever David said, however good May was with her, Eloise belonged to someone else. They would never be rid of Céleste. Apart from that, would David and she be up to protecting Eloise from being ostracised when the truth of her birth came out. David and Céleste had not even been married when she was born. And now she would be being brought up by another woman.

No, it wouldn't work. As much as it broke her heart, May

recognised that she had to let her and David go. They had their own lives that she did not have a place in. She would have to tell him.

33

Edinburgh, 2019

Their first evening together had been a strain, largely thanks to Andrew. He began by being pleasantly garrulous, entertaining even. Even Lorna laughed once. But it wasn't long before he drifted towards boring then incoherent then virtually comatose. Being at the heart of an unhappy marriage was difficult. Lorna couldn't hide her misery, although she did her best, talking furiously about anything that came into her head, semi-flirting with Ian which embarrassed him, irritated Isla and amused Charlie while ignoring Andrew as much as she could.

'Andrew! Time for bed.' Eventually Lorna tapped his shoulder.

He reared up as if he'd been poked by a cattle prod.

'Not yet. Still early. Nightcap, anyone?'

Ian joined him in a whisky – just to be polite, despite Lorna's badly hidden sigh of frustration.

In the morning, everyone bar Charlie began the day pussyfooting round each other in the kitchen while Lorna drummed up a restorative breakfast.

'I'd forgotten how a teenager can sleep,' she said, putting the toast into two toast racks for each end of the table.

Isla took her buzzing phone from her skirt pocket, too late to answer, surprised to be called so early. 'Odd. That was Di, my neighbour. I can't imagine why she'd want me. I hope nothing's happened at home. I'll just go upstairs and call her back.'

In her room, glad of an excuse to escape, Isla stood at her window and stared out at the garden as she made the call. She and Di had made friends the day she moved into Walton Street and Di, as wide as she was tall and with a pudding basin haircut dyed a dirty blue, had arrived on the doorstep with two mugs of tea and a packet of biscuits. Their friendship had quickly extended to weekly get-togethers, visits to the cinema and the occasional concert. If ever either need help, the other was always ready to oblige. However, things had changed when Tony came on the scene.

Isla was aware she hadn't paid her friend as much attention as she should recently and Di's disapproval of the new set-up was evident in the way she looked at Tony, as if he was something nasty on the bottom of her shoe. Making matters worse, Isla had an uncomfortable feeling the party wall between their bedrooms wasn't quite as thick as it might be. She had asked Di round a number of times, but either Tony had organised something so she had to rearrange or he was so casual, it was embarrassing. When she mentioned it, he was shocked. 'You're imagining it. I like her.' But that wasn't the Tony she knew and loved in private at all. Di had been understandably upset and distanced herself from them. Nevertheless, she answered Isla's call straight away.

'Are you all right? Has something happened?'

A thrush landed on a branch of the apple tree outside and began singing its heart out.

'I'm fine.' Di's sharp little voice was loud and clear. 'But exhausted thanks to the party that was going on at yours all last night. Have you come back early to celebrate something?'

'A party? No, I'm in Edinburgh.'

'Believe me, it's true. Fenton called the police at two thirty.' Fenton was Isla's other neighbour, a philosophy don, who usually kept himself to himself. 'One or two people left then, but the noise went on long after.'

'I'm so sorry.' Isla was puzzled. 'Let me call Tony and find out what's happened. It won't be happening again, I promise.' The thought of her home being besieged by strangers was more than she could bear. What could Tony be thinking of? She remembered the voices she'd dismissed when she last spoke to him. 'I'll call you right back.'

She sat on her bed and called Tony. No reply.

Downstairs in the kitchen, she explained what had happened.

'You haven't got squatters, have you?' asked Lorna, immediately putting the fear of God into Isla. Could they have moved in while Tony was out?

'No. Not possible. Tony's staying there.'

The complicit exchange of looks between Ian and Charlie was maddening but she didn't pick them up on it. Watching them together since he'd arrived had given her such pleasure. He had taught Charlie some complicated card game for two that had them shouting and laughing while Isla and Lorna were in the kitchen. He was at home here and made everyone laugh with his backstage stories that inevitably involved exposing one star or another, to everyone's gasps of disbelief. Charlie obviously worshipped him.

During the course of the morning, she called Tony three times but it rang out every time.

She phoned Di again.

'I can't get hold of Tony. He must have gone out. If you do see him, could you possibly ask him to call me?'

'I doubt if I'll be able to do that.' Di sounded even more judgemental than usual, which irritated Isla.

'Oh, don't be difficult, Di. Please. I want to sort this out.'

'It's not because I don't want to but because I've already seen him this morning. He was leaving your house with two large suitcases. A young man was parked, engine running, half up on the pavement ...' Her outrage at the offence almost made Isla laugh. Di was such a stickler for the rules. 'I ran out to tell him to move on when Tony came out of your front door. When I asked him about the party he just said, "Don't worry, I won't be coming back so it won't happen again."'

Isla was quite still, confused. Something was wrong. 'Are you sure that's what he said? That he's not coming back?'

'Certain. He chucked the cases in the boot, climbed in, and they roared off.'

Isla put a hand to her throat as she felt a rush of nausea. 'That can't be right. You must have misheard.' A hollow echo of what she had said to Charlie. Her heart was telling her one thing while her head was screaming out another. No, no. There would be an explanation. Di had got it wrong. She would call Tony and sort everything out.

'I'm so sorry but I really didn't . . . I did take a photo of the car though. Part of my building evidence for the council.'

But Isla hardly heard her. 'I'm sorry, Di. Can we talk later? I'm going to try him again.'

But she knew what would happen and, sure enough, his phone rang then switched to voicemail.

She couldn't believe this was happening. She didn't want to. The money she had given him to invest for her . . . She saw things with appalling clarity. What a stupid thing to have done. How could she have been so blind? But they were planning a future together. She stopped herself.

He had never said that.

A shared future was in her imagination. Her world had changed irrevocably over twenty-four hours.

She tried his number several times more. His failure to answer only confirmed her worst fears, no matter how much she didn't want to believe them. She looked up his new company's website, rang the contact number to be told it had not been recognised. Her online bank account confirmed the money had been safely transferred to his account.

But none of this tallied with what she knew to be true.

Although what Di had seen meant he must have gone away. With two cases containing what? But he would be back, she told herself. He would have to be.

Late-morning, when she was alone in the kitchen, she called Di again, this time to ask her to let herself into the house to check everything was more or less as she left it.

Twenty minutes later, Di called back. 'I'm in the house. I can't see your collection of Beatrix Potter figures though.' Those thirty little Beswick figures had taken Isla years to collect and should be safe in the museum, but she couldn't let them go. 'Or the snow globes. There are a couple of pictures missing: the angels over the mantelpiece and that woman's portrait in the hall. And the dining room table. There may be more but only you'd know.'

Isla felt as if a bucket of cold water had been emptied over her.

'And ...' Di sounded suspiciously as if she was rather enjoying her role in this. 'There's an envelope addressed to you in the kitchen. Handwritten. And it's not in the pile of post but separate with a set of keys.' Apart from Di, the only other person with a set was Tony. They had to be his.

'Could you read it to me?' Isla didn't want to share her humiliation but she had to find out what had happened. She was too far away from home to come rushing back. She had to talk to Aggie as well as being at her eighty-fifth birthday celebrations on Sunday.

'You're sure?'

'Quite.'

'Okay. Here goes.' There was the sound of tearing paper as she opened the envelope. *'Dear Isla.'*

Business-like. No dearest or darling. Isla braced herself.

'I'm a coward. I didn't mean to get so involved. Perhaps I shouldn't have come for the weekend but I couldn't resist. And I wanted the money of course . . . You haven't lent him money?'

Isla couldn't bear Di's incredulousness on top of her own. *Just my hard-earned savings*, she thought. *Just my retirement fund.*

'Only a little,' she said.

'More fool you. There's more. *I don't like feelings that get in the way of what would otherwise be a simple business proposition for me so it's time to move on. I've enjoyed our time together but perhaps I shouldn't have let it go so far. But without an inheritance, why wait around? I'm taking a few souvenirs. Don't try to find me. You won't. Have a good life.'*

There was a silence as both women absorbed the implications of the letter.

'Well!' Di spoke first. 'It looks like you've been well and truly had.' She was never shy of speaking her mind.

'Yes, but I can't . . .' This couldn't be happening. Isla leaned forward and put her head on the cool kitchen counter, grateful not to be told how Di had never trusted him or that she could have told her so. What an idiot she'd been. She saw it all too clearly. Tony was nothing but a common conman. He had targeted her, picked her up in the Ashmolean, discovered her mother had just died, leaving her, he thought, an inheritance. As good, she had savings. He'd taken her well and truly for a ride and walked away with her twenty thousand pounds, two of her precious collections and God knows what else. How could she have been so stupid? After all these years of caution and non-commitment, she had fallen for the wrong man. How she had misjudged him. How she thought she had loved him. She heard a sob. Hers.

'You should call the police.' Di was still there, waiting. 'Now.'

'And say what? That I'm a silly old woman who's been taken in by a fraudster?' She could imagine their scorn. She blinked her tears away. He would not make her cry on top of everything else, dammit.

'I won't hear that.' Di brought her back to earth, even if she didn't know the half of it. 'Just because you fell for it . . . you won't be the first, and you won't be the last. He's stolen from you. And remember I've got the photo of the car they drove off in, and its number.' She read it out. 'A grey Toyota Auris. He won't have reckoned on that.'

Isla's fury at being taken in, her humiliation, her shock were momentarily mitigated by the possibility of catching up with him. 'You're brilliant. Thank you.'

'Thought you'd never say it. Get on and make the call.'

'Perhaps I should come back?' Though she hated the thought of missing Aggie's celebration. How dare he rob her of that too?

'Why? He's gone. You can't miss your aunt's party. She'd be so disappointed. That would be letting him win. I can let the police in if need be.'

Isla had never been more grateful for Di's clear thinking. 'I'll call them now.'

Within a couple of hours, the police had been round to Walton Street, Di had shown them all they needed to see. Isla would make a formal statement on Tuesday when she was back. She was left feeling hollow inside. All that trust and love for nothing. She had come so close to committing herself emotionally, overcoming that bit of her that always held back. And the money. How would she make it up? Although the police had been confident they would trace the car, thanks to Di's quick reactions, and she might be able to get some of it back.

From now on she would be independent, giving nothing of herself to anyone again. The whole affair was a horrible wake-up call to the fact that she might be seen as a vulnerable older woman. Not the way she had ever considered herself. The humiliation she had felt while telling the police that she had let this man into her house, given him money, a holiday and what he walked away with could not have been worse. As she explained to the patient, unshockable voice at the other end of the phone, she heard herself sounding increasingly lunatic. No, she hadn't met any of his family or friends. Yes, she had transferred the money to an account her bank said had now been closed; no, she hadn't asked the full name of his business partner; no, she didn't have an address for where he had been living when she met him. The more he asked the more inept her replies seemed, each of them demanding the question, *Why not?*

She tried to do justice to Lorna's soup and bread and cheese lunch but her appetite had deserted her. Hearing what had happened meant the others were sympathetic. Even Charlie, whose instinct had been proved right.

Afterwards, Ian took Isla to one side. 'We need to talk.'

'Not "Can you talk to me?"' Isla attempted a joke, but it fell flat. 'That's what you always say to me.'

'It's not like that, this time. I know you've had a terrible shock but we've got something to tell you.'

'At least you can't make things any worse.'

He took her into the living room where Charlie was sitting in the window seat and shut the door. 'Sit down.'

'What is this?' She sat in the sofa which meant she could see her granddaughter. 'Now you're worrying me. Although nothing you can say will outdo what's just happened. I feel as if someone's hit me with a plank.'

'And will do for a while, I'm sure.' He sat beside her. Still wearing the same cologne, she noticed. Charlie crossed the room to take the chair by the fireplace and swung her bare legs over its arm so she was facing them. She was wearing her impossibly short shorts again and a baggy sleeveless T-shirt, her hair loose over her shoulders.

'Go on.'

'You're not going to like this – or maybe you will – but it's about Tony.'

'Not more.' Her voice wavered. 'Perhaps I can't take any more after all.' She stood up to leave the room. She was not going to cry in front of them.

'Sit down and listen.' He grabbed her hand but she resisted sitting back down beside him again, confused by how close she felt to him, confused by how drawn to him she felt.

'Charlie and I have done a bit of research—'

Charlie curled up her toes and, with a shake of her head, shielded her face with her hair.

'For God's sake, Ian!' Isla exploded with rage. As if this morning wasn't bad enough, he was bent on making it worse. 'Don't drag Charlie into it. Why are you doing this?' She'd rather spontaneously combust than any hear any more bad news.

'In fact, she dragged me into it.' Ian cast a reassuring smile at his granddaughter. 'Why do you think I turned up after you'd so resoundingly told me to stay away?'

'I thought . . .' But what could she say? Charlie had been right all along. 'I'm sorry I didn't believe you about Tony.'

Charlie looked at her knees, running a finger round her kneecap. 'Doesn't matter. I'm kinda sorry I was right.'

'But why come up early?' She looked at Ian. 'You didn't have to.'

'Why? Because we care about what happens to you. Unbelievable isn't it?' That matinée idol smile. It had worked on too many women. It wasn't going to work on her again.

'I don't need you to care though.'

'Actually you do.' He and Charlie nodded at each other. 'I've made a couple of phone calls and done some googling with Charlie's help. She was worried about you.'

'Don't be angry.' Charlie's eyes were wide in appeal.

That brought Isla up short. If anything she should be worrying about her granddaughter, not the other way round. 'And?' she said cautiously. 'Go on then. After this morning, nothing could come close.'

Except, from the concern written on Ian's face, perhaps this was going to come closer than any of them would like. She took a deep breath, readying herself for whatever it was.

He took her hand, which she snatched back immediately. 'Go on.'

'I was looking through Marchams online catalogue and saw a picture that was so like the one May left you. I remember it from David's study of course. It had a reserve of £3,500.

'Do you think it's mine?' If so, she had to have it back.

'I'm pretty sure, but the sale took place on Thursday.'

While they were in Lancashire.

'So we'll never know.' She heard herself groan at the loss.

'Don't lose heart, old thing.' Ian was bullish. 'I called them. An old friend works there.' Of course. In his antiques sideline, Ian maintained plenty of old friends in odd places. 'I told him that I thought there was a strong possibility the picture was stolen property – if Charlie hadn't alerted me, I would never have known.'

Charlie gave a pleased little smile at the acknowledgement. 'And?'

'If you can prove it's yours, they'll release the name of the buyer to the police and you'll get it back. They've alerted the buyer in the meantime. Unbelievably, the money hadn't been transferred to the seller. Very slack. So the whole deal is frozen until things are worked out.'

'Aren't you pleased?' Charlie chipped in, obviously excited about the success of their sleuthing.

'Pleased? I'll be thrilled to have it back.' And the thought of getting back at Tony in however small a way was delicious too. If only there could be other ways. She hugged Ian then stretched out her arm for Charlie to come and be included. Being knotted up with the two of them was the best feeling she could have. When they disentangled, Charlie was laughing and she could have sworn Ian had a tear in his eye, the old ham.

'Thank you both so much.' She was overwhelmed by the thought that the two of them had teamed up for her. How Charlie, who had seemed so indifferent to her at the start, had proved to be such a determined soul. In future, she would definitely be seeing more of her. If she could offer her the sort of retreat that Aggie had offered her when she needed it, she absolutely would.

34

Paris, 1955

The evening following the proposal, May returned to David's apartment for supper. As she walked through the narrow streets, avoiding urchins playing on the pavement, glancing into the shop windows, she felt the magic had left Paris. She didn't want to refuse David, but she had to. For Eloise's sake.

At first, while busy with the baby who refused to go down, they didn't speak although David, like May, must have felt the unsaid pressing to be heard. Eventually she dropped off, and the two of them sat down to eat the ragout she'd made and the two cheeses he had brought home.

'Well?' he said, expectant, excited.

She screwed up her courage, her fists clenched under the tablecloth where he wouldn't see. 'I can't. I'm sorry.'

His face crumpled with disappointment. 'But why not?'

She began to lay out the reasons that had presented themselves the night before. He sat quite calmly listening until she felt she was gabbling nonsense, then said, 'Shall we have coffee? Then I can think.'

By the time she had made it, he was in his favourite chair in the living room, staring into space. She put the cup of coffee at his side, his favourite puff-pastry biscuit, a *palmier*, in the saucer. She sat across the room from him in the chair with the uneven springs, one of Céleste's fringed shawls thrown over its back to disguise how dilapidated it was. At least she would soon be free of reminders of the woman who had preceded her.

She started going over all the concerns she had about taking Eloise home with them. 'I don't want us, and especially Eloise, to be the focus of local gossip. I hate the idea of those tongues wagging. And Céleste . . .' She paused, waiting for David to say something. Being in the same room as him was making her doubt all her reasons for not marrying him. With every moment she was becoming more certain that marriage to David was what she wanted. That, and a family of her own.

Finally David spoke. 'Eloise is so young that she won't remember any of this.'

May sat straight, slopping coffee into the saucer. 'But Céleste . . . She will.'

'She doesn't care.' Once again, that sadness was just beneath the surface. 'I tried to contact her today, to tell her that I'm going back to Scotland, but she's somewhere near Nice, modelling.'

'She's doing well then.' May attempted to mask her resentment with a show of admiration.

'Who knows?' He rubbed his right eyebrow, as if it

would help him see things straight. 'But she's doing what she wants to do.'

So why shouldn't they? Why should she and David have to take second place?

'Darling, why don't we get married before we go home?' He sprang to his feet, alive at the idea. 'We can pretend we married months ago in secret and that Eloise is yours. No one will know any different.'

'But that's . . .' She stopped, lost for words, stunned by the suggestion. 'But we'd be lying to everyone.' Although would they be able to get away with it?

'Only we would know that. You can tell Madame you want to go home. She doesn't need to know any more than that. And who from here will follow us? We don't have to tell anyone where we're going and the waters will close over our heads. We'll soon be forgotten.'

'And at home?' How tempted she was. She should have known that David would come up with a solution to all the hurdles. But, but, but . . . something still stopped her.

'Everyone at home will believe us because that's what we'll tell them and that's what they'll expect. Our parents will be shocked and mebbe hurt that we didn't tell them so . . .'

'We could say the magic of Paris swept us away.' She began to get caught up in the fantasy.

'There might be a few naysayers but if we stick to our guns, they'll come round. They'll have to.' He stood up and walked to the casement window, staring down at the courtyard below.

'I'm thinking of Eloise.' She went to stand behind him, putting her arms around him, smelling the smoky scent of his tweed jacket. 'Of her future.'

He turned and kissed her forehead. 'I know. And I love you for that.'

'What if Céleste has a change of heart?' Her greatest fear smashed his plans for their future together into smithereens. 'You can't have both of us.'

'I don't want both of you,' he said, stroking her hair, her cheek. 'I want you. But I can't keep her from her child if she wants to see her.'

May didn't look at his face but she could hear the note of yearning.

For the rest of the evening they went round and round in circles. With every suggestion David made, the more May realised how impossible a future was together and yet the more she wanted that future. The obstacles seemed insurmountable.

Two days later, David arrived home from work early. May had just got in from taking Eloise to the doctor for a slight cold. He was ashen-faced, his eyes red as if he had been crying. He looked broken.

'Whatever's happened?' She rushed to help him, taking his bag, and guiding him inside. Eloise balanced on her hip, reaching up to pull at her hair.

He let her lead him into the main room where he fell into his chair, looking up at them, his face glazed with pain. May propped up Eloise in the corner of the opposite chair and gave her a rattle. Usually David would pick her up, smother her with kisses and tickle her until she couldn't stop laughing, but today he ignored her, staring ahead, apparently lost.

'David! Tell me.'

He clasped May's hands so tight the bones felt as if they might crack.

'David! Please.'

'She's dead.' Tears began to roll down his cheeks.

May stared in horror. She had never seen a man cry. David's whole body was wracked with sobs, uncontrollable in his grief.

Only one person's death could possibly make him react like this. 'Your mother?' she asked gently.

'No! Not her, thank God.' He blew his nose and tried to gather himself together. 'Céleste was in an accident.'

So Céleste was gone.

May tried to dispel the shameful feeling of schadenfreude that nipped at her. How terrible it would be to rejoice in someone else's death. But how could she ignore the implications? The real hurdle to them being a family was cleared. Did that reaction make her a terrible person? She mustn't think about that now. Instead she sat and comforted him until he was ready to talk. She made him tea from the PG Tips his mother had sent him. She went to his chest of drawers and took out two big cotton handkerchiefs. She stroked his back, cradled his head. Waited.

Gradually he recovered, blew his nose a final time, took

the pipe she passed him and lit up. They sat quietly, him exhaling smoke into the room while she sat at his knee, until eventually he was ready to speak.

'What happened?'

He blew a smoke-ring and they watched it dissolve.

'She was with Jean-Luc in his car. They'd probably had a long day shooting, she'd often start at the crack of dawn. Apparently they went off the road last night somewhere in the mountains near Eze and plunged down the mountain-side. They must have been on their way back to the coast. They weren't found until this morning. Neither of them survived.'

Hearing what had happened was a shock. May could imagine the beautiful couple in an open-top sports car, Céleste's hair flying out from under a headscarf, her head thrown back laughing, her arm round the driver who was slim and impossibly handsome, like Louis Jourdan, the film star who had been so good in *Three Coins in the Fountain*. Wendy and May had been to see it twice. Something happened. Perhaps he took his eye off the road for one fatal moment, responding to something she had said. Perhaps they were tired. Perhaps he went to sleep at the wheel. The car was hurtling over a barrier and rolling over unstoppable, their mouths wide in a scream, eyes terrified, bodies, bits of metal, flames everywhere. May put her hands over her mouth, shut her eyes against the vision. 'That's dreadful. I'm so, so sorry.' But she was aware any words were inadequate.

So it was over. Her petty jealousy of Céleste, her waking fear of her return to reclaim David and Eloise could be forgotten. Her prime concern now must be to help David through his grief. Not for a moment did she worry that Céleste's death might alter his feelings towards her except to bring them closer together. She would be there for him and Eloise as she had been since the beginning. They were her future now and she was not going to let them go.

A week later, they walked over the Seine on the arched seventeenth-century Pont Royal and into the Tuileries Garden to mingle with the crowds enjoying the spring sunshine. They walked down the central gravelled walkway towards the round pond, the spectacular Place de la Concorde in the distance. How May would miss the grandiose lime-stone buildings, the wide boulevards, the atmospheric windy streets of the left bank, the food, the brasseries, the boats on the Seine – she had to stop herself from going on and making herself sad. She looked around at the people, families, young lovers, old men with sticks, children on scooters, others running around, donkeys giving rides and, of course, the boules players. She would never forget the elegance, the excitement and the enchantment of Paris. Eventually they stopped by May's favourite statue in the Grand Carré, a bronze of a tiger carrying a peacock to her cubs. It spoke of everything about motherhood to her.

They sat on the grass with Eloise sitting between them, wearing the little pink smock dress that May had spent nights sewing. When they were settled, David broached the subject again. 'I've been thinking about us.'

'Mmm? What's that?' She handed Eloise her rattle, fearful of what he was about to say.

The trees were in leaf, plants flowering in the borders, all heralding the advent of spring. Could this symbolise a new beginning for all of them or would it mark the end? May had to take David's lead now.

'Everything's different now Céleste's dead, but I haven't changed my mind. There are just the three of us now and I want nothing more than for us to be together.' His fingers fiddled with some blades of grass.

His words were like a fresh breeze that blew the cobwebs from May's mind.

'For Eloise's sake, we should think about the best way of doing things.' He caught her up so she sat on his lap, and he kissed the top of her head. 'I thought we might get married in Gretna on our way home. It's always struck me as being rather romantic.' He looked at her sideways hoping she would agree.

She caught her breath.

'And then we'll go home and no one will be any the wiser. We can put all this behind us and start again. Will you?'

She let Eloise grasp her finger and put out her hand to stop her from tumbling to one side. 'I can't think of anything I'd like more.'

No parents, no London, no Aunt Jess. But a future as a family with a man she loved.

'If we're convincing enough our families will believe us. If we say nothing to anyone, we may even begin to believe our story ourselves. I have one more suggestion.'

He'd obviously been thinking about the arrangement hard. She was a little disappointed it was all about the strategy and not about the romance. She looked at Eloise who was entranced by a couple of puppies so bouncy that they'd tangled up their leads. All May wanted was to be a mother. David was offering her that chance. But if they were going to do this, she wanted everything to be perfect for all three of them.

They walked on for a long time, wrestling with their plans.

While they did so, life in the city continued. Busy, colourful, fascinating. She held David's hand, feeling his fingers entwine in hers. *We can do this*, she thought. *We can.*

35

Edinburgh, June 2019

At the garden gate to Braemore, Isla stopped the car and took a breath. Every time she had come here as an adult, she experienced the same sense of reluctance that stopped her from going any further up the drive. When she was a child, she might have been nervous about her mother's mood but as she grew up and understood a little more what she was walking into, she had to prepare herself for criticism and the feeling she wasn't good enough. She would prepare, telling herself that she would not rise to the bait over the subsequent forty-eight hours, or however long she was staying. And now, after everything that had happened that day, she was having to prepare herself again, as if sensing something bad was about to happen. Whatever Tony had or hadn't done, he was not going to stop her from doing this.

'Come on.' Charlie took the lead and jumped out to open the iron gate that had lost its habitual squeak. 'I want to see. And if you're not up to it, I can ask the questions for you.'

They drove up the gravel driveway to the house, a

honey-coloured stone mansion. The windows shone, the paintwork was in good order. Isla was impressed that her aunt had managed the upkeep of the family home so well. A newish silver-grey VW Polo was parked by the door. Aggie must employ a team of gardeners to keep the huge garden from going wild. Over the left-hand hedge a couple of horses looked up to see what was happening at their neighbours'. Isla imagined the field filled with new houses. They couldn't let that happen.

'What's she like?' Charlie whispered.

'You're just about to find out.' Isla reached up and pulled the bell. They heard it echo through the house, then steps tapping on the stone flags towards them. The door opened and Aunt Aggie stood in front of them, wreathed in smiles.

'Come away in,' she said. 'It's so good to see you, Isla dear. You probably don't remember me? But I love your hair.' This to purple dip-dyed Charlie who was staring at her in amazement. Isla, used to Aggie's idiosyncrasies, saw her through Charlie's eyes, as if for the first time. Not many women in their eighties dressed so flamboyantly. Her wide yellow slacks and cornflower-blue duster jacket were accessorised with strings of different-sized coloured beads. Her hair was silver, cut short and gelled on end. On her nose were her usual dark-framed specs. 'Come, come.' She took them into the comfortable tartan-carpeted living room on the left of the hallway. Nothing much had changed since Isla's last visit. The heavy dark furniture was all in the same place. The same pictures hung on the walls. The old chintz sofa had been replaced by a stylish grey one that looked infinitely more comfortable with lots of coloured cushions thrown on it. Upmarket art, gardening and interiors magazines were scattered over the faded pink velvet ottoman. She took them through the open French windows to the terrace where the wooden table was laid with a white linen tablecloth held in place with a series of dragonfly weights, laid with porcelain plates and cups and saucers. The fine china had been in the family for as long as Isla could remember, only brought out for best.

'You make yourselves comfortable and I'll get the tea.' Aggie disappeared inside.

Isla was about to follow her to offer help when Charlie tugged at her arm. 'Are you going to tell her about Tony?'

'No. I'd like to try to forget him till I get home. Let's concentrate on her and what we've come for.'

'Is that where you put on your plays?' The mound that had seemed so large and theatrical when they were children had shrunk with time into more of a bump. 'I remember it being so much bigger, even though I've seen it loads of times since. How funny.' But like inside, everything else outside was pretty much the same. The borders were a riot of colour, beautifully tended by someone. The wooden swing still hung from the beech tree. The old potting shed which Morag once corralled for the injured pigeon and her procession of small pets was still there but painted a chic Scandinavian green. Through the centre of the lawn ran the quarry stones that stopped your feet getting soaked in the endless winter rain.

Just then a sleek grey cat strolled down the garden towards them. Charlie tiptoed to meet it without frightening it away, her hand held out.

'Bilbo, my faithful companion,' said Aggie, introducing the animal as she reappeared with a trolley on which was a pot of tea, and plates of tiny sandwiches, drop scones and slices of fruit cake. 'He's a Russian blue.' She began to unload the contents of the trolley onto the table. 'There's no point having tea unless you go the whole hog.'

Once they all had full cups and plates, and had covered all the bases, Aggie sat back and gave Isla a once-over. 'So? You said you wanted to ask me something? Not about May again, I hope.'

Isla had been deliberately vague when she had phoned her aunt the day before, given her reaction the last time they spoke about her. She hadn't wanted to give Aggie time to think about what she was going to say. So much had happened since then, she didn't have the energy to question her. But, having come this far, she couldn't give up now.

'I'm afraid it is,' she said.

'We think you might know some answers,' said Charlie. 'Otherwise it's a mystery forever, and that's not fair on Gran.'

Isla was surprised but grateful. Charlie had read the situation so well.

Aggie's beady eyes studied her. 'Mmm.'

With a strong sense of foreboding, Isla ploughed on. 'You were always so good to me when Mum was being difficult.' She chose her words carefully. 'Do you remember? Your flat was a special place for me.' A place she would love to be at that very moment – where she could escape from the real world.

'Of course I remember.' The warmth of her smile was the same as it had always been. 'I didn't like the way she picked on you sometimes. I didn't think it was fair. Anyway, it was lovely for me, on my own and no children, to have you in my life. I was being quite selfish, I assure you.'

'But why *did* she pick on me? Why didn't she like me?'

Aggie looked as if she was about to say something, but Isla hadn't finished. 'I've got a note that was hidden in the picture she left me. It's in French, from someone called Céleste.' She didn't miss the flicker in Aggie's eye that showed the name had registered. 'I know Mum was in France, working as a nanny, and we know she met Dad there but I can't put the pieces together. Aunt Aggie, you must be able to fill in some of the gaps.'

The teapot rattled against the cup as Aggie poured. Isla watched as her aunt quickly regained control.

'I hoped you might be coming to terms with her will.' Not even she could sound convinced.

'How could I? I don't think I ever will unless I understand. I've tried to remember an incident, something I said, anything that would explain her attitude towards me. But nothing so far makes me forget or forgive so I need an explanation. Please.'

Aggie put down the pot and offered Charlie a sandwich. Charlie was so intent on what was being said that she almost didn't take one. She reacted just before the plate was removed, examining the one she had chosen.

'Cucumber,' said Aggie briskly. 'I used to make them for rehearsals. The actors always loved them. Once—'

'You're the only one who might know,' said Isla, bringing her back to focus.

'I can't.' Aunt Aggie lifted her cup to her lips. 'I promised.'

'You promised?' So she did know something. Just as Ian had been sworn to secrecy. But why? 'Who did you promise? Mum? Dad?'

She gave an almost imperceptible nod.

'But they're dead,' said Charlie, not intimidated by Aggie's glare. 'They won't know what you say now, and Gran badly needs to. If I can get that, then you must too.'

They both looked at her, surprised. Isla wanted to hug her, but limited herself to what she hoped was a grateful smile.

'You're a very astute young woman.' Aunt Aggie put her head to one side as she considered her again, taking in the ripped jeans, the teeny T-shirt, the purple-tipped hair and the subtle but present make-up. 'And of course you're absolutely right.'

'Is there something that I ought to know? That perhaps Lorna and Morag should know too?' Isla felt she was on the brink of discovery.

'There is.' The words were exhaled as if they cost her aunt a huge effort. 'But May made me promise under pain of death. Even though she's gone now.' Her voice was heavy with sadness.

'Paris,' said Isla, encouraging her. 'Is that where it began?'

Aunt Aggie nodded. 'You know too much now and you're not going to give up until I tell you, I see that.'

'If she gives up, I won't. Not now,' said Charlie.

'I see how much you need to know but it's a long story.'

'We have all the time.' Dread tempered Isla's excitement. What if what she was going to hear made her feel worse still? But, she swiftly rationalised, any explanation would be better than existing in the limbo of not knowing. Whatever it was couldn't make her feel worse than she already did. When all the participants were dead, nothing could be that bad. Could it? 'Please.'

'Yes. Please,' echoed Charlie who couldn't hide her impatience.

'Very well.' Aggie cleared her throat. 'I hope we won't regret this. You're sure?'

'Quite.' Isla made herself sound more certain than she felt.

'Definitely,' said Charlie, wincing as the other two stared at her. 'Sorry.'

Aggie took a deep breath and settled back in her chair. She clasped her hands as if she was praying, her eyes shut. 'Very well then. When we were young, May was sent to Paris to be a nanny and to learn French.'

'We found that out at Morag's.' Charlie was triumphant.

'The idea was that she would learn French, then go to London to find work as a translator. I've no idea how the family was found but they put a roof over her head, gave her a job and some money in her pocket. Afterwards, our Aunt

Jess, who lived in London, would have helped her find work and digs of some sort. But May never went. I went instead a couple of years later and that's where I got involved with the theatre. I had a lot to thank her for really. Have I told you about my interview with Joan Littlewood?'

'Yes, several times,' said Isla, keen to get her back on track. 'Why didn't she go?'

Aggie waved a heavily ringed hand in the air. 'I don't know much about what she got up to in Paris but she told me snippets – the most memorable bits perhaps. She worked for this family, looking after their little boy. He was called ...' She looked to the sky for inspiration. 'No, it's gone. She loved Paris from the moment she got there. She and an English girl called Wendy got in with a couple of American boys, students I think and they fell head over heels for them. Wendy went to America and married hers. She and May stayed in touch for years afterwards. What happened between May and her boy ... ?'

'Max?' asked Charlie, just ahead of Isla.

Aggie shrugged her shoulders. 'Mebbe. I think so. She wrote to me about him once or twice but when she came back she wouldn't talk about him. She was very good at keeping her own secrets, was May. But I could tell something had happened and that it mattered a great deal to her. We'll never know what it was. Men come and go at that age. Later too.'

'Speak for yourself!' Isla teased her.

'Oh I do, my dear. I do.' She dabbed at her mouth with

a napkin, smudging her lipstick into the creases at one side of her mouth.

Charlie's eyes were wide.

'Yes, well.' Aggie gave a winsome smile. 'Enough said!'

'So she met Dad there?' Isla nudged her back to the story. 'But the passport Lorna found said he went there the year before her.'

Her aunt raised her eyebrows. 'You have been doing your homework.'

'We tried, but the clues have been pretty thin on the ground.'

'Yes, she did meet David in Paris. He was there before she arrived. They must have met soon after she finished with the American boy because about a year later she was back here, married to David.' She stopped as if that was the end of the story. 'There.'

She paused for dramatic effect.

'But it's not as simple as that, is it? Something else happened, I can tell.' Isla had rarely felt impatience like this but was aware that if she pushed too hard her aunt might clam up completely. She had the stubborn streak that ran through the family. She poured her another cup of tea to keep her going. But Aggie enjoyed a good story and, once started, was ready to go on.

'The fuss it caused, you've no idea. Mummy was so upset that they hadn't even been told. May wrote to them to say they were coming home but not that they were married. She calmed down a bit when she realised David was an Adair. If the marriage was good enough for them, it had to be good enough for her.' Aggie ran her fingers through her hair so it was more unruly than ever. 'The neighbours were impressed all right, once the gossip had died down.'

'Who was Céleste?' So far, nothing Isla had heard explained her mother's will or the picture. She felt, if not in the dark, in the shadows still. 'I saw you recognised the name. There was a note from her hidden behind the picture Mum left me. Does she have something to do with any of this?' Her hunch that it all tied together somehow was still strong. 'It must be significant, otherwise why single it out for me?'

'Perhaps she was someone May met in Paris,' offered Charlie. 'A friend.'

'But how will we ever find out?' Isla put down her cup. How could a painting be a clue to the way her mother had treated her? That didn't make sense and yet something told her it was important.

'It might not mean anything,' said Charlie, reaching for a slice of fruit cake.

'I promised,' Aggie said again. She stood up and walked to the edge of the terrace, looking down her garden to the old oak tree at its end.

Isla and Charlie stared at her, the cake halfway to Charlie's mouth.

'For God's sake.' Isla couldn't bear the suspense any longer. 'Don't do this to me. You've always been there for me. Don't let me down now. If there's something you know that I should know, please tell me.'

Aggie sat down, a hand clutching the beads round her neck as if they were a lifeline. 'You may not like it.'

'But it'll be better than not knowing,' said Charlie.

Isla had had almost enough knowledge for one day but she wanted everything Aggie could tell them all the same.

'All right, I give in. I always told May she was wrong to keep the truth from you, although I won't be responsible for what happens next.' She cleared her throat. 'Céleste was David's girlfriend.'

'Dad's girlfriend?!' said Isla. She had been so sure she couldn't be. Equally, she had never considered her father's life before he married May. Wasn't their young marriage when his adult life began? Whatever he had got up to before that can't have mattered that much.

Aggie's eyes were shut, her hands now twisting together in her lap. 'Yes. She was French. A very beautiful model. May told me that he'd met her here in Scotland on some kind of assignment, long before May met him. They were in love. He followed her back to Paris . . .'

'In 1953,' said Charlie.

Aggie nodded. 'He absolutely adored her and believed they would get married there.'

'*Je t'aime de tout mon coeur, pour toujours*,' whispered Charlie. 'Didn't last long then, did it?'

'Once she was back in Paris, she didn't want to know. There wasn't a place for David in her world, a world she didn't want to let go. Think of the time, Paris was the centre of fashion thanks to Dior and his New Look – such

356

thrilling times. Imagine David being part of that scene. No, you can't.'

'Poor Dad.' Isla could easily imagine him lost and lonely in Paris, a fish out of water.

But Aggie hadn't finished. 'And then she got pregnant. Getting pregnant wasn't part of her plan at all. By then she was already having an affair with a photographer she worked with and David was clinging on as best he could. He had found a job in Paris and he believed she would come back to him. Poor man. He worshipped her.'

'A baby?' Isla was shocked. Somewhere in the world she and her sisters must have a half-sibling that no one had told them about. Why would her parents keep something like that a secret from them? How could their parents have thought they wouldn't want to know?

Aggie nodded. 'Eloise.' She gripped the edge of the table, pressing her fingers into the crisp white cloth.

Isla looked down at the paper-thin skin of her aunt's beringed hand, marked by age, knuckles slightly swollen. 'What happened to her?'

Aggie looked as if she was summoning up every bit of strength she had to finish the story.

'Céleste didn't want anything to do with her baby. She was too young, too beautiful and too successful to be tied down by domesticity and motherhood. There wasn't room in the world she inhabited for a baby. How exciting Paris must have been then. It was her time. Those dresses . . . Givenchy, Dior, Patou – can't you see. And the city itself . . . a far cry from Dunfermline.'

'But what happened to them?' Isla imagined her father rejected and morose, hidden away in a rooftop garret somewhere, his heart broken. 'How does Mum fit in?'

'You've asked me to finish the story but let me tell it my way.' Aggie clicked her fingers as if she was summoning memories on command. 'Céleste was killed in a road accident in the south of France. She had gone on an assignment with her photographer lover and never came back.'

'That's sad.' Charlie spoke. 'But the baby? Where is it now?'

Isla put her arm round her granddaughter's shoulders and hugged her as they waited for Aggie to tell them.

'By then, David had met May and she was helping him by looking after Eloise. He needed her even more then.'

'What about Céleste's family?'

Aggie shrugged. 'No idea. They were never mentioned. And this is the difficult bit so let me ...' She closed her eyes. 'Were they both on the rebound? I don't know. Did they ever really love each other? I don't know that either, although May told me she loved him. They decided to marry and to bring Eloise home to Scotland. They married in Gretna on the way and told everyone the baby was theirs. They lied about when they met, and nobody bothered to work out the dates, and if they did it was better not to say. What was the point? He had made an honest woman of her. Done the decent thing. And of course Céleste was never part of the story. Years later, after David died, May told me the truth.'

'But what happened to Eloise? She couldn't have been that much older than me.' Isla's head was spinning, her heart racing.

'Come on, Gran.' Charlie's voice broke through. 'If I can work it out, you can.'

Eloise. Isla. Not such different names. But that was impossible. It had to be.

'I'm the baby, aren't I?' she asked in a small voice. 'Céleste was my mother.'

'I did say you might not like it.' Aggie put her hand on her knee. 'But yes, there you have it.'

Isla took a deep breath, trying to calm herself, to slow everything down. 'So I could never have known my real mother if she died so young. Mum stepped in and pretended I was hers.'

Charlie was staring at her. 'Wow!'

'They told no one and nobody suspected a thing. But Isla dear, she adored you as if you were her own. People were shocked that May would get pregnant before being married but they were pleased David had done the right thing. Some thought it was romantic.'

Thoughts and memories were rushing through Isla's head so fast that she was finding it difficult to hold on to any of them. 'So she left me out of her will because I wasn't hers?' The explanation didn't lessen the pain that came with such rejection. 'I don't understand. Why take me on and then reject me? What happened?'

She was aware of Charlie sitting absolutely still beside her, listening to every word. For once, her phone had remained in her pocket all the time they had been there.

'I'm afraid what happened was that she grew jealous of

you – is jealous even the right word? I don't know.' Aggie looked to the sky as if she might find the answer up there, before continuing. 'As you got older, you grew more like Céleste. Your face and your figure. Though you had your dad's red hair.'

Isla raised a hand to her head. She could hear her father's voice. 'Call it Titian, May. Such a special colour.'

'May believed Céleste was the love of David's life. Whatever she did, she could never quite measure up. However hard she tried, however many children they had together, however devoted she was, the ghost of beautiful Céleste was always there. Competing with a dead woman who will never be anything other than beautiful and young was impossible because she was never going to win. You were a constant reminder. If Céleste hadn't run away and been killed, her life might have been very different.'

'Why? She would still have met Dad, wouldn't she?' Isla was reeling, at the same time trying to imagine what it must have been like for her mother.

'Maybe, but he would never have asked her to look after you. She would never have fallen in love with you – and she did, you know – or David. She wanted a family of her own but she would have gone to London as planned and things would have been very different. For her and for me. Aunt Jess could only take on one of us. She made that clear.'

'So I stopped her from having a different life.' But plenty of women could blame their families for that. Except they didn't.

'They made a pact not to tell anyone the truth about you. No one.' She threw her hands in the air. 'Their first thought was to protect you.'

Isla couldn't believe what she was hearing. Her life was based on the most fundamental of lies. She had been brought up believing May was her mother when all the time, she was not even related to her. No wonder she looked so different from her sisters. No, half-sisters. She had no idea how to react.

But Aggie wasn't waiting for a reaction as she carried on, the wind in her sails now the truth was out. 'May couldn't help herself. When she saw David looking at you, she imagined he was remembering your mother. When you went into your mother's world of modelling and acting – that was another blow. Especially when he was the one encouraging you. She wanted David for herself, but Céleste never let him go. Or that's what she believed.'

'Did she actually say that?' Of all the people in the world, Isla couldn't imagine May opening up and confiding her innermost feelings to anyone. Not even to her husband. By the time Isla knew them, they were so buttoned up, so apparently incapable of strong emotion.

'After David died, I moved in here. She was broken by his death and that's when she told me. After sixty years of sitting on it together, he had left her with a secret that was too much for her to carry alone. She had to share it with someone. But she made me promise that I would never tell anyone. Of course I agreed. However difficult she could be, she was my sister and in trouble. When she died I wanted to tell you then but I was torn ... so torn. To be loyal to my sister or to be loyal to you?'

As Isla was torn between Helen and Charlie. She understood.

'But you're right.' Aggie nodded towards Charlie. 'The living have to look after the living. There you have it.' She stood up again but this time turned towards the house. 'A drink? I think we deserve it, don't you? I'm glad it's all in the open.'

'So the picture ...' Isla was slow to work it out.

'The picture was a present from Céleste to David. The only thing of hers he had. She couldn't give it to you without an explanation so she left it to you in her will instead.'

The picture was the only thing she had that had come from her birth mother, via David then May. It was the one thing that tied them all together. May must have understood that. And Tony had taken it with him.

36

When they got back to Lorna's, Isla couldn't face her sister or Andrew. 'Just tell them I've got a headache. I'll be down later. I'll tell her then.'

'Don't leave me alone, Gran, please.' Charlie grasped her hand and pulled her back from the staircase. 'He gives me the creeps.'

'I won't be long. Promise.' Isla's hand was on the bannister. She didn't want to show Charlie how devastated she had been by hearing the truth. Her emotions were all over the place. Mixed with the anger she felt towards her parents for their misguided secrecy and their assumption they could play God over her life was a grudging respect for her mother and a new understanding of sorts. If only they could have talked and May explained. Isla wouldn't have thought badly of her. Times had changed but her parents had been locked in the past. She felt terrible sadness for them.

'You look pale.' Ian came into the hall. 'Are you okay?'

'Not really.' But she did have the explanation she wanted. 'Céleste.' She said her name out loud. 'Ma mère.'

All this time, she had been the cuckoo in the family

nest and when she began to look and behave like her birth mother, May had almost tipped her out. *'That's the French in her.'* She heard her voice at last. So that's what it meant. But May was the one who gave her a family, love, and who made her the person she was. Nothing could take that away. If only she had found the right moment to explain, perhaps some of the hurt could have been avoided. 'Ian,' she said, her voice unexpectedly unsteady.

'What is it?' He was all concern.

'Can I talk to you?'

They looked at each other in surprise, then both smiled. Ian touched her cheek and looked her square in the eyes. 'You've never said that to me before. Never.'

'I've never wanted to till now.' And she did want to. She couldn't think of anyone else who would appreciate what this news meant to her more than he would. She didn't need advice but a sympathetic listener who knew her and her family and, for once, he was the one. The way he was looking at her told her that.

'Then we'd better make the most of it. A walk, I think, so we're not interrupted. Charlie! Take your phone to your bedroom and make the most of it. When we come back, we'll be back to business as usual. Hold Lorna at bay.' He held out his hand like a policeman stopping traffic. 'I don't know what's been going on, on top of everything else, but she can wait.'

Charlie shot upstairs like a rocket, feet barely touching the ground, her phone already in her hand. At the top, she turned round. 'Can I tell Mum?'

Isla hadn't got as far as thinking about Helen, but why shouldn't Charlie break the news? After all it was all in the family. 'Why not?' Charlie had helped her and giving her that responsibility might be a good thing. 'Make sure you tell her I'm fine and I'll call her this evening.'

'I will.' And her bedroom door slammed behind her.

'Tell her what?' Ian's hand was on her waist but she didn't move away. His was the touchy-feeliness of his profession, not to be mistaken for the real thing. Not anymore. 'Whatever it is, you're not okay, are you?'

'Today's all been too much. First Tony – I'm upset but more than that I'm so angry, with him and with myself—'

'My poor Isla. Don't.'

'And now this. Aggie's just told us May wasn't my mother.' There, she'd said it. 'That's what's behind all this.'

For once Ian was speechless. She felt the pressure of his hand increase but this time she walked away from it towards the front door. 'Let's get out of here. We'll go to the Hermitage. I'll tell you all as we walk. Jock!' The old dog ambled from the kitchen (Lorna would be pleased) and waited for her to put on his lead.

They walked down the road, Isla talking all the way. At the coffee house, they turned left past its busy garden and into the welcome shade of the trees. Sticking to the main path, dappled with sunshine, they carried on until they reached a bench overlooking the stream. To their right a family crowded round a picnic table, staring briefly as Ian and Isla sat down.

Ian proved to be exactly the listener she knew he would be. He heard her out without asking too many questions. They sat for a while watching the water, listening to its shallow trickle over stones, contemplating all she had said. Being with him, Isla felt her equilibrium returning and was able to relax.

Eventually he spoke. 'So you're Eloise, and you're half French by birth. That explains everything. French women definitely have something the Brits don't.'

'Idiot.' She punched his arm.

'Seriously. So she told Aggie that, as you got older and more like your real mother, it made her more aware of what she could never be. Or, more importantly, of what David would never have.'

'Thinking she had to live up to a dead woman must have been so hard. I wonder how well she knew Céleste. I can't even ask her about her. I've been presented with a mother that I could never have known. I can't even mourn her.'

'I know.'

The feel of his arm round her shoulders gave her the comfort she needed.

'Do you think Mum and Dad were happy? You knew them.'

She couldn't bear the idea of her parents' marriage being under such pressure as the secret they shared drove them apart instead of keeping them together. No wonder he retired alone into his study so often while she took to her bed or withdrew into a mood.

'I hate the idea of him yearning for something he couldn't have.'

'How difficult that must have been for her.'

'Do you think they believed their own lie in the end? That can happen.'

'Everything Aggie's told you suggests that however hard they tried, Céleste wouldn't let either of them go.' His voice had deepened as if he were in an ad for a horror film.

'You just can't help yourself, can you?' Isla teased.

'That's what first loves have a tendency to do: cling on. You know that. ' He quickly looked away from her. 'David was probably as happy as he was ever going to be with May. Whatever happened, he was going to be disappointed. That's what happens. From what you've said, Céleste had already decided she didn't want a life with him. Or with you.'

'That hurts.' She kicked at a stone by her foot. Except did it hurt? Did it really? Or was hurt what she thought she should feel? But this was a very different feeling from the inner turmoil and pain Tony had inflicted on her. She watched a pair of Jack Russells chasing after each other and couldn't help smiling at them.

'Look at me.' He waited for her to turn and face him, eye to eye. 'You are who you are. You're right. And you must hold on to that. If we don't accept the cards we're dealt, we'll all go mad. May and David did their very best for you, and even if she did become jealous because of your increasing resemblance to the woman she imagined he still loved, well . . . that wasn't your fault. Although loving a dead woman does sound a bit of a stretch.'

'Just because *you're* always looking to the future.'

His shoulders sagged. 'Oh, I wouldn't say *always*.'

Her heart stuttered as he held her gaze for a few moments longer than necessary. 'Oh, please. Don't start.'

'What?' He held up his hands, all innocent. 'You're lucky Charlie got his measure.' Where had this sudden desire to protect her come from? After all she'd managed without it for years.

Isla groaned. 'I know.' She wound Jock's lead round her fingers. 'I trusted him, like a fool. I even invested in his new business.'

'Jesus, Isla! Have you learned nothing in your long life?'

'Don't. I've been looking after my own money for years and I thought I knew exactly what I was doing. But I took Tony at his word without doing any independent investigation into the company. Of course I did. We were going to be in business together.' She hit her palm with her fist.

'And the account's been emptied and closed?'

'According to the police. No. I've waved goodbye to my savings.' She looked up to see Jock sitting too close to the nearby picnic table, eying up a piece of ham in a child's hand. 'Jock! Come here.'

The dog dragged himself away with as much reluctance as a hungry Labrador could muster.

'Do you think I could trace my French family?' she asked as they walked back towards the main road.

'Do you want to?' Ian stepped close to her to let a couple with their arms wrapped round one another pass. He was so close she could see the thin white scar he had gained from a sword-fighting accident when he was playing Tybalt.

'Oh, I don't know. Probably not. What would be the point? Even if any of Céleste's generation are still alive, I won't mean anything to them. They'd have come to look for me if I did.'

'Maybe they did. Maybe they agreed to stay away. After all David was your dad and May was, as it turns out, your step-mum. Not so far from being a mum.'

'Completely different, in fact,' she pointed out. 'You don't have to protect her.'

'But they had every right to bring you up. And, if I may say so . . .' He nudged her in the ribs. 'They did a pretty good job. And the French in you is definitely a good thing.'

Lorna took the news in her stride. 'That explains everything, doesn't it?'

The two sisters were making a start on the vegetable curry for supper, with a bit of sporadic help from Charlie who had to keep stopping to go and check her phone.

'If only they were alive to ask what really happened.'

'Would that help? You know what they did and that says everything.' She put the knife down and leaned against the island. 'We're your family – me and Morag, Helen, Mike, Charlie and Aggie. We're not going anywhere.' She put her arms out for Isla to step into. Unlike the hug when they arrived, this one was full of warmth and love. Isla closed her eyes, surprised and pleased by the change, and returned the embrace. Lorna was right. There was no point digging up more of the past when there was nothing any of them could do to change it. Acceptance was what she had to work at.

When she opened her eyes Andrew was hovering in the doorway, still in his fishing gear, his face redder than ever from the sun. 'Getting on all right then?'

'Thanks.' Isla stepped away from her sister. 'Yes, we are.' She looked at Lorna. 'Better than for a long time I'd say, wouldn't you?'

'Yes,' Lorna turned away from her husband. 'We just need to break the news to Morag.'

We?

37

The following evening, Isla was in the garden at Braemore again. This time Lorna came too. Isla guessed that was because she wanted to be sure they discussed the paddocks. To give her her due, she had kept quiet about her marital problems and her solution to them since Isla had been knocked sideways by Tony's deceit and then Aggie's revelations. Their relationship might never be easy, but they seemed to have come to an accommodation that would see them through. May might have driven them apart but she had also driven them back together again. Lorna had been only sympathetic and supportive when she found out they were half-sisters. Family did come first for her, when it suited. Her future with Andrew might be rocky; but if only a way forward could be found that didn't involve breaking up Braemore.

When Isla had asked about her conversation with Morag, Lorna had been evasive.

'Let's just say we spoke. She was as shocked as we were by what Aggie told you. Like us, she'd never suspected a thing. They kept their secret so well.'

'But you are speaking to each other?' On top of everything that had happened, that would be the best news.

She frowned and screwed up her nose. 'We both said things that can't be unsaid.'

'Even though we were all upset at the time.' Wasn't that a consideration?

'Even though. I still want to sell Braemore and Morag doesn't.'

'Have you explained why?' That would be the first step on the road to getting her way.

'No. I don't want her to know.' Lorna clenched her fists.

'But she's the one person who needs to know.' Sometimes her sister could be so short-sighted.

'I said no. I wish I hadn't told *you* now.' Her face was set, her unhappiness plain.

There had been no budging her.

As the two of them sat with Aggie on the terrace in the early evening sun, reminiscing about the old days, talking about their mother, a sense of belonging and well-being stole through Isla, overtaking those feelings of hurt and loss that had been eating away at her. Or was that Aggie's famously strong G 'n' Ts? She didn't care.

'When you dropped the jelly just before Mum's fiftieth party . . . the way the gate creaked so we couldn't escape the garden without them knowing . . . those amazing costumes you made for our summer play that had a bullfrog in it – do you remember?' And they kept on coming.

Eventually Lorna decided they should go. 'You want to

be at your best tomorrow, Aunt Aggie.' Her opportunity to discuss the paddocks had escaped her.

'I'm never less than at my best,' Aggie said with a wink as she pulled her gaudy kimono top round her. 'But Isla, dear, I do have one thing left to tell you. Perhaps I should have said something earlier.'

Isla sagged in her seat. 'I'm not sure I can take any more.'

'I don't think you'll mind this too much. Lorna, would you mind giving us a moment.'

'Sure, I'll go inside.' She bent down to pick up her bag, but Isla stopped her with a hand on her wrist.

'No. There have been enough secrets in this family. I'd rather we had everything in the open from now on so there can be no more misunderstandings. Lorna?'

Lorna settled her bag on her knee. 'Okay.'

Aggie shifted in her seat, the sun catching the diamante on the arms of her specs. 'Well, if you're absolutely sure, dear.'

The sisters looked at each other and nodded. The temptation for Isla to change her mind was sharp but short-lived.

'Perhaps I should have told you this yesterday. I made one promise to May that I broke then. But I made another that I fully intend to keep.'

Now she had the full attention of both women.

'May left me half of Braemore so that I would have somewhere to see out my days. She couldn't have been kinder, and she wanted me to have half of it so she could be sure that no one would try and sell the place and siphon me off into a home.' She winked at a startled Lorna. 'But she had me promise that when I die, which I surely will in the not too dim and distant, that I would leave my share to you, Isla.'

Lorna gasped.

Isla swallowed. 'But why?'

'She wrote me a note that I've got here for you. I found it after the will was read and thought it was stirring up more trouble by telling you after you'd all fallen out, but I kept it and looked it out last night. She was just putting in writing what she had already asked me so that I wouldn't forget.' She passed Isla a small sheet of the blue Basildon Bond paper May always used for her letters. Beside her, Lorna was tense with anticipation. At least she was managing to stay silent until they had grasped the full picture.

Gingerly, Isla unfolded the letter.

Aggie – I've thought long and hard about this. I know it might cause ripples between the girls but Isla deserves this. Promise me you'll leave her your share in the house when you go.

Isla looked at her aunt, who was fiddling with her rings, not engaging with either her or Lorna, then back at the paper.

I dare say this will seem perverse but I'm not leaving you and the girls a quarter share of Braemore each because I want you to have the major share so that you can live there for as long as you need. The girls shouldn't be able to push you out - just thinking ahead! David's family home has been very good to me and I'd like you to benefit too, before the girls do. You've been the best sister I could have wanted. Moving in here was the best thing you could have done for me when I was brought so low: companionship, laughter and your cooking! Love, too. You alone know most of the truth of what happened to me In Paris, how I met David and fell in love with him and Isla (Eloise). We didn't want her life trailed by the gossip that would inevitably accompany her if we told the truth. Nobody needed to know. I've loved her as my own but I know I haven't always been fair to her. I should have been able to shrug off David's love for Céleste, but somehow it got harder, as you know and perhaps made me little bit mad. I hope that this will go towards making things up to her. Do this for me, Aggie. Mx

Isla passed the note to Lorna without a word. However well meant, May was still stirring the pot, but this proved that she had loved her, despite everything, and that made up for everything else. Now everything was clear.

As Lorna read, her face tightened, a little tic began beside her left eye. 'Well! That's as unfair as not leaving you anything.' She passed the letter back to Aggie who had stopped her fiddling. 'I'm beginning to think our dear mother didn't love any of us. She's still playing us.'

'Don't say that.' Aggie stopped fiddling with her rings. 'She's trying, in her own way, to do the right thing.'

'You can say that because you've got the house.'

'Lorna!' Isla wanted to shake her.

'It's true. And you and Morag won't help me. I know you won't.' She looked as if she might cry with frustration. Of course she was devastated because it dealt a death blow to her plans to free herself from her marriage.

'I'm sorry but I'm not going to ask Aggie to do anything other than May asks her. I think that's fair.'

A sigh of relief and a breathy 'Thanks' came from her aunt as she clasped her hand in gratitude.

'Of course, you're not.'

'Don't do this, Lorna. Please. But it does change everything. Don't you see? Aggie and I can lend you the money you need.' She remembered that Tony had made off with most of hers.

'Don't!' Lorna shook her head in weary resignation.

'What money?' Aggie's ears were too sharp.

Isla was not going to be put off. 'You've got to explain. In due course, I'll ask a lawyer if I can share my half with you and Morag so we end up with equal shares of Braemore. I'm sick of all this wrangling. I'm sure May was trying to do what she thought was best in her odd mismanaged way – if Aggie says so, that's good enough for me – but I'm equally certain that Dad would have wanted to split the ownership between the three of us. So I'm going to be grateful to her but respect him.'

'Big of you.' Lorna rubbed her hands together.

'There's no need for that! Sarcasm doesn't suit you.' Aunt Aggie suddenly came to life, startling them both. 'All Isla's doing is trying to make right what my silly, impulsive sister did. It's regrettable, I agree. She had the best of motives, but just didn't think it through to its conclusion. Too caught up in the wrongs of the past and trying to right them. It's generous of Isla to try to straighten things out fairly, although I've no intention of clearing the path for you all for some time. None of this is her fault, so give her a chance. What we don't need is you making things more difficult than need be.' She stopped abruptly as if surprised at herself.

Lorna stared at her, fingers tapping her glass.

Isla held her breath and waited for the explosion.

But none came. Instead she bowed her head. 'I reacted too quickly.' She put her hand to her head, ruffling her hair as if that would sort out her thoughts. 'I don't want to fall out again either. Aggie's right, it is generous of you. Thank you. But what will I do now?'

'You'll tell Aggie what you need the money for, however hard that may be, and hope she might help you.'

Lorna closed her eyes, swayed back and forth, then began to talk. When she'd finished, Aggie was leaning towards her.

'Of course I can help you out. You three are like daughters to me, and I always want to help you if I can.' She chuckled.

'I have to confess I was wondering if you'd stay the course with him. You'll be so much happier without.'

Isla watched as they hugged. The weight that had sat on her shoulders for so long, the fear that she wasn't loved, was lifting. That letter had finally given her the truth.

38

The weather held. The garden at Braemore was ready for a party. Vivid coloured bunting was strung between the trees. Tables had been set out round the edge of the garden so they benefitted from the shade of the trees. Each was laid with plates, cups and saucers, and bright paper napkins with a mini milk-bottle of garden flowers at its centre. Aggie's friends had done her proud.

Ian had set up the bar on one side of the French windows where bottles of fizz sat on ice and champagne flutes shone. Jugs full of home-made lemonade and ice were protected by beaded lace covers. On the other side, a string quartet, young friends of Aunt Aggie from the Music School, were tuning their instruments.

Charlie and Isla had been there all morning, helping wherever they could. Isla took such pleasure in seeing Charlie joining in, so unlike the girl she'd teamed up with two weeks earlier who would have sat in a corner glaring at her phone. How she wished Helen could see her now. She looked around for her, to find her taking selfies, pouting in front of the party background. At least she had ditched her shorts for a pretty strappy dress. When she caught Isla watching her, she came over. 'I'm just waiting for Ian.' No ageing 'grandad' used for him. 'We're popping out to get a couple of things for Aggie.' She couldn't stop grinning as if she had just been told the best joke.

It was lost on Isla. 'Shouldn't you have done that a bit earlier?'

'Oh, Gran.' She pouted again, lips glistening, skin smooth with beautifully blended foundation, eyes large with mascara'd rims and a cat-like flick at the corners. 'I had to do my make-up and he wasn't ready.'

'But the guests are beginning to arrive.' Nothing made Isla more nervous than the beginning of a party and the awful premonition that half the guests wouldn't turn up.

The quartet had struck up as a sprightly-looking elderly couple came round the corner of the house carrying a beribboned potted plant that they gave to Aggie, who was looking particularly splendid in a bright patterned kaftan with kimono-like sleeves, wide bangles rattling, huge beads gleaming. She took it with a cry of delight.

'Are you coming?' Ian materialised beside them. 'We'll be late.'

'You can't go now. The party's just beginning.' Isla wanted them there with her.

'We won't be long. Aggie wanted us to pick something up for her.' The conspiratorial wink Ian gave Charlie made Isla immediately suspicious.

'What? Can't I come with you?' Never mind the party after all.

'No! You're needed here. There's something that has to be picked up last minute.' Ian looked muddled by his own explanation. 'You'll see when we get back.'

'Just some ice cream, Gran.' Charlie pulled a face at Ian's back to show how hopeless she thought he was being.

The two of them went off, leaving no time for further questions. Moments later, Isla heard the car leaving but her curiosity was soon forgotten as Aggie's guests began arriving in quick succession. Soon the lawn was filled with Aggie's friends, some from her theatre days, some from the bridge and poker clubs, neighbours in the street and their grown children. What a turn-out! Everyone had made an effort to dress up. Drinks were handed round and soon the lawn was alive with people. Isla helped Aggie's friends transfer the food – a whole poached salmon, various quiches, cheeses and numerous salads and crusty baguettes – from the kitchen onto the long trestle tables near the house so everyone could help themselves and take their plate to whichever table they wanted to sit at. Isla went round encouraging people to get their meal, or helping one or two of those who were chair-bound, before the sun dried everything up.

Ian and Charlie had been gone for ages. They must have had to drive miles to pick up the ice cream that they didn't really need.

Once most people were settling down, a commotion at the French windows signalled Lorna and Andrew's arrival as he tripped over the step and righted himself by clutching on to one of the chairs on the terrace. Fortunately a woman of considerable girth was sitting in it, so it held fast while Andrew steadied himself. Lorna poured him a lemonade and handed it over. As Isla went across to greet them she caught him taking a hip flask from his pocket and slipping a good slug of something into his drink. The sooner Lorna was free of him, the better. Now Lorna was assured of the funds she needed, she could make her plans and would tell Andrew when they were in place.

'I can hold it,' he said as Isla came over. 'She just doesn't think I can.'

'Whatever,' she said, shepherding him towards Jeannie, the cleaner who had been at Braemore for so long she was almost a member of their family. She would know what to do with him. She caught up with Lorna at the mound they once used for a theatre.

'Remember when you were Puck and got stuck in that tree?' She pointed at the laburnum with branches that drooped over the edge of their stage.

'When I was meant to fly out of it but my tights got caught? Dad had to come and rescue me. God, I was cross.' They laughed, Isla glad that their new relationship was holding firm. 'Where's Ian? There's something I want to ask him.'

'He's gone off to get something for Aggie.' They both swung round as a school bell rang.

Standing in the French windows was Ian. 'Hear ye, hear ye. I present you with not one but two special unexpected guests.'

Aggie's hands were clasped. 'She's come?'

'Morag Adair, Aggie's niece all the way from Derbyshire!'

Isla turned to Lorna whose face was twisted in an expression of anticipation, pleasure and fear. She clasped her hands in front of her. 'She came.'

'You knew?'

'I invited her!'

Morag's eyes were roaming the garden until they fixed on Isla and Lorna. She had changed out of her usual farm clothes and was in a neat pair of trousers and a loose shirt. She waved and came over.

'I wasn't going to come but Lou persuaded me that I was being a stubborn bitch. If you could pick up the phone to me, then the least I could do was come.'

Another ring of the bell stopped her in her tracks.

Why did Ian have to be such a showman? Isla looked at the one cloud in the sky. But she also knew Aggie would appreciate the drama.

'And now we have Helen Belton who's flown in from the States.'

Standing beside him was Helen, looking radiant, in jeans and a white shirt, her hair cropped into a pixie cut that made her look younger, her arm round Charlie's shoulder. All three of them were beaming as if their faces would split, so pleased with themselves for creating a surprise that had Isla pinned to the spot. Aggie's face was a picture of delight as she opened her arms in noisy welcome as everyone started clapping.

The three sisters walked towards the house while most of the guests went back to their conversations.

As she crossed the lawn, propelled by Lorna, Isla felt dazed. So much had piled onto her in the last few days that had both crushed and lifted her. She couldn't tell whether she was coming or going as so much of what she thought she knew had unravelled round her. But within that confusion there were certain constants that she had been in danger of forgetting.

Charlie and Helen were running towards her, Ian just behind them. Before she knew where she was, they had swept her into an enormous family hug, something they hadn't all done together for years. Isla let herself sink into the enveloping warmth of her family. This was what love was. This was what would sustain her through the rest of her life whatever happened to her. They would always be there supporting her. She was lucky. Despite the down-turns, and she had experienced quite a few, the upsides like this were what one waited for. Eventually she extricated herself. Helen was standing in front of her, glowing with health and success.

'But you're meant to be in America,' Isla blurted.

'Aggie and Charlie both called me and told me everything that's gone on. I'd finished my last meeting so changed my flight and flew in to Edinburgh this morning. I've been hiding out in a hotel. Poor old you. It must have been such a shock. And as for Tony . . . what can I say?'

'Thanks to Di's quick thinking, the police say there's every chance they'll trace him. Though it'll probably be too late to get back the money I gave him.'

Helen gave a shake of her head to show she couldn't believe how gullible her mother had been.

'I know. Don't say it.' Isla didn't need anyone else to tell her what she had repeatedly berated herself for.

'Are you surprised, Gran?' Charlie was hopping up and down with delight at her part in the deceit.

'Blown away.' That was exactly the feeling: light, unencumbered, but thrilled. 'I never suspected a thing. You've been brilliant.'

'I'm so proud of you.' Helen put her arm round Charlie and kissed the side of her face. 'I even like the hair. Purple suits you.'

Charlie positively glowed.

'That was the whole plan.' Ian looked monumentally pleased with himself. 'We decided you needed a bit of family love-bombing in the circs. So here we all are.'

'And Morag, too.' Isla looked around her. Her sister was standing apart from the chattering guests, waiting until Isla was ready for her. When she saw Isla look up, she came over, smiling broadly.

'Sounds like you've been having a bit of a rough time.' They kissed cheeks.

'You might say. Rotten choice in men, *again.*'

'Oi! Watch it!' Ian hadn't been standing far enough away. But that ageing film-star smile showed he took the joke in good heart.

'And thanks for smoothing things out over Braemore. That's generous but will keep the peace.'

'We'll make a three-way decision about what to do with it when we need to. And looking at Aggie, that won't be for some time.' They turned to see her laughing at something someone in the groups of friends surrounding her had said. 'I absolutely promise,' said Isla. This was one promise she intended to keep. 'At least we're speaking to each other again.'

'We are. But don't expect us all to be bosom buddies all at once.' Morag was as bad as Lorna. 'Let's just celebrate our new half-sisterhood.' She went off to get three glasses of fizz.

'She's so pig-headed.' Lorna sniffed.

'Pot. Kettle,' said Isla. The fact that her sisters had colluded to be here for her meant everything. She wasn't expecting miracles but perhaps time would better mend the rift.

The rest of the afternoon went past in a whirl. She talked to many of Aggie's friends but most important of all, she had time with Helen.

'So, America. How did it go in the end?'

'Brilliant. I met everyone I needed to, spent time with my US agent. And I'm ready to go. I can work from here with the occasional quick visit. Until they start filming. I thought I'd take Charlie with me next time.' Her eyes shone with excitement. 'What *have* you done to her, Mum? She's undergone some weird transformation.'

'Nothing special – just introduced her to a conman and let her share the discovery that my mother wasn't my mother at all.' Anything else was too much detail for now. 'She's been great. You should try to spend more time with her.' As she said it, she could have bitten her tongue. The last thing Helen would want was her advice.

'Mum, don't. I've just said I'll take her to the States with me – *if* she gets her act together.'

'Don't expect too much too soon.' From where they sat, they could see Charlie sprawled on the grassy mound, engrossed in something on that small screen, her thumbs moving fast over it, quite oblivious to what was going on around her.

'We're going to Greece for two weeks next month – all three of us. Mike's back on Tuesday – at last. Being away gave me a bit of perspective and I'm determined we do this together. Mike's promised not to take on another job till after the holiday and I got a great last-minute booking.' Her excitement was contagious. 'In fact why don't you come too? A villa on Spetses.'

'I've just been away.' Although her holiday had been far from how she had originally planned it, she had no desire for another so soon. 'I want to go home, straighten out the mess in Walton Street and make it mine again.' She wanted to remove all traces of Tony from her home and restore it to the haven it was before he entered her life. 'Then I'm going to concentrate on Fernleith.' Just the thought of the Grade 2 listed building that had been given over to the collections of toys was enough to steady her. At least Tony had been unable to take that from her. She needed time to take on board everything that she had learned in these two short weeks and to regroup and find herself again.

'You're sure? We'd love to have you.'

'Certain. You should have time together and I should get my life back on track. I feel like such a fool.'

'But, Mum, you liked him. That's allowed. You weren't to know.'

'That doesn't stop me feeling stupid. Sad too, though.' For all that he'd taken from her, Tony had shown her she could perhaps love again. She would miss that sense of a relationship with another person that gave such warmth and confidence, even if it had been misplaced this time.

'Maybe you'll meet someone else.' In the background, someone had put Dean Martin's 'Everybody Loves Someone Some Time', one of Aggie's favourites, on the old record player and a couple of her friends were dancing on the terrace.

'Ever the optimist. I don't think I'll go looking for a while.'

'Are you dancing?' Ian had approached them from behind.

'No, it's just the way I'm standing.' The old family joke cracked them all up.

He held out his hand. 'Come on.'

She looked around to see if there was an excuse, but Helen was walking towards Aggie who was pulling out a chair for her at her table. Lorna and Morag were sitting talking together over the prone body of Andrew who was asleep on the lawn. The plates and leftovers had been taken inside and only the hard core of guests remained. By the time they reached the terrace, three couples were swaying side to side in time to the music.

'We can do this,' said Ian, sensing her reluctance. And sure enough they could.

As one song changed to another he put an arm round her waist and took her other hand, leading the way. They knew each other well and fitted neatly together. With him, she felt no pressure, no need to be perfect. They had ridden out so many storms and yet still stood to tell the tale. She closed her eyes and let herself sway with the rhythm of the music. The one place she was safe and loved was at the heart of her family – nothing could replace that.

'Mmm, this is nice,' she heard him say.

She stepped out of his arms and stood with her hands on her hips. 'Don't you ever give up?'

'Not while there's still hope,' he said, grinning that grin. 'Oh, come on. Where's your sense of humour?'

He reached out for her and she stepped back into his arms, looking up at him. 'There ain't no hope, sunshine.'

'More's the pity.'

The music changed again and she found herself flung backwards as he caught her up in a jive. By now the terrace had cleared and the remaining partygoers stood round the edge clapping as Ian threw her around and the steps of their favourite dance came back to her.

Out of the corner of her eye she could see the rest of her family laughing and applauding too.

Home. However long it had taken to get here, this was where she was meant to be.

Acknowledgements

Every novel of mine relies on a team of people who help with research and who keep me on the straight and narrow.

Huge thanks are due to –

My agent and friend, Clare Alexander, has been tirelessly supportive and always has my back. Clare Hey, my patient and perceptive editor without whom this novel might never have seen the light of day. I've been welcomed by her team at Simon & Schuster where I must give a particular shout out to Sara-Jade Virtue, Jess Barratt, Alice Rodgers, and the eagle-eyed Sally Partington.

Helping me with research into the world of teenagers were Charlotte Pearce, Maggie Shipp, Miranda McMinn and Lucia Hagan, Louise Candlish and Greta Burton. Jane and Jeremy Rawkins walked where I couldn't during lockdown and reported back in detail. Elizabeth Buchan who talked through plot lines and read an early draft. Michelle Gorman who read another and made some fantastically astute suggestions. Thanks to you all.

Finally as always my family and friends who put up with

me during the writing of this novel which went through its ups and downs, and particularly my husband Robin who read and advised so brilliantly.